THE ACCIDENTAL MARRIAGE

A GRUMPY BILLIONAIRE ROMANCE

NADIA LEE

The Accidental Marriage

Copyright © 2025 by Hyun J Kyung

This book is a work of fiction. The names, characters, places, and incidents are products of the writer's imagination or have been used fictitiously and are not to be construed as real. Any resemblance to persons, living or dead, actual events, locales or organizations is entirely coincidental.

All rights reserved. No part of this book may be reproduced, scanned, or distributed in any manner whatsoever without the prior written permission from the author except in the case of brief quotation embodied in critical articles and reviews.

Trademark Notice: Nadia Lee is a registered trademark in the United States. (Reg. No. 7,040,051)

www.nadialee.net

1

ARES (10 YEARS OLD)

"I love you, Ares. You know that. I'm doing this for you. For *us*. Don't you want to be together? Don't you love me?"

I feel sick to my stomach as Mom's fingers dig into my shoulders. Her ice-blue eyes, too wide and too bright, like they're on fire, won't let mine go. Everyone tells me I have her eyes. *Do I look this crazy and scary?*

Just the idea makes me feel cold, like I'm about to throw up. I don't want to scare anybody with her kind of craziness, especially not the girl I met since Mom brought me here.

I can't afford to give in to the urge to hit Mom. It'd only get my hands tied to the old wooden chair, too. So far Mom has left my arms free, but tied my torso, legs and ankles tightly to the chair. I've tried to get free, but can't. Mom's a good sailor, and knows a lot of ways to knot a rope. Maybe I should've gone sailing with her a few times when she asked so I could've learned how to undo her knots. But by the time I was old enough, my parents' marriage had begun to fall apart, eventually ending in gunshots, a 911 call and a lot of ugly publicity that Grandmother says brought shame to the family. Now they're in the middle of a vicious divorce. Well, Dad is forcing it, even though Mom doesn't want to leave him.

And now she's trying to avoid it by kidnapping me. She would've gotten the twins, too, but I fought and made it impossible for her to grab all three of us. Bet she regrets that. I'm stubborn, but I'd give in if she'd threatened to hurt Bryce and Josh.

She must see something in my face, because she relaxes her grip and pulls back, giving me some space. Finally, I can breathe without smelling that gross floral perfume. Even the shampoo she uses smells like flowers—makes me want to puke every time her pale golden hair brushes over me.

The air inside the cabin is stale, like old bread. A small window behind me is open to let fresh air in, but it isn't enough to hide the smell of old fungus. Twigs and dirt cover the floor, and the dusty spider webs over the fireplace mean that nobody's been here in a long time.

If only I could get loose...! The door is just a few feet away, right behind Mom. I doubt she stays anywhere near the cabin after her daily visits. There isn't any electricity here—I haven't seen any lights, and when the sun goes down, the cabin plunges into absolute darkness. The pitch-black nights combined with the sounds of rustling animals and bugs are torturous enough to make me want to agree to whatever Mom wants, which is why she's doing this—*in the name of love.*

Mom sighs harshly and looks around. Then she gestures at the plate of freshly baked cookies with a maternal smile, her exasperation disappearing faster than a drop of water on a hot pan.

My empty belly twists hard. The cookies smell *so good.*

"I brought them for you." Mom's voice is calmer, more in control. I don't trust it. She always appears sane and sweet, like those fairytale villains who pretend that they're good guys before they show their real selves. "Why don't you have some? You haven't had anything to eat in the last five days."

"I'm not hungry." But my stomach *really* hurts. I've never been this hungry before, but I'm not gonna let her see it.

Of course, my belly decides to growl. Triumph flashes in Mom's eyes. "Was that a sad little sound from your tummy?" She shoots me a teasing smile. "Are you *sure* you don't want—"

"I don't like cookies." My voice is shaky with betrayal and helplessness. I never expected Mom to drag me to some cabin in the woods. Our fight made her lose Bryce and Josh, so she then put something in my food that left me unable to think or move. "No more defiance," she said with a soft *tut-tut*.

Once I figured out that the food was making me unable to fight, I quit eating. I don't care how bad the hunger gets; I'd rather die of starvation than be under her control like that. I might not understand everything, but I know enough to realize she wants to use me to get Bryce and Josh—and manipulate Dad. I overheard Grandmother say Mom wasn't getting anything—no alimony, no custody. Words I know because our whole family is lawyers.

Mom cradles my face in her delicate hands, stroking my cheeks and chin with a tenderness that makes my skin crawl. Her unblinking blue eyes focus on me, studying my eyes, my nose, my mouth. "You're so much like your father. He's the only man I ever loved," she whispers, her gaze softening briefly. "Flowers. Fireworks. Torrid confessions and whirlwind trips everywhere so we could mark the world with our passion. You're the fruit of that love."

I grit my teeth, trying not to throw up. If I weren't hoping for the girl's secret visit again, I'd puke up the uncomfortable acid in my belly.

I don't know who she is—she wouldn't even share her name. She's much smaller than my twin brothers, and they're two years younger than me. She has messy golden hair, a pointed chin and different-colored eyes, one green and one blue. Dirt and leaves stick to her bare feet, and her skin is almost as pale as the grass-stained white dress she wears. She looks like some kind of a wild forest fairy, except she's always carrying Wonder Bread and bottled water.

Three days ago, the first time she broke into the cabin, she asked me if I was hungry. I was starving after not having eaten for two days. She gave me a slice of the bread, and I gobbled it down and regretted it when it was all gone within a second. She nibbled on a slice of her own, focused on chewing like it was the most important thing in the world. She offered me another slice. "I can't give you more because it's for the whole week. But if you want, I can come by tomorrow."

Then she shared her water with me. She kept her promise to come back. But she wouldn't tell me her name, even when I threatened to call her "Bread Fairy."

That only made her giggle. "Ew."

"Then what? Princess?"

"Nope." She tilted her chin up. "Princesses have no power."

"Yeah they do."

"Haven't you read any fairytales? They get bossed around. I wanna be a queen. Nobody tells *them* what to do."

"So you want to be called 'your majesty'?"

"Nope. Just 'Queen' would do fine."

"Of course. Queen Wonder Bread," I said, making it sound all formal, and she giggled again.

She tried to undo the knots, but gave up. I felt disappointed, but Mom's too good. Still, I like it that the girl tried.

From our conversations, I figured out she was an orphan who got stuck with an aunt and uncle after her parents and grandfather passed away. They must be pretty poor to leave her barefoot and in the same stained white dress all the time. When I leave this place, I'll take her with me and ask Dad to foster her. I'll make sure to protect and take care of her. That's the least I owe her. She'll look really pretty in new dresses and shoes. And she'll be happy to have something other than Wonder Bread and water. I don't know if her aunt and uncle are sending her to school, but she can start. My family always pays its debts.

"You don't have to eat if you aren't hungry," Mom says suddenly, breaking my train of thought. Her smile says, *Aren't I reasonable and considerate?* "But I'll leave you those cookies, just in case you change your mind. I made them with love, so you should—"

Her phone rings. She checks the screen, eyebrows pinching slightly. *Is it Dad, demanding to get me back?* Bryce and Josh ran while we were still in Los Angeles. They should've been able to make their way back. All they have to do is say that our father is a lawyer at Huxley & Webber, and people will know exactly where to take them. It's one of the largest and most prestigious law firms in the country.

"I have to go." She softens her abrupt tone with a smile. "Be good, sweetie. I'll be back soon." She puts her hands on her knees, bends down and looks tenderly into my eyes. "You know what? Why don't we grab some burgers later? You'd like that, wouldn't you?"

Suddenly, she goes behind me and grabs my hand, yanking it back at an unnatural angle. Pain shoots through my shoulder. I cry out, tears springing to my eyes, and feel something icy circling my wrist. She grabs my other hand, pulling it back. Something cold and hard wraps around my other wrist with a metallic click—then she lets go and the throbbing subsides. I wiggle my hands, then realize *she's handcuffed me.* I glare at her with all the hate in my heart.

Her eyes flick in my direction. She doesn't seem bothered by my blatant loathing. She takes the cup of water on the table and grabs my jaw tightly, exerting pressure until my mouth opens. She pours the water into my mouth. Desperate, I shake my head and try to spit it out. Half the liquid gushes down my chin. Tsking, she pinches my nose. Out of reflex, I swallow twice—it's either that or suffocate. I hate her for doing this to me, and hate my body for giving in so easily.

When there's no water left in the cup, she throws it on the floor and places a quick kiss on my head. I spit at her, hitting her cheek. Her expression turns blank, and she swipes her fingers over the wet spot.

"I'm doing this for you, Ares—for our family. You'll thank me when we're back together again." It's scary how sincere she sounds. The rusty hinges on the door creak as she opens it and walks out, slamming it shut.

I glare at the slab of wood, then at the giant, snarling iron wolf above. Its jaw is wide open, the teeth sharp. Inside its mouth is a capital H, for the Huxleys—my family. If Mom wants to show her fealty to the family, she's doing it wrong. Grandmother hates it when the family coat of arms isn't faithfully replicated.

But even if Mom replicated everything faithfully and promised to live by the family motto—*pietas et unitas*—Grandmother would never welcome her back. Hell, Dad won't let her through the gates to the house.

The slant of the sunlight says it's late afternoon. Mom stayed longer than usual. *Did Queen give up and leave?* She might have. Mom never lingered for so long. Bet she wants to know why I'm able to resist the various treats and drinks she leaves out. As far as she knows, I've gone five days without food or water. I should be dying for her poisoned crap.

The shadows slowly get longer. My head feels fuzzy. *Queen isn't coming.* Why not? Was she peeking inside and saw what happened?

Dad says a man's worth is determined by the confidence he inspires in others and how well he protects what's important. My total helplessness probably doesn't inspire any confidence. Weak, pathetic and useless. That's what I am.

Darkness starts to creep inside the cabin. I squeeze my eyes shut. The sounds of the forest animals seem particularly loud today, and my skin crawls with chills, then something hot and uncomfortable skitters over my spine until my body spasms. My head hurts, like a sliver of rusty metal is sliding between my eyebrows. I realize I don't even care about the bread and water Queen carries. I just want to see her—to feel like I'm not alone. Just to glimpse a sliver of goodness and sanity. All my thoughts grow hazy, then scatter like broken marbles until my head goes blank and darkness envelops me.

⁓

A SHARP SLAP. Another. They send ripples through my mind, pulling me out of the drug-induced haze.

"Wake up! We gotta go!"

I try to focus through the haze. Another slap, this time harder than the ones before.

"Come on!"

"Queen?" I cough. The air is acrid with dust and smoke. A pale orange light casts shadows on her small face.

"You have to get up!"

I start to tell her I'm tied up until she shows me a small fruit knife.

"I cut you free." She sounds inordinately proud, then clears her throat. "Not your arms, though."

I'm stunned. I start to stand, then stumble and collapse on my knees. My legs are stiff from being bound for so long. Nerves prickle like millions of needles. I hiss with pain.

She grabs me. This close, she smells like lemon and bread. "We have to *go*. There's a *fire*."

Must be the source of the light in the cabin. She tugs at my arm again. I fight the effects of whatever Mom forced down earlier. Queen did her part, and now it's my turn.

The smoke is thicker. The air feels like sandpaper against my throat and lungs, making me cough again—violently. I swallow, but my mouth might as well be full of cotton. It's hard to balance with my hands tied behind my back.

Her skinny arms wrap around mine, and she drags me toward the door. I go with her, as the fog from the drug lingers, trying to overpower me again.

The door is banging open and closed from the wind generated by the fire. The metal wolf over it comes loose, swinging crazily on one nail, and then drops. Queen pushes me to my left. The wolf's jaw falls on her shoulder, then the head rolls down my arm, tearing the skin. Searing pain yanks me out of the haze.

"Are you okay?" I demand.

Tears form in her eyes, but she doesn't cry. She just sets her mouth in a tight line and nods. In that moment, she doesn't seem like a little girl, but the queen she said she wants to be. And I want to be her knight and keep her safe.

"We have to run," I rasp.

She nods, but doesn't let go of my arm. Pain and anxiety pinch her expression, and I force a smile to reassure her. Doesn't matter what Mom fed me; I'm going to do everything I can to protect my Queen.

We rush out together.

The night sky isn't black anymore. Orange flames lick at the trees around us. The air is hot and thick. I look around, searching for a way out, but the only thing I see is fire and more fire. My right arm throbs, but I don't make a sound. I can't complain when she hasn't said a word about her own shoulder injury.

She points. "There's a lake that way."

We hurry and cut through a dry, grassy field, the scorching air at our backs. I don't know how long we run. It's impossible to tell when I'm only awake due to terror and a sense of responsibility for her safety.

Finally, we reach the "lake." It's more like a small pond, but good enough. If the fire gets any closer, we can jump into the water to avoid getting burned alive.

My legs finally give out, and I fall to my knees. I can't keep my head up without feeling like it's about to explode with the sharp, pounding pain. I lie down and close my eyes, focusing on breathing. I hate Mom for drugging me. For making me feel helpless and useless and weak.

The dress rustles as the girl crouches next to me. "Are you okay?" she asks.

I'm too out of it to say anything.

"Don't die," she whispers.

I crack my eyes open. She looks down at me, her brows knitted with fear and worry. The fire casts an orange halo around her, making her look like an angel.

I nod. "I won't. I promise."

She gives me a relieved smile. I should smile back, reassure her, but all the strength in my limbs drains away and everything goes black.

When I open my eyes again, I'm in a brightly lit hospital room. Dad, Grandmother and Aunt Jeremiah stand around my bed, looking worried.

"How are you feeling?" Dad's voice is shaky. I've never heard him sound like this before.

"Tired. Otherwise...okay." I add the last part for Queen if she's listening from somewhere in the room.

Dad doesn't believe me. "You've been unconscious for three days."

Three days? I look around, but don't see anyone else. "Where is she?"

"Who?"

"The girl who saved me. She led me to the lake."

My aunt and grandmother exchange glances. I'm too exhausted to figure it out, but they're hiding something.

"There wasn't any girl," Dad says finally.

"No way. She was there. And she got hurt, trying to save me."

"It was just you, passed out by the pond." Grandmother's voice is firm and assured. "We didn't see anybody. If we had, we would've brought her in to be treated."

"I don't believe you."

"It's true," Aunt Jeremiah says. "But once you get better, I'll personally help you find her. I promise."

My outrage at their denial dies. She rarely makes a promise, but when she does, she keeps it. There's no point in insisting on finding Queen right now. "Did you catch Mom?"

The Accidental Marriage

"We'll deal with her." Grandmother says it calmly, but the sharp glint in her eyes promises retribution. "You just focus on recovering."

"Where did you find me?" I ask, hoping for some clue as to who Queen is.

"A forest in Oregon. About an hour from the state border." The vindictive flash in Aunt Jeremiah's eyes says she's going to fuck Mom up. Nobody touches one of the family and gets away with it.

But we also don't ignore it when somebody's helped one of us. So why are they so reluctant to talk about Queen?

Four days later, I get discharged. I try to look for her, but not even the firefighters who found me know anything about her. Aunt Jeremiah hires a team of private detectives, and they also return with nothing. Queen might as well have been a figment of my imagination. My therapist implies as much. He says it's a "coping mechanism," something to keep my sanity intact. "One of the ways our mind protects itself."

But...

As I stare at the long, ugly scar on my arm, I know I didn't imagine that night. Or the drugs Mom put into my food and drink to keep me under control. If Queen hadn't cut me loose, I would've died. If she hadn't pushed me out of the way, the wolf might've fallen on my head and killed me on the spot.

I think of her shoulder injury. Wonder if something happened to her while I was out cold—

I hate Mom! I *hate* her, hate my weakness, hate that I lost Queen and can't find her again. So much for being her knight. I don't even know if she's okay. Her aunt and uncle couldn't have been treating her well, not with those old clothes and how dirty she was. She really needs more than Wonder Bread and water. And a better dress than the stained white one she was wearing. And shoes. And school. And the pretty things that girls deserve.

No matter where she is, I pray that she's okay—and that her goodness comes back to her a thousand-fold.

2

ARES

—TWENTY-TWO YEARS later

"It won't be possible for you to make junior partner. Thought we should inform you before the official announcement," says Catalina, my grandmother and the matriarch of the family.

Her voice is supposed to be soothing, but it only pisses me off. "Are you shitting me?" I say in a flat monotone, unmoving in my seat. My eyes scan TF, short for The Fogeys—what my brothers, cousin and I call the elders behind their backs.

Grandmother sits at the head of the table, her jet-black hair pulled into a chignon. It's the style she's favored since her years as a highly successful prosecutor in L.A.—it makes her appear both stern and elegant. Her skin is pale with very few wrinkles, and she's in a cool blue dress that intensifies her eye color.

To her right is my father, Prescott Huxley, a senior partner at Huxley & Webber, who wields his tongue like a scalpel to shred his opposing counsels into little, mewling ribbons. His hair is as dark as Grandmother's, but he keeps his cropped, all clean cut and controlled. He has a booming voice, but rarely raises it. He doesn't need to in order to get attention. His confidence alone is sufficient. Not only that, he's in one of his black three-piece bespoke suits he reserves for court appearances, although he had no such thing today. He silently munches on a miniature tiramisu from the dessert trays before him, his pale gray eyes on me. The delicate sweet looks awkward in his large hand, but he adores the little desserts Grandmother serves when the family gets together.

Aunt Jeremiah sits opposite him, her hair once again dyed a deep, rich red—which inspired a joke that her hair periodically turns that shade from being drenched in the opposing counsels' blood. Also a senior partner at Huxley & Webber, she believes in winning at all costs and commands both respect and fear. She's drinking a glass of Merlot and puffing on a cigar. Her son Huxley thinks she only smokes cigars to celebrate a victory, but she also indulges when she's feeling particularly tense. Her well-fitted, hand-stitched ebony skirt-suit projects power and control. Complete overkill—I should've realized this wasn't going to be a friendly evening chat.

"We wouldn't joke about your career." My father pushes the dessert tray in my direction, as though a bit of sugar will be enough to coax me into a better mood.

"Why can't I get the promotion I deserve?" I demand.

"You aren't *owed* a promotion," Aunt Jeremiah points out.

"My clients love me, and I draw new clients. Not only that, I bill more hours than anybody else, and the work is exceptional. People respect it."

"Yes, but you don't know how to balance your life. And you do the bare minimum of mentoring," Dad argues.

"I aim for quality *and* quantity. Just ask." The junior associates never complain about me. Most compete to have me on their side.

A short silence falls over the table. Grandmother adds more sugar to her tea and stirs it in.

"You know I deserve this promotion," I say. "Ethan fucking Beckman is making junior partner this year."

Grandmother frowns. Ethan Beckman is my nemesis and the right-hand man of John Highsmith, a name partner at a rival firm. He loves stealing our clients and doing everything in his power to fuck up our cases. Everyone at Huxley & Webber loathes him. "Be that as it may, you exhibit an unhealthy obsession."

"What unhealthy obsession?" I demand. I'm the opposite of obsessed. I do everything in my power to stay as detached as possible from everyone, except family. Hell, I've only had four girlfriends.

"The girl from Oregon."

I freeze. *Queen.*

"We're worried about you." Grandmother closes her eyes briefly and sighs. "I know you're still looking for her."

"She was there."

"Ares, your mother *drugged* you." Grandmother sounds pained.

"Are you saying I was delusional?"

Dad clears his throat, his eyes soft with sympathy. He's speaking as my father, rather than a senior partner. "You said you ate the girl's bread." His eyes fall on the tiramisu in his hand. He places it on a napkin.

It's clear that he doesn't believe me. He doesn't think I'm lying, necessarily, but he's convinced I couldn't have overcome my hunger and thirst in the face of the treats Mom left out for me. In order to protect myself, I made up the girl and the bread she brought.

My hands clench. *I'm not crazy.* I didn't make up anything about what happened.

"If she was there, we would've found her by now. Jeremiah looked for her, too, remember? Her people are thorough."

Aunt Jeremiah gives me a sympathetic look mixed with pity, then looks away in discomfort. Compassion really isn't her thing.

But her feelings aren't my focus right now. Bitter disappointment curdles in my belly like milk gone bad. "You want me to give up on her."

"We want you to live in the present," my father says. "It isn't healthy. It's been twenty-two years."

"Bullshit." I lift my gaze at the coat of arms above the wall behind Grandmother. A trio of silver wolves snarl on a shield with the family motto in all caps: PIETAS ET UNITAS. Loyalty and unity. It's embedded in us. Even before we're born, the family has special canes crafted for us with a Huxley wolf as the knob and the motto engraved along the body so we never forget.

Of course, loyalty and unity are reserved for the family, but as far as I'm concerned, Queen is more than family. She was my savior. How can I abandon her just because the search is taking longer than I'd like? How can I call her "not real" just because The Fogeys insist?

"I'm a Huxley. I don't give up."

Dad downs his whiskey. He's stressed. Aunt Jeremiah swirls her wine glass, her unblinking eyes on me. Grandmother merely taps the table.

"Even if you may never be a partner?" Grandmother says finally.

"Even then." My eyes slide over to Dad. "There are other firms." A bluff. I can't imagine myself anywhere but Huxley & Webber. It's a family legacy, something I've rightfully earned through my hard work. However, you can't negotiate from a position of weakness.

Grandmother inhales sharply, her face stiffening. "You'd betray the family for her?"

I give her a hard look. "Didn't you betray me first by denying me the promotion I deserve?"

"Fine. Get married and settle down."

What the hell? "Where am I going to find a wife?" I demand, wondering if they're trying to maneuver me into an arranged marriage the way they did with my cousin, Huxley.

"That's not our concern," Grandmother says nonchalantly. "But prove to us you aren't mad with obsession. Marry a good, respectable woman. Have a good, respectable family of your own."

"I'll marry a woman that fits your criteria before the annual review, and you'll make me a junior partner this year," I say.

"*If* you marry by then." Grandmother arches an eyebrow in a cool challenge. "But can you?"

"Don't ever underestimate my will, Grandmother." I look at the two elders seated on either side of her. "Father. Aunt. It won't even take a month."

"Then we'll expect to be introduced to your wife in thirty days." Aunt Jeremiah's placid smile says the sky will fall first.

3

LAREINA

—TWENTY-SEVEN DAYS later

"I don't know when she's going to be up. But we can't drag her out to get the marriage license like this. She looks like a bleached cabbage," my aunt huffs, probably complaining to her husband or stepson Rupert.

I stay limp on the bed, but crack my eyes open surreptitiously and scout the area as much as possible. The bed's large, probably king-size, and we look to be in at least a two-bedroom suite in a hotel. Aunt Doris, holding a phone to her ear, undoubtedly booked and paid for it with my money. Continuing to play Sleeping Beauty isn't such a bad idea when my head hurts from whatever their doc injected me with so I wouldn't fight back on the flight from Nesovia to Vegas.

"Can't we just slip some cash to the clerk?" Rupert's nauseating voice comes through on speaker.

"And get arrested?"

"We gotta hurry up. There's only six months left," he says impatiently.

"You don't have to remind me. If you'd been able to butter her up...!" She lets out a soft growl of frustration. "Just how hard is it to say some sweet nothings and seduce her? It isn't like she's surrounded by boys!"

True. Since my aunt and her family can't have their source of income fall into someone else's hands, they made sure to keep me away from not just boys, but most girls my age as well. I have no bestie I can call and pour my heart out to, and the only classmate I sort of know is Ethan Beckman, who was in the classic art course I took online. But since then, we've lost contact. *Thank you, Doris.*

Nesovia has some of the shittiest and most archaic inheritance laws in the world. Until I'm married or turn thirty—whichever comes first—I can't control my own money. So Doris, as my sole living blood relative, has had control over my sixty-billion-dollar inheritance since I was eight.

Initially, she was good to me, always making sure to treat me as well as Rupert, although she told me at least once a week that Rupert saved me from the forest fire twenty-two years ago. The constant reminder was irritating, but Doris claimed it was to help me remember even though the details never seem to add up. Besides, I just can't imagine Rupert lifting a finger for anybody unless it benefited him. And he was only ten back then, too young to understand the complexity of my inheritance situation.

Everything changed when I overheard her and Rupert a couple weeks before my thirteenth birthday. They were disappointed I still couldn't accept how Rupert saved me from a horrible death—being burned alive is pretty shitty, after all—and somehow failed to fall in love with him. So they wanted to engineer a heroic scenario, which they'd make sure would be embedded in my memory forever. The plot was simple, albeit clichéd. I was to get kidnapped and Rupert would rescue me. Doris believed I'd fall in love with him for sure and marry him as soon as I was old enough. Then they could rightfully take full control over my trust.

I should've kept my mouth shut and played them. But my youthful brattiness and inexperience made me lash out. Doris took away my phone and started to control me, including putting drugs into my food. Unlike me, she understood the importance of managing public perception.

While living lavishly on *my* money, she goes on TV and other media to brag about how she's fighting for girls in Nesovia to gain agency. Her dream is to leave a name for herself—a legacy of her own, since Grandfather refused to let her run Hayworth Shipping. Of course, if she really believed what she spewed, she would've handed me the reins over my finances when I turned twenty-one.

"I tried, but she's impossible! She's probably a lesbian!" Rupert shouts in impotent fury.

I'm not. But I could be if he were the only man left. Hell, entering a nunnery would be a better option.

"She's too stupid to know when somebody's flattering her!" he adds. "And *stubborn*. She won't accept my explanation."

"About what?"

"That what she overheard back then about the abduction plot was a misunderstanding."

Won't accept it because he's too stupid to make me believe it. Lies only work if you're sincere in your deception—you have to believe your own bullshit. Sadly, his contempt and derision for me are obvious every time we interact. He could drop to his knees, kiss my feet and call me his goddess, and I still wouldn't believe him.

And his girlfriend, Parker Jacoby, hasn't helped the cause either. Rupert and Parker pretend they're just friends—probably what they agreed to do in front of me—but she's too impetuous and impatient to play her part with any consistency. Every time Rupert isn't around, she shows off the fancy jewelry or purses he bought for her, doing her best to provoke me.

Her face turns red every time I respond along the lines of: "Things you bought with *my* money. So technically, it's me who gifted you. No, no, no need to thank me, Parker. I don't want your body. You aren't my type, even if I were inclined to play for the other team. I prefer my bed partners intelligent and disease-free."

It's oh so satisfying to watch the steam come out of her ears, especially since she can't do anything about my mockery. Telling Rupert would only earn his anger. She told me he's only marrying me for money. Once he's in control of my inheritance, he'll get rid of me and marry Parker in a ceremony that will put the British royal family to shame. Clearly, she thought the revelation would upset and humiliate me. But you can only get upset if you have expectations. And those vanished years ago when I overheard Doris and Rupert talking about fake-kidnapping me.

It's sad how low people can stoop for money. On the other hand, I guess sixty billion can negate pretty much anything, including one's conscience.

"You should've just slept with her and gotten her pregnant!" Doris says.

So now rape is being packaged as "sleeping with"? Even more astounding—she actually believes that I'd have married Rupert if he forced himself on me! What century does she think we're living in?

"I would have if she didn't carry that damn fruit knife everywhere."

I almost killed him when I slashed at his neck with it. When he came at me again, I threatened to cut my wrists. Since then, he's quit trying to force me physically. Anything that could cause my death isn't worth the risk.

He continues, "But if you want, I could do it now."

Dread unfurls, tensing every cell in my body. Doris probably took my knife away. *Damn it.* Is there anything I can use as a weapon in the room? There has to be a minibar with a corkscrew in this place.

"Never mind." Doris sighs impatiently. "You're going to marry her before midnight anyway." A sharp ping from the phone. She looks at it, then gets back to Rupert. "I have to take care of this. Think of some good way to get her to agree to get the marriage license."

"Fuck. Grandfather shouldn't have let the money go to charity if she dies."

"Shut up. What if somebody hears?" she hisses.

"Like who?"

Like me? I think, feeling the weight of my aunt's gaze.

"A big ring might do the trick," she says. "Something really ostentatious."

Translation: I have no taste to expect any better. But then, that's the public persona I've cultivated, because eccentricity is one of my most important tools of survival. And to be honest, it isn't that difficult to be a tasteless heiress when I don't have any. Taste, that is. I didn't inherit any of my artist mom's discerning eye or talent. One of Doris's frequent lamentations is, "Susan wasted six years trying to impart some of her artistic genius on you. She should've just settled in Nesovia after marrying William, rather than frittering away our money taking you to all those fancy museums and exhibitions."

Tiresome how everything's measured by money. Mom wanted to create memories with me and protect me from the worst laws of Nesovia. She didn't come back until Grandfather altered his will and trust to protect me as much as possible.

"Why? I already bought her one for the engagement!" Rupert says.

The engagement? When did he ask me to marry him? I move my left ring finger and realize *there's a ring there that I didn't have before. Oh my God.* Did he propose during the flight when I was out cold from the drugs administered by their "doctor"?

"Just shut up and do as I say. Or maybe buy her some gourmet chocolate. No girl can resist that."

This girl can. I haven't touched food from them for years now. I filch meals from the staff in the mansion and throw wild parties that I never attend but are beloved by other idle and aimless heirs and heiresses. Acting eccentric and unreasonable has its benefits. No matter what I do, nobody questions it anymore. They just chalk it up to me being me. *Too much money, too little control.*

I add fuel to the fire by devoting most of my free time to painting whatever moves me at the moment. Although I didn't get Mom's talent, she tried to teach me before she passed away. Every time I complete a piece, Doris replaces it with a blank canvas, saying art is a good way to vent my emotions. She clearly doesn't understand I'm not dumb enough to fall for her faux concern and encouragement. I always rein myself in just enough to ensure nobody will consider me clinically insane. Getting locked up in an asylum? *No thanks.*

The mattress dips. Cool fingers skim my forehead. "Why can't you just accept our story about the fire? Rupert isn't a bad catch. You should totally be in love with him." It's less a lament than resentment. Doris would love nothing more than for me to slavishly agree to everything Rupert wants. *Gross.*

The mattress springs back, and a few minutes later the door opens and closes. I count to ten, then open my eyes. Just the bed, an ornate ceiling fan with gold foil, a giant TV and a vanity.

I'm alone. *Perfect.*

I sit up, my bare feet touching the thickly carpeted floor. Doris hates giving me shoes, as though they'd allow me to run away. I grab a bottle of Evian from the minibar, bypassing a pitcher of water by the bedside stand. I'm not touching anything that isn't sealed.

The mirror shows a pale woman in a white wedding gown. It's designed to cover my shoulders, arms and back. Modesty isn't the point, but covering the hideous burn scar on my shoulder is. It's as big as my palm, but I can't remember how I got it. You'd think a trauma significant enough to mar such a large patch of skin would've left a lasting impression. But no.

Doris told me it's from the fire, where Rupert rescued me. Without his pulling me out of the flames, the injury could've been more significant—or worse, I could've died. Rupert didn't get any scars or injuries from it—how lucky. I was supposedly hospitalized for a week, unconscious and feverish. Bet Doris and Vernon were biting their nails, since they need me alive to get my money.

The burn mark doesn't hurt or anything, but Doris, Vernon and Rupert act like I'm running around with a used sanitary napkin stuck to my skin every time they see it. Maybe it looks that awful to them, but I don't think it looks quite that horrible. Hard to say, since I'm probably not the most objective when it comes to my own scar.

But does the dress have to be so hideous? With such huge, poufy shoulders and lace on the sleeves and so many layers of chiffon—to the point that the skirt looks like a cross between a tutu and a rococo-style dress?

The lipstick on my mouth is bright red—ridiculous for my ghostly complexion, but then, Doris isn't known for her taste, either. But she is good with hair. My platinum mane is twisted into an elaborate style with a few tendrils framing my face. If I had a bit more color in my cheeks, I could pass for a radiant bride.

I look down at my finger and scowl. There's a diamond solitaire stone set on a plain platinum band. About as interesting and creative as Rupert himself.

All right. Time to grab my passport from the safe—where Doris always stores important documents—and get out of here. I'm only six months away from my thirtieth birthday and freedom. No way am I going to be forced into marrying Rupert. I don't know exactly what Doris is planning, but she'll stop at nothing to get her hands on my inheritance. And neither will her husband Vernon, who would make your average bribe-taking banana republic politician look conscientious.

I quietly head into the living room. Nobody's around. I reach for the safe. It's a simple four-digit combination type. I press 0-8-2-5, the birthday of Doris's favorite actor, Sean Connery. She isn't aware that I know it, but then, I've become very good at playing dumb and biding my time. Doris has grown "protective" after the fruit knife incident and put multiple bodyguards on me to keep me safe. But they're actually spies, reporting my every move and ensuring I don't do anything to harm myself. If I die too early, my money will go to a charity in America she can't touch.

For this trip Doris brought two guards—probably the only ones she could bribe to look the other way as she forces me to marry her stepson—and they're stationed outside the suite. When Doris, Vernon and Rupert aren't around, they look at me like I'm a piece of meat. I call them Creepy and Creepier because the latter copped a feel a couple of times while "helping" me to my room after Doris put something in my drink. No matter how careful I am, it's impossible to avoid all poison and drugs in the food and drinks—another compelling reason I need to get the hell away from my so-called family.

The safe clicks open, and I take out my passport and stuff as much cash as I can into my bra. The glint of Rupert's diamond ring catches my eye. Making a face, I yank it off my finger and place it where my passport was.

"Sayonara, fuckers."

I reset the safe with a satisfied grin. Doris likely feels secure, thinking the bodyguards won't let me leave.

She doesn't know there's more than one exit to a hotel.

I head out to the balcony, where I discover that it's late afternoon. The suite is on the seventeenth floor. The hotel exterior is ornate with gargoyle bas-reliefs, horns and talons as big as my forearms sticking out. Four such carvings, then a balcony. I look down. Lots and lots of little balconies underneath...and people and cars as tiny as ants.

My heart races, blood whooshing through me. *Holy shit.* That's high.

I close my eyes to create a strong visual. First up: me as a bloody pancake on the sidewalk. I shudder. *No, no. I'm too young to die.*

How about... *Me as Mrs. Rupert Fage?* My stomach roils, and I start to gag as acid sloshes in my belly and begins to climb to my throat.

That does it. Death is preferable to being married to that piece of shit. I didn't avoid him for over twenty years just to be forced to be his missus. Parker is welcome to that cootie louse.

Carefully, I reach over and grab the closest horn, then swing my leg up until my bare foot finds solid purchase on the knee of the gargoyle. Gritting my teeth, I pull myself up, then over. The desert wind blows, pulling at my hair and dress, as though telling me to go back to Doris's luxurious prison.

No thanks.

I slowly and carefully make my way over. My muscles burn as I clench the horns and fangs with all my might. Holy shit, this sort of stuff looks so easy in the movies. At least the stone used for the carving is rough, and I can get a decent grip. Otherwise, I'd definitely slip and die. I inch my way over...

Careful... Careful...

Don't be afraid, I tell myself. Seriously, death is shitty, but not as terrible as it appears. Should I fall, Doris, Vernon and Rupert would become destitute fairly quickly. I looked up the charitable organization that would get my entire sixty-billion-dollar fortune. The Pryce Family Foundation is run by a woman named Elizabeth Pryce-King, and she doesn't look like a pushover. The best part is that she has no connection to anybody in Nesovia, and Doris has no way to influence her.

My pulse pounds in my head, and my mouth is completely dry.

Come on. Just a little bit more...!

I stretch my leg as much as possible, and my toes touch the railing. Air rushes out in a big sigh of relief, but I still maintain a tight grip on the gargoyles. Can't screw up the last step.

Clenching my teeth, I throw myself at the balcony and safety. At the same time the double doors open, and a dark-haired man in a charcoal-gray suit steps out.

I yelp, and he spins in my direction, his eyes wide in shock and alarm. I crash into him, wrapping my arms around him in a death grip. He staggers back a few steps, until his back hits the doorjamb.

"What the hell?"

"Shiii—!" I put a hand over his mouth, looking back at Doris's suite. "Not so loud."

He stares at me with wide, blue-gray eyes. My heart still pounding from the crossing—*but I'm safe now*—I take a moment to gather my thoughts. A neighbor wasn't part of the plan. Given how extravagant Doris is with my money, I thought she might have rented every room on the floor, just to show how important she is.

The man's tall—at least six-five—and my toes barely touch the floor while my arm's looped around his neck. Smells good, too—something woodsy and spicy with a hint of warm flesh.

The few thoughts I've gathered scatter as I look at him. He is simply *beautiful*, something I never thought I'd ever consider any man to be. A lock of dark hair falls over his high forehead. Thick eyebrows are slanted slightly upward, three deep lines settling between them as he studies me, the intensity in his eyes sending scalding shivers down my back. His cheekbones are just high enough to balance his stunning features, perfect spots for a woman to lay affectionate kisses. His mouth is still pressed against my palm, and my pulse speeds up for reasons that have nothing to do with the exhilaration from my daring escape.

I should say something. I'm the only one with a free mouth. "Look, if you don't scream or anything, I'll let you go. Deal?" I whisper.

His gaze glides to the gargoyles...then to the balcony on the other side. He takes my wrist firmly, then lowers my hand. Um. Guess he could've always freed himself. "Did you just come from the next suite?"

I nod with a smile full of pride, a sentiment he doesn't seem to share. The lines between his eyebrows become trenches. "Are you *crazy*?" he demands.

"Maybe?" I shrug, then look up at him. "Which way should I answer to get you to cooperate?"

4

ARES

THE WOMAN'S question leaves me speechless for a moment, and as a Harvard-educated lawyer, that doesn't happen often. *Cooperate?* With her? For what purpose?

Her eyes are unusual—one blue and one green, just like Queen. Although my heartbeat picks up at the thought, logic quickly kills the hope. I've found several women with such eyes who turned out to be nothing special or outright scammers, even though I'm careful not to reveal why I'm looking for her. And there's no way *this* woman is Queen. My girl was brave, not insane.

Thick, dark lashes make the woman's eyes appear large and innocent. They don't seem crazy. On the other hand, Dad didn't think Mom was crazy either until she decided to be crazy in love, *literally*.

"You do realize there are things called doors and hallways, right? You could have just knocked like a rational human being." Then I wonder...is this woman from my uncle?

I've only had four girlfriends, but that should be enough for Harvey Dunkel to know my type: a willowy blonde with blue or green eyes, although the lady in front of me is a bit too skinny for my taste. She has a heart-shaped face with a slightly pointed chin, which gives her a pixie-like appearance. Her platinum hair is set in a fancy style with flowers, suitable for a wedding. She's even in a floor-length white gown layered with lace and chiffon. It's almost as though Harvey saw into my memory and created an adult version of Queen as closely as possible.

He's been doing his best to get in touch with me, ostensibly to get me on retainer to help him extend his "empire" into the United States. Says he'll pay me in cash or women, or both. "Once you truly learn the pleasure of female flesh, you'll never look back," he said.

Disgusting.

Where he got the nerve to try to hire the firm is beyond me. The details of the negotiations and deals made after I was rescued are all secret, even to me, bound by an ironclad non-disclosure agreement. Mom never got arrested or served time. Somebody else did, though— some low-level thug who apparently wanted to ransom me to turn his life around. I protested, but the cops didn't buy my story. My cousin, who saw the kidnapping, was in Switzerland to attend boarding school, and Grandmother didn't allow any law enforcement agents near my twin brothers, claiming the experience was too traumatic for them to recount.

But Dad's divorce went through, and he got everything he wanted. Mom stayed away all these years, despite my doubts. She was convinced she loved us, was ready to do anything to make the family whole. It was in her eyes. How could she suppress such an overzealous belief so easily?

"Doors? Hallways? For you, maybe. Not for me. There are guards outside the room next to this one." The woman's matter-of-fact statements pull me back to the present.

"Guards? Are you a criminal? Somebody who needs to be kept under watch for the safety of others?" Wouldn't surprise me a bit. Crazy hot chicks are the worst. I've seen Mom's photos when she was in her twenties. She was stunning, and look how she turned out.

The blonde blinks, then laughs softly. "I wish. That sounds so much more glamorous than being locked up for money."

Reluctant concern stirs, and suddenly I feel like a dick for being so cynical. She must've been desperate to cross over the way she did. And I know what that's like. "Are you in trouble?" My voice is gentler.

"Not if I can make my escape before my aunt or cousin come back." She looks up at me. "If anybody asks, you didn't see me."

"What are you going to do?"

Her smile grows sunny, but it's the sunniness of a woman who knows she has to rescue herself because nobody else will help. "If I try to go out through your door, the guards will notice. So I'm going to get to one of several doors down first."

I direct my thumb behind me at the other balconies. "That way?"

She nods solemnly. "That's the only way."

Just to be sure, I look down. As I suspected. No net. No cushion to catch her if she slips. "Are you out of your mind?"

"I've thought it through. If I die, nobody gets my money, so I win."

What the fuck? "Try 911."

"Won't work. Do you think this is my first time?" She sighs.

An inexplicable ache tightens around my heart. Her predicament vaguely reminds me of being tied up in the cabin by Mom. Just because her family is keeping her in a nicer jail doesn't mean she's free.

"Kind of a Pyrrhic victory." I hope she'll listen. She might be stronger and more agile than she looks, but one mistake and she's done. I don't want that on my conscience.

"But still a victory." She shrugs, her eyes surprisingly devoid of insanity, even if the words rolling out of her mouth are anything but sane. "Scorched earth."

"No."

She pulls back. The retreat might as well have plunged me into a vat of icy water. I clench my hands to avoid reaching out for her, unsure why I'm feeling this way. Nothing makes my skin crawl like people touching me, especially women. When they get clingy, wrapping themselves around me in what they undoubtedly believe is a sexy, affectionate way to keep me tied to them, I want to retch. It reminds me of the way I was bound, constricted and helpless. But with this one, I want her to hold on to me. The feeling is unnerving.

"Don't tell me you're sending me back to my aunt. I'm not marrying my cousin, even if he is technically a step-cousin. They just want to use me for my money," the woman says, raising her arms in a defensive gesture. For some reason, it irritates me.

"Of course not."

Slowly crossing her arms, she looks at me up and down. "I don't think you're strong enough to carry me over there." She jerks her pointy chin in the direction of the balcony on the other side.

"Even if I were, I'm not reckless enough." I shudder inwardly. "I actually value our lives."

Her mouth forms a small O of surprise. "Why would you care?"

"Because I'm a well-adjusted human being? Anybody would."

"No, they wouldn't," she murmurs softly, but I shake my head. She must have super-shitty relatives to feel this way.

"I'm strong enough to carry you out of here if that's what you want," I add before she proposes something insane and inane to escape her aunt and cousin. If anything happens to her, I'll get tangled up with law enforcement as a witness, and I need to be back in L.A. tomorrow. At least, that's what I tell myself as I scrutinize her. "Get all the flowers and crap out of your hair," I say as I drag her inside, so she won't even think about climbing over more gargoyles.

"Okay." She yanks them out of her hair, which falls in long waves down her back. "Now what?"

I pause, taking her in. Untamed tendrils frame her face, her cheeks rosy from her earlier exertion. The white gown sports gray smudges from the stone carvings outside. The slightly disheveled appearance looks so much like little Queen. She never told me her name before disappearing. If only I knew it. Perhaps then it'd be easier to locate her.

"What's your name?" I ask, wondering if she'll be reluctant to share, like the little girl was.

"Lareina."

Her prompt response sends a ripple of disappointment. Of course it's not *her*. How would she have made it to Vegas or be in the predicament Lareina is in? She wasn't the kind of person you'd lock up for money. Hell, she wasn't even confined—she roamed freely in the forest.

"You?" Lareina says.

"Ares."

Her eyes sparkle. The light chips away at my general reluctance to get involved. "Like the god of war."

"Like that." I haven't done anything to pay for the kindness Queen showed me because I wasn't able to find her. So maybe I should pay it forward by helping Lareina out, just this once. After tucking a wayward tendril behind her ear, I step closer to the door. "Have the guards seen you in the dress?"

"Don't think so. My aunt wouldn't have put me in it until after she checked in. Too attention-grabbing."

"Okay, good. Now. Play along."

She nods.

"What do you mean, you're *rethinking our marriage*? Everyone's here already, including my grandfather! His heart won't be able to handle the stress!" I raise my voice enough that even if the people outside won't be able to make out what we're saying, they'll know we're arguing.

She covers her mouth, her eyes wide.

"I don't give a shit if you still have feelings for Ethan!" I add.

"Who's Ethan?" she whispers.

I give her a look.

"Right." She nods. "Just wondering, since you said it with such fury. It sounded very real." She pats me on the shoulder and gives two thumbs up.

"Pay attention," I say, then raise my voice. "We're going to the chapel even if I have to drag you naked!" That should be enough theatrics if anybody's listening.

Mischief twinkles in Lareina's eyes. "Now what? Do I strip?"

The idea of her nude body heats the tips of my ears, although I know she's just messing around. "No." I bend down and, as gently as I can, toss her over my shoulder. She gasps, then presses her hands on my back. Her palms brand me, sending a warm tingle to my stomach. I clench my teeth.

"Wow. This is just like a movie," she whispers.

"Act like you're angry. Resist and don't let anybody see your face," I direct her, more to ignore the fiery sensation of her touch on my back than because I believe she needs instructions. Then I throw the door to the suite open and walk out.

There are a couple of men in black suits outside the door next to mine. Their earpieces say they're hired guards. Probably decent quality. They stare.

Lareina flails and squeals without saying anything. Smart girl. If those men had any interaction with her, they'd recognize her voice.

"What are you looking at?" I spit tersely, letting my aggression show.

"She's blonde," one of them whispers to the other.

"Never seen a blonde before, dickhead?" I raise my voice, not even bothering to be civilized. Everyone in my family says I have a resting asshole face, and when I let my temper go, I apparently look like a sociopath.

They flinch, then glance away.

I hit the button for the elevator, which thankfully opens quickly. An elderly couple is inside. "Eloping?" the man asks.

"Something like that," I say. Lareina keeps quiet, but quits moving her arms and legs. Probably to save energy.

The elderly lady opens her mouth, probably to probe. I give her my least friendly expression, the kind I reserve for the opposing counsel I plan to eviscerate before the day is over. She closes her mouth and looks away. No small talk. Perfect.

In the lobby, I gesture at the couple. "After you."

"Good luck," the man says awkwardly, and they exit. I follow them out, cutting a straight path through the busy, marbled lobby to the revolving door. People stare, but don't dare approach. The I'm-going-to-shove-your-deposition-up-your-ass mask works wonders to keep people away. The exception is the women Harvey occasionally sends to butter me up. Nothing short of a gun in their face makes them back off. Not even then in some cases. Harvey's people are nothing if not loyal.

Out on the sidewalk, I choose *left* and start off. I carry Lareina over my shoulder for some time before finding a chapel to set her down in front of. "Here. You should be okay now."

She pushes her hair up. Her cheeks and neck are flushed. Not even the oncoming dusk can hide the brilliant twinkle in her eyes. "Thank you. I wouldn't have been able to escape so easily without your help."

"It was nothing." I start to turn away.

She waves with a big smile. Her disheveled appearance bothers me, though. No purse on her either. I should just go, but I don't want her to be totally helpless. *I'm just paying it forward, making the world a slightly better place, just like Queen did.*

I pull out several hundreds from my wallet. "Here."

"Oh no. I couldn't possibly. I have some cash." She points to her rather modestly sized chest. Just how much can she hide in there? "I'm all set."

"You sure you're going to be all right?" I should really go now, but feel uneasy, like I'm leaving a helpless child by a pool. *Damn it. Stop getting involved more than necessary.*

"Of course. Thank you." She goes on her toes and places a quick kiss on my cheek, then pulls back just as swiftly, waving and walking toward the pedestrians.

I press fingers against the spot where her lips touched, which prickles.

She's already disappeared into the sea of tourists. A sudden sense of loss presses down on my heart, and I shake my head. Uncharacteristic of me to be this sentimental. It's the unsettling feeling I get around the anniversary of Mom's kidnapping each year. It has nothing to do with Lareina.

My phone buzzes with a text from the latest PI I hired to track down Queen.

–Greg: Couldn't find anything. Interviewed people who used to live in the area twenty-two years ago, but they don't recall any girl matching the description.

"Come on, Queen. It's been over twenty years. Don't you think it's time to show yourself? Perhaps give a little hint as to how you're doing?" I just want to know if she's okay. And that Mom and her people didn't do anything to her. Although Harvey promised me to keep Mom in check, I don't trust him. Not really, anyway. He'd sell me out in a heartbeat if it would earn him a buck.

I let out a long breath. Lareina's completely gone from view. Putting away my phone, I start back to the hotel. It's time to get ready for the bachelor party.

5

ARES

Music throbs, the loud beats pounding through my body. Barry, an associate at the firm, is getting married, and he rented an entire club for his bachelor party. As I walk along the dark corridor, the specially mirrored walls show my reflection. The way my eyes glow makes me falter for a second, and I avert my gaze, staring at the wooden floor. Everyone says I have my mother's eyes. Every time I look at my reflection, I feel like I'm looking into her face, eerie in its love and madness, and the scar on my arm throbs. When I brought up the pain with my doctor a few years ago, he said it was a phantom pain, just psychological.

Thanks, doc, for making me feel so sane.

Wonder if he shared his opinion with Grandmother or Father. That could explain their concern that I might be insane—no, *obsessed*...although in my family, the words can be used interchangeably.

Once I'd calmed down after the ridiculous dinner where they insisted that I give up on finding Queen and get married to get promoted, I grudgingly accepted that their concern is partially driven by guilt. They were supposed to protect me back then, and I should've never been left to survive on my own in the fire. But that doesn't mean they get to brush Queen off as a figment of my imagination and do their best to convince me of that.

Barry has apparently snagged himself a nice woman. My own hunt for a wife isn't going as smoothly as I'd like. Most associates at the firm are reluctant to refer suitable candidates, assuming they're aware of what's going on with me and The Fogeys. They probably don't want to get involved in the family drama. The women I get matched with through various online dating sites and apps so far have been the equivalent to what's left after a two-week clearance sale—ill-fitting and unsuitable, even at seventy-five percent off. The Fogeys would never accept one as "good and respectable." And neither would I.

If I get really lucky, I might run into a suitable woman tonight. A cursory glance says there are more women than men here. But upon closer inspection, they're all strippers, given how little clothes they have on. Should've known. This is classic Barry. I don't know how he plans to stay faithful to just one woman when he's an equal-opportunity lover.

It's okay, I tell myself. I have a few more dates set up for the next three days. The Fogeys never said anything about a ceremony. I just need to produce a lawfully wedded wife.

The phone buzzes, and I glance at the screen.

—Unknown: I love you, my little prince.

This is the third time I've gotten a strange text like this. I block the number. It could be my persistent ex, although the "little prince" part doesn't really fit. On the other hand, who can tell what the hell goes on in her head? In her world, she's a princess who can do no wrong, and anybody who disagrees with her is a problem.

It's too bad none of my exes fit Grandmother's conditions: good and respectable. I boasted I could find a bride in a month, but one that will work? That's proving to be much harder.

On the other hand, I'm not looking for the love of my life or a soul mate. Just a presentable wife for The Fogeys to accept until I get my promotion. If we happen to fall in love, fine. We can continue. Otherwise, we'll quietly get divorced. By then, I'll be a junior partner and the Fogeys won't be able to force a demotion on me over a divorce. If they do, I'll sue the damn firm and Dad as well.

"Hey, you made it!" Barry booms. Almost as tall as I am, he's solidly built, with broad shoulders and massive arms and legs from playing football for the University of Georgia. A knee injury ended his athletic career, so he focused on academics and went to Yale Law. A tuft of bleached yellow hair, an excessive tan and a slightly goofy grin make him appear mildly dim-witted, especially when he lays it on thick with a Georgian drawl, but he's one of the meanest lawyers at Huxley & Webber. He slaps my back twice, having quickly deduced that a man-hug is not the way to go with me. Like I said, smarter than he looks. And he's already soused.

"Wouldn't miss it for the world."

"I don't believe you. Bet you were doing billable work until two seconds ago," he says with a tipsy laugh.

I shrug. "I bill, therefore I am." The previous legal team for one of our clients screwed up an overseas leveraged finance deal, which means that now *I* have to fix it. As complicated and frustrating as it is to navigate the bureaucracies of multiple countries, work is a great balm for the soul. It doesn't betray you or let you down.

I don't mention that while I was doing the work, I was also thinking about ways to find a wife in under three days. Barry wouldn't know a respectable woman if his life depended on it. His fiancée is a fluke. Wouldn't it be convenient if an acceptably decent woman just jumped in front of my car? That actually happened with one of my cousins, but I doubt I'll be that lucky.

Four scantily clad strippers push a giant cake into the room, setting it in front of an enormous champagne fountain. The guys are already drunk, hooting and yelling in good spirits. Although I paste on a smile for Barry's sake, this isn't my kind of scene. Half an hour, then I'm going back to my room to wrap up the contract amendments. I start to reach for a glass of champagne, and the top of the cake opens and a well-bronzed blonde in a tiny bikini with nipple tassels pops up. "Ta-da!"

What the fuck? My hand drops without touching the flute. Dread, resignation and irritation pump in sync to the music as my latest ex shimmies in the cake like a Hawaiian dancing doll. Her tits bounce in every direction, much to the excitement and delight of the intoxicated men. If anybody recognizes her, it's impossible to tell with the deafening music and noise.

Then Barry squints. "Isn't that Soledad?"

I sigh. "Yes."

Soledad is the only child of a billionaire venture capitalist who also happens to be a client of Andreas Webber, one of the name partners at the firm. She supposedly took one look at me and fell in love. She pursued me relentlessly for six months until I agreed to a date just to get her off my back.

And it went all right. Despite my misgivings, she was actually pleasant. Even carried on an interesting conversation. The second date was better, and she kept calling and texting to set up times. I even thought she might be the one I could carry on with long term, since she isn't the kind of woman Harvey can manipulate...

Then we hit the third month, and everything went to shit.

"Ares, I love you!" she screams over the music.

My skin crawls at her wide grin. She'd make a great Joker.

"Wow," Barry says. "She loves you."

I clench my fists. "No."

Apparently, Soledad can read my lips from across the room. "Don't be cruel. You know my heart is true!"

"Her heart is *true*," Barry informs me.

"As true as a beachfront property in Nebraska." There were several reasons for our breakup—such as her sudden meddling in my private schedule, as well as rapid-onset jealousy and clinginess. She even demanded to know who Queen was—much to my shock, since I don't discuss her with anybody, especially not my exes. But the deathblow came when I caught her in bed with a gigolo. She was wrapped around him like a starved boa constrictor, calling him Ares.

I remember standing there quietly and watching for a moment. Intellectually I understood I should be upset, but inside there was nothing. Her antics and endless demands had exhausted me. It takes too much mental energy to rouse anger for a woman you have no feelings for. Besides, it wasn't my bed, it was hers. And she was welcome to invite whomever she wanted.

I merely stepped into the walk-in closet to take the two suits I'd left there. The gigolo noticed me before she did and ran out with his clothes faster than I could say, "Defamation lawsuit."

As I came out, she hopped off the bed and grabbed my arm. I yanked it out of her grasp without a word. She wasn't worth the effort.

"Aren't you mad?" she demanded, standing in front of me without bothering to cover herself.

"No." I paused, mildly curious about something. "Is his name really Ares?"

She turned red. "*No!* I was pretending he was you, since you're so cold in bed!" She pointed at the newly created hickeys on her neck. "You see these? He did them! For me!" Her eyes were open so wide that I could see the white on all sides. *Deranged.* "Because he cares about me!"

Her shrill declaration tightened my gut, but also reaffirmed that I'd made the right decision to end the relationship before she became even crazier and clingier. "I'm happy for the two of you." I left, blocked her number and promptly forgot about her.

So why the hell is she here? "Did you hire her?"

"Nope." Barry raises his right hand. "I solemnly swear on my mother's grave."

"Your mother's healthier than a horse and will probably outlive both of us."

He grabs a glass of whiskey from a tray. "Here. Drink this." He gestures at my ex. "She's crazy, we all know that. I'll have security throw her out."

He pulls out his phone and starts to make a call. Soledad drags herself out of the cake, her movements awkward, since the tiers are so high. She looks worse than the ghost girl crawling out of a TV in *The Ring*.

Soledad runs toward me. "Ares!" She throws herself at me.

I sidestep, and she stumbles, bumping my drink and almost spilling it. She manages to right herself with a pout.

"Why are you so mean? Are you still upset about that guy? Forget about him. The hickeys are gone already." She pushes her hair back, revealing her neck. "We can start fresh. I'll let you put *new* hickeys here."

"New hickeys! And on the same spots. Well, that *is* a temptation. But I'd rather not contract some yet-to-be-discovered strain of herpes."

"I'm clean!"

"As clean as a fraternity's bathroom floor after a mixer." I can't do this sober. I knock back the whiskey fast. "There's no fresh start. We're done."

"Don't be silly! I love you! I came here for you. For you and our future baby!" She puts a hand over her belly with a smile that's clearly meant to be shy but only serves to make me recoil. "Imagine. Our family of three!"

The bright sparks in her eyes mix with Mom's expression when she looked at me in the cabin, and I just can't.

Soledad comes closer, and I put out one hand to stop her and grab another drink with the other.

"Come on, baby! Your uncle said he'd love to welcome me into the family!" she yells over the music.

Uncle? There are only two people I would consider an "uncle." Ted Lasker, Aunt Jeremiah's former lover and the father of her only son Huxley...or Harvey Dunkel, my mom's psychopathic younger brother, whose life goal is to take over his family's mafia empire and expand it far beyond the borders of Nesovia.

Ted would like Soledad because she's what he would deem "hot," but he has zero influence over my family. He's never been part of it, and Aunt Jeremiah doesn't give him time of the day unless he pays or it's one of his ridiculous birthday parties. That leaves Harvey, who somehow seems to believe he has a familial tie with me because neither of us cares for my mom.

But he's mistaken. The depth of my loathing for her is unmatched. I hate everything to do with her, including myself. Half the time I don't even like my own eyes. Sometimes I can't look at my face because I'm afraid there's more of her there.

Soledad wraps her arms around mine, and I can't seem to move fast enough to pull away. *What the hell?* She isn't that quick, and I have great reflexes.

"Come on," she whines nasally, tugging at me. I should resist, but inexplicably my feet follow her lead. The gears in my head turn slowly, as though they're in a pool of cooling molasses.

She walks me out of the club. A few guys glance at me, but once they see that I'm with "a stripper," they shoot me knowing smirks and turn away.

Damn it. The smog of the city hits me. The neon lights seem to sear my eyeballs, and I squint. Music, laughter and conversations buzz in my ears like angry bees. Soledad tugs at my arm. "This way, my love."

"Not your love," I say even as my body follows her. *What's going on?*

"Yes, you are. You drank my love potion. I put it into your drink. Smooth, huh?"

"No. You're fucking crazy." As insane as my mother.

Humming, Soledad leads me down two blocks until we reach a steakhouse. She opens the door and steps inside. If her bikini shocks anyone, nobody shows it. The maître d', crisp in a black-and-white suit and a bow tie, gestures at her to follow.

"Look at this! I can't remember the last time we had a date," she coos.

"Because we broke up." My body might be doing her bidding, but my mouth remains independent. Dad would say it's the Harvard training. Grandmother would credit my work at Huxley & Webber. Thank God for this small favor. If I couldn't even talk back, I'd want to jump off a balcony.

Balconies... Wonder how Lareina is doing? Now, *she* was somebody worth dredging up some concern and emotion for. At least she wasn't clingy. No. She was too...*not* clingy, which was vaguely irritating now that I recall. And yet she was desperate enough to climb over those gargoyles. Did she have some kind of circus training? A cat with nine lives?

"Come on." Soledad's annoying voice breaks my train of thought. She pulls me through the dark restaurant and the aroma of sizzling meat, potatoes and herbs. The band on the small stage sings of unrequited love in a jazzy tune, and patrons toast each other and dine with gusto. Faces blur, and the music grows faint in my head.

The maître d' opens a door at the end of a hall, and Soledad and I are in a private room with a cherry table, two new glasses and a bottle of Hibiki.

At the other end sits Harvey, his black suit hugging his powerful shoulders and draping down to the trim waist. His mahogany hair is slicked back to show a neat forehead with a faint hint of a horizontal wrinkle. He has pale amber eyes with heavy lids, nothing like Mom's.

He took after his father and got the narrow, straight nose and thin lips.

Two beefy bald men stand to each side behind him. Probably his right and left hands. They look like crosses between a human and a pit bull.

Great. So Soledad is in cahoots with Harvey. Figures. She's too stupid to know you don't get involved with a mob boss's heir.

Harvey smiles. "Good to see you, Ares."

I sigh. "Can't really say the same."

Soledad interjects, "I did it!"

Harvey's snakelike eyes flick in her direction. "You did. Now wait outside."

"What? No! I want to have my say first."

"Business first." He signals the man to his left, who immediately steps forward and takes her arm.

"Let me go!" She turns to me. "Ares, you aren't going to let them manhandle me, are you? I'm the love of your life!"

She could be the salvation of humanity, but I'd still let them. She's the one who set me up. "Get her out of here," I say to the man.

"You asshole!" she screams. "You know why I hired that other Ares? Because he would've defended me!"

"For a fee," I mutter.

"You're such a shit!" She kicks so hard, her silver heels fly off. The man drags her out. She resists, but she might as well be resisting a rhino.

As soon as the door closes behind them, the room plunges into silence. Harvey gestures at the seat opposite him. "Please."

The last thing I want is to sit with him. But my ass is already lowering itself into the armchair. I'm sure Soledad's "love potion" came from him.

He pours the Hibiki into the two glasses. "To our family."

"We aren't family," I say, raising my glass. Thankfully I have enough self-control to avoid going along with his unspoken suggestion and drinking it. What the fuck did he have Soledad feed me?

"Sure we are. *Pietas et unitas,* and all that."

"Loyalty and unity extend to the Huxleys. Not a Dunkel."

"Don't tell me you're still upset about your mother."

"She should've gone to jail," I seethe. "Or better yet get, locked up in a dungeon. I know you have a couple in your compound."

He shoots me a hooded look over the glass. "She's too fragile for it."

Recalling her wild expression, I snort. "Right. Fragile. She single-handedly kidnapped me, drove me to some godforsaken place in Oregon, then left me to die."

"The fire was an accident." He sighs, full of a regret I don't buy. "She paid a heavy price for it."

"By having somebody else take the fall for her?" I sneer.

"She's been confined."

"Did she get tied to a chair and fed drugged food? It seems like the family thing—drugging people."

"You refused to take my calls, and I don't want to hurt you, not the way your mother did. I care about you and our familial bond. No matter how much you deny it, the Dunkel blood flows in your veins. That makes you one of us."

"I'll never be one of you."

His lazy smile says, *We'll see about that.* The man to his right places a black leather folio in front of me and opens it. It's a standard retainer agreement on official Huxley & Webber stationery. *Motherfucker.* He came prepared.

His goon puts a pen in my hand.

"Sign it."

Harvey's soft command tugs at me, and my fingertips whiten around the pen. The goon moves my hand until the tip of the pen is at the signature section. *Oh hell no.* My family can find all sorts of loopholes to break out of contracts, but a retainer agreement is another matter. Even if we do it legally, it can create a negative perception, and sometimes that's more important than the truth.

"This is coercion. And the retainer is just going to be another worthless piece of paper when it's proven I was drugged," I say.

Crossing his legs, he swirls his whiskey. "How confident are you that you can get tested before it's gone from your system?"

Fuck.

"Just sign it, Ares. The law firm will love having our business. I promise it'll be lucrative. A great, long-lasting partnership founded on blood ties and boundless profits."

My fingers twitch. The pen shifts on the paper, leaving a short line. *Sign, sign, sign,* the voice that sounds just like Harvey urges in my head. Nausea roils. Sweat pops out on my forehead and back. There's a great reason I shouldn't sign, but what...? My thoughts grow unclear.

"Come on," Harvey says gently—a paternal figure leading a lost youth back home. "You don't truly believe your mother just gave up on you and your brothers, do you? The agreement between our families stipulates that she's free to reach out again when all the boys reach the age of thirty, and your brothers just celebrated their thirtieth birthday last month."

I stiffen. Grandmother and Father seemed a bit tense at the party, but I assumed it was simply a management problem at the firm. After all, the Huxleys' relationship with the Webbers has become awkward, and things are still shaking out.

"Bullshit," I say finally. "My family would've called for a restraining order in perpetuity."

"Wanted to. Couldn't. Not when she threatened to cut her wrists." Harvey's smile doesn't reach his eyes. "Zoe's hard to stop when she's motivated. And your grandfather loves her. A mystery, isn't it?"

For this, the family would've extracted something from the Dunkels. Still... *Fuck.*

Then I recall the text I received earlier. *My little prince.* Mom would call me exactly that...

"She's trying to find a way to get to you. My men tell me she's going to use young, beautiful women this time. She's been busy with her little side business in gambling and lending and got her hands on women so desperate they'd do anything to seduce you and bring you back to the fold and the love she's been saving for you." He waits for his words to sink in for a moment.

It takes a while, with my head so foggy. But when I process it, nausea roils through my gut.

Harvey continues, "I can keep them away from you. Keep you insulated and safe. You don't want to be Zoe's little puppet, do you?" He gives me a Satanic smile, bargaining for my soul. "Sign the retainer. I promise you won't regret it."

I shouldn't. I can't. "I need to pee."

"What?" Harvey squints at me.

I jump to my feet, but his goon pushes me back down into the seat. His meaty paws are strong, and he doesn't mind being rough.

"Sign first," Harvey says.

"Pee first," I counter.

The muscles in his jaw flex. "Ares—"

"I'm going to pee on the contract if you don't let me go to the bathroom *right now*."

"You wouldn't."

I reach for my belt buckle. Harvey scowls, his expression somewhere between disbelief and horror. I unbuckle, then begin to lower my zipper.

"Fine!" He turns to the goon. "Take him to the bathroom." He looks at me coolly. "Once you're done, you'll come back and sign like the good nephew that you are."

A thin smile curves my lips, although my head feels fuzzier. I observe the scene like it's happening outside of my body.

The goon takes me by the arm, and we leave the room. Soledad jumps up from a chair and lunges at me past Goon Number Two. *Ugh.* I don't have the mental energy to deal with her right now.

Putting two fingers on her forehead, I push her back into her chair. "Stay."

"Ares, you know I love you, right? You won't forget about me?" She looks at me tearfully, but her mouth is twisted into a weirdly manipulative smile. She probably has some ground pepper in her purse to rub into her eyes. Should've given up when she was ahead. Her profession of love only strengthens my resolve to make my escape.

"I'd rather cut off my dick than be with you."

"You can't say that!"

"Don't like it? Talk to Harvey about the defective 'love potion.'" *Drive him crazy with your nasal whining.*

There are two ways you can score a win. One: crush the opponent's spirit with a show of overwhelming force. Generally how I prefer to be in courtrooms and other professional settings. Two: feign incompetence and weakness to make the opponent underestimate you and lower their guard. Works great when you're dealing with somebody who thinks he has the upper hand.

I stumble a little, moving as though I'm feeling woozy. The neckless goon knows I've been drugged, but he probably doesn't know with what or exactly how it affects me—my uncle isn't the sharing type. So I'll put on a show.

The bathroom is all black and reflective, with stall doors going from floor to ceiling. Very civilized, very private. The asshole pushes me toward a urinal. "I need a stall." I point at the biggest one with a blue wheelchair logo on the door.

"You only need to pee," he says in a gravelly voice.

"I have a condition. Paruresis."

"What?"

"Shy bladder syndrome. Can't pee with you staring." I give him a meaningful look while swaying slightly.

He looks horrified. "I'm not staring at your dick."

"Don't believe you."

"What the fuck? You were about to take out your dick in front of Harvey."

"He's family. Probably changed my diaper when I was a kid." I lay it on thick, slapping his solid shoulder. "Look. Just let me pee in peace, okay? To be honest, I kinda need to poo, too."

His face scrunches.

"Full disclosure is important. You should know—I'm a lawyer."

He glares at me. In fact, he looks like he wants to murder me, but Harvey needs me to sign the retainer agreement. I give the goon a cheeky grin, then stumble into the stall and lock it with a loud click. The automatic flush goes off. Fantastic.

I look around. What can I use to surprise attack the asshole outside? Can I take out the toilet paper holder? It's metal, and long enough to hurt if I jab it into his eyes. But am I going to be quick enough? I was slower than Soledad at the party, and since then the drug has had more time to spread through my system.

I look up and see a long window across. It opens, and I think I can push my head and maybe shoulders through if I grease myself.

Desperation can be a great substitute for grease.

I don't have to have any grease. Besides, I don't want to leave my clothes behind. I step on the toilet seat and slide the window open. It creaks a little.

"What's that?"

"A fart, okay? Whatever your boss gave me is making me gassy."

A sound of disgust. I grin, then hoist myself up. Just because my reflexes are slower doesn't mean my muscles are useless. Doing gymnastics for six years and practicing aikido and judo since I escaped the burning cabin have made me pretty agile.

I stick my head out and look around. A small alley. Underneath the window is a big dumpster, probably for the restaurant. I experimentally push myself up, trying to fit my shoulders through. The frame scrapes my clothes and skin. Something gets caught, and I wriggle and yank at my jacket. The toilet flushes.

"Finally! You done now?" the goon calls out impatiently.

"Mostly!" I yell back, then shove myself out.

Carefully, I twist and turn. Something cracks, but I don't pay attention, since it isn't me. Finally, I get my torso through and turn, hanging from the window. My foot touches the dumpster cover. It flexes a bit under my weight; I hop down. My balance isn't quite perfect, but I manage to stay on my feet. *Yes!*

This must've been what Lareina felt when she managed to escape her terrible aunt via the balcony. Wonder how she's doing now. Hopefully she wasn't caught.

I trot toward the main drag and people. Harder for Harvey and his men to act recklessly when there are so many witnesses. The lights halo, and my eyes refuse to focus correctly, just like the time I had them dilated for an examination.

Blinking, I stumble into the crowd. Nobody seems to notice anything off about me. Harvey is smart. He would never give me something that would earn me a hospital visit.

Moving behind a gay couple with bulging arms and legs, I pull out my phone to dial. Except the battery's down to nothing. *Damn it.* I could have sworn I charged it before leaving the room. Scowling, I put it away. No calling for help tonight.

I walk a few blocks, and then see a tall, bald man in a black suit in the crowd. *Is that the asshole who dragged me to the bathroom?* He swivels his nonexistent neck left and right.

Shit. I turn around and start moving toward a brightly lit building to my left. Every nerve bristles with apprehension. How much of the alarm I'm feeling is real and how much is from the drugs? I don't want to move too quickly in order not to get spotted, but then the goon sees me. Being as tall as I am makes it hard to blend in to a crowd. I pick up the pace, but the goon increases his speed as well.

It seems like a futile effort. Frustration swells in my chest. Why the hell didn't the family ensure nobody associated with the Dunkels could get near me?

My eyes refuse to focus properly, but I'm close enough to see that the place I've been walking toward is a casino. I start to push the door open, and a cool hand closes around my wrist.

6

LAREINA

This must be how Jerry felt, running and hiding from Tom, I decide, thinking about one of my favorite cartoons. After leaving Ares, I've been walking around, entering and leaving various stores and casinos. Since I only have a limited amount of money, I haven't bought anything except for a bottle of water and a big, floppy hat with two mini-sunflowers on one side.

Doris, Vernon, Rupert and their men are looking for me. Every time I spot one of them, dread slashes at my gut. They don't seem to recognize me—maybe it's the loose hair or maybe it's the hat. I also ripped off the sleeves of my dress and the two outer layers of the skirt, so it's as limp as old lettuce, rather than the poufy dandelion puff it started out as. I considered buying a set of new clothes until I realized I'd have to ask somebody to help me out of the dress, and didn't want anybody to see my scar.

Still, it's only a matter of time. They're determined to find me and force me to marry Rupert. I hadn't really thought things through when I fled the room. I need to do more than just run; I need to permanently stop them. The only way to do that is to get a husband of my own choosing who won't throw me under the bus for my aunt.

Why didn't I realize this sooner? Then I could've asked Ares if he wouldn't mind being a husband in name only for at least six months. I could've offered to reward him handsomely for it, too.

Yes, he's a stranger and I don't know anything about him. But he helped me without asking questions or demanding compensation, which was surprising. In my experience, people don't lift a finger to assist unless there's something profitable in it for them. Someone like Ares is likely altruistic and trustworthy, at least enough that I could trust him for a few months until I'm safely in control of my inheritance.

My grandfather despised Doris and did everything in his power to ensure she couldn't touch the inheritance or kill me. Her bad-mouthing her brother—my dad—and mismanaging a small subsidiary he put her in charge of didn't help. Grandfather loathed men *and* women who overestimated themselves. He told me that as soon as I was married or came of age, I needed to get a lawyer specializing in tax, estate planning and other financial matters and ensure that Doris and her family couldn't leech off me.

How and where can I find a suitable groom? I look at the crowd milling on the night streets of Vegas. Couples, more couples, groups of women... a few guys who could be single, but I don't like that they look like they just finished high school. Some Elvis impersonators. Should I hire one of them to be my fake husband?

And is a fake husband going to be enough? Won't Doris check? I would if I were her. What if she tries to invalidate my marriage? I know nothing about the legal requirements for marriage in the States.

Argh. So irritating.

I wish I'd somehow found a way to keep in touch with Ethan. He's in the States, and it's possible he lives in Vegas. If he's single, he could help. Or maybe he could refer me to a single friend who isn't a greedy sociopath. Ethan seemed like such a nice guy. Smart, too. Knew a lot about art. And saying his favorite artist was my mom during our first-day introductions endeared him to me.

It's sad that he's one of my closest friends and I've never even met him in person.

Then I see *him*—Ares! And he's coming toward me! He's walking a bit unsteadily—maybe had too much to drink? He's looking around, squinting under the neon lights, then flinches when his eyes land on a guy several feet behind him. The man starts after him, but Ares also begins walking faster.

Is he in trouble? The man is coming up quickly. I trot to Ares, spreading my arms as though to hug him. As curious I am about what's going on, I want to help him first. That's the least I owe him for his act of kindness earlier.

But before I can reach him, he makes a small turn and starts to push the door of a casino to his left. Acting on instinct, I grab his wrist. His whole body stiffens, his bright blue eyes boring into mine with the ferocity of a cornered lion. Shivers skitter along my spine, and my mouth dries. This isn't the kind of reaction I expected.

The reflection of Ares's pursuer grows closer in the glass door. First things first: time to rescue Ares.

I paste on a bright smile. "Hey, baby, I've been looking everywhere for you!" I twirl in my dress. "Like my wedding gown?"

Recognition flickers in Ares's wide eyes. "Lareina?" he says, incredulous. "What are you doing here?"

"Getting the perfect wedding gown!" It's an easy lie, and the truth would definitely attract nosy eavesdroppers.

The stalker is still coming toward us, but looks a bit uncertain now. Ares's eyes flick to the glass door too, and his mouth tightens. I have no clue who the creep is, but Ares obviously wants to lose him, and there are certain distractions that make people look away. Like a fairly intense public display of affection.

Smiling, I put my hands on Ares's cheeks, feeling the day's growth of beard scratching my palms. He looks down at me in confusion, but I give him no time to ask questions before I pull him down for a kiss.

The sacrifices I make to keep him safe.

I've experienced a kiss before, when Rupert ambushed me on my sixteenth birthday. All I remember of that appalling incident is that his breath held a hint of onion and Tic Tac, and his mouth was wet, slimy and slightly cool. His tongue didn't feel any better as he shoved it between my teeth like a squirmy salamander.

Ares's large hand supports my back out of reflex, the touch hotter than a brand and inexplicably delicious. The hard muscles of his chest and legs press against me, cradling me. My heart rate picks up and starts to race. A wild cocktail of anticipation and jitteriness pulses in my veins. He smells so good—something spicy and woodsy and safe and exciting, all at the same time. Butterflies fluttering in my belly, I brush my mouth against his. His lips are surprisingly soft and hot. Searing tension winds around my gut, an illicit thrill sparking along my back. Goosebumps rise on my arms, and I slide them upward until they're looped around his strong neck.

His mouth remains closed, and I freeze with my tongue pressed against his lips. Now what? Shouldn't he make the next move, since I already did my part? Or is he waiting for me to do everything?

I open my eyes, and realize he hasn't closed his. Surprise lingers in his gaze, pupils dilated. Abrupt annoyance and embarrassment heat my face. Obviously, I'm the only one who felt anything. Did the contact feel like a squirmy salamander for him?

Forget it. I purse my mouth and pull away. I'm not desperate enough to continue with a guy who's grossed out by me.

Suddenly he cups the back of my skull, threading his fingers into my hair. His mouth claims mine, open and carnal, stealing my breath away. I don't even realize I've parted my lips until his tongue glides inside, stroking me and sending delicious sizzles all over. My head spins, and I grip his shoulders to anchor myself. His body was warm earlier—now it's *scorching*. The air in my lungs grows thick, and I stroke his tongue with mine, curious if it'll feel as amazing for him.

A soft groan vibrates in his chest. He pulls me tighter, and I feel intoxicated, high on newly discovered sensations. My cheeks burn, and I wish we could get closer. Much closer. My breasts ache, pressed against his torso, and the tips tingle. An unfamiliar throbbing starts between my legs. An almost irresistible urge to wrap one of them around his waist scrapes along my nerve endings, but I restrain myself. That seems a bit too much, even in Vegas.

My head grows lighter and I slump, slightly dizzy. He holds me tight. Is it from not having eaten much all day? But the weakness in my limbs seems somehow different from the effects of not having eaten.

"Breathe." Ares has my head resting on the spot between his shoulder and chest. I sense his pulse, his quickened breathing. The world quits spinning, although I'm still overly hot and sensitive all over. "What was all that?" he asks.

"Distraction? Reinforcement?" I say vaguely, looking around for the stalker. "That freak who was following you is gone."

Ares sighs, then runs his fingers through his hair with an irritation I can't understand. "Kissing a strange man isn't the smartest move," he says as he puts a hand on my back and starts to walk along the Strip. His gait is off…a little awkward and slow, like he's fighting sleep or extreme fatigue. *Does he feel weak in the knees from the kiss like me?* My cheeks warm at the possibility.

"You aren't exactly a stranger," I say. "I know you, and I told you quite a bit about myself earlier."

He looks at me seriously. Thoughts flicker in the depths of his eyes, but he doesn't say anything, as though he's trying to sort himself out first.

"Besides, you helped me earlier, and I wanted to return the favor," I add. *Does what I'm saying sound weird?* By now, most people probably have close friends and boyfriends. I don't have anybody I can call a friend. Aimless trust-fund babies make up my social circle. They're great for inviting to wild parties to cement my reputation for unpredictability, but nothing more.

His shoulders deflate for some reason. Maybe he expected a better explanation…?

"That thug was expecting a lone man, obviously, not a man kissing a woman in a wedding dress. The guy after you probably thought we were newlyweds and decided he'd made a mistake. Happens a lot in Vegas, I heard. Eloping, I mean, not getting chased by bad guys."

A corner of his mouth twitches in a small smile. "And yet here we are."

"Can you tell me who that was? You don't have to if you don't want," I add in case it's too private, although I'm dying of curiosity. Ares doesn't seem like a criminal, but…you never know. If he's in trouble, maybe I can hire a lawyer to defend him and get him out of whatever mess he's involved in. Rupert bragged his attorneys could get him out of any jam on a technicality.

"My uncle's man. He wants me to work for him."

The Accidental Marriage

My heart softens with sympathy. He too has a shitty relative. "And you don't want to."

"Hell no." Ares shudders. "That would be my idea of hell. He's not a nice man." The finality in his tone says he's not discussing his uncle anymore. "How about you? Did you figure out how you're going to get away from your aunt?"

"Not yet. Her family and guards are still looking for me." I make a face. They won't give up until they get their hands on my money permanently.

"Need help?"

"Are you a lawyer specializing in estate and tax law?" I tease him a little, since I doubt he's volunteering to marry me right now.

He frowns. "No." We walk in silence for a few moments, and then he stumbles.

"Are you okay?"

He closes his eyes briefly. "No."

"Drunk?" There's a whiff of alcohol on him.

"No. The uncle I told you about? He put something in my drink to make me malleable."

I inhale sharply and scrutinize him. Bloodless complexion. Beads of sweat popping along his hairline. His pupils are wider and more dilated, his eyes glassy. "Do you need to throw up? Maybe sit down?"

He shakes his head. "No. Too late to purge it. Just have to avoid him until the drug wears off."

"Jeez. I thought only I had relatives with a propensity for drugging people." I put my arm around his waist. He's too big for me to really support, but hopefully I can help him balance better.

We turn left, and I stop, air catching in my throat at the sight of a tall, beefy man with an earpiece and sharp cheeks. He's scanning the crowd with narrowed eyes, so I turn my head to the side, making sure my hair curtains my face.

"What's wrong?" Ares says.

"One of my aunt's guards." It's the one I dubbed Creepier.

Without thinking, I pull Ares into the closest establishment, praying Creepier didn't spot me.

"Hello! Here for your marriage certificate?"

49

An Asian lady smiles sweetly at us from behind a counter, her short, bleached hair falling around an oval face with soft, rosy cheeks.

"Did you already apply online?"

Oh shit. This is the place Doris wanted Rupert to drag me to! I'm sure they did, in fact, already apply online, but there's no way I'm telling this kind lady that. I'd rather twerk naked in front of a church on Sunday while belting a Cardi B tune.

I glance at Ares, then at the door. Creepier is probably still outside looking for me. Creepy could be coming. Worse yet, Rupert could be rushing here right now to get the marriage license.

But can I ask Ares to go along? He might not want to—

"No," he says to the woman.

"I guess you didn't know about the program. It makes it so much quicker. But it's okay. I can still help you. Oh my goodness, what am I doing? I'm Pippa!" She extends her slim hand, long nails shining with fresh polish. "Let's get started."

7

ARES

Pippa seems like a nice woman. Asks questions, all enthusiastic and sweet, as though we're her best friends reaching a major milestone in romance.

Lareina, too, is agreeable. And inexplicably sexy. Her voice is velvety, which feels good to my ears when she speaks, but I also sense a bit of steel underneath, which makes me respect her. Spinelessness is pathetic. Thinking back on the way she climbed over those gargoyles to reach my balcony, I'd say her balls are bigger than a lot of men I know.

She casts me sidelong glances from time to time, as though to gauge my reactions. Am I supposed to do something when she gives her name or birthday? We're almost the same age, although she looks much younger. And more finely made, with a delicate arch to her eyebrows, the sweet, straight slope of her nose, a soft, full mouth and the supple lines of her long limbs. Her fingers are pale and slim as she lays them on the counter and fidgets a little.

Before I can think, I have my hand wrapped around them in a comforting gesture. She looks at me, her eyes wide. Hasn't anybody ever tried to make her feel better? Or warm her surprisingly cool hands?

She must've had a lot of shitty boyfriends. A ball of acid forms in my stomach at the possibility that she might've been forced to date that step-cousin of hers, who obviously has to be a dick.

"So that'll be—" Pippa's request for money, very polite and professional, jerks me out of my random reveries. Her eyes are shining, silently wishing me and Lareina a world of joy as long as we can pay the fee. The situation seems a bit absurd. What happens if you're too poor to afford a marriage license?

I almost wish I could declare myself too poor to pay the fee, except Aunt Jeremiah would immediately spot me the cash. She can be such a bitch. The Fogeys act like they're concerned, but they only worry about me the way they want. If they really cared, they wouldn't insist I get married to get promoted. Or worse, demand that I give up looking for Queen.

The lights are too bright, and Pippa's smile is too white. Her face seems to melt a little, like one of Dali's clocks. I touch my temples to anchor myself—before my head flies away like a balloon or drops off my neck to the floor. Either possibility seems likely.

Lareina reaches into her bodice for cash. I put out a hand for her to stop, and reach for my black AmEx. *But wait.* Harvey is a sneaky asshole; he might be monitoring my credit cards—illegally, of course. Just because he wants to hire a lawyer doesn't mean he's law abiding. I pull out a wad of cash and slide it to the clerk. Can't let a woman pay, especially someone who's helping me. Also...that kiss was amazing.

"You thought it was amazing too?" Lareina says, her cheeks pinkening.

I start. *Did I say that out loud?* Her eyes sparkle as she waits for a response, and I say, "Didn't you?" The hot excitement from the moment is still buzzing in my blood.

Lareina's face turns redder. *Cute.* I grin. *Adorable, in fact.*

Perhaps you can marry her and get promoted! my mind says.

No. I need respect and indifference in my marriage with a wife who embodies the tranquility and social acuity that The Fogeys are looking for. Lareina doesn't fit the mold. A woman headstrong enough—and crazy enough—to climb across the outside of a hotel to reach the next balcony is bound to be wild and disruptive, even if she is a great kisser.

And even if I do want to kiss her again.

Pippa grabs the money with a prehensile gusto that reminds me of an eagle's talons. Or a velociraptor's.

A dinosaur? My head is a mess right now—which I hate. I keep my thoughts *pristine* and *organized*. No smiling at a woman I've known for less than twenty-four hours, thinking she's cute or adorable. And no reliving the kiss we had to share to escape. And most definitely no hoping we can kiss again.

Fuckin' Harvey. Just what the hell did he feed me?

"You guys are super sweet!" Pippa says.

"Thank you!" Lareina beams.

"We hear that a lot," I add on impulse. *Shut up.*

I shove the license into my pocket and escort Lareina out. The wind chills my face and hands as we make our way down the street. She shivers in the dress. I shrug out of my jacket and drape it over her shoulders.

She looks up at me. "What about you?" she says, even as her fingers curl around the lapel of the jacket. She really is adorable. And transparent.

"No problem." Wonder what she'd say if I told her I wanted the jacket back. Would she pout? Or just hand it back with a sniff? Whichever way she responds, it'll be cute. It's hard to resist teasing her. "I'm a man. Men don't get cold."

The sound of her laughter rolls around me, sending a strange, tickling sensation to my heart. Absurdly enough, I want to just let go and join her mirth. The impulse is both exciting and sobering. I'm too much like my mother to relinquish control.

Perhaps I should give Lareina my credit card so she can find a place to stay. But Harvey's people might be monitoring—

I wince as my head pounds. It's like having a hangover. *What the hell kind of drug is this?* Hangover pain without any of the fun?

"Are you okay?" she asks.

"Yeah. Just...a headache." I'm going to murder my uncle. Actually, I can't kill him. If he goes, Mom will get a shot at taking over their "family business." And my mother plus the power of the mafia would be too dangerous. My brothers and I are older and wiser, but so is she. She wouldn't use a method as crude as kidnapping again, especially when it failed the first time.

She got herself some hot women to seduce me. Or at least that's what it sounded like based on Harvey's warning, but they could be after Bryce and Josh. I should warn them.

But first... I inhale and try to organize my mind. I need to get Lareina settled somewhere safe, then hide from Harvey until I'm a hundred percent back to normal. Afterward, I'll deal with Soledad and Harvey for conspiring to fuck with me, and see which of my dates, scheduled for the next three days, will make a satisfying wife for The Fogeys. As for the marriage license in my pocket, I'll get rid of it once I'm back in L.A.

Suddenly, Lareina stiffens and throws herself at me, burying her face in my chest. "Rupert," she whispers. "And Doris. My step-cousin and aunt."

She shudders. Not sure if it's out of fear or revulsion. Could be both. Either way, I hate that she feels either of those things at all. I pull her tighter, shielding her from her enemies.

"You here to get married?" somebody says from behind me.

I turn and face a skinny, black-haired man sporting a used car salesman's ingratiating smile. He looks like he's eager to unload a shiny Mustang with a rusted-out engine.

Before I can say no, he continues, "I'm Jonny. You guys look so good together, standing there so affectionate, just had to ask. The couple that was booked to come in just canceled. Bride caught the groom getting a hummer from a hooker. Apparently, the bride sucks at it—pun absolutely intended!"

The man laughs uproariously, slapping his knee, weirdly sincere in his amusement. Lareina and I just watch. He finally straightens up without a trace of awkwardness.

"Since we're free... What do you say? Dan-tatata. Dan-tatata!" He sings the opening to "Here Comes the Bride" then shifts his attention to Lareina, who's raised the lapel of my jacket to hide as much of her face as possible. "Your girl here is already dressed. And you don't look bad. It'll be a wedding you'll never forget. Guaranteed!"

My gut really likes the idea. Why *wouldn't* I want to have a wedding I'll never forget? But at the same time, my brain says, *No, no, no!*

Lareina's too wild and hot to make a good wife who can be respectful and indifferent.

I narrow my eyes and try to recall the women I've booked to check out in the next few days. A lawyer. An accountant. An aspiring model. An influencer. Other than their occupations, nothing comes to mind. Not even their age range or faces, even though their profiles featured both. Meeting them is going to be a chore that takes time out of my already tight schedule.

What if none of them works out? You gonna give up on being a junior partner?

I scowl, not wanting to face that possibility.

Lareina is right here. And you already have the marriage license. Marry her and you can be a junior partner.

But is she a wife respectable enough to satisfy Grandmother? another voice argues, although it's growing increasingly faint.

I look at Lareina's wrinkled and stained dress, recall her climbing across the hotel wall, then pulling my head down for a kiss. Compare the images to Grandmother's cool, composed presentation.

Probably not. But does it matter that much? We can solve each other's problems. A husband from a powerful legal dynasty will keep her greedy relatives away. And a wife means promotion. Lareina can just put on a designer dress and smile prettily.

Suddenly, marrying this woman doesn't seem so terrible. My workaholic heart even points out that I can cancel all those dates and spend my free time doing billable work.

"I won't even charge you the rush booking fee," Jonny says, probably worried that we're taking too long to decide.

"Rush fee, my ass. You wouldn't have any work without us," I say. "So shouldn't you give us a discount?"

"My man." He wags a finger with a big grin, flashing yellowed teeth. "You think you're pretty smart, eh?"

"I know I am." Harvard undergrad. Harvard Law. Huxley & Webber. Countless high-profile clients and cases won and settled. And I play a mean hand of poker against my brothers.

"He really is clever," Lareina adds, her words slightly muffled against my chest.

"Fine, fine. Hey, I can be nice about it, right? Tell you what: ten bucks off, but not a penny more or I'm gonna lose my shirt. Come on." He starts to reach for Lareina, then glances at my face, changes his mind and gestures for us to accompany him. "This way." He points to a squat white building in front of us.

How could we have missed it? A garish neon sign bleeds blinding red and purple against the black sky. Strangers in the Night Chapel. Their specialty seems obvious.

We walk through a faux-medieval wooden door that has a black iron support beam across it, held by big black rivets. There is lots of red and white velvet. Fake blue flowers sit in a few white vases decorated with golden ribbons. The ceiling is arched with panes of...vinyl covers of Frank Sinatra records?

Jonny thrusts his palm out. "Payment's upfront. Five hundred bucks."

"Seems high for the venue." I'm certain there won't be any food or drinks. At least nothing decent enough for me to touch.

"Got your wedding bands? I didn't think so. We provide them, included in the cost."

"Gold?" Lareina asks.

He sniffs. "Of course. Together with certificates of authenticity. Now, cross my palm. Cash or major credit card. No financing, though."

I'm skeptical about the pricing and the bands, but hand over the cash. You can't have a wedding without rings. Even Huxley, who was forced into an arranged marriage, had rings. Of course, he had his custom-made at Sebastian Jewelry. I'll upgrade our hardware as soon as we're back in L.A.

Directly behind the altar is a stage, and on it is a Frank Sinatra impersonator, complete with a white fedora, shiny black leather shoes, and a pinstriped pale-beige suit that's just a tad too large. At the sight of us, the band starts up, and he belts out "Love Is Here to Stay," his raspy voice booming from the surround-sound system.

Horror slaps me hard. I glance at Lareina to make sure her ears aren't bleeding, then touch my own. No blood. *A miracle!*

"Go on," Jonny says, elbowing me. "March on up to the altar."

"What happened to 'Here Comes the Bride'?" I ask, still shell-shocked.

"It's more unique this way, don't you think? I promised you a ceremony you'll never forget."

Well, that's true. The volume of the faux Sinatra's singing is inversely correlated to his ability. He's not only off-key, but the melody is unrecognizable. His range is unbelievably limited—he can handle maybe four notes at best—so when he can't hit a high or low note, he substitutes one he can manage, then compensates by singing louder. Where he ought to croon tenderly, he bellows like a shipwreck victim who's just spotted the coast guard.

Lareina is staring with a mixture of horror and incredulity. "I feel like they should pay us," she yells over the singing.

"It's just one song." At least, I *hope* he doesn't try for another. It'd be against every international convention on human rights. Hell, forget international—it's against the Eighth Amendment. I can sue his ass for violating my constitutional rights!

"Could've been lovely. I like the lyrics."

She looks down at her hands, her eyes wistful, and I want to punch the Sinatra impersonator for ruining the song.

"Maybe we should go somewhere with better music?" Her eyes dart back and forth between the exit and the altar. Jonny subtly shifts his weight and puts himself between us and the door, then mouths, *No refund.*

I narrow my eyes. Nobody stands between me and what I want. Should I push this asshole out of the way? It wouldn't be hard. Bryce, Josh and I grew up wrestling and busting each other's chops, and my brothers are bigger and stronger than Jonny.

But Lareina's greedy aunt and step-cousin could be loitering outside. What are the odds I could take her step-cousin and the "guards" her aunt brought with her? I'm good, but against three guys, two of whom are pro?

Now I wish I'd taken up the offer to go to Thailand for a year to train with a kickboxing master, rather than heading straight to Harvard undergraduate to please my grandmother. Constitutional law is my superpower in court, but it doesn't do much outside of it.

And if I fail, what happens to Lareina? Abused even worse by her relatives for money, undoubtedly. I look at her pretty face again, the wide, innocent eyes and sweet curve of her lips. I'm not sure how much she's worth, but I've seen people give up their dignity and humanity over a few thousand dollars. Once her relatives bleed her dry, she'll be nothing more than an inconvenience to them.

Can't let her suffer. The thought crystalizes and occupies the center of my mind, spreads to my heart with firm conviction.

The impersonator ends "Love Is Here to Stay" and starts singing "Fly Me to the Moon." *Oh, hell no.* If he finishes this song, we're flying straight to the asylum.

Grimly, I put an arm under Lareina's knees and pick her up. She gasps and wraps her arms around my neck tightly. Her warm weight feels so good, reminds me I'm holding a real, flesh-and-blood woman, not some figment of drug-induced hallucination. She smells faintly of lemon and something else, sweet but not saccharine. I practically run to the altar just to end the song.

When we come to a halt a foot away from the singer, he stops. "Hello," he says with a grin.

"Hey."

His grin widens, and his chest expands. If he tries to go back to singing, I'm going to nut-kick him so he'll have something to screech about for real.

Perhaps he senses imminent danger to his family jewels, because he doesn't try to finish the song. "I'm so glad you could join us. Every couple deserves a Sinatra moment."

"Yeah, and fuck the Universal Declaration of Human Rights."

He wags a finger. "No fucking anything that isn't your bride here. We run a wholesome establishment." Faux Sinatra peers into my eyes for a second. "Jesus, what did you snort? You're higher than the Hubble, aren't you?"

Ha! A high would at least feel good. And less dangerous than whatever Harvey gave me. "Not high," I shoot back.

"Can you make it quick?" Lareina says, sounding anxious.

"You not going to put your bride down?" Sinatra asks.

I frown. I like the feel of her way too much. "Do I have to?"

"Uh..." A shrug. "I guess not. Since you want it quick, give me your license?"

She reaches into my jacket pocket and hands it to him. "Are you legally able to do this?"

"Of course!" He puffs his chest out. "I'm a properly licensed and vetted officiant, and proud of it, too!"

"Proud of your singing, too," I mutter under my breath. Or at least I thought I did, but I must've spoken too loudly, because he hears me.

"Damn right. Everyone does Elvis here. Super boring."

Thank God he didn't go for Elvis. It would've been unbearable.

Sinatra looks at me. "Do you take this woman to be your lawfully wedded wife, to have and to hold, in sickness and in health, in good times and not so good times, for richer or poorer, keeping yourself unto her for as long as you both shall live?"

I open my mouth. "I—" *Oh shit. Prenup!*

No wonder I've been feeling off. I'm worth over two billion, thanks to the huge trust my grandmother on my stepmother's side left me. Marrying without one would be stupid.

"Wait!" Lareina says suddenly. "I forgot the prenup!"

Wait, what? "What?"

"I should be protected, don't you think?"

Most people don't think about one. I doubt her inheritance is bigger than what my zaibatsu grandmother left me. "I'm worth about two billion," I say, trying to play it safe—I haven't checked my accounts in a while. But the amount should be pretty close, plus or minus a few million.

She looks at me like I'm joking. Sinatra rolls his eyes with a loud snort.

"Very funny," he says. "Like billionaires get married here. And like they dress like *that*. Besides, if you're smart, you would've done the paperwork before, not now."

"Are you calling me stupid?" I scowl.

"Course not." His arched look says, *Yes*. "And the prenup? What do you think I am? A lawyer? That's way above my pay grade!"

"Maybe you should consider offering a legal-service-plus-wedding package," Lareina suggests. She's quite kissable when she's serious, so why not just skip all this and go straight to the part where I kiss the bride? This ceremony is already a mess. Might as well just do the good part—

Sinatra waves his hand. "Forget it. I'm feeling generous, so I'm gonna accommodate you. *For free.*" He turns to me. "Do you take this woman to be your lawfully wedded wife, to have and to hold, in sickness and in health, in good times and not so good times, for richer or poorer, *and not take any of her shit,* as long as you both shall live?"

What the hell? This is *sooooo* not legally binding. I should tell him so, but somehow my mouth won't obey. Besides, saying yes seems like the best idea ever, especially when Lareina looks up at me with shining eyes and a pretty smile, like she actually is a happy bride. A teeny voice in my head says I might as well burn my law degree if I say yes, because I'm being stupid and leaving myself exposed to all sorts of legal issues down the road. Yeah, that's true, but the urge to please Lareina is irresistible. It's just a simple yes, not castration. "I do."

"And you"—he turns to Lareina—"do you take this man to be your lawfully wedded husband, to have and to hold, in sickness and in health, in good times and not so good times, for richer or poorer, *and not take any of his shit,* for as long as you both shall live?"

"I do!" she says with more enthusiasm than I expected. "But is it really okay to just add that to the question?"

"No," I mutter.

At the same time, Sinatra booms, "Of course. As your celebrant, it is within my power. Also, it's a solemn promise between you and God."

I stare at the man. There's nothing godly about his presence or talent or the ceremony.

"I now pronounce you husband and wife."

A beat. Where's the "you may kiss the bride"? That's the most important part of the wedding.

Before I can bring up my objection, Lareina says, "Where are the rings?"

"Oh. You paid for those?" Sinatra's eyes shift left and right. "Gimme a sec. Most people don't buy 'em here."

Jonny runs up with two rings. They look more silver than gold. "Genuine white gold!"

The Accidental Marriage

"And I'm Santa Claus," I say.

"Are you saying this isn't gold?"

"If the shoe fits..."

"It's real gold. We guarantee it. Everything sold here comes with a week-long warranty."

I should argue that the law governing merchantability requires that they guarantee it for more than a week. But why debate the point when I'm going to buy a set of better rings anyway? Even if it does annoy me that Jonny and the fake Sinatra are selling me fake goods...

I lower Lareina, hating how suddenly cold I feel without her in my arms. My mouth tight—she really deserves better hardware, platinum at least—I put the smaller ring on Lareina. The size is just right, and the entire event of the day since I met Lareina feels destined. Like the way I met Queen.

Wonder how she's doing? Hopefully her aunt and uncle are treating her well, better than how Lareina's being treated. At least no one would be hurting Queen for an inheritance, given how poorly she was dressed and nourished.

Lareina slides the ring onto my finger. The thing is so cheap it's painful, but seeing the matching one on her finger somehow makes it okay.

Sinatra signs the certificate and jots down a few things on the lines. Then he flashes it at us. "See? All legal and proper. And now"—he makes an elaborate flourish with one hand, building the moment—"you may kiss the bride."

Finally.

I start to dip my head to taste her mouth. She looks up at me, her eyes shining.

"I'll serenade you as the photographer commemorates the moment," Sinatra says.

The moment shatters. "Please don't." I link my hand with hers, then dash out before he can finish "Fly Me to the Moon" and permanently scar both of us for life. No amount of therapy could cure us.

Jonny doesn't try to stop us this time. "Happy wedding night!" He waves with a huge grin.

I kick the door open, and we run smack into a pasty man standing right outside. Short, strawberry-blond hair is gelled to his skull. Hyperpigmentation mottles his nose and face, and pale lashes surround reptilian green eyes. His shoulders are somewhat narrow underneath an ivory tuxedo complete with a white peony boutonnière.

"Hey!" he yells, then starts to shove us away. His eyes widen when they land on Lareina. "You!"

"Yuck," she says.

"Who are you?" I step forward, shielding her with my body.

"I'm Rupert Fage." He announces his name like I should know it.

"And that matters because...?"

"I'm her *fiancé*." He drags the last word out, emphasizing each syllable.

"My step-cousin," Lareina clarifies. "The one I was drugged and dragged to Vegas to marry. Remember what I told you before?"

"Yes. The penniless loser who wants your inheritance," I say.

His face turns interesting shades of red and purple. "Stay out from this!"

"Can't. She's my wife now."

"Your *wife*? Is this a fucking joke?" His eyes drop to my finger and hers. "That's some cheap shit! It can't be legit."

"Take it up with the state of Nevada." My head is growing increasingly fuzzy. Rupert is right about the rings, though. They aren't just cheap shit. They look like it too. "But if you don't know, no state in the U.S.A. has a law specifying the price of a wedding band."

"You can't get married!" he screams, his chest heaving.

"But she already did. And there's no room for another ring on her finger." I link my hand with hers, bring it to my mouth and kiss the fake-gold ring—the best five hundred bucks I've ever spent—giving him a stare full of challenge. Veins bulge in his forehead, and little blood vessels turn the whites of his eyes red. His nostrils flare. Pop a couple of horns on his forehead, and he'd look like a mad-cow-diseased bull ready to charge. I smile over Lareina's wedding band, hoping my silent provocation pops one of those bulging veins.

"You can't do that! You stupid bitch, you'll ruin everything!" He jumps forward to grab Lareina.

I step right in front of him. "Back off."

"You *fucking back off!*" He shoves at me, then swings fast and hits me unexpectedly hard in the gut.

My equilibrium is off from the drugs, and the sudden attack makes me stumble, then step on something jutting out of the sidewalk and land on my ass. The fall doesn't hurt, but the abruptness of it leaves me frozen in shock for a moment. Talk about no dignity. *Shit.*

"Are you okay?" Lareina says, bending down to peer at me, her heterochromatic eyes wide with concern. With the blinding yellow and red lights glowing behind her, she looks like a haloed angel watching over me.

Like the girl who came to rescue me out of the shed in the burning woods.

I run my fingers along her soft cheek, brushing the pad of my thumb across her trembling lips. "Queen."

"Ares?"

Rupert grabs her arm and yanks her up. "You whore, I'm going to make you pay for what you've done."

She tries to pull away from him, swinging her arm to loosen his grip. "Stop it! Let me go!"

"You're going to annul this fucking marriage!" he says, and shakes her, spittle hitting her face.

Asshole. Although my vision and balance are still a little off, and the drugs are still gumming up the gears in my head, everything starts to crystalize. My day has been leading me to this.

I push myself up. "Let her go."

"Fuck you," he sneers with the confidence of a man who feels strong and powerful over others. Delusion springs eternal. "Get lost before I kick your face in."

I roll my shoulders. "I'm sure you'll try."

He scoffs, his grip on her tightening. "Whatcha gonna do, loser?"

"Be her knight and protect her." The words slip out as naturally as breathing.

"Knight?" He laughs. "Your armor looks a little rusty, bud—"

I kick his elbow, forcing him to let Lareina go. Then I smash my fist into his face. His head snaps back, blood spewing from his nose and mouth in a satisfying crimson fountain. "Principal." His legs go wobbly, and I kick him in the gut so hard he folds in half at the waist. "And interest."

He collapses and doesn't get back up, but then, I'd be shocked if he did. Lareina starts to touch my face. "Oh my God. I'm so sorry. Does it hurt? Do you need anything?"

I grin lopsidedly. She's so cute when she's worried, especially about me. Knights are supposed to get banged up for their queen. Hell, it's an honor. "No. But I'd really love it if you could hold me for a bit."

"Of course." She embraces me, wrapping her arms around me like a warm cocoon. Her lemon scent tickles my nose, and her hair is like warm silk lying over my hands. I'm supposed to keep her safe, but somehow the world feels at peace as long as she has her arms around me.

I hug her back tight, then close my eyes and drop my guard.

8

LAREINA

Ares slumps in my arms. Just how hard did Rupert hit him?

I wish my step-cousin were a stick-armed dork, but he's shockingly strong from years of practicing karate. The punch to the stomach must've hurt Ares. A lot.

Hot emotion fisted my heart when he stood before me like an impregnable wall and said, "Be her knight and protect her." I don't know how much of it he meant, since he's becoming more and more out of it as the evening wears on. He's been sweating nonstop, although I don't think he realizes. His complexion isn't the best, either, especially compared to how he looked this afternoon. A hint of ash under his tan makes me wonder just what he was forced to take. He kept muttering to himself about his mother and family. Lots and lots of talk about laws and something about dinosaurs. Then random stuff like needing "better hardware."

"Hey," I say softly. "You okay?"

He merely shakes his head. "Where are we going next?"

"Not sure. The hotel, maybe?" Exhaustion weighs me down. Besides, it probably isn't a good idea for him to be out and about like this, not when he's unwell. When Doris and her cronies drug me, it tends to get worse—a lot worse—before it gets better.

"But your relatives are there, right?"

"Probably, yeah." Or not, since they aren't thinking about anything except catching me and forcing me to marry Rupert. They'll be even more desperate now that they know there's some competition.

"We can go to a different hotel."

"True. Vegas is full of hotels. I'll pay." Ares has been paying since we met. He even tried to give me money earlier.

Was he thinking about being my knight at that point, too? Thousands of butterflies flutter in my belly, and I press my lips to savor the warmth coursing through me.

"How am I going to let you do that? My wife doesn't pay. I have money."

"Fine, half. The vow said no taking each other's shit."

He slowly shakes his head. "Not legally binding. Need a separate contract. I'll take care of it—soon as I feel better."

"Why? Because you're worth two billion or something?" *Two billion, hahaha.* It's sort of cute. Reminds me of a little squirrel I saw on YouTube guarding his acorn stash.

Ares's expression is serious. Guess my humor didn't penetrate. "It isn't just about money. Not having one could mess up a lot of things. Like what happened with my parents' marriage."

"Was it bad?" I ask cautiously. I'm curious about his family, but I don't want to look like I'm prying.

"Awful. It's a miracle nobody died." His words are more slurred now.

Wow. Must've been a *nasty* fight. Doris gossiped about a friend's divorce, breathlessly relishing how bitterly the couple fought over every penny. They even argued over who should get the dog—and the husband suggested they divide the poor Scottish terrier in half because that would have been better than letting the wife have custody. Apparently, it's normal for a couple breaking up to get that nasty, and that was one of the tamer cases. They probably fought over each grain of soil in their garden, too.

"A prenup would've helped, but they didn't have one. Love at first sight. Eloped in Tenerife. Passionate and classy beginning, messy and ugly ending. Dad should've known better." Ares sounds regretful. Maybe even a little angry.

Explains why he wants one, then. Well, I want one too. No more leaving myself vulnerable to others' whims. Ares saying he'd be my knight and protect me is thrilling and stirring, but Doris expressed a similar sentiment when I became an orphan and Grandfather passed away. She squatted so she could see into my eyes, then hugged me tightly. "My poor child. I'll keep you safe."

What she meant was: "I'll keep you alive so I can use your money."

I look into his glassy eyes. I doubt he'd take my money—he said he has two billion, a huge contrast to Doris and Vernon, who have enough to be okay, but not live in the kind of luxury they believe they deserve. He might want more, once he realizes I have about thirty times his net worth. But hopefully I can get the inheritance and prenup—post-nup?—squared away before he becomes greedy.

If he becomes greedy.

We start walking. Gotta put some distance between us and Rupert before he regains consciousness. "We'll sign a prenup. But I need my own lawyer for that."

"Yes, my dear," Ares says with a crooked grin.

"And you can't change your mind about 'not taking my shit.'"

"Of course."

A beat of silence. "You aren't asking me if I'm going to change my mind about not taking your shit."

He cocks his head. "Are you?"

"No. But shouldn't you worry?"

"Should I?"

I narrow my eyes. "You're more pleasant when you don't answer everything with a question."

A lopsided grin splits his face. "That's unbecoming. I apologize, but I'm an agreeable kind of guy. Why would I worry about you changing your mind? My wife should spend my money." His pupils are even more dilated, and he's probably being amenable without realizing what he's agreeing to. Likely he also forgot our marriage isn't technically real, even though the state of Nevada recognizes it as legal.

We slip into a glitzy hotel and get a room. "The nicest suite, please," I say. I want to be able to splurge on *myself*—and someone *I* like—for once. *Oh, wait.* I need to economize. "A two-bedroom suite, actually."

The clerk takes our IDs, then demands plastic. Sadly, I don't have a credit card on me, so Ares gives them his expense card with the company name embossed in front.

"Can you do that?" I whisper. "We aren't working. Are you?"

"No, but I don't have enough cash and it's linked to my company, so my uncle can't trace it. I'll take care of the charge later," he says with a shrug. "You want a suite, and we don't have enough cash to cover it."

I frown a little, but let him. The concierge rushes out to escort us to our suite. How nice. Did the hotel Doris book offer the same service? If so, how did she explain the fact that I was drugged?

Or maybe people don't care. Sort of like how most staff at my house have looked the other way, all the while either knowing or suspecting something nefarious was going on. The ones I bribed cared, but then, they were paid to do so.

We go inside the suite. The concierge hovers. "If you need anything—"

"We're good." I smile. "Oh, if anybody asks about us, we aren't here. I have a stalker I'm trying to shake off. A very persistent ex, you know what I mean."

"Of course. Certainly. How awful," she says with all the assurance she can muster. Don't care if she thinks I'm weird.

Then I remember the creepy guy who was after Ares. "And my husband, too," I add quickly, then flush at how intimate "husband" feels on my tongue. It's super weird when I haven't even had a boyfriend or a fiancé. Nobody ever proposed to me, and I feel cheated out of the entire courtship process.

After the woman leaves, Ares stumbles to bed.

"Wanna sleep?" I ask.

"Yes."

"I don't think they provided any pajamas."

"'s'all right." He toes off his shoes, then starts to unbutton his shirt, his fingers surprisingly nimble. Given how his reflexes seemed off, I assumed he'd fumble with the buttons. Then I could've helped—

Stop it.

But the kiss was amazing. And he thought it was great, too. We could kiss again. Or maybe do more than that.

And let him see your horrific scar? He might just puke all over it.
I hate it when my mind won't let me ignore reality.
Because nothing can defeat reality.

The burn on my shoulder from the fire twenty-two years ago has grown increasingly fouler over the years. The gouge marks haven't faded one bit. Instead, they stretched out as I grew bigger. They look like teeth, and there is something that looks like an *I* between them. Doris said it's terrible that I have a scar I can't get rid of, because no man will want a woman so damaged and disfigured.

"Thank God for Rupert! If he hadn't rescued you, it could've been worse!" she told me more than once, in case I ever forget it's her stepson who saved me from the fire.

She and Rupert hypothesized the *I* probably stands for something awful, because why else would anybody brand me with it? The mark has to be shameful, and I should reflect on what I did to get it.

But nothing comes to mind. Whatever happened to scar me must've been horrific—enough to be permanently etched in my brain or permanently deleted from it. The therapist Doris hired said it's probably the latter. He told me I should hide the scar to alleviate my sense of shame and try not to think too much about how I got it. "The *I* could be anything. Or nothing at all."

Easy for him to say—it's not on his body. At least it isn't a *J* for Jezebel. What other bad things start with an *I*? If it were an *H*, I might've guessed "hoe," but that seems a little off. Too plebian and silly. If you'd go this far, you would do the *W* for whore.

Shoving aside the unpleasant thoughts, I lie on my side of the bed and watch Ares get undressed. More buttons come undone, revealing more of his taut, golden skin. From the sexy way his suit fits him, I figured he was an office worker, but the lean muscles on his chest are thick, the ridges on his abs deep and shadowed. A sprinkling of dark hair dusts his belly, then disappears below his belt.

Cuff links clink on the nightstand on his side. The shirt drops to the floor. I let out a soft gasp at the sight of long, twisted burn scars that stretch from the top of his shoulder all the way to his wrist. They're slightly raised and pale, except for several gouges that are a shade or two darker than his regular skin. No hair grows on the paler scars, which covers at least a quarter of his right arm.

He doesn't seem to notice my staring. Or maybe he's just ignoring me. His expression doesn't show anything other than methodical calmness as he sheds his clothes. He unbuckles and drops his pants. His lower body is even more muscular and powerful than his upper, taut muscles rippling as he moves. The kick he delivered to Rupert must've hurt like hell. It's too bad he didn't kick him in the balls. If Rupert got his balls busted for real, he might decide to leave me alone.

As Ares shifts, I spot a small, triangular burn scar on his upper thigh. Did he get it at the same time as the ones on his arm? Does he remember anything about the incident that gave him those marks? Or was it too traumatic? To be injured like this would be pretty bad, wouldn't it?

"How did you get them?" I blurt out before I can stop myself.

He knows what I'm talking about. "In a forest fire. Would've been worse if somebody hadn't saved me," he says quietly.

"Do they bother you? Like... Do you think, um...they're gross?"

"The scars?" He sways and frowns, looking down at his arm. "Do *you* think they're gross?"

I shake my head. "You survived whatever hurt you. As far as I'm concerned, that's all that matters."

The tension in his brow eases. "Well then. I won't worry about them, unless you want me to cover them up."

"I don't." I lay my hands over a pillow and rest my chin on them. My gaze falls on the silver wedding band. Even though his uncle fed him something, he didn't have to marry me. He still had enough wits about him at that time, and he could've said no. So why say yes? "Do you think I'm pretty, Ares?"

"Yes," he says promptly.

"Even if I have some burn scars of my own?"

He nods. "Yes."

"You didn't ask me where or how big."

"Do I need to?" He tightens his lips in confusion. "I think you're amazing just the way you are. Gutsy and smart. Pretty." He smiles then plops on his side of the bed. "You think my scars are fine. Why do you think I'd care about yours?"

"Because I'm a girl...?"

He snorts. "What you are is silly." His eyes start to droop.

I shift and watch him succumb to sleep. He's beautiful, his eyelids fluttering as they close. The tension on his face melts away, leaving the stunningly gorgeous features, from the slanted eyebrows to his full, relaxed mouth. His entire body slowly goes limp, like a high-performance machine powering down.

The wedding gown isn't that comfortable, but I can't undress myself without help. Doris picked this particular outfit not just because it's pretty, but because it leaves me helpless.

I think you're amazing just the way you are. Gutsy and smart. Pretty.

Recalling Ares's words brings a smile. Nobody's ever called me pretty without reservation. And smart! Doris had me homeschooled mostly, although she was forced to enroll me in a few online classes on subjects she couldn't manage. But I never did well enough to get into a decent college. I could only do an online college, and Doris allowed it because it would have looked bad if she hadn't let me attend it.

My husband thinks I'm gutsy and smart and pretty!

Joy and anticipation cartwheel in my heart. For the first time, I feel like my life is finally on the right track.

9

ARES

"We gotta go before they catch us."

A woman extends her hand. I stare at the long, slender fingers, the paleness of her translucent skin. Her unbound golden hair billows in the chilly breeze, obstructing my view of her grownup face. She's in a white dress like before. The petals of a little pink flower tucked behind her ear flutter.

"Queen?" I murmur. It doesn't matter that I can't see her face or that we're grown up now. From the way my heart picks up speed and every cell in my body calls out, I know it's her.

The Fogeys are wrong, I think triumphantly. She's real, and she's here now.

"Come on. We can't just lie around here all day. We have to go."

Go where? The smell of dirt and vegetation surrounds me, just like twenty-two years ago. I have no idea what's going on, but I trust her.

I shrug out of my jacket to put it over Queen to keep her warm against the wind. But just as I get close enough, flames engulf us.

The old scars on my arm and thigh throb as though they're being seared into my skin again. I clutch my arm and hiss.

She turns around, hair still blowing and obscuring most of her features. "Are you okay?"

"Yes." I can't whine about the old injury, not when she was hurt worse back then. I have to be strong.

She nods, then takes my hand. Her palm is surprisingly cool against my skin, and prickly sensations spread through me. I try to squeeze my fingers, but somehow they won't obey. The right half of my body stays still, refusing my commands.

Queen tugs at me, but no matter how willing I am to go with her, I can't. The fire around us expands, widening until I can't see its limits, towering over us like a flaming deathtrap.

Shit.

"Go without me," I say.

"No. I'm not leaving my knight behind."

My chest tightens. It's my job to keep her safe. "Queen—"

Her fingers rest over my lips, cutting off the rest. The scent of lemon tickles my nose.

"You'll be okay," she whispers, then crumbles and disappears before my eyes like a pillar of ashes.

"No!"

A slender rope wraps around my shoulders. Need to push it away, but I can't. I'm bound tight, like before in the shed, when Mom tied me to the chair.

Somewhere in the fire, Mom's manic chortle rings. Helplessness pummels me, and I grit my teeth. I haven't spent all these years in vain. No way is she going to win. Adrenaline surges, drying my mouth and at the same time sending my heart rate through the roof. My skin grows taut, as though it'll split in half at any moment.

"You lost," Mom says, standing like a dark monster, backlit by the sky-high flames behind her. "Give in, Ares. Accept my love, and we'll be family again."

"Fuck you," I grind out, only to have her throw her head back and laugh in triumph. "I'd rather die first."

"My poor little prince." She runs her index finger along my cheek. The touch is like a snake crawling over my face. She leans closer and closer until I can see the blood-chilling madness in her blue eyes. "You won't be able to get anything you want without a wife by your side. So take my girl. Have her bear your children.

The family line must continue." She shoves a disheveled blonde at me.

"Never!" Shuddering, I flinch away and suck in air, frowning at how cool it feels in my lungs.

An ivory ceiling. Soft cotton sheets underneath. I'm naked, except for my boxer shorts. A hotel room, but not mine. *How the hell did I end up here?*

The last thing I remember is Harvey trying to force me to sign the retainer. I'm pretty sure I escaped successfully. His goon wasn't outside the window, but after that...

No idea.

The more I try to recall, the hazier my memory becomes. And a figurative ax is grinding into my skull. Just what did Harvey feed me?

I wish I'd been able to find a lab or something last night to do toxicology. If I go to the police now, they won't find anything. Harvey's too smart to use anything long lasting.

I pray I managed to evade him and his goons, because there's no way I'm providing legal advice to the mob. Grandmother revealed that one of the biggest reasons Mom wanted to marry Dad was that she was planning to rope Huxley & Webber into representing the "family business," a.k.a. the Nesovian mob her family runs as it extends its tentacles into the United States. Huxley & Webber represents clients in all industries, but we don't do organized crime in any shape or form. As a former prosecutor with a sterling reputation, Grandmother refuses to ruin the family legacy that way.

Water and aspirin, then coffee. Afterward, call Dad and Grandmother, explain what happened and put everyone on alert. Harvey won't stop with me. He'll go after Bryce and Josh as well.

I start to get up, then stop when I finally realize something is wrapped around my arm. Weird. I can't stand anything restricting my limbs, and I rarely let anybody loop their arms around mine. It must be Harvey's drug that made me not notice.

Ice skitters down my spine at the sight of a tangle of golden hair and a white gown. Harvey's warning about Mom's plan to have ultra-desperate women manipulate me back to what she calls "family" reverberates like an emergency alert. If Mom were normal, I'd brush his words off as nonsense. But I can never underestimate her deviousness or tenacity.

Besides, the end of my nightmare floods into my head, flashing like a big warning. My gut tightens.

I lift my head, trying to figure out what the hell is going on and who the woman wrapped around my arm like a squid is. And just what—

There is a silver ring on my left hand.

It glints in the morning light.

No. No fucking way I eloped!

I want the promotion, but not to the point of eloping in Vegas while high on Harvey's drug. I couldn't possibly have dragged myself into a chapel with some strange woman, could I? Sudden alarm clenches around my throat. I jostle the woman and hop off the bed, then turn on the lights.

"Hey," comes a soft grumble.

The voice is low and raspy, surprisingly pleasant to my ears. She turns around and shoves the hair out of her face. Her winged eyebrows pinch together, small nose wrinkling and mouth pursing until it resembles a rosebud. Finally she opens her eyes, one blue and one green, and blinks at me.

"Lareina?" I say, dumbfounded.

"Yeah. What's the matter? Did Mr. No-Neck chase us here?"

"No-Neck?" What kind of trouble are we in? The lack of control over the situation is worse than listening to a screeching violin. Or Soledad.

"You know, the guy you were running away from."

Harvey's asshole. "How do you know?"

"Cuz I'm good." A lazy, satisfied grin splits her pretty face. "He tried to catch you, but I got you instead. You said you'd managed to escape before somebody could make you sign something or other."

I let out a sigh, my shoulders sagging. At least I didn't do anything irreversible with Harvey.

"You're welcome," she adds. "It was karma. You helped me, I helped you."

Doesn't that seem a little too convenient? She just happened to be in the suite next to mine, then after I helped her leave the hotel without getting detected by her money-grubbing relatives, she just happened to run into me while I was out of my mind from whatever the hell Harvey fed me? And then she just happened to fall into bed with me?

I look at Lareina's slim hand. A silver ring—one that wasn't there yesterday—glints on her finger as well. She gazes up at me, her eyes hopeful.

Does she expect me to say "thank you"? Drop to my knees and vow undying gratitude and offer to do anything she wants?

My help was genuine. But hers? After the encounter with Harvey and the warning about Mom, I don't dare take anything at face value. Some might automatically believe that Lareina really wanted to help, but I've never been that lucky. Queen was the only exception.

The real question is: who does Lareina answer to? Mom? Harvey? Or herself? And if the answer is the last one, where do I fit in her scheme? Nobody marries a stranger just *to help*. She wants something.

"By marrying me?" My skepticism is sharp enough to cut.

She opens her mouth, but her belly interrupts with a loud growl. Her cheeks flush. I smirk at the convenient timing. I start to say something cutting, except my stomach lets out a matching growl.

Seriously? Fuck you, biology. But once my body starts to protest the lack of food, I realize I'm famished. I probably haven't eaten anything. I wouldn't have touched anything Harvey might've offered, and Lareina was obviously too busy dragging me to a sleazy chapel to feed me.

"Food first," I bite out, annoyed I need to eat at all when I'd rather continue the interrogation. "What do you want?"

She presses her lips together in concentration as though I just asked her to recite the entire California state constitution. "Whatever you're having is fine," she says finally. "I need to shower, too."

The way she scrunches her face is cute, making her look like an annoyed bulldog pup for a moment. I forcibly remind myself that she won't seem so cute once I've had coffee.

"Shower first, then food and conversation?"

I nod, frowning at her choice of words. "Conversation" makes it sound like we're a normal couple. "Ladies first," I say before she can offer to wash with me. I need some time to myself to gather my thoughts and come up with a preliminary plan.

"Don't worry. The suite has two bathrooms," Lareina says before disappearing.

Why did she get a suite this large if she needs to cling to me?

I check every drawer, closet and storage space. No purse, phone or tablet of hers. No locked safe, either. I don't think her dress has a hidden pocket or anything. *Weird.* I can't think of *anyone* who goes around without a phone. You might as well leave your life behind.

What wouldn't I give to be able to remember last night! It puts me at a huge disadvantage, not knowing anything. I don't trust anybody to tell me the full truth.

Lareina comes out of the bathroom, still in the wedding dress. "I need your help with the buttons in the back." Without waiting for my reaction, she turns around and gathers her hair to the side, revealing the elegant line of her slender neck and spine.

I'm no stranger to feminine wiles. One of the things women do is act like they need help, then go all flirtatious, angling their bodies in the most provocative ways to showcase all their assets. I generally feel nothing but annoyance at those tactics because I'm too smart to fall for them.

But right now, my mouth is dry. Lareina's brisk, businesslike manner says she has no ulterior motive except to get out of the dress, even though I know better than to accept that at face value. Nonetheless, the room feels warmer all of a sudden.

Satin laces have come undone and hang from the holes on either side, but the dress is also held together by endless, tiny pearl buttons and hooks. Whoever designed it didn't want the bride to be able to get out of it—or wanted the groom to rip it off like tissue paper on the wedding night.

Since there doesn't seem to be anything else she can wear, I unbutton them, moving my fingers carefully to avoid touching her. But the warmth from her skin can't be denied. It sends a tingling sensation through my body—one that gathers in my dick. I can't tear my gaze from her as more of the taut expanse of creamy skin is revealed. She smells more like a woman than citrus in the morning, and I want to bury my nose in the soft curve of her neck and inhale, then press kisses all over, stamp her as mine.

The urge grows stronger, and before I can draw another breath, she takes a step away. "Thanks," she says with a quick smile over her shoulder, then disappears into the bathroom, closing the door behind her.

Only then do I realize I was very close to kissing her. It leaves me feeling unsettled. My stepmother Akiko might call it "love at first sight," since she still believes in things like true love and happy endings. But I'm a realist. It isn't like me to feel this way. The remnants of Harvey's drugs are probably still affecting my judgment.

Everyone is aware I'm particular about women. Most of my friends can't believe I've only had four girlfriends, none lasting more than a few months. But I just couldn't deal with them when they said they'd developed feelings for me. Every time they looked me into my eyes and said they loved me, all I saw was the unwavering determination in Mom's gaze when she told me how much *she* loved me, how she'd do anything to be with me and how much she wanted me to understand she'd kidnapped me for my own good.

That's when I end the relationship. And I can't even look at another woman for a while afterward.

Nobody really understands why I dump my girlfriends as soon as they start to say they love me, although The Fogeys seem to believe it's because of my obsession with finding Queen. Most people just assume I'm an asshole who's easily bored. Mom and Harvey couldn't have anticipated my uncharacteristically libido-centric reaction to Lareina...

Could they?

Or is Lareina the first in a long string of women they're ready to throw at me, hoping one of them will stick? Can't put anything past those two. Harvey made it sound like only Mom would stoop to using women, but he used Soledad without a second thought.

If only I knew Lareina's true motivation, my situation would be much easier to handle.

After instructing the hotel concierge to send breakfast in half an hour, I head to the unoccupied bathroom and brush my teeth. I shy away from the mirror, not wanting to see my reflection with its similarities to Mom. Everyone, even my grandmother, who has a heart

The Accidental Marriage

colder than a block of ice, says Mom is a stunning beauty, and I have my mother's looks.

I glance down at the scar on my arm. If the wolf's head had grazed my face instead, would it have been better? That way nobody would ever say I looked like Mom.

Stop it. The therapist helped me see that such self-destructive thoughts aren't helpful. The goal is to avoid getting entangled in Mom and Harvey's schemes, not fantasize about being harmed or disfigured.

A hot shower almost makes me feel like myself. The first-aid kit in the cabinet has a few packets of aspirin. I rip up two and swallow them. Hopefully they'll kick in soon. Gotta be at one hundred percent when I'm about to face Lareina and tease out what happened last night.

Shrugging into a bathrobe, I go to the living room and check my phone. No battery. *Great.* I look around and eventually spot a charger at the workstation. I plug my phone in and wait for it to get enough juice to load messages and missed calls.

Three texts from Barry, who was curious where I went because he wanted to try his luck at a roulette table with the women he met, with me by his side. I'm apparently his lucky charm.

Ten from an unknown number, which all say something along the lines of, *Where are you? I'm the only one who can protect you from your mother.*

Harvey. *No, thank you. You just want to establish a foothold in America, then launder hundreds of millions of dollars with my expertise.* For some reason he seems to believe that just because we share a blood tie, I will never betray him. What stops me from fucking him over is that I haven't figured out how to stick the knife in without anybody knowing. The mob would come after me if I did. But I'd sell him out for nothing if I thought I could get away with it.

One from Akiko, asking me to be careful and stay safe. I used to think she was being a little ridiculous until I realized this is how she shows she cares. She believes that America isn't like Japan, with "so many dangers lurking everywhere."

Two hundred texts from an unknown number. *I love you.*

Revulsion whirls in my gut.

Don't you love me?

I think I'm pregnant with your baby!
Your baby needs you!
Just imagine our bright future, a family of three!
We'll be the envy of the world!
Another one pops up: *I'll never stop loving you. You know that, don't you?*

Soledad. It's as though she knows how to say all the wrong things. Disgust clutches my chest and nausea roils in my stomach.

"Are you okay?"

I start, then jerk my eyes from the screen and look at Lareina. She's in a bathrobe, probably with nothing on underneath. *Stop thinking about her naked body.* The scent of the hotel shampoo and soap wafts over—the same as mine. Also not something to dwell on. Her damp hair hangs loose around her pretty pixie face. She looks younger without the makeup—more touchable. Her naturally pink lips are full and seem eminently kissable.

Don't look at her mouth either.

She continues to stare up at me expectantly.

"What?" I say, feeling a little ridiculous. I don't lose my train of thought or lose my place in a conversation. You can't if you want to be a good lawyer.

"I asked if you were okay."'

"Of course." My answer is more out of habit than anything else. It's always easier to say I'm fine than not.

She tilts her chin skeptically. Those heterochromatic eyes probe into mine, like she's a lawyer not believing a word out of the witness on the stand. "You shouldn't say something you don't mean."

10

ARES

I scowl, mostly out of reflex. I'm not used to people probing so openly. Not even Dad or Aunt Jeremiah do it—they're afraid of reopening old wounds. And because sometimes it's easier to just pretend everything's fine rather than dig too deep.

Lareina lifts a hand toward my face, and I frown harder, torn between the desire to have her stroke me and to evade her altogether. Her presence is unsettling, throws my equilibrium off, leaving me feeling vulnerable and unprotected.

When she drops her hand back to her side, it isn't relief, but disappointment that floods me. I realize I wanted to feel her touch more than I was honest enough to admit. Uncertainty casts shadows in her eyes, and I get a strong urge to comfort her.

Stop. I don't know where this unfamiliar drive is coming from. But if Lareina is Mom or Harvey's agent, they did far better than I ever thought possible. I better watch my back. And if, by some one-in-a-million chance, Lareina is innocent, there's still danger. Women who can make you act out of character are fatal. Just look at how things turned out for Dad when he met Mom. A woman who inspires respectful indifference, possibly tinged with some mild affection, is ideal, the kind I'm aiming to find and spend the rest of my life with. Dad's life with Akiko is exactly like that, and all the proof I need.

Just as I open my mouth, there are three hard knocks at the door. Lareina jumps, casting a furtive glance in that direction. Her fingers dig into my sleeve, her entire being focused on the door. It's damn good acting, designed to make me feel sympathy.

"Relax. It's just breakfast," I say in a rather cool voice to let her know her antics won't work.

Her cheeks flush as she looks up at me. "Sorry," she says. "Didn't mean to do that." She pulls away as though embarrassed to have been clutching me. I roll my shoulders, trying to ignore the bereft sensation.

Trying to restore my equilibrium, I head over to the door and check the peephole. An elderly, uniformed staff member is standing over a tray cart.

As soon as I open the door, he rolls the cart in and sets it up in the living room. Two bowls of fresh berries and whipped heavy cream, a basket of croissants that smell like heaven, various jams and salted butter, coffee, freshly squeezed OJ and sparkling water. French toast topped with powdered sugar and berries with maple syrup on the side complete the spread. And bacon, of course.

Perhaps I went a bit overboard when I placed my order, but I'm sure I can finish most of it. Besides, Lareina is hungry, too. She's literally licking her lips, staring at the food with the intensity of a starved dog.

After the man leaves with my signature, I pull a chair out for her, then immediately regret it. I need to be a dick, not a nice guy. The problem is Lareina. Showing her little courtesies comes instinctively.

She sits down, and I pick up a coffee pot, deliberately pouring myself a cup, but not her. It's *much* harder than expected. But damn it, if she wants some, she can serve herself. I pour enough syrup over my toast to drown it and take a big bite. I'm starving. I also take a chunk out of the bacon on my plate and several gulps of coffee. *Ah...* This is what it feels like to be human again.

Lareina pushes her food around. Her mouth grows tauter and tauter, and an inexplicable tension pulls her shoulders toward her ears.

"What's wrong? Not to your liking?" I ask, almost relieved. I've finally found a reason to dislike her: she's a picky princess. "Should I have ordered you fat-free yogurt or something, your highness?"

"No. Um..." She pulls her lips in, her eyes darting back and forth between my food and hers.

What is this? When a woman thinks this hard and hesitates this much, nothing good ever follows. I brace myself.

"Mind if we swap?" she says suddenly.

"Swap...?"

She points at our plates. "Food. I keep thinking yours looks more delicious."

I look at hers, then mine. They look about the same, except for the fact that mine has a bite or two taken out. "Is it because there are a couple more slices of strawberries on my French toast?" I look at the bowls of fresh berries and cream on the side, hinting that she can just grab those.

"I think it's better this way. And you get more food. I'm sort of hungry, but not, like, super hungry." Except the intense focus in her eyes says she's starving.

What's going on?

She reaches over and swaps the plates. "Thank you for understanding." Then she scarfs down half the French toast before I can blink. If this is the latest seduction trend, she needs to quit watching so many stupid videos on worthless social media sites.

Finally, she makes a slight choking noise.

"You don't have to shovel it in. *I'm* not stealing your food," I say.

She shakes her head. "That's not it." She pours two OJs and pushes one toward me.

"I don't drink fruit juice."

"You don't?"

"No. It just came with the breakfast."

"Oh." Lareina looks down at her glass and purses her lips. Her expression reminds me of a kid being told she isn't getting a Christmas present.

I should just ignore her and go back to my breakfast. But I can't stop myself from reaching for the glass and taking a sip. *Ugh. Tart.* Not my thing.

She leans forward. "You like it?"

Does she want me to say I love it because she's the one who served it? "No."

"Great." She beams, then reaches for my glass. "I'll take it, then."

Uh... *What?* "You have yours."

"I know. But you said you don't like it. Wouldn't want to waste this one." She grabs my glass and takes a sip. If she'd pressed her lips where mine touched, I might've thought she was attempting to flirt, clumsily so. But no. She's acting too casual now.

Perhaps my suggestion that she can slow down penetrated, because she's eating at a more normal pace now, and bothering me for a different reason. It's just standard breakfast—and yes, it may seem more delicious due to our hunger—but her cheeks flush, and her eyes half close with every bite she takes. When she munches on the bacon, bliss transforms her face, making it glow as though she's just had the best orgasm of her life.

My tongue stops registering taste and texture as all my overheated blood heads to my dick. I eat mechanically, totally focused on her. If she's reacting like this to food, what's she going to be like in bed? A screamer? A moaner? Will she cling? Bite? Scratch? Does she like to wrap her legs around her man? Did her exes give her orgasms on a reliable basis?

No, probably not, I decide. If they had, she wouldn't be deriving this much pleasure from the food. Even the OJ is making her hum a bit.

When she reaches for the glass again, the ring on her finger—the same as mine—winks. The sight should cool my blood, but instead, it sends an unfamiliar sensation through me.

"Tell me what happened last night," I say.

"You don't remember anything?"

"No. Not really."

"You punched my step-cousin out."

Her eyes sparkle with sheer admiration as she looks at me across the table as though I'm her knight in shining armor. I don't usually like it when women look at me like this, but with her... I feel ten feet tall. The realization is terrifying, like being trapped on a roller coaster that's about to drop.

The Accidental Marriage

"You know, the asshole I was almost forced to marry so he could steal my money," she says.

The one she supposedly crossed the hotel wall to escape from.

"But it was too late for him because we'd gotten married already," she says. "We were walking out of the chapel when he stopped us."

Weird. How loopy was I that I agreed to marry her, just like that?

"By the way, your punch was justified because he hit you first," she adds. "He knows karate, so he hit you pretty hard."

I cock an eyebrow. He must be shitty at karate, because I'm not feeling it. If Josh or Bryce had punched me, I would've been bruised for days.

"He went down like a misfired rocket." She lets out a laugh, which puts a reluctant smile on my face. "Hopefully, he and his parents won't bother me for a while."

"Why not?"

"Because you and I are married now?"

"The ceremony alone isn't legally binding," I inform her.

"Don't worry." She's all sincerity. "We got a marriage license first."

Isn't she thorough? "Who told you to get a license?"

"No one. It just happened. You were there, too. And you insisted on paying for it."

I can't picture myself doing that. But I don't remember, so I can't deny it. She could lie about everything, including her relationship with Mom and Harvey—or lack thereof—and I wouldn't know any better. *Irritating.*

"A fake Frank Sinatra sang for us, too, which makes it extra airtight because he's a licensed officiant."

I frown. *A fake Frank Sinatra?* Fucking Harvey. It isn't like me at all to marry a woman I don't know, even if I was high. He was probably willing to keep me all night to force me to sign the retainer agreement. Bet the drug he fed me was to make me malleable and nod and agree with him, regardless of whatever warning signs might have been there.

"Can I suggest something?" Lareina asks.

"Sure." She might finally tell me why she's gone after my bachelorhood while I was out of it. I pull one of the cream-laden bowls of berries close and start to eat.

She eyes it longingly. I push the other bowl toward her, but she doesn't touch it. Instead, she continues to look at mine, then swallows hard.

I don't know what this...fetish is, and shouldn't care. But her longing gaze is driving me crazy. A starving stray dog would be less overt. I swap the bowls.

"Thank you." The smile she gives me is like the sunlight pouring in through the window behind her. I stare, dazzled. My heart pounds, the rapid beats reverberating through my body. I reach for my coffee to shake off the strange agitation.

"As I was saying…" She pops a strawberry into her mouth and sighs softly. If she wants me to give her proposal proper consideration, she needs to quit making that orgasm face! "I'd like to propose that we maintain our marriage."

"No." My response is instant and firm. I look at the cheap ring on my finger again. It's nice enough that she helped, but I'm not staying married to a woman who throws me off like this. And although I only have two more days until my deadline, I do have more dates set up. Surely one of them will work out.

My personal goals are simple: marry a woman who doesn't throw me off, get promoted and live a good, uneventful life.

"It'd only be for six months, until my thirtieth birthday," she says.

"What happens after your thirtieth birthday?"

"I'll be one hundred percent free to do whatever I want."

"Hmm. And what would I get out of it?"

"Money." Her answer is prompt.

Doesn't she know how much I'm worth? She spoke of having her own inheritance, but I doubt it's much. Large inheritances tend to be held in complex trusts that are designed specifically to preserve the wealth for the beneficiary and their descendants for generations to come. They can't be undone with something as simple as a marriage.

"I'll make it worth your while," she adds.

"Don't want it." My response is as decisive as hers.

She cocks her head, the berries on her fork forgotten. "Everyone wants money."

"Not me."

"Oh." She looks down, then scoops up strawberries, making sure they're laden with cream, and brings them to her lips. She puts them in her mouth, then licks the cream on one corner. The sight of her rosy tongue is shockingly erotic.

Fuck. My libido is out of control, and I'm sober. How crazy was it last night when I had no control?

"What do you want, then?" she asks warily.

"Absolutely nothing you can give me. You aren't what I have in mind for a suitable wife or ideal marriage."

"I'm not?" Her eyes widen, then she bites her lip, looking away briefly to hide the uncertainty in her expressive gaze before raising it to meet mine. "What's wrong with me?"

I open my mouth to respond, then change my mind. It'll be less hurtful to tell her what I have in mind for my future. "I want a marriage of respectful indifference with someone who has a busy life of her own. She and I care enough about each other to be considerate, but never cross the line into being nosy or controlling. Pleasant dinners when neither of us is working late. Annual vacations to someplace pretty and relaxing. Well-raised children, likely to head to Harvard or Yale Law and take over Huxley & Webber when they're ready. Unfortunately, a marriage with you wouldn't offer me any of that."

Or anything of value. If Soledad were a normal human being, I might assume my marital status would discourage her, but she's a self-centered sociopath and won't care. Mom won't give up whatever horrific plot she comes up with to reunite the family just because I'm married. And Lareina doesn't fit the image of a "good, respectful woman" The Fogeys have in mind.

"I can be respectfully indifferent," she protests. "And I can get a job and stay busy. I promise. Plus, I'm totally open to giving you children."

I return to my food. "No."

"I'll even let you ask me for a favor later, as long as it's not illegal or something."

Her plea is difficult to resist, but I'm not letting myself get suckered by a pretty face and the sexual need she arouses in me. "Still no."

"But you told me last night that you wanted to be my knight and protect me," she says in a small, shaky voice.

What? Be her knight and protect her... That's a sentiment I've had for Queen...and Queen *only*. I've never expressed it to anyone else.

I lift my gaze from the plate and look at Lareina. Her eyes shimmer with unshed tears of frustration as she looks out at the Vegas sky, then at her fingertips.

My mind conjures how sassy she was after the hair-raising balcony stunt she pulled yesterday. Something about her spirit and appearance reminds me of Queen, even though I know it's not her. But this reaction...

You crushed her, asshole. Congratulations. With your sterling personality and charm, where are you going to find a wife? You only have two days left before the month is up. The Fogeys picked the timeline, knowing you'd fail. And you will fail and never make partner.

I get up and pace. Sometimes I really hate my conscience. "Your condition is that we stay married for six months?"

"Yes. Well. And as long as you agree that it doesn't cross any inappropriate boundaries... I wouldn't want to be disrespectful or clingy, but...can we have sex while we're married? Other than just for making babies?" She peers at me to gauge my reaction. Thankfully I'm done with coffee, so I have nothing to shoot out of my nostrils. "I think our chemistry is pretty good."

Suddenly the air feels too thick. I feign nonchalance, sit down again and slowly chew on some raspberries to buy time. "Is it?"

"Don't you remember?" She smiles, then bites her lip. The bright sparkle in her eyes and the flush in her cheeks make her look like a teenager in love. "You said the kiss we had was amazing."

I raise an eyebrow. I remember nothing, and it's infuriating. But that kind of praise is unlike me. It's my policy not to discuss or analyze bedroom technique. If it's good, the relationship proceeds. Otherwise, it ends. No point in putting things into words.

Perhaps it was too good to go unremarked upon, my worthless libido says.

The silence stretches, and she gives me a narrow-eyed stare. Slight irritation begins to infect her gaze. "Well...?"

"Well what? I have nothing to say." Outrage flashes, and she bristles like a furious—but cute—guinea pig. I already made it clear I don't remember what happened last night. Is she probing to test me, or is she just trying to take advantage of the fact that I don't have full information? If I had all the memories of last night, I wouldn't be so guarded. Since I'm feeling perverse, I add, "Maybe the kiss wasn't memorable enough to leave a lasting impression."

She gasps, then glares at me like I'm the most awful person ever. "You know what? I think I was far superior to you. You were just, you know, *okay*, despite having a lot of experience compared to me. It was my first time kissing somebody."

She might as well have sucker-punched me in the solar plexus. "*First time?*" I choke out. "How old are you?"

"Twenty-nine. And what's up with the reaction?" Her tone is aggrieved.

"You're twenty-nine and never kissed anybody until now?" *How can that even happen?*

"Basically. Also, not now. Yesterday."

"Are you telling me..." There's only one—almost unbelievable—conclusion. "You're a virgin?"

She nods. I search for any sign of deception or amusement, but she's dead serious. What the...?

"Why do you want to give your virginity to me?" I ask, even as my dick hardens. Sexual excitement that she wants to be with me for her first time and be mine electrifies my blood. Something must be defective, because I've never cared about such things as virginity. I expect a woman to be experienced, especially at our age. But being Lareina's first feels as special as being the first to step into a field of freshly fallen snow.

"Well...you *are* my husband. And you're an *okay* kisser," she says primly, her chin tilted up.

"There are words other than 'okay' to describe my kiss. Heart-pounding, magnificent, carnal, orgasmic—"

She ignores me and continues: "But if you're awful at sex, we'll stop. I've abstained for twenty-nine years. I can go for another six months, then divorce you and get myself a proper man with satisfying technique."

"Awfully eager to divorce, aren't you?" *Is this some kind of reverse psychology?*

"Well, I can't be with a man who doesn't satisfy me in bed. You said a marriage of respectful indifference, not sexual frustration. I mean, we aren't even in love with each other."

"Okay. What if *you* can't satisfy *me*?"

She stares at me wide-eyed. It's obvious that the thought has never occurred to her. *Talk about confidence...* Or is it arrogance? "Then six months later we divorce."

"Well, I haven't gone without for that long." A lie. I've gone for months without a woman every time I broke up because just thinking about their obsessive clinging destroys my sexual appetite.

Lareina finishes the berries. "I don't think I'll be a problem, since you thought a simple kiss was amazing. But if you're worried about your prowess, you can always audition."

"Audition?"

"To prove yourself worthy." She holds my eyes in challenge.

Does she think she can play with fire and remain unscathed? I toss the napkin on the table and stand, then stalk toward her.

Her tongue darts out, swipes over her lower lip before disappearing. She tilts her chin higher and looks at me with eyes dark with anticipation. "You can try kissing me again."

"Kissing is anemic."

Despite the hotel shampoo and soap, there's a faint whiff of lemon and something sweet and hot coming from her. She exhales, the warm breath just the tiniest bit shaky. Her long, thick lashes flutter a little as she stares at me. I put my hands on the arm rests, caging her. The pulse in her throat throbs, and I lower my head, brushing the tip of my nose against hers. A tremulous inhale; her throat works as she waits for my next move, and I enjoy her subtle responses. Her lips part. The heat from her body is sweet and intoxicating. I angle my head, press kisses along the taut line of her pixie-like jaw.

"Are you going for my chin?" Her voice shakes, the pulse in her neck beating wildly.

I chuckle. "Who says the mouth is the only place a man can kiss a woman?" I rain kisses on her hot cheeks, then smooth forehead and cute nose, and she lets out a soft whimper. *Get a proper man with satisfying technique, indeed.* I have no idea how the kiss went yesterday, but the

The Accidental Marriage

one right now is going to be seared into her mind, and she won't even *think* of using shitty sex as a reason for divorce. I'll make sure of it.

She shifts a little, angling her face, chasing my mouth. Instead of giving her what she wants, I kiss the corners of her gorgeous eyes. Amazing how beautiful they are, how expressive.

She tunnels her hand into my hair and tugs me down. Triumphant, I run my tongue over her lips.

A soft sigh, and our breaths mingle. I take in the air between us and stroke her pillowy mouth with mine. Excitement breaks throughout my body, making every nerve ending prickle with life. Her fingers dig into my forearms, and I deepen the kiss, invading her mouth with my tongue. Hers glides against mine, and an electric ripple runs down my spine. The flush on her cheeks deepens until they're almost crimson.

Another sound, half sigh and half moan, comes from her throat. She flexes her fingers, then tilts her head back to offer me better access. I cup her nape and plunder her, taste the sweet syrup, berries and spice. She kisses me back, more enthusiasm than technique, but the raw display of desire is sexy as hell. My blood runs hotter than ever, pooling into my now-rigid dick.

If I had a condom, I might be tempted to carry her to bed. But I don't —and pregnancy would be stupid in a temporary situation like ours.

I cradle her face with one hand, swiping my thumb slowly over her cheekbone. She leans into my palm, wrapping her hand around my thick wrist. Tenderly I trace the shell of her ear and she shivers.

Sensitive. Mmm.

I take the earlobe between my lips and suck, running my teeth along the tender flesh. She moans softly, tilting her head to the side. "Oh my God, Ares. Okay, you pass," she says, her lips wet and swollen.

I laugh darkly. "Sweetheart, I'm just getting started."

11

ARES

Lareina's eyes grow wide, a question fleeting in their depths, as though she can't believe what she just heard. Or perhaps she just can't digest my words at the moment. But surely she didn't think she could throw out a challenge and not be met with some pushback?

I trail more kisses along the taut skin of her neck, inhaling her scent. She smells so good—shampoo and citrus and warm female flesh. Tastes amazing too, like her skin was soaked in honey. Shivers run through her. She moans softly, one hand digging into my hair and the other clutching my shoulders.

My callused fingertips graze along the delicate lines of her collarbones. I keep my touch featherlight, teasing. She moves her legs restlessly, breaths shuddering in and out of her as she loses herself in the fire I'm kindling in her blood.

Wherever my fingers touch, I follow with my lips, licking and sucking. The more I taste her, the more I crave her. She's like fine whiskey in my blood, fiery and intoxicating.

Moaning, she shifts in her chair, squeezing her legs together as though to ease an empty ache. Carnal triumph curls in my belly at her reaction. I draw the lapels of her robe aside, revealing the sweet slopes of her breasts. Her nipples are the color of ripe raspberries. My mouth waters. She's feminine perfection, supple, warm and stunning.

She twists subtly under my hot gaze, her body undulating, beckoning me. Her lust-glazed eyes beg for more.

She says she's never done it, but she's more sensually demanding than any woman I've been with. The stark honesty in her desire is the hottest aphrodisiac.

I raise my hand, letting it hover over a breast, so close that I can feel her body heat, but not touching. I look at her, cocking an eyebrow in silent inquiry. I don't just want her to want it. I want her to *admit* it.

Her throat works as she swallows, then nods.

"Good girl," I say, voice full of wicked satisfaction.

I close my hand over her breast. Our marriage may be fleeting, but for the moment, Lareina is mine.

Mine to possess, mine to devour, mine to defile, corrupt and worship.

I knead the silky weight gently, stroking the upper and lower curves with my thumb as though they're the wonders of the universe. Her eyes flutter shut as she throws her head back and squirms. A rosy flush in her cheeks spreads all the way to her chest. Her breathing grows shallower, and my cock hardens impossibly at the signs of her rising arousal.

Her eyebrows knit, as though she's torn between the desire to keep going or stop. Maybe she wants both at the same time, from the way she's biting her lip.

I bite back a curse as she digs her fingers into my shoulders, then arms, silently begging and urging. The movement is earnest but clumsy. Shock colors the small gasps and moans tearing from her gorgeous mouth. She says she's never had sex, but she's twenty-nine. She couldn't possibly—

"Have you ever fondled yourself?" I ask.

She blinks, her eyes hazy with need. "What? No."

"You've never even masturbated?"

Her cheeks grow redder. "No."

I narrow my eyes in disbelief. "Why not?"

"Don't want to get caught. People tend to barge into my room, and—"

"Nobody's barging in now."

"I thought we were supposed to be kissing? Masturbation isn't a kiss." Although her voice is breathless, she tilts her little chin primly, her eyes flashing with a challenge.

I pinch her nipple, drawing a long moan from her. "Neither is this," I taunt her, gently tugging at the tip.

Her back arches like an electric jolt is running up her spine. Her legs rub against mine restlessly.

"Take your hand and touch your breast. Experiment. Make yourself feel good for me, baby," I whisper, as wicked as the devil tempting the innocent.

She stares at me as though I've suggested the unthinkable, but I merely look back at her, silently promising a reward for her compliance.

Licking her lips, she raises a shaky hand and cups her breast. The vision of her smaller and softer fingers kneading the creamy flesh overheats my blood. Uncertainty and desire war in her blue and green eyes.

"This is weird," she whispers.

"Does it feel bad?"

She considers, then shakes her head. Still, her movements are too tentative. I take her index finger and rub it across her nipple. It puckers and beads under my gaze and the touch. A shudder runs through her, her finger growing tense under mine. Her legs squeeze my hips. Vulnerability and lust mix in her gaze, and her pelvis undulates, testing my already slippery control.

I take a tight rein over myself. No way am I letting a virgin make me lose it. It isn't about my ego or her challenge. I want her to feel good, experience the carnal pleasure between a man and woman.

I want her to feel glad she chose me to be her first.

"How does it feel?" I ask, as I continue to run her fingertip over her nipple.

"Amazing," she says shakily.

"Good girl." I shoot her a smile, appreciating her honesty. The naked sincerity in her response stirs a protective instinct in me, and I want to spoil her senses.

I rub my cheek against the soft mound of the breast I've been toying with. When my stubble brushes against the nipple, she writhes in shock, her cry loud with pleasure, tinged with apprehension.

"What's wrong, wife?"

"It's just... It feels too intense." She flushes. "Maybe a little scary?"

Her response is like a bucket of ice water. I can't treat her like my exes who've had plenty of experience. Am I being too rough, too inconsiderate?

I realize I'm inexperienced about being somebody's first. Sudden vulnerability and anxiety clench around my heart, making it ache.

She looks at me shyly. "Can you kiss me?"

I take her mouth tenderly, fusing my mouth with hers in a sweet gesture of mutual pleasure and reassurance. She wraps her arms around me and kisses me back, her tongue stroking mine. Her honeyed flavor intoxicates me, and I continue to kiss her while I stroke her, exploring her sensitivity.

I trail my mouth along the high cheekbones, the taut line of her jaw and the fluttering pulse point in her neck. The breaths she lets out are shaky with building pleasure. She still clings to me as though she's lost in a big, turbulent sea, but only blissful need sparkles in her eyes—without any hint of apprehension.

Yes.

I travel lower, shower her breast with hot kisses, then suck her nipple into my mouth, wanting to push her higher. She cries out at the wet heat. I nip gently, then lick to soothe. I put my hand over hers, which is lying limply over her other breast, then massage the soft mound, rubbing the pad of my thumb over the rosy peak.

I shift my eyes upward and meet her gaze, dazed with pleasure and greedy for more. Her whole body shivers, her hips rocking against me. From the way she hangs on, I don't think she realizes what she's doing, simply riding the building wave of ecstasy.

The sight is magnificent. I laugh softly, her nipple still in my mouth. The vibration seems to drive her even crazier with need. Her fingers rip at the armrests.

I pinch her other nipple. "Ride it out," I order her, letting her know it's more than fine. "Chase the orgasm."

"I can't," she whimpers. Tension winds around her tightly, but she resists, uncertainty fleeting across her face.

"Sure you can." I squeeze her small hand over the breast, giving it firm pressure, then suck on her nipple hard, my cheeks going hollow.

She screams, her spine arching. Every muscle in her body tightens—and then she turns to a soft goo as a satisfied sigh comes from her sweet little mouth. Her eyes remain closed as she savors the descent from her climax.

Her first orgasm.

The idea wrecks me. Exhilaration pumps through my heart. My cock is so hard, it's painful. At the same time—

"That was fun, wife." I force a light grin to hide my rising possessiveness. Her coming just from my playing with her tits is probably the hottest thing I've ever seen. How could she have denied herself for so long when she's this sensitive? She wants sex from me? *Fine.* I'm going to enjoy spoiling her in bed, filling her senses with pleasure only *I* can give as her husband.

"Fun...?" she repeats weakly.

"Uh-huh." I press a kiss on her still-trembling belly, then pull her closer until she's perched at the edge of the chair, her legs spread wide with my hips against hers. Her robe is mostly undone. Meanwhile, mine is still neatly tied at the waist, although there's no way she can miss the thick length throbbing against her wet core.

I place my hands on her warm knees and spread them wide. The slick flesh between her thighs pulses, and I can't look away from the sight of her need. Her muscles tremble again as expectation builds, her chest rising and falling rapidly.

Anticipation and embarrassment war over her flushed face. Her toes curl and uncurl, and I can't help but smile.

My eyes on hers, I press my mouth over her pubic bone. Her scent is stronger here, hot and sweet. She swallows, licks her lips. I cock an eyebrow, my mouth unmoving. I want her to give her a chance to pull back.

Except she doesn't. She stays immobile, holding her breath. I wrap my fingers around the sides of the chair, and she takes in my face, poised over her most sensitive, untouched flesh.

I'm dying to taste her, make her feel good, feel her spasm under my mouth and tongue. *Steady*, I tell myself. I want her to admit she wants this. I want her to know who's giving her oral for the first time.

I drag a finger down the folds, from the tip of her clit all the way to her opening. Her muscles clench, and she lets out a soft sigh, her hips jerking. I smile at the glistening fluid on my fingertip and lick it with even a bigger grin. "Sweet." I slide my eyes toward her. "You've never tasted it, have you?"

She shakes her head.

I push the finger into her again, more deeply. Her muscles contract around it. Holy shit, she's tight. And so hot. I burn as I look at her. "Want a taste?" I offer her the finger.

Her eyes on mine, she nods. I gently brush my finger over her lips, smearing the clear liquid over them like lip gloss. She flicks her tongue out for a taste, then frowns a little. "Salty."

I laugh softly. "You're wrong, wife."

The proprietary way "wife" slips from my lips this time stuns me. Surprise flickers in Lareina's eyes as well, quickly followed by a vulnerable hope.

Suddenly I don't want to deal with any sort of expectations from her about our future. We've already established that we're going to divorce, and it's best to stick to the plan. Sexual compatibility is no reason to stay together, even if my cock has never been this hard before.

No. This moment is all about sex. I close my mouth over her. Taste her slick honey. Her arms shake, her fingers digging harder into the chair. My breath fans against her worked-up flesh. When I run the flat of my tongue over her folds and tease her clit with the tip of my tongue, the muscles in her legs quiver. She clenches the chair, letting out uneven, labored breaths.

Her eyes flutter shut. She bites her lip as though she's trying to control how much pleasure she'll allow herself to feel—she won't be caught unaware like before, getting thrown up in the climax.

Oh no you don't.

I pull her clit into my mouth and suck hard, then use my tongue like I'm rolling a piece of candy. She twists at the onslaught of pleasure, crying out. Her heels dig into my back, and I work her harder, loving her naked reaction, reveling in making her lose her mind with bliss.

Her legs quiver as she tries to close them around my head. *Oh yes, baby, yes. Rock yourself against me.*

I push a finger inside her, parting the tight flesh. She trembles, squeezing her dripping pussy around my digit. I push it even deeper, until I find the little bump.

I rub it and am rewarded with "*Oh my God!*"

"It's Ares, baby," I say with a laugh.

She twists under me. "Stop. It's too much, please," she sobs, although her legs are clenched tight around my head, and her fingers are dug deep into my hair, pressing me tighter against her. Then she cries, "Please, *please!*"

My lips and tongue give her what her body is demanding. She tenses, then bows her back as she climaxes again with a sharp cry. Her grip on me is almost painful, but I love her unabashed enjoyment of the orgasm.

As she floats down from the high and relaxes, I lift my head, then run the back of my hand over my wet chin and mouth before ravaging her mouth. She tastes like a woman well pleasured, all soft and languid like heated honey. It goes straight to my head, driving me wild. She wraps her legs around me as I pick her up, and we fall on the bed together.

My robe parts, my cock pressing against her soaked flesh. It feels so damn good that even my scalp tingles. My dick pulses against her, like it has its own heart beating inside. I continue to kiss her, my tongue stroking hers, as I fight for control.

She seems determined to destroy it; she clings to me, digging her nails into my shoulders. She presses her feet flat on the mattress and rocks against my cock. Electric jolts shoot through me, one after another, to the rhythm she sets.

Siren. Mine.

"Yes, Princess," I groan.

"Not Princess. *Queen*," she corrects me breathlessly. "I've always hated the term princess—pretty but helpless."

My muscles tense. Every time she talks like this, it reminds me of Queen, except she isn't Queen, and I shouldn't confuse the two. Queen wouldn't show up this easily into my life again. Not after being hidden for twenty-two years.

Focus.

Not wanting to associate my temporary wife with Queen, I bury my face in the crook of her neck and rock harder and faster, making sure my cockhead bumps her clit each time. She lets out a whimper, then slaps at my shoulders as though to protest that she can't endure another orgasm.

Yes, you can and you will.

I pull her earlobe into my mouth and nip.

Every cell in her body clenches, and she sobs as another peak wrecks her. She holds me as though she will never let go. Her desperation should make me pull away; instead, it pushes me over the edge.

A deep groan tears from my throat, and I lose myself in climax as shudder after shudder racks me. When I can drag air in again, I push myself up on my hands and take in the sight of my cum splattered all over her belly. My mark on my woman in the most primitive sense. She flushes under my gaze, and there's a hint of vulnerability in her eyes as she looks down for a moment. My skin feels overly tight, like it can't contain the abrupt swelling of possessiveness.

I cradle her face, kiss the tip of her nose and forehead, while smearing more of my cum all over her like a wolf marking his territory. She doesn't protest. Instead, she kisses me back just as passionately.

"Did I pass?" I ask after a while.

She blinks slowly. Then a mischievous grin curves her swollen lips. "Lemme think about it."

I cock an eyebrow, taking in her heated face. "Need more demonstration?"

Her cheeks turn rosy again. Need glimmers in her eyes, followed by a hint of surprise. "How could I want more?"

"Because it feels unbelievably great?" I tell her, lightly flicking my index finger over her small nose.

"Yes, but... No. I don't need more."

Her firm rejection sends an unexpected—and uncharacteristic—disappointment through me. I've never craved more time in bed with a woman before. If the other party didn't want it, no big deal.

"We need to get out of Vegas before our stalkers find out where we are," she says, then gives me a saucy look. "But later…we can investigate the matter between us more thoroughly."

12

ARES

When Lareina cleans up and comes out of the bathroom, I lower my coffee mug and stare. Her golden hair loose around that pixie-like face with its large blue and green heterochromatic eyes and the white dress on her, she looks awfully like—

Not Princess. Queen.

Her breathless correction ripples in my head. Something about the way she said it made me think of the girl who said, "Just 'Queen' will do fine," so regally. For a moment I thought she was Queen until I reminded myself she couldn't be out here. Besides, if she were in Vegas, wouldn't the investigators I've hired over the years have found her by now? I had them try to trace her from Oregon, and they found nothing. Clues came every so often, but none of them turned out to be anything.

Still...

Could Lareina be Queen?

I send a quick instruction to Greg: *Look into Lareina Huxley's background.*

–Greg: Huxley?

His confusion is palpable. He knows there is no such Huxley in the family.

—Me: My wife.

—Greg: Her maiden name?

He's too professional to betray himself this time. I frown as I realize I have no clue. She mentioned getting the marriage license, so it must've been brought up, but of course I remember nothing, which is irritating.

"What's your maiden name?" I ask abruptly.

"Hayworth," she says. "Why?"

"Curious. You're my wife, and my family might ask." I text it to Greg, asking him to make it quick.

As soon as I put away the phone, Lareina walks toward me. "Can you button the back for me?" She turns around. Her arms are twisted awkwardly to hide as much skin as possible.

"Too late to be modest," I say as I button the bodice. The image of my cum on her belly floats up—and all the blood in my body flows down.

I was too impulsive earlier, letting her goad me. Our having sex basically means I have accepted her proposition, and can't change my mind now.

Despite the unease in my heart, I console myself with the fact that Lareina will take care of the problem of my finding a wife. Although she's a bit eccentric, she's pretty. Plus she's a blonde, which means nobody will question our relationship. And our sexual compatibility is a *major* plus. Virgin or not, I'll enjoy our time in bed.

Besides, this marriage doesn't have to be forever. The firm will complete the annual review in three months. Then, in the subsequent four weeks, it'll announce all the promotions. So in four months, I'll have no use for her anymore. Since she wants to be at least thirty before she goes back to being single, I'll be magnanimous and give her the extra two months she needs.

I make sure to brush my fingertips against every inch of her warm, exposed skin, delighting in her nearness. I never understood why my cousin loved to put things on his wife so much—isn't the point to get her naked?—but now I see the charm. "Your back is beautiful. All smooth and creamy."

She stiffens for a second. *What did I say?*

"I'm not showing you my back," she says, sniffing. "Only a man would undervalue modesty."

"Not just any man, but your husband," I correct her.

"If I tell you to walk around buck naked—"

"Wanna see it right now?" I finish the last button on the top, then pull her back until her backside bumps against my half-hard cock.

Gasping, she turns around. "Aren't we going home?"

I place a firm kiss on the back of her neck. "Yes." I need to get away from Vegas, put some distance between me and Harvey—and possibly my mother, who might be in the city searching for me. Once again, I question the unforeseen forces of the universe: *Why couldn't I have been blessed with a normal mom and uncle?*

I have my original hotel's concierge check me out, pack my things and send them directly to my home in L.A. Then Lareina and I head to the airport, where my private jet is waiting. I let out a soft sigh. The crew is mine and loyal. I don't just pay them handsomely, but make sure they and their family are well taken care of. Harvey or anybody else won't be able to bribe my crew and fuck me over.

Since it's just two of us, the jet takes off quickly, just the way I prefer. Lareina looks outside as we climb, then studies the plush leather seats with interest. "Ooh, this is nice! Does it turn into a bed?"

"No. But there's a bedroom in the back."

She trots away to explore, while I pull out the documents from the bag the concierge sent over. The flight to L.A. will be about an hour, and I want to finish the docs I need for filing.

After a few minutes, she comes back. Her eyes sparkle as she looks at me. "We should go to Europe on this plane."

"I don't have time for a honeymoon."

She rolls her eyes. "I don't mean *now*. It would be too clingy. But later. It can be our divorce-cation!"

I glare at her, oddly irritated by her mention of divorce. "You don't go on a divorce-cation with your soon-to-be ex-husband."

"You do if you plan to remain friends with the ex." She leans over. "Aren't we going to be friends?" She's so close that I can smell the berries on her breath, the lemon on her skin. Her eyes are wide, and my shadow is reflected in their clear depths. She appears so guileless. My protective instincts stir.

Then I think of my parents. And all my exes who started out okay but devolved into clingy, creepy messes as soon as they decided they were in love with me. "No. We'll be enemies for life." It comes out more tersely than I intend.

Lareina pulls back. With the growing distance, I'm no longer reflected in her eyes. Her sweet scent retreats, leaving a void.

Before I can process my reaction, the cabin attendant serves us bowls of warmed nuts and sparkling water. Thank God for the interruption. Why the hell was I thinking about my wife's scent, of all things? Or what's reflected in her eyes?

I have a few walnuts. Lareina watches me for a while, then takes a cashew from my bowl.

"*What's wrong with yours?*" What excuse will she give this time?

She squirms a little. "Not enough cashews," she says.

I eye the two cashews on the top of her bowl. "Let me guess. Mine looks better."

"Something like that." Smiling sheepishly, she swaps her bowl with mine.

I go back to the documents. *Let her have the damn nuts.* As far as habits go, it isn't too bad. Not like ordering a salad, stealing half my fries, and then getting upset when I order a side of fries for her, which one of my exes did all the time.

Soon the plane lands in L.A., and my apprehension regarding Harvey dissipates, as though being back on my home turf has restored my footing. Lareina deplanes ahead of me. She's pretty on the gray tarmac, in spite of her long, unbound hair blowing everywhere and the smudged, wrinkled dress hanging limply on her frame. As the SoCal sun hits me, the surreal, fairytale-like daze from Vegas vanishes, leaving me sharp and clearheaded. Regret and remorse twine around my gut like twin snakes. *What was I thinking when I agreed to her ridiculous proposal?* Now I'll have to live with her, share my house with her.

Having a stranger in my sanctuary feels violative. My house is my own, and I don't let anybody in, other than family and staff for maintaining the vast mansion. My exes didn't last long enough to move in with me, and they certainly never got to set a single foot inside.

I suddenly realize that I've never pictured my future wife inside my home. The respectful marriage I envisioned would take place at some abstract location, but not my home.

Suddenly, Lareina stumbles with a small yelp. I lunge forward to catch her.

"Are you all right?"

"Yeah. I just..." She pulls her dress up, revealing her bare feet and a jagged rock.

"Where are your shoes?" I straighten and start to turn toward the plane. Is this another of her weird habits and fetishes?

"I don't have any."

"What? Did you lose them yesterday running away from your cousin?"

"No. I never had any. Doris—my aunt—likes to keep me barefoot, thinking it'll stop me from running." Lareina snorts, then laughs to herself as though the entire belief is absurd.

Damn it. Can't believe I didn't notice. *She walked all over Las Vegas without shoes.* I drop to my knees, then take a narrow foot in my hand. It's slightly cold, with hard calluses on the side. I check the sole to see if there's some injury she isn't telling me about. A small scrape, but it doesn't look infected or anything. I run my finger along the scarlet line, and she immediately yanks her foot out of my grasp.

"Stop! I'm ticklish," she says.

"Hush. Does it hurt?"

"Only a little, if you touch it."

I *tsk*, shaking my head.

She blinks. "Are you *mad* at me?"

"No. I'm annoyed with myself for not realizing sooner. And I want to punch your aunt for not giving you shoes."

"Really? But she's a woman."

"So?"

"I thought men don't hit women."

"I'll hit anyone who's the enemy." Another hard-learned lesson from Mom's kidnapping. Looking at her angelic façade, nobody would ever think she was capable of hurting her own child. She taught me women can be just as vicious as men. "Enemies are supposed to be brought down hard and fast, not given another opportunity to hurt you."

Lareina smiles. "Thank you. That's actually nice to hear. Sometimes people defend her, saying she's just a woman doing her best. I always hate that."

"And you should. A woman doing her best wouldn't leave her niece shoeless." I examine her other foot. Again, the same—cold and callused, with a red sole from walking all over the city.

"Are you buying me a pair?" she asks.

I gesture at the crew for a first-aid kit, then grab a big Band-Aid for the small injury on her foot. "A closetful."

Laughing, she takes a step toward our waiting car. I pick her up and carry her toward it instead.

"Ack." She loops her arms around my neck. "What are you doing?"

"Not having my wife walk around the city barefoot."

"It's only to the car." She tilts her head.

"Not happening. Princess carry."

"Queen carry!"

Her insistence that she's a queen sends shivers through my chest. "Why do you want to be a queen?" I ask, outwardly indifferent, although my pulse picks up speed.

"Because she's the *boss*."

The answer is so similar to the one Queen from Oregon gave. It makes my heart skip a beat.

"Plus, I'm too old to be a princess," she adds matter-of-factly.

"A woman is never too old to be a princess," I say firmly, amused by her attitude. She's not even thirty, although from the way she's described her life so far, her experience might be less than a typical woman in her late twenties. "Besides, a princess gets a prince. Ever think about that?"

"Princes are overrated. Unless he's ridiculously handsome, sweet, rich, moral and—"

"Good in bed?"

She flushes, but nods. "I was getting around to that."

The crew put my bag in the trunk and the driver opens the door.

"You don't know how to drive?" she says, eyeing him.

"I only arranged for a pickup in case I was hungover and tired." Barry's parties are wild and never end before the sun rises. Although I make it my policy not to get wasted, I wanted to be prepared, just in case.

I put her in the car, then climb in. She sits with the dress spread primly around her legs, totally composed.

So far, nothing except my initial refusal to go along with the marriage seems to throw her off. But I want to upset her equilibrium as she's done to me. I pull her onto my lap, eliciting a satisfying gasp.

"We don't have to pretend anymore," she whispers into my ear. Her eyes dart to the front seat. "I don't think he's paying attention."

A smile tugs at my mouth. Funny how she's acting shy all of a sudden after demanding from me *satisfying* sex or else. "My family needs to believe this marriage is real. So you'll cooperate."

She frowns. "Why does it matter what they think?"

"Because they're hoping I'll bring home a nice, respectable wife."

"I don't think nice, respectable wives sit on their husbands' laps."

"Do you have a lot of experience with married life?"

Her mouth purses. "No, but I've never seen a married couple sit like this."

"I have."

She ignores me. "My aunt and uncle didn't. My parents didn't, either. At least, I don't think so."

"You don't remember?" I say in surprise, keeping my arms around her because the weight of her feels good. And it's only until we arrive at my place.

She doesn't make any move to squirm off my lap, and gazes off into the distance. "There are a lot of things I don't, although I get a warm, fuzzy feeling right here"—she places a hand over her chest—"every time I think of my parents. They passed away from food poisoning when I was little. But I recall Mom taking me on her travels and teaching me how to draw. She was an amazing artist, and she was always generous with praise. Apparently, she refused to live in Nesovia until Grandpa did more to protect me and my inheritance."

Fucking Nesovia. That explains a lot about her predicament. That country is ridiculously medieval in its attitude toward women.

She continues, "After we finally settled there, Dad taught me to ride, since he wasn't much of an artist." She smiles a little. "Lady was a wonderful pony. All white, with a beige spot on her forehead. I used to say that was where her invisible horn was, because I was convinced she was secretly a unicorn princess hiding from her evil stepmom, and my parents indulged me."

"They sound like lovely people," I say softly.

"They were. Not sure what happened to Lady after my grandfather passed away. I didn't have much time to spend with her. On top of that, I was too upset and traumatized, and Doris kept me busy with school, tutors and therapists who were hired ostensibly to help me overcome my grief. I hope she sold Lady and found her a great new home. I don't even care that she might've made a profit from the sale, as long as Lady had a good life."

Her wistful tone sends a ripple through my heart. I squeeze her hand, trying to comfort her. "I'm sure she did."

She rests her head on my shoulder. The gesture feels shockingly natural, which is weird and uncharacteristic for me. Normally I don't care for women leaning on me. It means they're starting to develop feelings, which means they're beginning to become obsessed. And then there's the clinging and sobbing about love and just generally being nightmarish.

But with Lareina, having her lean on me a little doesn't seem so terrible. *Just until we reach the house. I can indulge her for that long.* Besides, she smells good, so it isn't such a hardship.

"I miss Mom and her paintings," she continues. "And drawing."

"Are you any good?"

"No." She makes a face. "Mom always said I was amazing and talented, more so than her. But apparently I suck at it."

"Do you paint often?"

"Yeah. Doris begrudges spending money on me—but not art supplies, especially after a conversation with my therapist. It supposedly helps me stay calm and dream of an escape and a better life. He thinks that since I'm reluctant to open up to him, he can use my art to see into my mind. But I doubt he's good enough to figure anything out, paintings or no, and I need something to keep me sane when things get too stressful and unsafe."

Unsafe? "Did they hit you?"

"No. But they wanted to pair me up with Rupert. Badly."

"Did he...try to force himself on you?"

"He tried, but failed. I slashed at him with a fruit knife I had, and he got scared. He tried again, but then quit when he realized I wasn't going to give up my knife, and he might never get his filthy paws on my inheritance." She snort-laughs at the memory.

Her laughter horrifies me. She's laughing because that's the only way she can cope with the trauma.

She adds, "I made sure to have a knife, but I also threatened to jump off the balcony if Rupert forced himself on me, which scared them. They couldn't afford to have me dead and lose my inheritance, so Rupert behaved, sort of."

"I'm going to murder that son of a bitch."

"Get in line. I plan to make them all pay." Her tone is shockingly light, and her eyes show no hint of rage as she straightens her knees before dropping her feet.

I can't process her reaction at all. "You aren't upset?"

"Is the past worth being so angry about right now when my belly is full of delicious food and I'm with a husband who can keep Rupert away from me?"

I frown at the question.

"Not really," she answers without waiting for my response. Her practical outlook is stunning. Perhaps her therapist really *is* good, even if he can't figure out her situation with Rupert and all.

"But enough about me. I can tell it's just making you gloomy," she says. "Tell me about *you*. I feel like I should know something about my husband."

A clumsy attempt at distraction, but I humor her. "I'm a lawyer. My entire family is, actually, except for my stepmom and my cousin. I have two brothers—twins. Bryce and Josh. Hard to tell them apart, and they're both dicks unless you're family. And one aunt. Jeremiah is her name."

"Sounds like a man's name."

"Yes, but we don't mention that because it was Grandmother's decision. She wanted her daughter to be strong and powerful."

"And is she?"

"Oh yeah. Anybody who fucks with her finds out very quickly."

She smiles. "You like her."

"I do. Sharp as a tack, and mean as hell. If you have her on your team, you're golden."

"Must be lovely." Lareina bites her lip, then lowers her voice. "Is her husband the one who drugged you and tried to make you work for him last night?"

I snort, thinking about Aunt Jeremiah's scandalous baby daddy Ted. A lot of people in the family think she only slept with him to see if he was as good as rumors made it sound. But we'll never know the truth because she never talks about it. You'd have better luck prying open a clam barehanded than squeezing information out of Aunt Jeremiah when she doesn't want to share. "No. She's never married, and even if she had, she wouldn't have picked a man who goes against the family's interests. Harvey's from my biological mother's side."

"Doesn't he know offering you a lot of money would've been more effective?"

I chuckle dryly. "Money doesn't motivate me."

"Ah. The two billion."

My spine stiffens. "How do you know that?"

"You told me."

"I must've been more out of it than I thought. Did I say anything else?"

She gives me a long look, tapping her chin. "Quite a lot, actually," she says slowly. "Give me a moment and I'll tell you what I think was important."

Her teasing tone makes me want to kiss her. I wrap my hand around the back of her neck and pull her close. Our lips fuse; I pull her tongue into my mouth.

A delicious gasp tears from her throat, and her hands fist on my shoulders, as though she can't decide between pushing me away or pulling me close. I stroke her tongue with mine unhurriedly, drawing out her reaction. Although the fists on my shoulders don't relax, her mouth softens and she kisses me back. Her breathing grows shallower, and the heat from her skin is scorching. There's an inexplicable addictiveness to her, and it's both exhilarating and terrifying.

She squirms to get more comfortable, the movement rubbing her thigh against my already hard dick. Hot blood rushes through my veins, and it's all I can do to swallow the groan building in my chest as I plunder her.

After a bit, I vaguely register that the car has stopped moving. I open my eyes, see the front entrance to my home and reluctantly pull back from Lareina.

She looks at me, her eyes glazed with arousal. It might be her lack of artifice and shield that makes me prone to lower my guard with her. I understand it's a bad move, the kind that would earn me a loss in a chess game.

I get out first, hit the entry button for the house on my phone, then carry her inside. The huge double doors open automatically at our approach, showing the spotless foyer with its contemporary chandelier, all crystal and smoked glass. Bright sunlight pours in through the skylight, casting a halo around her. She looks at me with a shy smile, and behind her, the family's coat of arm glints. PIETAS ET UNITAS. Above the motto, snarling wolves flash their fangs, reminding me of the wolf's head in Mom's cabin.

Complex, contradictory emotions stir in my heart. I want to hold Lareina and push her away, protect her and hurt her, keep her both close and at arm's length. If I didn't have any emotional baggage, I'd just revel in how beautiful and sweet she is, but there's a tinge of trepidation that she's too different from the others.

"Your home is pretty," she says softly.

"It's all right," I say. I've never given much thought to the mansion, purchasing it because it had the right specs, right price tag and right zip code.

I carry her to the kitchen, since it's time to grab a late lunch, but the scent of a cigar hits me. I freeze at the sight of Aunt Jeremiah at my kitchen island. *What the hell is she doing here...?*

She's in a white bathrobe, her blood-red hair held by a black headband and some kind of green goo on her face. A wisp of smoke rises from the lit cigar in her hand, and a glass of Merlot sits in front of her.

She turns to me. If she's cocking an eyebrow, it's impossible to tell from all the goo. Her eyes flick to me, then to Lareina, then take in our outfits.

"Well, well, well. What do we have here?" she says drolly. "Did you elope with Barry's fiancée?"

13

ARES

"Who's Barry?" Lareina asks.

"The groom." My aunt takes a sip of wine—*my* wine.

"I thought his name was Ares."

"I *am* Ares. She's talking about somebody else," I say. Facing my aunt unprepared with Lareina wasn't part of my plan for the day. I was going to talk to Dad and Akiko first.

I place Lareina on one of the stools, making sure there's an empty one between her and Jeremiah. My aunt has many admirable qualities, but nurturing and welcoming aren't her forte.

"So who is she and why is she here?" she asks me, as though Lareina weren't right in front of her.

"I'm Lareina. And I'm Ares's wife."

"I see." Aunt Jeremiah continues to study Lareina, her eyes narrowed.

Lareina merely looks back with a smile, which sparks a reluctant respect. It isn't easy to remain serene—and very few people manage to keep themselves together when faced with my aunt. She's a scary cross-examiner. If the family hadn't been so focused on its legal empire, she could've had a career at the CIA or NSA, interrogating terrorism suspects.

She turns to me. "So this is the answer to our objection to your promotion?"

"Yes. Lareina is a nice, respectable wife."

"Mmm." Noncommittal. So typical of my aunt, since she hates being pinned down until she feels she has sufficient data to make a decision.

I check to see the damage she's done to my groceries. Although she broke in and helped herself to my wine, she hasn't contributed a thing to my pantry or fridge.

I quickly toast a couple of bagels, then load them with cream cheese and smoked salmon slices with a few gherkins. I hand a plate to Lareina along with a bottle of water. She sips slowly, but doesn't touch the food.

"Picky eater?" Aunt Jeremiah's tone would be conversational to most, but not to me. There's a tinge of surprise that I'd be with someone who's so particular. She's seen me with my exes. "Inattentive, uncaring workaholic asshole who might be fun to screw but is bad for everything else and certainly not worth the fuss" is what she called me some years ago after my third romantic relationship ended. My ex at that time made a scene in the Huxley & Webber lobby every day for over two months, and I walked past her, seeing through her as though she were a stranger.

"Not really," Lareina says. "Just not that hungry yet."

I bite into my own bagel sandwich. *Time to rescue Lareina.* "What are you doing here, Aunt Jeremiah? Where are your clothes?"

"The pipes in my bathroom sprang a leak that went unnoticed, and made an unholy mess at my place. The plumber said repairs would take a while. Obviously, my house is uninhabitable until he's finished."

"And...?" I prompt her, still unsure why she's *here*, in my home.

"So here I am." She smiles creepily through the green goo. There's a reason smiley faces are yellow.

"No hotels?"

"Couldn't find anything I liked. You know I'm discerning."

"Why not Ted?" I say.

"He's hosting an orgy at his place this weekend."

I give Lareina a reassuring smile. We aren't as weird as that sounds. Orgies! Avoided!

Her eyes skitter from me and my aunt, then drop to her plate. Some impression to make on a twenty-nine-year-old virgin. Jesus.

"Why not Hux?" I say irritably, referring to her son. Ted was too lazy to use his creativity, so he named the child Huxley after Aunt Jeremiah's surname. He fits so many criteria for deadbeat fathers—except for the fact that he's rich as hell and financially generous with his seven sons.

"He absolutely refuses to share his place with me. Says he's married. Needs his privacy. Ridiculous." She puffs, then waves her cigar irritably.

"So stay with Dad." I take another bite.

Her back stiffens. "That insufferable know-it-all thinks that the ruling in—"

"Got it," I interrupt before she starts in on her thesis about the constitutionality of some really old and obscure case. Dad and she often disagree on the most abstruse points of law, and being that they're both headstrong lawyers, neither will give an inch. But it's really for the best that she doesn't stay with Dad, for Akiko's sake. My stepmother isn't a lawyer, but both Dad and Aunt Jeremiah try to drag her into their arguments, wanting her to judge the validity of their legal theories. Since Akiko hates to cause disharmony and hard feelings, she absolutely detests it when they bicker and does her best to ply them with saké, hoping good alcohol will dull their sharp tongues.

Aunt Jeremiah flicks her eyes at Lareina, then at me. "Why is your wife looking at you like a dog watching its owner eat?"

Lareina turns redder than a tomato. "I'm not."

"Of course you are."

Now she turns so crimson that I'm afraid she's about to burst with embarrassment or anger. "Hey, I can look at him any way I want. He's my husband."

Aunt Jeremiah's eyes narrow. Nothing good follows when she gazes at you like that.

"Did you want something to drink other than the wine, Aunt Jeremiah?" I ask, getting up and heading to the fridge.

"You know, maybe I'll go upstairs and let you two talk," Lareina says. "Maybe being able to climb a flight of stairs without spilling any water will convince your aunt that I'm not a dog." She picks up my plate and bottle and leaves before I can say anything.

"Look what you've done," I say to Aunt Jeremiah.

"She stole your plate!"

"She's worried I'm not eating enough, so she left me the untouched plate." I pull Lareina's plate toward me and start biting into the bagel like there's nothing wrong with this. I don't understand Lareina's weird obsession with swapping plates either, and don't want to get into it with my aunt. I make a mental note to talk to Lareina about it later.

Aunt Jeremiah glances toward the now-empty staircase, then turns to me. Her gaze is intensely focused. "Where did you find her?"

"Vegas, the City of Fast and Furious Marriages. Where else?"

"Be serious."

"Oh, I am. As you, Dad and Grandmother wanted, I'm *respectably married*." I spread my arms dramatically.

"Why did she marry you, then? You didn't have time to draft and sign a prenup, did you?"

"No. She married me out of necessity. The foundation of our marriage is solid."

Aunt Jeremiah snorts. "What happened to Soledad?"

"We broke up. I caught her fucking a gigolo."

"Why on earth would she do that?"

"Something about it being the best way to get me back."

"Good God." *What a dumbass,* her tone says. "But Lareina? It isn't like you to rebound. You didn't really care for Soledad, did you?"

"Not really. And no, Lareina isn't a rebound." I tell her what happened, leaving out all the details of Lareina that would prevent me from presenting her as a nice, respectable wife to The Fogeys.

"So you traded a moron for an eccentric." Although my aunt used a more politic term, it's clear what she really wants to call Lareina is "weird" or "crazy."

"She saved me from Harvey. How could I not fall for a woman who kept me safe?" I lay it on thick.

"That doesn't mean *she's* safe." She frowns. "Besides, you said she's from Nesovia, which is a nasty country for women. Her aunt probably won't give up so easily. I had a client from there, in a similar situation. A jewelry heiress. She got out of it by arranging for a marriage with her cheating fiancé's brother. It was quite the drama."

"Are you talking about Lucienne Peery?" I ask.

My aunt nods.

"Did she get what she wanted?" I ask, somewhat curious.

"Of course. I'm very good at giving my clients what they desire. Besides, her husband hired John Highsmith." She chortles, clearly reliving destroying the client's husband, then grows serious. "I should've warned you that Zoe might try to approach you again when Josh and Bryce turned thirty. Keeping Zoe away from you for life wasn't something we could pull off. Prescott wanted to walk, but we needed other guarantees from Vincent," she says, referring to my maternal grandfather.

"Mom won't get to me like before."

"She's more motivated. So is Harvey."

"Aren't they always?" I mutter.

"It's different this time." She puffs thoughtfully. "The rumor is that Vincent is sick."

"Finally?" I met him once after the fire that nearly killed me. He was built like a thousand-year-old oak, thick and powerful. I marveled at how he could end up creating somebody as delicate-looking as my mother.

"His last wish is to see you and your brothers. By that, he means have you join the family fold." I can hear *dream on* from her tone. "He allegedly said whoever could bring you and your brothers into the family would be his heir. Your mother has always wanted to prove herself to her father, and she won't pass up this opportunity. Harvey hates her, but most importantly, he knows what'll happen to him if she wins, so he'll do everything in his power to ensure *he* wins. And then..." Aunt Jeremiah pulls a finger across her neck.

That explains why he allied with Soledad and drugged me. He prefers to be more refined in his methods, believing himself to be a man of great sophistication.

"Soledad is a bitch, and she'll pay for what she's done," she continues coolly. "But I'd be careful about your wife, too. Her story is unfortunate, but your due diligence isn't finished yet. She's from Nesovia. Who knows what kind of connection she might have with the Dunkels? The country has a clean and proper Chamber of Commerce image, but underneath it's corrupt as hell. A lot of their industries and politicians have mob connections. And your mother is from one of the most prominent mob families." She pats my hand, which is a shock. For her it's practically a hug and vow of unconditional love. She does loyalty well—it's the first half of the family motto—but love isn't part of her repertoire. "If you need me, you know where to find me."

14

LAREINA

I BLINK, coming awake slowly. Every shade between white and black seems present in the room. Even the cool, silky sheet underneath me is a dove gray.

I'm still in the dress Doris got me. And from the way the sheets have the same smell as Ares, I'm in his bed.

Just what happened yesterday? I was so hungry after we got home, and I didn't want to deal with that aunt of his, who seemed so suspicious of me. She obviously thinks I'm after his money—he probably didn't tell her I agreed to the additional marriage vow of not taking his shit. Or maybe she's too lawyerly to accept that.

When Ares got distracted, I took his water and plate—subtly, of course, and naturally, like I mistook his for mine—then found a small reading room and ate.

Once my belly was full, all the tension slowly seeped out. After all, I wasn't just married, but actually *away from Doris and her family's power*. It would take time to find me, and even if they did, I was certain they couldn't just barge into Ares's home and try to steal me away. And they couldn't force Ares to give me up to them.

I'm safe. The two words rang in my head as I looked up at the snarling wolves over PIETAS ET UNITAS. Exhaustion overwhelmed me, and I gave in to it, truly relaxing for the first time. I probably fell asleep and didn't notice anything when Ares brought me to his bedroom.

What time is it?

I check the clock by the night stand. It reads twelve past ten a.m. I overslept.

Where's Ares?

I get up and listen for a moment. The mansion is eerily silent. Part of me wants to snoop. It's a habit I developed early, to scout my surroundings just in case I needed to make a quick escape.

But that would be rude here. And unnecessary. I'm sure I can ask Ares to show me around later.

Since I'm itching to get out of the uncomfortable wedding gown, I step into the walk-in closet, hoping to find something to put on. A light comes on, and in the ivory center island is a gorgeous glass case with bright spotlights over it. I step closer, curious what's inside. Jewels? A collection of fancy watches?

Nope. Over the soft crimson velvet lies a long cane. *Pietas et unitas* is etched in fancy silver filigree. A silver wolf's head sits on the top, where you'd wrap your hand. The name *Ares Joseph Huxley* is engraved on the latch of the case. Must be some significant family item, on par with an irreplaceable heirloom. Ares must prize it, too, for it to take such a prominent place.

I look at it for a while, my heart beating a little too fast and funny, my mouth bone dry. The wolf's head faces me, its eyes and fangs furious, as though it'd bite my neck. I shake my head. Probably just thirst making me feel off. My throat is parched.

I tear my gaze from the cane and look around. Suits, suits, dress shirts, shiny men's shoes and...some expensive-looking watches. I don't think there's anything I can wear, even temporarily.

I head to the kitchen, hoping there's more of the bottled water. After water, I'll get a lawyer. No, actually, fresh sets of clothes and shoes first, *then* a lawyer.

On the kitchen counter is a bottle of water and a small, sealed package of cereal. I pour it into my mouth dry, then read a yellow sticky note on the granite. Ares's handwriting is surprisingly neat. I thought a lawyer would have crappy handwriting because he'd have a secretary to write his memos and so on.

> Left you some food. Hope it's suitable. It's in a sealed package. I noticed you seem okay with food and drinks that are factory sealed.

I blink, surprised and touched that Ares noticed *and* cared enough to leave me something I can eat. I was planning on either not eating anything until he came home or going to a restaurant and asking the server to taste my food for me first.

The rest of the note reads:

> A newly activated phone, since you don't seem to have one. (If I'm wrong, just ignore it.) Your passport is in the upper drawer of the nightstand on your side of the bed. Clothes and shoes in the living room. Try them on, keep what you like and set aside what you don't. The personal shopper will come collect what you don't want next weekend. Take the credit card and buy us new wedding rings, since my family will want to meet you soon. At work now. If you need anything, text me. My number's already in your phone.

Huh, so he noticed I'm phoneless. Thanks to Doris, I've gone without for over fifteen years.

Is this part of being "indifferent"? I thought he wouldn't notice—or care even if he did.

I pick up the sleek teal phone, already in a case and with a clear protective cover on the screen. My heart flutters at finally having a tool in my hand that can help me connect with the world. The credit card he mentioned is a black American Express. I run my index finger over his name: Ares Huxley. *My husband.* The thought sends a warm ripple through me.

I know Ares asked me to text him *if I need anything*, but I have to text him my gratitude now. If he questions me, I'll tell him I *needed* to say, "Thank you." Besides, being polite isn't clingy. It's respectful, which is one of his requirements for our marriage.

–Me: Thank you so much! I love the phone and breakfast! You're amazing!

I stare at the screen for five heartbeats. He doesn't respond. Probably busy. And if he's in the office, so is Jeremiah.

I, on the other hand, am alone in this big house. Nobody to hover over me, watch me, report my every move or try to force me or manipulate me. Even the air is lighter and more wonderful in Ares's house.

For six months, this could be mine, as long as I toe the line. He wants me kept busy with a life of my own. Probably doing something that doesn't overlap with his in any way, shape or form. Easy. I'll just paint for the next six months, since it isn't like I can put together a résumé and start a job anytime soon. I don't even know how to drive, so it'll be best to do something that doesn't require commuting.

And what else did he want...? Caring without being nosy or controlling. Based on his tone, he seemed to value the boundaries more than the caring, so when in doubt, pull back.

Dinners can be arranged... But who's going to prepare them? If I'm supposed to be busy with a life of my own, I can't be expected to cook, right? I'll ask him, but takeout or eating out might be best. Actually, takeout or delivery, because he might get weird about my need to swap plates. When I was in Nesovia surrounded by household staff who treated me like dirt—not realizing that the money that paid their salaries came from me—I stole their food without a twinge of guilt or awkwardness, since I didn't give a damn what they thought. But I care about Ares's opinion of me.

Anyway, no annual vacations, since I'm not going to be around for a year. He didn't even sound enthused about the divorce-cation. No kids, obviously. That's for him and some subsequent *real* wife. But oddly enough, the idea pierces my heart like a needle, making it ache.

I don't understand. *Why do I care?* Ares is a super-nice guy, but he's only going to take up a short chapter in my life. Given how he told me I don't offer any of the things he needs in a wife, I need to make sure I

The Accidental Marriage

don't get too attached. Even if he's going to be my first. It's only logical I want my first time to be with a man I find attractive and who is good at sex. And squirmy salamanders are the last thing on my mind when Ares kisses me.

I take my time finishing the cereal, then head to the living room. Ares has a beautiful, albeit boring, home. Didn't anybody tell him he can have colors other than white, black and gray? Despite large windows and skylights to take advantage of the California sun, the dreary color scheme makes the place feel as cool and austere as a monastery. At least the leather chairs look plush and expensive, but also exude an air of *don't even* imagine *parking your unworthy ass on us*. Actually, everything in his house has an aura of look, *but don't touch*.

Probably not intentional. Just look at all the beautiful red, pink and purple blossoms in the garden surrounding the house. I glance down at my phone, at the pretty teal.

The sunken living room is enormous, with four sectionals and two fireplaces. In the center is a huge pile of boxes. Next to them are multiple clothes racks, where hundreds of dresses, shirts and pants hang. Are they what Ares referred to as "clothes and shoes" for me?

I thought he ordered a couple of T-shirts and shorts and shoes, not cleared out a department store. Granted, I came here without anything but the clothes on my back, so I need more than most people. But...this is going overboard.

Shaking my head, I rummage through the boxes and find a pair of super-comfy flats in blue, then pick out a pink baby-tee and denim shorts. Ooh, a cute tote in lavender! And a wallet! I pull out a few pretty pieces of lingerie. I've never owned anything this fancy before. Doris might've spent money to put me in a "nice enough" dress to avoid speculation and gossip, but she always bought the cheapest and ugliest underwear for me, since nobody was going to see it.

I pull out a silky emerald gown and a cute red dress with spaghetti straps, then change my mind about the latter. The back is too low, and it'll show the scar. I select a burgundy dress that stops an inch above my knees with decent back coverage in case Ares and I need to put on something a bit more formal.

As I walk by the kitchen with my new clothes, shoes and so on, I pick up a pair of shears. Then I stride past Ares's bedroom and choose a guest bedroom two doors down. It has a fully stocked en-suite bathroom with fresh towels and toiletries. I hang my new stuff in the empty walk-in closet, then gleefully proceed to cut the wedding gown Doris chose for me into ribbons.

Buh-bye, past! Don't let the door slam you in the face, Doris! You either, Rupert and Vernon! Actually, I hope it hits you and breaks all your noses! I won't be paying for your rhinoplasty! Whee!

The tatters of the dress lie at my feet. I kick them away, then decide to keep kicking, just because I can. *Ah! Doesn't that feel* great!

Finally free of the godawful dress, I shower using the orange-scented soap and shampoo, and put on the clothes *I*'ve selected. Although I'm in a simple shirt and shorts, the pretty underwear makes me feel sexy. And only the Chosen One will be able to see what's underneath.

I smile saucily at my reflection in the huge mirror in the closet, then shove the black card into my wallet. Time to busy myself shopping for rings like Ares wanted. Except...he didn't tell me how to get to a mall or anything.

—Me: How should I get to the jewelry store and get the rings?

—Ares: Take the Maserati in the garage.

—Me: Not a good idea. I don't know how to drive.

There is a pause.

—Ares: You don't?

—Me: My aunt didn't even let me wear shoes in case I'd run. She wasn't going to teach me how to drive.

Another pause.

—Ares: All right. A driver will pick you up in an hour.

—Me: Thank you.

I wait, but there's nothing more. Is he already back at work? And would thanking him be against the respectful indifference code?

I reread his last text, brow furrowed. *Ares, Ares, Ares...* It's like a heartbeat as I tap the corner of the phone. I don't like the name. He deserves something more fitting.

I change his name on my phone to "My Knight" and save it with a smile.

Exactly one hour later, a black limo stops in front of the main entrance. *Wow. Fancy.* I thought Ares would send me a yellow cab, like you see in the movies.

The uniformed driver opens the back door with a smile. He looks to be in his fifties, with warm brown eyes and a lot of smile lines. "Where to, Mrs. Huxley?"

I stare at him blankly for a moment before realizing. It's a bit startling to be called that, when all my life I've been called Ms. Hayworth. "What's the best high-end jewelry store? I need something that'll impress my in-laws," I say.

"Sebastian Jewelry or Peery Diamonds. You can't go wrong with either. Masako Hayashi also does some great custom work."

"Peery Diamonds." I feel like I should stick with a girl from my own country. Lucienne Peery was one of the most high-profile heiresses in Nesovia. She left and married an American billionaire. It made the news back home, and every celeb gossip rag talked about it with breathless titillation and derision. They seemed unhappy nobody was invited to the ceremony, and even less happy that she moved to the States to be with her husband when she should've stayed in Nesovia and contributed to the country's economy.

Why should she, though? The country treated her like shit. They treat all women with money like trash. I won't go back once I take over my trust. I'm not sure where I'll settle down. Ares might object to my staying in L.A. after our divorce, so I should look around.

I add that to my mental list of tasks. Freedom is great, but it also comes with a lot of things to do.

Peery Diamonds turns out to be housed on the first floor of a massive gray and white stone building. Every window is spotless and showcases gorgeous gemstones sparkling on dark, cushy velvet. A diamond and sapphire set catches my eye. The design is too classic for my taste, but the sapphire's precise shade of blue exactly matches Ares's eyes. Plus the sapphire is *enormous*, twice the size of a quail's egg.

Want, I think, but shake my head. Ares needs me to get wedding bands, not other stuff at Peery Diamonds.

I step inside the store, my flats hitting the immaculate marble floor. A Mozart violin sonata floats in the air, elegant and tasteful. The air smells of a subtle fragrance that's both opulent and calming, the kind of scent you'd expect at a high-end retail location.

Just being inside soothes your senses and makes you feel like a VIP. No wonder Parker acted like she was *all that* every time she went to buy jewelry from Peery Diamonds, then pitied me for having never been despite all my wealth. Where she got the chutzpah to brag when it was *my* money that paid for her excesses is beyond me.

Bitch. If I run into her again, I'll tell her exactly how I feel, but with extra smugness, since she'll be completely cut off from my money. The second I get a hold of my fortune, I'm evicting Doris and her family from my home. Then I'll charge them for all the things they've stolen from me. They pretend to be innocent, but I know they've been selling the antiques my parents collected. *Assholes.*

A brown-haired clerk in a crisp black-and-white suit comes over. "May I help you, ma'am?" He flashes a clean-cut smile that is polite without being overly friendly.

I glance at the nametag. "Yes, Jasper. I need wedding bands. Ideally with sapphires like the ones there." I gesture at the set I admired earlier. "But obviously the stones can't be so large."

He smiles. "I understand." He's started to lead me to a massive display behind him when I see a tall blonde coming out of one of the private rooms. Despite her height, she's in high heels that make her tower over the male managers, and a ruby anklet draws eyes to her slim ankle.

Lucienne Peery—Lucienne Lasker now. I haven't seen her in about five years, but she looks great. Confident and *in charge*. But then, she got married and took over her family empire. Her husband, from what I read, doesn't interfere in her business or financial decisions. Freedom does that to you.

"Lucie," I say.

She stops, then turns to me. Her eyes narrow for a moment, then widen with recognition. "Lareina Hayworth?"

I grin. "The one and only."

"Oh my *God*! What are you doing here?"

She puts gentle hands on my shoulders, then slides them down my arms as though to confirm I'm real. Although we didn't spend a ton of time together, the horrible restrictions on young heiresses in Nesovia tended to make us feel a certain type of bond.

"How...?" She still looks stunned. "Last I heard, you were too sick to travel. You had to be in Nesovia to recuperate."

"That's what my aunt told everyone." I shrug. "But as you can see, I'm not sick. Or in Nesovia."

"You should've texted that you were here in L.A. I was worried when you were carried out like that." Lucie was present during the last overdosing incident. Doris acted out of impatience and went too far. Although I'd been vigilant, I didn't realize she'd resort to bribing the kitchen staff at the restaurant. I collapsed after taking three bites of steak. The only person who hurried over to check on me was Lucie, who happened to be dining there as well. And she called for the ambulance, while everyone else just stood around and watched.

After that, I quit eating out unless somebody else took a bite and made sure it was safe. It doesn't matter that the chances of Doris tampering with my food are one in a million. It's now more psychological than rational. And I doubt therapy will fix it. The phobia is now as instinctive as a fear of spiders or snakes.

"It was just some minor food poisoning," I say breezily. No point in getting into the gruesome details. They'd only distress her, as someone who was in a similar situation—although as far as I know, *her* family didn't try to slow-poison her.

"What are you doing here? What brings you to L.A.?" she says as she leads me to a private room and has me sit with her on a soft leather couch.

"Shopping for rings for me and my husband." I show her the cheap ring on my finger. "Can't wear this, can I?"

Lucie lets out a horrified gasp. "No, most definitely not. Where did you even *find* that? It looks like stainless steel."

"Seriously?" I examine the band more closely. "The guy selling it swore it was white gold."

She snorts. "And I'm a unicorn."

I laugh. "Well. It wasn't that expensive."

"Better not have been. They'd have to pay me to wear it."

"You have an image to maintain as a jewelry mogul." My gaze drops to her ring. It's made with a gorgeous sapphire and a diamond, encircled by tiny diamonds. "Like that. Very unique."

She smiles. "I know, right? My husband's design." Her gaze softens, and all of a sudden, she's just a girl in love.

I envy her. What wouldn't I give to find a man who'd love me unconditionally and support me? Sebastian Lasker is a wealthy man with his own career and interest, and has no desire for anything of hers except her heart. The story of their marriage was one of the most sensational news items in Nesovia for a while, especially since both Lucie and her husband are young and beautiful. And there was a Hollywood glitz angle, since her husband is the son of a famous Hollywood movie producer.

"How romantic." I exhale softly.

"You can do something similar."

"As much as I'd love to have something custom-made, I don't have the time to wait. Who knows when I'm meeting his family?"

She lets out a wistful sigh. Guess she can't understand the point of giving up an occasion for pretty jewelry. "You could go ahead and order a set, and then we could give you one to wear until the order is completed."

A great idea, but Ares and I won't be married for more than a few months, so it seems like too much effort. "It's fine. Maybe next time."

"*Next* time?" She stares at me for a moment, then lowers her voice. "Is this a marriage of convenience?"

"More or less. My step-cousin was desperate to marry me, and I basically had no choice."

"Rupert, right? Rupert Fage?"

"Yeah."

Lucie narrows her eyes. "Never liked that guy. Always so..." She thinks for a moment. "It's like he has dollar signs in his eyes."

"Like in a cartoon," I say, snapping my fingers and laughing.

"Exactly! Besides, doesn't he have a girlfriend?"

"Yes. Parker Jacoby. She was willing to let Rupert marry me so he could 'take care of' my finances. Apparently, the plan was to divorce me and marry her once he got all my money."

Lucie laughs derisively. "The things women like her dream about."

"I know, right?"

Jasper brings in a tray of bands, placing it discreetly on the table in front of us. I sweep my gaze over them until I see a set of platinum bands with three beautiful sapphires. I pick one up and scrutinize the stones under the light. They're the exact shade of Ares's eyes.

I smile. "This," I say to Jasper.

He nods politely.

"Good choice," Lucie says. "You always did have great taste."

"Got it from Mom. I miss her so much."

"She was a great woman. I adore her paintings."

I nod, wishing my parents were alive. Then I wouldn't have been abused by Doris or her shitty family.

"By the way, do you have a lawyer?" Lucie asks. "Or do you need a referral?"

"I don't have one yet. But I'm going to need one. I just married Ares Huxley on Saturday."

Lucie gasps. "Really?"

"Yes. Why?" I ask warily.

"I didn't realize he was the marrying type. He has a rep."

"For...?"

"Being peculiar. I hate to be uncharitable, because he's one of my brothers-in-law's cousins, but I also don't want you to get blindsided. There's a chance he'll recognize you're wonderful and fall in love, but there's a greater chance he won't." She takes my hand and pats it. "He apparently can't stay in a relationship for more than a few months. Whenever the woman falls in love, he ends it. Doesn't matter how much she begs and pleads. He's done."

"Ah..." I let out a noncommittal sound as I connect the dots. Ares was specific about the kind of relationship he wanted, and obviously a woman being in love with him is the opposite of respectful indifference. I just didn't realize he was dedicated to that sort of future, to the point that he'd drop girlfriends. Based on what he said, I thought it only applied to marriage.

Note to self: *Never fall in love with this man.* If I do within the six months, he'll divorce me before I have the chance to wrap up everything with the trust. And if I do afterward... Well, I'll be the loser, since he'll break my heart.

"It's transactional," I say placidly. "There's no chance of love or losing my head over him."

She gazes at me for a moment. "I see. Well, good. Anyway, since he's your husband, I can't recommend Jeremiah Huxley. It might be a little weird or even awkward."

"Wait, *she's* your lawyer?"

Lucie nods. "Yes, and I love her. But there are other good lawyers around. Like John Highsmith. He's fantastic, and one of the few who can make sure you don't get screwed, not even by the likes of Huxley & Webber." She pulls out her phone. "Let me make a call for you. And give me your number so we can keep in touch."

15

ARES

"When do we get to meet the bride?"

My grandmother's voice comes from the phone. My eyes slide to the clock on the desk in my spacious office at Huxley & Webber. Eleven thirty-six a.m. An exceptional display of patience on her part. Or perhaps Aunt Jeremiah didn't text her last night.

But knowing how my aunt is with Grandmother, my money's on the former. Given her regular routine, Grandmother probably spent the morning trying to figure out who Lareina is and just when and how I had the time to meet and marry someone.

"When would you like?" I ask.

"Before the month's up, since that *is* the deadline."

"Then tonight?"

"Excellent. Akiko was quite excited about hosting a dinner."

Ah. She was busy plotting a little get-together with my stepmother. Should've known. The Fogeys love throwing those at me and my brothers.

"We'll be there. Seven?" I start to type a text to Lareina so she can plan the rest of her day accordingly.

"Yes." Grandmother hesitates. "Are you in love with your wife?"

My fingers still. "Grandmother."

"I just... I just want to know if she'll be good for you. That she can make you happy." There is a thread of wistfulness and guilt in her normally cool, impassive tone. "You, of all the children, Ares, deserve to be happy. You've suffered so much."

I soften my voice. "Grandmother, I'm content. Lareina is the *nice, respectable wife* you expected of me. I'll be even happier when I make junior partner."

She lets out a soft chuckle. "Fine. But I meant what I said about nice and respectable. I don't want you to marry just anybody for the promotion."

"Seriously? Then you shouldn't have tied my promotion to having a wife."

"If you'd quit looking for the girl—"

"I will *never* stop looking for her." I see my brothers at the door. "Gotta go. See you later."

As soon as I hang up, Bryce and Josh walk in. They're identical twins with dark eyes and even darker hair, the polar opposite of Mom, which I envy. Although they don't always have the time to go out and enjoy the sun, their skin is more or less golden all the time. Since it's a Huxley custom, they're in three-piece suits, shoes impeccably polished. When they have their hair slicked back the same, it's almost impossible to tell them apart. Even I have trouble.

Bryce is in a pinstriped charcoal suit, Josh in all black. The latter has a meeting with a client who needs extra care and reassurance, and he likes to look as somber as possible on such occasions. Aunt Jeremiah advised him to smile a lot at the client, as she's somewhat vapid, but he declined, saying he didn't want to encourage the woman.

They close the door behind them. Josh takes a seat, but Bryce doesn't. Instead, he paces like a big cat in a zoo.

Josh and I wait. It's not a good idea to jump in and start a conversation when Bryce is like this.

"You got married?" he says finally.

I stretch my legs out and cross my ankles. "You heard?"

"Of course we heard. I thought we were going to be your best men." Josh sounds reproachful. "Don't you think it was a little fast, even for the promotion?"

Bryce's eyes fall on my ring. "Jesus. Was the ceremony legit? Did you fake being poor?"

"It was quite proper," I say. "And no. The situation was a little tense. I didn't have a lot of cash on me, but still had to get married quickly." I get puzzled looks from my brothers and hold up a hand to forestall them. "But to answer your real question, yes, my wife knows I have at least two billion to my name."

Josh stares at me, then covers his face with a hand.

Bryce stops pacing. "Who did your prenup?" He sounds genuinely hurt. Prenups are one of the things he does. He drafted one for our cousin when he got married, and undoubtedly expected to do mine.

"Don't have one. The officiant allegedly added 'not take the other person's shit' to the vows."

Bryce looks flabbergasted. "And you went along with it?"

"What the fuck is *wrong* with you?" Josh demands, his eyes sharp. "What happened to your common sense and brain?"

"I was drugged, that's what happened," I say.

Josh's jaw drops. "She *drugged* you?"

"No. Harvey did, using Soledad."

That stops them. Bryce takes a seat. "What the fuck?"

"Don't worry. I've already contacted the police. She's going to pay."

Josh cocks an eyebrow. "How?"

"I'm sure the surveillance cameras at the party caught everything. Barry's a player, but he's also a fanatic about covering his bases." One of his former football teammates got accused of sexual assault. Unfortunately, there wasn't any video, and it became an ugly he said/she said publicity nightmare for the guy. Even after he managed to clear his name, it was too late. Every time somebody Googles his name, at least one article about the assault accusation comes up among the top three search results. "Soledad isn't exactly subtle. Or smart. She thinks her daddy can fix anything for her." She even threatened me with her dad after our breakup. She doesn't understand that I don't work for her father.

"How about Harvey?" Bryce says balefully.

My jaw tightens. "That's harder. He doesn't dirty his hands."

"Why is he messing with you like that?" Josh seethes. He hates our uncle—actually, everyone from our maternal family.

"Aunt Jeremiah tells me Vincent is sick," I say.

"So?" Bryce's indifference to Vincent's condition matches mine.

"What's the point of her telling you anyway? Are we supposed to go see him at the hospital?" Josh bristles. "If I see him in person, I might just end up spitting in his face." He's still resentful that Mom never went to jail for kidnapping me. Actually, so is Bryce.

Guilt still plagues them. They blame themselves for running when I fought Mom and bought them time. If they'd stayed with me... If they had been kidnapped and taken to the cabin, perhaps I wouldn't have suffered so much. They're certain that, if only they'd been there, I might not have made up the "illusion" of a girl who brought me food and water.

They don't realize that having them in the cabin with me would've driven me to greater despair and desperation. I'm the oldest. Back then I was much bigger and stronger, too. It's my responsibility to keep my baby brothers safe.

Pietas et unitas. Loyalty and unity. It doesn't merely mean being devoted to the family and putting on a united front. It's doing one's *duty* to the family. And I'm a Huxley to the core.

I look at my brothers with helpless affection, wishing I could erase the memory and its effect on them. But the only thing I can do is tell them the truth so they can be on their guard. "Vincent wants to see us. All of us. I guess he's decided he really misses his grandchildren now that he's facing his mortality."

"Fuck him. I'm not his grandson," Josh spits.

"When was he ever a grandfather to us anyway? He sided with Mom." Bryce's tone says there could have been no greater betrayal.

"He told Mom and Harvey whoever can bring us to him first can take over the family business."

"No way. Those sexist Nesovian assholes will never accept her."

"But it's enough to shake Harvey's legitimacy. There are bound to be others who want to usurp Harvey and take over," I point out. "He believes Mom's going to do whatever it takes to get what she wants this time—to bring us 'back into the family.'"

"You mean what she did twenty-two years ago wasn't bad enough?" Josh sneers.

I shrug. "He seems pretty certain she'll throw women at us this time."

"Because that's what he would do. Drugging you using Soledad? Seriously?" Bryce snorts. "I want Mom to escalate until whatever we do becomes justifiable self-defense. Although I wouldn't mind fucking up Harvey either." The sharp gleam in his eyes says he'd love nothing more than to strangle both our mother and uncle. "Why couldn't *our* mom be an orgy-loving, megalomaniac Hollywood movie producer?"

I laugh. It's a description that fits our cousin Huxley Lasker's father to a tee.

Bryce turns to me. "What about your wife, though? Is she, you know, *safe*? Not somebody Mom or Harvey got to manipulate you?"

"So far, so good. But it won't matter even if she isn't." The memory of Lareina's softness and sweet smile fleets through my mind, creating a sudden wave of hesitation. I forcibly remind myself of the purpose of our marriage and harden my jaw. "I plan to get rid of her as soon as I get the promotion."

∽

AFTER MY BROTHERS LEAVE, I realize I'm out of sticky notes. *Weird. Thought I had a new pad.*

Cynthia isn't available, since she took off early to visit her mother in the hospital. The poor old woman had a heart attack a couple of days ago, and my assistant is worried sick. The surgery apparently went as well as it could, given the patient's age and condition, but it doesn't sound promising.

I get off my butt and go to the supply room, opening the doors to three cabinets without finding what I want. The shelves are neatly organized, but where are the sticky notes? There only seem to be legal pads, pens, spiral notebooks—

"Hi. Can I help you with something?"

I start and turn around. A lithe blonde smiles at me, her moss-green eyes bright and friendly. Her hair is cropped to her shoulders and cascades a bit messily, half wavy and uncontrollable. A white sleeveless halter-top shows her slender shoulders and arms, and pink slacks fall straight from her waist. A pair of beige shoes with the tips worn white peek from under the hems. Not a lawyer. Probably office staff.

"Did I scare you?" Her smile grows a bit apologetic. "Sorry, didn't mean to. Just thought you might need some help after I saw you open all those cabinets."

"I'm looking for sticky notes." My tone is cool but polite. She seems cordial enough, but something about her rubs me the wrong way. It's possible I'm just paranoid after what Harvey and Aunt Jeremiah told me.

Not that I think Harvey or Mom would use the woman before me to bring me back to the *family*. The firm does background checks before hiring anybody. If there's any tie between her and the Dunkels, HR would've sent her a polite form rejection letter.

"Oh. Right here." She walks past me, her floral and citrus perfume tickling my nose. Not a hint of cigarettes. Interesting. She has a raspy voice that might be due to smoking.

She reaches into a cabinet I opened just moments ago, then stretches, pushing her arm deep inside and fumbling. As she does so, the thin center strip of her top shifts, revealing an old burn scar on her left shoulder blade.

Everything inside me freezes as I stare at the white, puckered patch of flesh. Is she...

Queen?

Her eyes aren't dual-colored, but sometimes colors change as people grow older. My heart starts to race. I flex and unflex my hands as little tremors start in my gut and spread all the way to my extremities.

Finally.

Even though excitement pulls at me, caution wins out. There have been women pretending to be Queen before. But none of them ever had something this concrete. The exact nature of Queen's injury isn't something I've shared with anybody.

Still, it could be a coincidence. With Mom and Harvey back in my life, ready to mess with me and my brothers, I have to be extra careful.

The blonde lets out a satisfied huff, pulls her arm out of the cabinet and turns to face me. "Here." In her outstretched hand is a sticky note pad.

I don't immediately take it. "How did you get that scar on your back?"

She blinks, then turns red. "You saw?" A hint of reproach ripples in her tone.

"Sorry, but yes. I mean, it's there."

Her flush deepens. "I got it as a child in a forest fire."

"What were you doing in a burning forest as a child?"

"My family went camping, and we got caught."

"I see. Well, Southern California *is* kind of famous for fires."

"No, it was up in Oregon."

My heart races faster, but I manage to keep my voice steady. "Anyone else get hurt?"

"No. Thank God."

"So you guys were just at the edge of it?"

"I'm not sure. But I've been told my voice turned raspy from smoke inhalation." She frowns and gives me a strange look, as though she's just noticed how weird I'm behaving toward her. "Did that satisfy your curiosity?" Her tone is far less friendly now. Just polite.

"Just one more thing. Do you remember anything unusual about the fire? Did you meet anybody while camping?"

Her expression grows more cautious. "No. Honestly, I hardly remember anything about what happened. Likely due to trauma. It wasn't the best experience."

Disappointment buries the excitement. *Another dead end.* But then, why should I expect anything different? "Of course."

"So. Are you done with your cross-examination?"

I force a tight smile. "Sorry about that. I lost a friend in a forest fire when I was young, so I was... I apologize."

She clears her throat, the wariness in her expression easing. "It's okay." She places the sticky note pad in my hand. "Here's what you wanted. Anything else?"

I press the pad of my thumb against the sharp corner. The little pricking sensation says I'm not dreaming. "What's your name?"

"Kenna Miller."

"I'm Ares."

"I know." She slowly relaxes into a grin. "You're famous. Anything else you need?"

"No."

"In that case..." She walks out. "Toodle-oo."

I stare at her back, trying to see the scar that's now hidden again by her top. As unsettling sensations swirl in my gut, I realize elation isn't the only thing filling my heart at the possibility that I might've found Queen.

16

LAREINA

It's urgent.

That's all Lucie had to say to get me a same-day appointment to see a lawyer at Highsmith, Dickson and Associates. She was a little peeved that neither Highsmith nor Dickson was available. But I'm sure they aren't the kind of people you can see on little to no notice, especially when you aren't already a client.

Lucie has a meeting, so she leaves, and Ares's driver takes me to the swanky high-rise that houses the offices of Highsmith, Dickson and Associates. Soft gray carpet muffles my footsteps. Six enormous flower pots along one wall sport orchids that don't have a single scratch or flaw. There's a splash of blue in the décor, probably so it doesn't look too monochromatic.

I shake my head. The insistence on white, black and gray must be a lawyer thing.

An impeccably dressed receptionist in a smart navy suit smiles. "Do you have an appointment?"

"Yes. I'm Lareina Hayworth. Lucie Peery—Lasker—referred me here."

She taps on her tablet, then brightens. "Of course. Right this way." She stands and leads me into the inner sanctum of law offices.

Everyone's in a suit, light gray, charcoal or black. A few crazy rebels are in navy.

I stand out like a sore thumb in my pink top and denim. But then... I'm not the one asking to be hired.

The receptionist stops in front of an office and knocks. "Your two thirty is here." A beat, then she opens the door for me. "Here you go."

"Thanks." I walk inside the space with an exceptional view of the city. On the wall to the left hangs a colorful Lichtenstein—a replica, of course. The piece is rather startling amid all the black and white. Bookshelves groan under the weight of countless thick legal tomes. Those, of course, are a respectable black.

The lawyer at the wide cherry desk is in his early thirties, with neatly cropped brown hair and slender fingers. Gold-rimmed glasses sit on his face, and he lifts his eyes from the stack of documents on his desk. His mouth curves into a dazzling smile. "Lareina Hayworth! It's you."

I narrow my eyes. *Do I know this guy?* As I stare intently, he tilts his head.

"'The art is the most fundamental expression of one's soul.'"

I stagger back half a step as recognition hits me. "*Ethan?*"

His smile widens. "Yeah."

"Oh my goodness. Our art professor used to say that at least once a lecture!"

"Right? And now I can't recall his name."

It takes me a moment. "Sanderson."

He snaps his fingers. "Yes!"

"I didn't realize you were a lawyer here. I can't believe we're finally meeting each other in person!"

He stands, and we hug each other.

"How long has it been since that class?" I ask. "Ten years?"

"Yeah, about that long. I'm surprised you remember me. I wasn't entirely sure, because I never got a response to my emails."

"You sent me emails?" I frown.

He shoots me a slightly sheepish expression. "Yeah, to the address in the student directory."

I never got anything from him. The only thing that landed in my inbox during the class was correspondence from the professor.

Doris. Had to be her. Must've set up a block list or something to ensure nobody except instructors could get in touch, to keep me isolated and without support. It's one thing to know other wealthy trust-fund babies through parties. Those relationships tend to be superficial. But in a class setting? That's entirely different, with a possibility of deep conversations leading to genuine friendship.

"I'm sorry. I never got any of them."

Something flickers in his gaze, and his smile returns to being bright and warm again. "Probably some weird tech fail. Happens." He gestures for me to sit down.

I take an empty seat and cross my legs. "I guess." I shrug helplessly. As soon as I get my money, I'm going to make *sure* Doris pays for everything she's done.

"I really wanted that pencil drawing you promised me," he says.

It takes me a moment. "Oh, right!"

The professor gave us an extra-credit assignment where we had to sketch a classmate. I did a pencil portrait of Ethan, and the professor shared it with the class to illustrate what he meant by "deft capturing of key features." I was a bit surprised, then embarrassed, then pleased that he thought so, since other art experts and critics that Doris befriended said my drawings weren't that good. At the end of the class, Ethan asked me if he could have it, and I said yes. Since then…

I frown. Doris took all my artwork to the therapist, and I never got any of it back. "I'm sorry. I don't have it right now."

"Well, no, I'd imagine not," he says with a light laugh. "But you can give it to me later."

Assuming the therapist hasn't thrown it away. "How about if I just redo the sketch? I mean, if you're okay with it."

"Sure, that works." He smiles. "Anyway, what brings you here? Lucie says you need a lawyer?"

"Yes. I just got married—"

"Married?"

I nod. "And I need someone to draft a contract between me and my husband. A sort of prenup after the fact, I guess."

"You don't have one?"

"No. The wedding was, um, rather sudden." Ares said the impromptu addition by Mr. Sinatra wouldn't hold up in court, and I'm certain he's right about that. He's a lawyer, after all.

"Oh, wow." Ethan runs a hand over his face. "I didn't know you had a boyfriend. When we had that class on romantic love and art, you said you'd never experienced it—and didn't plan to."

"Nope. And I still don't. But that didn't mean I didn't want to get married. I've always wanted a *husband*." Someone other than Rupert, of course, so I could be free of Doris. I honestly believe if she could get away with it, she would've tried to marry me off to Vernon, except that bigamy is illegal even in Nesovia.

Ethan's gaze grows sharp as he regards me over steepled fingers. "So. You're not in love with your husband?"

"Love isn't necessary for a marriage of mutual understanding and benefit." Besides, even if I had such a romantic notion, Ares doesn't want it. He wants a cool, businesslike union, without cheating or anything that could cause public embarrassment. "You know how it is in our circle. And as a Nesovian, I need a reliable husband to take control over my money."

"Ugh. Horrible country. They updated their inheritance law not too long ago after Lucienne Peery's marriage made international headlines. I think the government was vaguely embarrassed at being outed on how badly they treat half their citizens."

"Does this mean it's going to be easier?" I ask, hoping.

"Of course not. Have you ever seen a government bureaucracy improve your life?" Ethan clicks and unclicks the end of his pen a couple of times as he considers. "Anyway... Who'd you end up marrying? Do I know him?"

"You might. He's a lawyer, too. Ares Huxley?"

"You married a *Huxley*?" I might as well have said I married a serial killer from the way Ethan's eyes bulge under pinched eyebrows.

I squirm, an odd discomfiture fleeting through me at the strong disapproval in his tone. Does he know something about Ares that I don't?

"We ran into each other in Vegas and, you know, hit it off," I say. "It seemed perfect." Well, *was* perfect when Ares told me he wanted to be my knight. Of course, he had to ruin it by saying he only wants an "indifferent" relationship, then confuse me by being considerate about my food issue, even though I never said anything explicit about it. Only an observant man who cares would do what he did. "Is there something about him I should be aware of?"

"Other than the fact that he's got a rep for being a dick, both in and out of court? No." Ethan's eyes narrow, but the gleam in them is tinged with satisfaction.

His reaction strikes me as odd, but maybe he and Ares have some sort of enmity? Possibly they were pitted against each other in court or something.

But Ethan also said "out of court." Maybe my expression is too transparent, because he adds, "He dates women, then dumps them as soon as they fall in love with him."

My face crumbles a little.

He spreads his hands, but not entirely without sympathy. "Lareina, everybody knows this. He's infamous."

This might explain Ethan's vague disapproval. "Don't worry. I don't plan on falling in love with him." Throwing myself at my husband when he specifically told me to stay respectfully indifferent would be beyond ridiculous and humiliating. "Nobody gets to break my heart without my permission."

"Good." A corner of his mouth quirks upward. "So. Exactly what do you need this contract to do for you?"

"Protect my assets against my husband and his family." Ethan gives me a vaguely horrified expression. I realize he might've misunderstood and hurriedly add, "Not that I think they're going to steal my money or anything, but a girl can never be too safe. Besides, *I* ought to have full control over my premarital assets, not my husband or his family. Right? So can you do that for me?"

A smile tinged with glee splits his face. "It will be my pleasure."

17

ARES

EVEN THOUGH IT makes more sense for me to go directly to my father's house from the office and have the driver bring Lareina, I make a detour to stop by my place. I want to check on her and make sure she's going to be presentable. Part of me would like to believe she'll behave, but my luck with women hasn't exactly been great. Furthermore, given her eccentric behavior, it's an open question as to what she'll find acceptable for the dinner.

Although it's technically a "family" dinner, dressing too casually would be awkward. Dad, Aunt Jeremiah and my brothers will show up in suits because they're coming directly from work. Grandmother will put on whatever dress managed to catch her fancy on her latest shopping spree. Akiko will pick either a dress or a kimono, depending on how she's feeling. If she goes for a kimono, it means ultra-formal and fancy. Dad told me he was pretty certain she'll spring for a new kimono she's been dying to wear.

Besides, even if I wasn't worried about Lareina's choice of clothing, I need to see her to give her the new wedding bands from Sebastian Jewelry I picked out in case the ones she got are unsuitable. My family will never believe we're married if they see our current cheap crap. Vegas, the city of fake Sinatras and fake gold. Even if we eloped and had

The Accidental Marriage

no choice at the time, The Fogeys would expect me to replace them as soon as possible.

I walk inside and spot a little purse on the kitchen counter. Must be what my wife picked out. Cute. It suits her.

I go to the living room to snoop a bit and see if she's spent most of her day sorting through what the personal shopper brought. Five or six half-open boxes litter the floor, and a few dresses lie limply over the backs of sofas. My personal shopper brought colorful items, it seems. He's been trying to get me to expand my color palette. He's crazy if he thinks I'm putting on a salmon-colored dress shirt, even if it was hand-stitched in Italy.

"Lareina, I'm home," I call out, then suddenly stop. That sounded a little too domestic. It's unsettling how naturally the words rolled from my mouth.

Footsteps come from the staircase. I turn, and my breath catches at the sight of her descending the steps. She looks like an angel. Her unbound hair flows down her back like a golden waterfall. The makeup on her face is light, making her look younger than her twenty-nine years. When she reaches the bottom of the stairs, she spreads her arms and twirls like a pirouetting fairy. The hem of her teal dress spreads out. "How do I look?" She gazes at me, her eyes sparkling with anticipation.

"Beautiful."

"Thanks!" She flushes, then hesitates for a second. "You look very nice, too."

What's the indecisiveness about? Since she tends to be blunter than not, I doubt she was trying to lie about how I really look. "Thank you." I reach into my pocket and pull out a velvet box. "Here. I got us rings." I pop open the lid, showing her a pair of matching bands. They're classy with small diamonds dotting the platinum.

Lareina leans forward to study them, both excited and dismayed. "They're so pretty. I didn't realize you were going to get rings. I bought some this afternoon." She looks up at me. "Do you think we can send them back?"

"Which ones do you want to send back?"

"Yours." Her answer is prompt. "Not because there's anything wrong with them," she hastily adds, "but I just like mine a little bit better."

"Let me see," I say. Although I want to tell her it's my job as a husband to provide the rings, I want to see what she bought. She reaches into her clutch and pulls out a box with a discreet Peery Diamonds logo on it. At least whatever's inside is going to be high quality.

She opens the lid and presents a set. "Here. What do you think?"

The rings, glinting against dark velvet, make my pulse skitter. The platinum bands are classic, like the ones I bought, but they feature exquisite, radiant-cut sapphires that seem to sparkle with their own inner fire. The blue is deeply saturated, and the shade reminds me of my mother's eyes and sends a small chill down my spine. Hiding my reaction, I force a smile, not wanting to upset Lareina. "They're beautiful," I murmur. "But why sapphires?" *Can we get different stones?*

"Not just any sapphires, but these. They're the *exact* shade of your eyes. I just had to get them."

I go still.

She smiles up at me. "You have the most beautiful eyes I've ever seen in my life. The shape, color, intensity—everything about them is divine. It must've been fate at work for us to meet and get married in Vegas the way we did—so unlikely and far-fetched but real." Her cheeks flush with shyness, but she doesn't look away.

I gaze deeply into her eyes—what she said about mine is exactly how I feel about hers. Her face shines with sincerity, not a hint of sarcasm or deception.

My lingering doubts about her true intentions quiet down. If she were somebody Mom sent, she'd never comment on my eyes. Mom has to have learned how much I despise them for looking like hers—her father Vincent came to see me at the hospital after the fire and remarked how my eyes look just like Mom's, as though that would soften me toward her. My reply was *That's why I hate them.*

"I know it sounds selfish. I mean, I doubt thinking about your eyes does anything for you, but if you don't mind... I'd love it if we could wear them," Lareina says.

When she asks like that, my heart feels funny and I can't say no. I also wonder what else she sees when she looks at me. Or is she like this because she has no clue about my reputation? "Jerk" is one of the kinder word people use to describe me. "Yes. That'd be fine."

"Great!" All the anxious trepidation gone, her smile grows brighter. She pulls the old ring off my finger and replaces it with the band from Peery. The size is just right. Either she checked before leaving or she has a great eye.

She does the same with herself and lifts her hand to admire the ring. "Wow. It looks even better on my finger." Her gaze softens as she gently caresses the blue stones.

Something hot and unbearably sweet clutches my heart and spreads through my body. It's like lust, but more intense and honeyed. A hand at the small of her back, I pull her to me until she bumps against me. Surprise flickers in her lovely blue and green eyes. A gasp tears from her parted mouth, and I slant mine over it. Her fingers thread into my hair as she welcomes me. The addictive fragrance of lemon and woman suffuses my senses, her warmth enveloping me.

Our tongues dance, and she clutches my head tightly, accepting my passion and taking what she wants from me.

Mine, mine, mine, my heart booms as it races faster. My turgid cock pushes against the confining fabric of my slacks. I trace the gentle slope of her back, then cup her taut ass and squeeze, drawing her in until she can feel my hardness.

Her breathing roughens; her fingers dig into my shoulders. Tremors run through her, and she moves clumsily against me, wanting more but unsure how to get it. And I want to give her the world.

My cock pulses against her warmth. She kisses me deeper, and our mouths fuse as though we'll never stop kissing.

I don't ever want to quit her. I maneuver us so she's pressed against the wall. She wraps an arm around my pelvis, and I instinctively stroke the taut, bare flesh of her thigh, loving the way she shakes for me.

She throws her head back, her lips wet and swollen. "Ares." Her voice is thready.

"Baby, my angel." I drop kisses on her smooth neck, where the pulse beats wildly.

A moan. "Don't stop."

I nip her neck. A shudder rips through her; her back arches. I cup her breast and watch her eyes glaze with need.

My phone pings. I ignore it and return to her breast and kissing her senseless. It pings again. A tension that has nothing to do with sex seeps through her.

"Dinner," she rasps breathlessly.

"Later," I say, not wanting this to end.

"But your family—"

Fuck. If we don't show up, The Fogeys will never let me hear the end of it. Especially since I boasted that I could find a wife within a month—everyone will join forces to deny me my promotion.

Pulling away from Lareina is actually painful. Now I understand why dogs look at you with such balefulness when they think they're going to get a treat but end up with nothing.

You're not a dog. You're a man in full control of his faculties.

Except that when I'm with my wife, I don't seem to have that control. Nor do I feel emotionally settled. Everything about her puts me off kilter. From the very moment she jumped onto my hotel balcony, she was disruptive.

If she's experiencing half the emotions I am, it's no wonder she thinks there's some kind of divine meddling involved in our relationship. I don't believe in destiny, but I can understand.

I pull out my phone and glare at the alert for the family dinner. Dad's assistant probably had it put into my calendar. Given my workaholic tendencies, Dad instructs his own assistant to ensure I show up when he needs to avoid disappointing Akiko.

My parents' house isn't too far. They upgraded decades ago for more space and better security. Part of it had to do with me. I needed to be with someone at all times for a few months, so they hired bodyguards. But after a few months, I couldn't be around anybody without feeling suffocated, including bodyguards. They were still around for my safety —I knew Dad and Grandmother wouldn't dare be lax with that anymore.

Although my brothers and I moved out, Dad and Akiko kept the house. The glitz and opulence suit them, and Akiko in particular is very fond of the neighbors on the infrequent occasions that they run into each other.

A black Maybach and a silver Maserati. My brothers are here already. Aunt Jeremiah's bright red Lambo is also in the parking area—blocking their cars. Parking like a dick is one of her things, like smoking cigars. She probably also wanted to subtly rebuke them for not doing more billable work.

I escort Lareina to the formal dining room, leading her through the wide hall with tall radius windows facing the garden on one side and recessed nooks holding a huge collection of Japanese Bizenyaki vases on the other. Earthenware hold ikebana, each with a few flowers in minimalistic arrangements. Given that my parents' staff isn't familiar with such art from Japan, that would all be Akiko's doing. Although the mansion is very Western, she makes the Japanese features fit in as harmoniously as if they were always part of the home.

Everyone is seated at the long table. As expected, Dad and my brothers are in suits. Aunt Jeremiah's in a blood-red pantsuit—probably a sign somebody died a gruesome death in a legal battle with her. My grandmother is in a formfitting black maxi dress that flatters her slim frame. And Akiko... Well, she's in a lustrous bronze silk kimono with intricate embroidery. A twisted black-brown branch cuts diagonally from the left hip to right calf, with crimson blossoms, birds and so on completing the design. The kimono is exceptionally fancy—I can see why Dad said she was obsessed with finding the right occasion for it.

As formal as the kimono is, my petite Japanese stepmom fully matches it. Her hair is pulled into a knot in the back, set in place with pins and fresh flowers that complement the outfit. And her posture somehow is both regally straight and yet at the same time embodies a certain willowy femininity. Akiko and Dad met soon after I returned home from the kidnapping, married a year later in a grand traditional ceremony in Kyoto, then held a special reception in L.A. for the people who couldn't make it to Japan.

Beaming, Akiko comes over. "Ares, you look so good! And is this your wife?"

"Hello." Although Lareina smiles, I can sense a hint of tension. I squeeze her waist in reassurance. She gives me a surprised glance, then smiles more genuinely.

"Oh my goodness. You're so captivating when you look at Ares. It must be true love." Akiko sighs like a girl a third her age.

"Welcome to the family." Grandmother hugs Lareina, placing an air kiss on each cheek. "I'm Catalina Huxley, Ares's grandmother."

"Prescott Huxley," Dad says.

"My father," I say.

Dad shakes hands with Lareina, his expression slightly guarded. He doesn't really believe I married out of anything but a desire to get promoted. He isn't entirely wrong. The promotion is a big part, but sometimes when I look at my wife, junior partnership is the farthest thing from my mind.

Aunt Jeremiah lifts her wine glass. "We already met." Her eyes flick up and down Lareina's outfit. "Nice dress."

"Thank you."

Bryce and Josh study her for a bit, like a team of predators eyeing some prey. I shoot them a warning look.

Finally, Bryce smiles. "I'm Bryce. This is Josh. If anybody asks, I'm the better-looking twin."

Josh scoffs. Lareina laughs. "Both of you are equally handsome."

"People who think that end up disappointed when they learn the truth," Josh says with a small grin.

"You know, I wasn't sure what to make, so I made a little bit of everything," Akiko says as we take our seats. "I hope you enjoy the feast."

"Thank you. I'm sure it'll be lovely."

Lareina's polite answer brings a huge smile to Akiko's face. "Aren't you a darling girl?"

Bryce and Josh press their lips together and glance at the luxurious table setting mournfully. I try not to sigh as well, regretting that I didn't stop by a McDonald's drive-thru and grab a burger before coming over. When Akiko decides to get fancy and "make a little bit of everything," it means we're going to get a single bite—possibly two—of each course. We've hinted subtly, and otherwise, that we'd like more food, although

Dad refuses to bring it up with her, saying he doesn't want to cause any friction with his wife.

For whatever reason, our diplomatic petition hasn't moved Akiko. She's decided she'll just add more courses to her dinners, which wouldn't be a bad solution, except there's been a concomitant reduction in the size of each item. Her portions aren't enough to fully satisfy Grandmother, either. I've seen her crunching on potato chips after one of Akiko's "feasts." But she apparently doesn't want to trouble Akiko either.

At least Akiko serves great saké. We all have cold saké and plum wine in a matching bottle set, and a glass of ice water.

The first course is served on a large, beautiful bone china plate edged with gold in a complex pattern. In the center are six bite-sized sashimi pieces—tai, salmon and ootoro—and on one side are edible garnishes composed of five green sprouts and three sesame-seed-sized pink flowers with a light drizzling of green and yellow sauces. It's artistic and pretty to look at if your belly hates food. What's even worse is that Akiko is an amazing cook.

Lareina stares at the plate, then leans toward me. "Does she know she can put stuff on the white parts?" she whispers, subtly gesturing at all the unoccupied space on the plate.

"Yes. Er, no." I pick up a fork. "I don't really know."

My wife follows my lead, then hesitates. Everyone eats, including my brothers.

"This is amazing, Akiko. I'm so glad I'm on a diet every time I visit. How else would I control my appetite when you serve the finest dishes?" Aunt Jeremiah says.

"Oh my goodness, Jeremiah. But you're so wonderfully slender! I'm not sure why you'd need to lose weight."

"You may have a point. I wouldn't want to stuff myself like a swine and have to replace my wardrobe. What a pity *that* would be."

Akiko smiles and nods. Aunt Jeremiah has no problem being a complete sociopath with the rest of us, but with Akiko, for some reason, she always pulls back at the last moment.

"But you *could*, of course. It's not like you don't make enough," Dad says, clearly feeling protective of his wife.

"It isn't about money, but time. Why do you always pick a fight with me?"

Her eyes gleam evilly. *Here we go again.* I gird my loins for another legal argument nobody cares about except my aunt and dad.

She continues, "You didn't get your ass kicked enough when you recognized the brilliance of my thesis on the—"

"In Japan we have a saying: *hara hachi bun*," Akiko says, almost in desperation. "Only eat until you're eighty percent full. I always believe we should have just enough to nurture our bodies without overfeeding." She nods, agreeing with herself. "Very good for longevity."

"I'm going to live forever," Josh mutters.

Bryce squints, trying to recall something. "Doesn't *hachi* mean *eight* in Japanese? Maybe she misunderstood and is only feeding us, like, *eight* percent—"

I feel Josh nudge him with his knee. Meanwhile, Dad pours plum wine for himself and Akiko.

Naturally, Lareina is merely poking at her sashimi and swirling it in the sauce.

"Don't you like fish?" Akiko asks, as though the thought had never occurred to her.

"Oh no, I love fish." Lareina smiles a social smile. "I just want it to absorb the sauce a bit."

"You don't have to. It's already topped with a bit of fleur de sel for optimal flavoring."

I have a bite of each—the ootoro is the best of the lot, the cold slice melting on my tongue—then swap plates with Lareina before Akiko grills her some more about her preferences. Every eye swings in our direction. Bryce and Josh silently communicate, *Your wife is going to stab you dead for stealing her food.*

Instead of making a fuss like everyone expects, Lareina relaxes as she pops the fish into her mouth. "I see what you mean," she says to Akiko. "It's delicious."

Normally Akiko would beam with pride. But right now, she's too busy being confused to react.

"Did you just take her food?" Grandmother says incredulously.

"You really want to eat *all* of your portion," Bryce advises Lareina, sounding ultra-lawyer-like. "Every course is just as spare—carefully portioned to keep you from overeating to ensure nobody develops gout. Which, by the way, doesn't run in the family."

"Thank you, but it's fine."

"Does she still want you to eat more?" Aunt Jeremiah asks me drolly.

Akiko looks at her. "Has he stolen her food before?"

"At that time, *she* took *his* plate," Aunt Jeremiah says.

"It was a mistake," Lareina says with a shrug. "Happens."

"And this time?"

"I just want my husband to have some more. I'm on a diet, too, Aunt Jeremiah."

My aunt chokes on her saké.

"Besides, my husband loves food, so why not accommodate him? It's what makes me a good partner and wife."

Horror and disbelief cross Bryce and Josh's faces. Josh surreptitiously pulls out his phone and starts typing.

My phone pings. I pull it out.

–Josh: What the hell has happened to you? You don't like women this saccharine and accommodating.

–Me: Says who? Don't be jealous. She's wonderful.

–Josh: You like spine and balls.

–Me: Maybe YOU like balls on your bed partners. Not me.

Josh lifts his head, looks at the ceiling and, elaborately casual, scratches his chin with his middle finger.

The second course comes out. It isn't any more bountiful than before. Exactly one broccolette—the size of Lareina's pinky—two tiny sweet-potato medallions and one shot-glass-sized piece of Romanesco sit atop three thin, wel- marbled slices of beef, each one bite-sized. Akiko must've felt generous to give everyone three. Usually, it's two. A dark demi-glace sauce is drizzled around the beef in a double circle, while the veggies get an ivory cream sauce that lies over them like snow. The plating is even more beautiful than before.

I quickly take a small bite out of each item, then swap plates with Lareina. Grandmother clears her throat with a small scowl. "Couldn't you just let her eat first and take her leftovers, rather than giving her whatever's left on your plate?"

"Oh, no. It's fine," Lareina says hurriedly. "It's better this way."

"But, my dear, it's really...odd. And, more precisely, ill-mannered."

Lareina drops her eyes. I give Grandmother a sharp look. "Your opinion isn't necessary. Or particularly welcome."

Lareina jerks her chin up to look at me.

Grandmother's face reddens. "Not her. *You.* You're the problem."

"I am *not*—"

"Please," Lareina says. "It isn't his fault. It's mine."

"You don't have to defend him, child." Grandmother straightens in her seat. "I never realized he had such a...fixation about giving his dates his leftovers. It shames me, but it also explains some things." Her reproachful eyes say *I'm* the reason I can't keep a girlfriend and haven't gotten married all this time.

"That's unfair." Lareina places her hand on my arm. The sapphires on her band seem to wink at me reassuringly. "I have a psychological hang-up that makes it impossible to eat something people haven't touched. Well, tasted, actually."

I already suspected as much, so I don't react. But I'm a bit surprised she's being so upfront about it to my family. I didn't expect her to reveal the secret when she hasn't even talked to me about it.

"Oh my..." Akiko breathes out softly. The rest of my family stare at Lareina with concern.

"Why on earth would you have such a hang-up?" Aunt Jeremiah asks.

"She doesn't have to tell you," I say. My aunt starts with an innocuous question, but then turns it into a grueling cross-examination if she feels her curiosity hasn't been satisfied. "It doesn't matter how or why she has the problem. It's *her* history, *her* trauma. Nobody else is entitled to know, and the only thing she's owed is our understanding."

"It's okay," Lareina whispers. "I don't want them to think you're being rude or weird to me."

The fact that she's revealing what is an undoubtedly painful past to defend me clenches my heart and squeezes all the air out of my lungs. "What they think of me is irrelevant. The family will accept me the way I am."

18

LAREINA

ARES SQUEEZES MY HAND, wordlessly communicating that I don't have to reveal anything I don't want to. Genuine concern infuses his gorgeous blue eyes. "Don't relive the trauma because of me," he whispers.

Warmth flows through me, as sweet as heated syrup. How can he be this nice when all he wants is respect and indifference? Or this is part of his being respectful?

Akiko looks vaguely uncomfortable, as though she can't believe Ares doesn't consider her close enough to know my past, while his brothers give off an "of course he doesn't care" vibe. His father and aunt tilt back their drinks, and Catalina sighs, apparently resigned to the careless impudence of *the family will accept me the way I am*.

I shake my head. Ares has been nothing but protective and nice. Even when he was drugged out of his mind, he fought Rupert for me. Said he'd be my knight.

He might not remember that, but he's continued to protect me and keep me feeling safe. Revealing my strange, unbelievable past is the least he deserves.

A little jittery, I turn to the others. My phobia isn't something I've discussed much once I realized that most people prefer to look the other way...or else express judgment and disapproval. Some even outright gaslit me, saying there was no way my aunt could be that evil and that I must be mistaken. Many of them worked for her—like the therapists I was forced to see—and others knew her. My reputation for being eccentric didn't help.

Almost unconsciously, I thread my fingers through Ares's and inhale. I'll stick to the bare facts and won't get emotional. If he and his family don't believe me... Well, at least I tried.

"I can't eat anything that isn't factory-sealed or already tasted by somebody. My aunt and her family tried to slow-poison me starting at age thirteen, just to keep me sick enough that I couldn't lead a normal social life or continue going to school like I should. I almost died a few times when they fed me a bit too much out of impatience—or sometimes malice because I was particularly difficult or threw a wild party behind their backs." I let out a small, humorless laugh. "Although they regretted it pretty quickly every time I had to be rushed to the ER. If I died, they'd get nothing."

"*What?*" Ares's fingers flex. He stares at me, horror slackening his face.

The room goes still, like somebody hit the pause button. It would be almost comical if my situation weren't so sad. The twins' forks are angled the same way, and Jeremiah's mouth stays parted. Prescott's hand clutches at nothing as it lies palm down next to the plate. Akiko has her fingers pressed against her mouth, and Catalina's head is tilted, her brow furrowed. It is, as the French say, a *tableau*.

The three wolves on the coat of arms behind Catalina, caught in mid-leap, contribute to the effect. *Pietas et unitas* glints, reflecting the chandelier's glow. *Loyalty and unity. Wouldn't it be great to be part of that circle?* I think with a tight longing in my heart. I wouldn't lean on them too much, but in some of those moments when I'm exhausted, just tired to the bone, I'd love to be able to rest my head on a shoulder and take a moment to catch my breath.

The tableau breaks, and I'm suddenly uncomfortable at being in the center of the Huxley family's intense scrutiny. I realize that I expected them to make light of the situation like everyone else, and now I'm at a loss when they don't. "I know it sounds far-fetched—"

"No." Ares's voice is calm, but underneath seethes a carefully restrained rage. "It makes complete sense. And now I know why you climbed over to my hotel balcony in Vegas."

"*What?*" everyone else shouts in unison.

"She used the gargoyle bas-reliefs on the hotel wall to climb from her balcony to mine. We were on the seventeenth floor," he tells his family.

The twins stare at me with something halfway between admiration and horror. Prescott opens and closes his mouth without making a sound. Jeremiah raises her glass in a salute while Akiko looks like she's about to faint.

"Why didn't you report the poisoning to the police?" Catalina's voice is hoarse.

"No phone." I shake my head, still feeling helpless at the memory. "Even when I said something, nobody wanted to help. My aunt controlled my money. And in Nesovia—where I'm from—young, unmarried women don't have many rights and are treated like children."

"Fucking Nesovia," Jeremiah mutters. "Still the same shithole."

"Sweetie, you'll never have to risk your life like that here," Akiko says shakily, then pours herself more plum wine. But she spills half the glass as she touches it to her mouth.

Ares grinds his teeth, his eyes burning with fury. The knuckles on his free hand whiten, although he's careful not to crush my fingers with his other one.

Even now, he's so thoughtful and protective. Does this mean the respectful indifference he asked for isn't what I think it is?

"Unacceptable," he grinds out, the word pulled out of him with great difficulty.

I open my mouth to tell him it's no big deal—and then I realize I'm totally wrong. I just *told* myself it was no big deal because I needed to believe it.

If I admitted to myself how horrible what Doris and her family did to me was, I would've been too furious with the injustice of my situation to stay rational and fool my aunt and her family and everyone working inside the house. If I hadn't been able to deceive them with my crazy acting, they might've done something drastic much earlier.

"You're right," I say finally. "It was unacceptable."

Ares's face contorts, crumpling like he can't decide between crying and screaming.

Oddly enough, the sight of his anguish both warms my heart and pains me. I paste on a smile. "It's fine. *I'm* fine. It's over."

"It was never fine," he says. "It's not fine."

My vision blurs for a moment, then his thumbs brush underneath my eyes. Hot tears cut two lines on my cheeks, and only then do I realize I'm crying.

"It was *never* fine." Underneath Catalina's soft voice is a razor's edge.

It makes me cry harder as I realize that, not only do these people believe me, *they're on my side*.

We just met, and I told them something completely outrageous, but they don't question the veracity or ask for proof. A simple account of my lived experience was enough.

The Huxley family's belief in me is a balm to my wounded soul. I can't remember the last time I thought people would take me at face value. So many have doubted and questioned the validity of my life situation that I just withdrew, unwilling to say too much.

"Why did they do that to you, child?" Catalina asks gently.

"Money. They wanted my inheritance, and they'd do anything to get it." The words flow more easily. "My aunt tried to manipulate me into falling for her stepson Rupert. When that failed, she had him sneak into my bed one night."

"Son of a *bitch*!" Ares explodes. Murderous rage erupts in the dark depths of his eyes.

I put a soothing hand on his forearm. "When that failed, she tried to force me to marry him by drugging me and bringing me to Las Vegas."

"Nesovia never disappoints." Jeremiah practically sneers as she says my home country's name. It warms my heart to know people like Lucie and I aren't the only people who find the customs and laws of the country vastly unfair.

"Your aunt seems to have gone through a lot of trouble to get your inheritance." Prescott's tone is cautiously skeptical.

"She's a greedy woman. Resents that my grandfather didn't leave her a penny—including the family business. She's always believed she could run it better than him or my dad. But when Grandfather gave her a chance, she crumbled." I shrug.

"Jealousy, greed and resentment make for great motivations," Catalina remarks, her gaze on Prescott. "People kill for far less."

"If Nesovia is so bad, why not just defect? If you have a decent amount of money, you can go anywhere," Bryce says.

"Except maybe Japan," Akiko murmurs. "But if you want, I could probably pull some strings and help. My family has some minor connections."

"Is that what we call the zaibatsu? Families with some minor connections?" Jeremiah says, which makes Akiko flush.

I raise an eyebrow. Zaibatsu are powerful conglomerate families in Japan, and I met a couple of people from one once when they came to Nesovia to negotiate a shipping contract with Grandpa. Based on how sweet and unassuming Akiko is, I thought she was an ordinary Japanese woman who happened to fall in love with Prescott.

"Why does she need to defect or go anywhere, including Japan? She's married to Ares now." Josh shrugs. "So just say bye-bye to Nesovia."

"The point isn't the backwardness of the country, although it's an important part of the discussion. But what I want to know is... Is there any hard evidence of deliberate poisoning by your aunt? Or anything else she's done to harm or coerce you?" Catalina says.

"She's an arrogant woman, and she used some of the maids at the house to buy the poison she used on me. But I can't be sure if anybody would testify. They might not want appear like they're betraying their employer. Although my aunt technically uses my money, she's 'the one who pays them.'"

"Anything else?" Catalina asks patiently.

"The doctors she had me see... And maybe the ER doctors who treated me when she fed me too much poison? I'm not sure if anybody would be able to help you build a case. It was a while ago, and the doctors didn't see fit to report the problem to the authorities." They were glad to take the money, but didn't want to do more than the bare minimum they were legally required to do.

"I know what it takes to build a criminal case," Catalina says. "I was a state prosecutor, after all. It bothers me that some people get away with the most horrible deeds because they get lucky, while their victims are left to suffer and cope with the trauma."

"If I could get some revenge, that'd be great. But right now, all I want is to be free of their control."

"You have me," Ares says, lifting our linked hands and kissing my knuckles. "I'll not only free you from their control, but we—the family—will avenge you. You're a Huxley."

19

ARES

My wife's eyes are swollen like a goldfish's from crying, although she doesn't seem to realize. But she couldn't look more beautiful to me. There's a glow to her now, like the dark clouds hanging over her have vanished.

The strength and steel nerves it must've taken to survive her horrific childhood—and after—awe me. I remember how I nearly went mad in the cabin with its tainted food and water and my mother telling me how much she loved me, as though to imprint my malleable young mind with the idea.

It still shocks me that nobody around Lareina tried to help or report the wrongdoings to the authorities. My estimation of mankind drops several more notches.

Once the truth of her past is revealed, she eats and drinks more freely. My family is solicitous. Instead of serving the usual saké, Akiko brings out a sealed jar, opens it and pours a cup for Lareina. Then, holding up a hand, she dips a clean chopstick into the saké and tastes it, then smiles. "All good."

"Thank you." Lareina flushes, then sips the liquor. "Wow! That's amazing."

"It's from my aunt. She got it in a town called Saijo. Very famous in Japan for saké."

The next dishes come out and the meal progresses. The family purposely keeps the conversation light and warm to make Lareina feel welcome and included. The saké puts a lovely rose in her cheeks, and she seems to enjoy the meal, as well as the dessert and cheese that end the dinner. Akiko serves four different cakes and tarts the size of my thumb and three different types of cheese imported from France and Holland. A well-aged port is passed around as well, and I take a sip before giving it to Lareina.

On the way home, she hums softly, her voice slightly off-key but pretty in its airiness. "Thank you," she says when we arrive. "For believing me and being on my side."

"You're my wife. It's the least you deserve," I say gruffly.

I help her out of the car, then keep my arm around her waist. Her warm, soft weight pressed against my side feels amazing. We fit perfectly, and I seethe for the hundredth time that I almost lost her because of her criminally insane aunt. Lareina is so slight, and I wonder if it's because of the poison her aunt added to her food. I wish I could go back in time and protect her.

A gentle smile splits her face as we enter the house and climb the steps to our bedroom. "You're a good man, Ares."

"I'm not. Not really." She might scream and run the opposite way if she could peer into my head and see all the horrible things I'm fantasizing about doing to her aunt, et al. Lareina said I hit Rupert in Vegas. I should've broken his neck. "Have you thought about what you might do to your aunt and her family?"

"Oh, hundreds of times. First, I'm going to take over my trust and completely cut them off. Then I need to audit exactly what they've stolen from my inheritance. They think they're slick, but I know they've been selling my antiques and paintings to set up a slush fund just in case they fail. I'll make them disgorge everything."

"Need help? I can arrange a team for you." I mentally flip through the entire firm and all the attorneys who could assist. Having Huxley & Webber on her side would ensure the total and utter annihilation of her aunt and family.

"Thank you, but I already hired someone."

"Who? Where did you find them?" *She found a lawyer already?* A quick Google search wouldn't have given her an attorney who can handle a complex cocktail of international financial, tax and inheritance laws. She's going to need a team of highly trained, capable people.

"Ethan Beckman."

What? The annoying, smarmy face of John Highsmith's sycophant pops into my mind. Where did she find him? How does she even know him?

"He came recommended. He works at Highsmith, Dickson and Associates," she adds, as though I've never heard of one of the most prominent law firms in the country. "Apparently a big and proper entity. I was going to ask for John Highsmith, but he was too busy to take my appointment. But Ethan was nice enough."

"I know what they are. I thought—" I realize I wanted her to discuss the matter with me before making the decision. Not because I want to meddle in her affairs, but because she knew she married into a cutthroat and capable legal dynasty. Wouldn't she want my advice before making her selection?

If she didn't want to entrust Huxley & Webber with her legal issues, I could've referred her to somebody less annoying than Ethan Beckman. Like Ken Honishi from Ellis & Honishi LLP. He's all proper, strait-laced even for a lawyer, but he harbors the viciousness of a barracuda underneath the spotless black Armani suit he wears like a uniform.

"I didn't want to bother you," Lareina explains with a smile. "You were at work and had things to do. And sorting out my inheritance will keep me busy, just the way it should be."

Something about the way she phrases that feels off, but I can't place my finger on it. Before I can sort out my feelings, she disengages herself from my arm and gives me a little wave.

"Anyway, good night." She starts to turn left at the top of the stairs.

"Our bedroom's this way." Catching her wrist, I tilt my chin to the right.

"You mean yours. I set up mine over there." She gestures behind her. "To ensure you have your space, and we can maintain our boundaries."

What the hell? What is she talking about? "My wife sleeps in my bed."

She considers for a moment. "Isn't that a bit clingy? Makes us too in each other's faces?"

Is that why she didn't say anything before hiring Beckman? Besides, what does being clingy have to do with her sleeping in my bed? "Isn't sex clingy too? And you can't *have* sex if you aren't in each other's faces." It's bluntly put, but I'm not sure where she's coming from.

She frowns. "Well. That's different."

"How?"

"We can have sex in my room or yours, then just walk back to our own rooms."

I scoff. "Ridiculous."

"Why? I gave it a lot of thought, and this way is logical. Plus it respects all our boundaries."

Our boundaries? "If you can still walk afterward, I didn't do a good job."

"That only happens in books." She gives me a flinty stare. "I've read romance novels, Ares. Being a virgin doesn't mean I'm totally ignorant."

"Not true. If you're blithely walking back to your room, it was we-should-never-do-it-again awful," I argue, even though I'm aware of my contrarian behavior. But I don't enjoy being told I'm not welcome to sleep in my wife's bed. So I remind her of the conditions she set out in Vegas regarding our sex life: If the sex is terrible, we won't be doing it again.

"Yeah, right." Skepticism flashes in her eyes.

It's both challenge and dare. I narrow my gaze. "Let me demonstrate." I throw her over my shoulder, the same way I did in Vegas when I carried her out of the hotel under the futile watch of her aunt's goons.

Lareina yelps, then slaps my back. "Hey, put me down!"

"Trying to conserve your energy."

"But my room—"

"If you can walk back to your room after we're done, I'll let you have it your way."

She gasps, then smacks my ass. Twice. She isn't strong enough to make it hurt, but it's still hot as hell. A kitty with her claws out.

"Keep that up, and you'll never leave the bed," I say lazily, then I slap her ass, which is nice and taut bent over my shoulder.

"You animal!"

"Guilty as charged."

20

LAREINA

Ares's dark laughter sends hot shivers down my spine. Oh my God, how did my considerateness turn into this?

After my meeting with Ethan, I've spent a lot of time thinking about what Ares said he wanted out of marriage, and I want to give him everything he wants. After all, he's giving me my freedom and agency over my money and body. And separate bedrooms seem more than reasonable. That way, none of us will appear clingy and ridiculous. And we can pursue whatever we want after work—aside from a few dinners he said he'd like to have with his wife—in peace without anybody hovering.

Ares kicks the door to his bedroom open. The bed is impeccably made—not by me, because, much to my shame, I realize I didn't bother this morning. *Already failing at the respect part,* I think with chagrin.

I squirm on his shoulder, trying to get down. He slaps my butt again, sending an erotic ripple through me. Embarrassment flames my cheeks. What is *up* with me? But at the same time, I can't deny being tossed over his shoulder like this is hot as hell. The sexy dichotomy of my husband in a hand-stitched three-piece Italian suit carrying me to bed like a barbarian is irresistible.

He stalks to the bed, moving like I weigh nothing. My entire body shivers at the demonstration of strength. He stops a few feet in front of the bed, and I bite my lip, ready to be thrown on the mattress, but instead, he gently sets me down on my feet.

His arm wraps around my waist as he pulls me to him. His thick erection pushes against my belly, and I gasp at the contact, looking up at him. His sapphire eyes are darker, like the endless depths of the Pacific, and he tangles his fingers in my hair, holding me as he plunders my mouth.

I kiss him back, loving the contact. When he ravages me with his tongue, I feel wanted and loved. The way he patiently draws my reaction and enjoyment makes me feel cherished and glad I'm with a generous lover.

He tastes so good—saké and man, darkly seductive and sweet. I rub my tongue against his, urging him, needing more. I want him tonight.

He unzips the back of my dress. The straps slide down, trapping my arms and baring my breasts to his hot gaze. My nipples are hard. Without breaking the kiss, he strokes the pad of his thumb over one tip, sending a jolt of electric heat that pools between my legs, leaving my flesh slick and achy.

I rock against him, wishing I could soothe the emptiness inside. He grips my ass, his palm hot through my dress, then closes his mouth over my nipple, pulling it deep inside. I arch my back, clenching his hair and holding on as honey-sweet pleasure seeps into me. My limbs grow weak, and I cling. He shows no mercy, his tongue stroking, his teeth nipping, and his lips soothing. He's determined to drive me insane.

"Ares..." I moan softly as my knees buckle.

"Still think you can walk, my love?"

Dazed, I blink up at his intense eyes. His mouth is wet and flushed, and need burns in his gaze as he waits for my answer.

I shake my head, burning up with the fire he stokes in my veins.

I rise up on my toes and kiss him. He picks me up, pressing the lengths of our torsos together, so with every step he takes we're rubbing against each other. Then he drops me on the bed.

I lie on the mattress, careful to keep my scar hidden from his view. My unbound hair spread on the soft pillows, I pant as I look up at him. The nipple he sucked on earlier puckers, feeling an extra chill.

My husband drops over me, his hands on either side of my hot face. His knees press into the spots next to my pelvis, caging me like he's a panther getting ready to devour his prey. Sexual excitement sparks, and I labor to draw in air into my lungs.

"You look like a pretty princess ready to be ravished."

"*Queen*," I correct him, although my voice is breathless.

Amusement, nostalgia and something else I can't fathom cross his gorgeous face. He gazes at my lips, my neck, my naked breasts before returning to my eyes. A tremor runs through me as I realize this is really about to happen. There's a smidgeon of trepidation along with excitement. Is it going to hurt? Romance novels always say it doesn't hurt, but I've also read the opinions of women on forums who say those books lie.

"Are you going to be fast and rough?" I whisper.

"No. It's your first time."

"You're *really* hard."

His mouth quirks. "It's just because I like you." He dips his head closer. The tips of our noses brush, and his heated breath fans my skin, sending a jolt through me.

He kisses me, lapping at my mouth like a soft knock, asking for permission to enter.

I part my lips, pull him inside. I cradle his cheek in an unspoken request to be gentle despite the need that's clearly driving him, dig my other hand into his surprisingly silky hair, then glide it down to the back of his neck.

He kisses me patiently. A drug-like bliss unfurls. He caresses my neck, his thumb over my erratic pulse, as though gauging my reaction.

My senses spin. Air thins as I kiss him back more openly and chase his tongue with mine, driving into his mouth and taking the pleasure he's offering. I twist on the sheet, wishing he'd do more.

His mouth on mine, he pushes the dress down. I lift myself to help, and the bunched clothes land on the floor, leaving me only in heels and a tiny thong. He slips his finger underneath the string, running it along my wet folds. Ecstasy shivers through me, but it isn't enough.

I break our kiss. "Ares, I want you."

The fire in his eyes suddenly burns brighter. The muscles in his jaw bulge, and his fingers twist the sheet. Is he losing control? I gaze up at him in anticipation, tinged with just a tiny bit of apprehension.

He pushes a finger into my slick depths. I gasp at the slight invasion, then squirm as he slowly moves in and out.

"You're too tight."

"Don't tell me you're too big to fit," I say.

He laughs. "Baby, no dick's too big to fit if the man knows what he's doing. It's a matter of making sure you're ready and can enjoy it too." He pushes another finger inside, then kisses the soft mounds of my breasts. The lazy thrusts feel so good—but so insufficient, much to my frustration. At the same time, the possessive way he latches on to a nipple and sucks arches my back, making me wish I could drive him as wild as he does me.

He lavishes attention on my other breast, then leaves a trail of burning kisses on my belly and below. He spreads my thighs with his shoulders and runs his tongue along my wet and overheated flesh. The strokes are searing; I twist and sob and beg. But he's relentless as he adds a third finger to my pussy and devours me at the same time. He finds the spot inside me from before and strokes it with his fingers while licking my clit like it's a tiny lollipop.

Lust overheats me, until even the soles of my feet seem to burn. "Please, please," I pant, although I'm not sure exactly what I'm begging for. I just know Ares is the only one who can give it to me.

He continues to torment me with his mouth and fingers. I'm out of control. My pelvis moves to the rhythm he sets, and I'm desperate to relieve the unbearable tension tightening in my core. I grip his hair and grind against his face, need overcoming any inhibition or shame.

Ares growls in approval, and the vibration tips the scale. An orgasm rips through me, tearing a scream from my throat. Air shudders out of me as I pant on the bed, eyes closed, savoring the aftereffects of the blissful storm.

"That was beautiful," he murmurs.

"That was *great*," I say, then grin. "But you're in too many clothes."

He cocks an eyebrow.

"I want to see you."

Heat flares in his gaze as he pushes himself off the bed and shrugs out of the jacket. A whisper of silk and it slinks unceremoniously on the floor. He unbuttons the vest, and it joins the jacket. The platinum and onyx cuff links drop with a carelessly elegant flick of his wrist before he turns his attention to the dress shirt.

With every button undone, more of his physique shows—the thick slabs of muscles on his chest, the ridged abs and the lean hips. He lets the shirt slither down, toes off his gleaming shoes and strips out of his slacks, socks and underwear, kicking them away like they're rags.

His cock juts out, the round, plumlike head dripping. It's much longer—and thicker—than I remember from Vegas. For a second, I wonder if my teasing remark about it not fitting might be somewhat prophetic.

But then he's on me, kissing me like I'm the only drop of water in a desert. My nipples brush against his chest, the motion teasing my already hyperaware senses. I rake his back with my nails, my patience running low. The man knows how to drive me wild.

His cock presses against the slick flesh between my legs. It pulses like it has its own heart, and I rub against it, enjoying its erratic twitches and searing throbbing.

"Vixen," he says.

"What you gonna do about it?" I grin. "I can still walk."

He reaches for a condom in the nightstand, rips open the foil with his teeth and rolls the rubber down the length of his shaft. I reach out to trace the veins, but he pulls back. "Not now."

I mock-pout, but he merely laughs and kisses me again, spreading my legs with his knees. A frisson of electric excitement shoots through me. Along with it comes an unshakable belief that he'll make it good for me. He's been generous, taking his time to prepare me, make me relaxed and feel amazing. I can't imagine this part being any different.

He pushes in. His hips move gently as he shallowly thrusts, slowly going deeper. I cry out as my inner muscles stretch to the max, and then a sliver of unfamiliar pain cuts through the haze of pleasure like a shiv.

Hot tears slide from the corners of my eyes to my temples. I try to wipe them away, suddenly embarrassed at crying when sex was something *I* demanded. Didn't I want to decide when, how and with whom I was going to lose my virginity? I've gotten what I wanted.

The Accidental Marriage

Although the pain is sharp and shocking at first, it isn't exactly unbearable.

He stops. "You okay?" he asks, his forehead touching mine.

I swallow, then nod. "I think so. Yes."

"You sure?"

He's fully inside me now, his breathing labored. From the beads of sweat popping on his hairline to the tendons standing out in his neck, it's obvious he's barely holding on to control. But if I say no, he's going to stop, hold me in his arms and soothe me. I know it as clearly as my own name.

I lay a hand on his trembling cheek and run my thumb over his lips. "Kiss me so it won't hurt."

A hint of relief flashes across his face, quickly followed by a tenderness that melts my heart. He cradles my face with reverence, as though he's holding the greatest treasure in his life, and fuses our mouths with a blissful sweetness that makes my heart skip a beat. He starts to move again with painstaking care, and I shove my fingers into his hair and continue to be lost in the kiss. He changes the angle of his pelvis with each thrust, some better than others... Until my vision whitens and I gasp against his lips with shocked pleasure.

He plunges into me a few more times, and my back arches at the unbearable bliss. What he's doing to me shatters my mind. I wrap my legs around his waist, pleading for him to stop and continue at the same time. He lets out a triumphant laugh and drives me harder and faster.

"Oh—my—*God*—"

"Yes, my queen, yes," he murmurs, his eyes glazed. He's just as lost as I am, and I revel in the fact that we're in this together.

An orgasm barrels into me like a locomotive. I scream, tightening my legs around him. Instead of letting go and joining me in the peak, he continues to drive into me, pushing me to another. I sob out his name, writhing, hoping to escape the grip of another orgasm, yet perversely hoping for it, too.

Ares gives no mercy as he propels me higher and higher, orgasm after orgasm spinning me out of control. When I don't have the strength to hold on to him anymore and my fingers lose their grip on his sweat-slickened back, he rams into me, powerful and fast, and I shriek with another electric climax, my vision dimming. He wraps me in his arms, burying his face in my neck and groaning and jerking and grinding against me.

Feeling boneless, I start to fade away...then feel a gentle kiss on my forehead.

Later in the night, I hear Ares whisper in his sleep. "Don't go, Queen."

21

LAREINA

Something wet and hot tickles the back of my neck. I burrow deeper into the blankets. I'm too exhausted to move. More sleep sounds heavenly.

Besides, it's too early in the morning. I'm sure of it.

More kisses. A warm hand on my belly...then slowly traveling up, up, up until it cups my breast. I ignore it and keep my eyes closed.

Gentle kneading.

"I'm tired," I whine.

"I know." Ares kisses me on the sensitive spot behind my ear, brushing his thumb over a nipple to tease. Despite the lingering sleep, the flesh between my legs grows slick. "You don't have to do anything but enjoy it." His whisper hits me like a darkly seductive promise. Except...

I scrunch my face a little. "Ridiculous. Besides, I'm dirty."

"I know you can be." There's a hint of laughter in his voice.

How can he sound so energetic and well rested? It's unfair. "I mean *I'm* not clean. I didn't clean up down there before falling asleep." *That should discourage him.*

"Oh, that. I took care of it. Don't worry." His tone is smug.

"You did?"

"Well, there's no one else around. And who else would do that but your devoted, care-taking husband when it became obvious that you were, you know, too exhausted to walk back to your room afterward?"

"Are you going to hold a grudge?"

"Never." He gives my breast a squeeze, and my breath catches. "Just stating a fact."

"You're annoying."

"Facts aren't annoying. They simply are."

"I didn't say facts. I said *you*."

"Let me make myself less annoying, then." He rubs himself against my backside. *Holy...* He's searing hot. Hard as steel, too.

"It's too early," I say, even though the signs of his desire have me wet.

"Let me do everything." He pushes my hair out of the way and drops an endless trail of kisses on my right shoulder.

My scar! I stiffen and simultaneously twist to stop him before he decides to explore my left side, where the scar is. "No. Not like that."

"I thought you said you were tired," he says lazily, probably assuming I'm just being contrary.

"Not that tired."

A wicked gleam appears in his eyes. "But too tired to do more than just lie there?"

"Well. Yeah." I put a hand on his chest to ensure he doesn't try to have his way with me. "Besides, why do you want to kiss my back anyway?"

"Why *wouldn't* I want to kiss your back?" A soft laugh. "Back... backside... You're pretty all over."

"No." It comes out a little more decisively than I intend.

He frowns.

"I don't like it when people see my back." The deepening scowl on his face compels me to explain, despite my general attitude to offer nothing. "Look. I have a scar I'm very self-conscious about."

The tension in his brows eases. "Can't be *that* bad."

I jut out my chin stubbornly. "I don't care. I don't want anybody to see it. That includes you, too." Most importantly him. It's possible he won't be weird about my scar. But I'm not ready to show it to him yet. At least his scar is sort of cool—like he got it fighting or something. Mine's just weird, like I was bitten by some kind of mythological fire hound.

"You're my wife."

His wounded tone makes me want to soften toward him, but I stiffen my resolve. "Think about it like Medusa's head. Something you shouldn't see for your own good." *Or mine.* "We shouldn't cross each other's boundaries."

The expression on his face falls further.

"I'm sure a man of your experience can come up with many ways for us to have fun without looking at my back." I'm flattering him to wipe the hurt look away.

Ares considers me, his mouth flat and eyes unreadable. I don't like it that he's unhappy, and I hate it that I broke our languid morning mood, but my scar is too important for me to stay mum about.

So what? You could've kept your mouth shut and just shifted around to hide your scar. Now he's going to just get up and leave. Doris's voice, judging me. According to her, I can't do anything right—a true failure of a human being.

Whatever. I'm not giving those years of being gaslit and emotionally abused the power to ruin my marriage with Ares, temporary or not. Later, when he's had a chance to calm down, I should send him a gift to cheer him up. Although... What's a suitable "let's not fight" gift that's respectfully indifferent yet thoughtful at the same time?

Finally, Ares's eyebrow twitches. "Yes, I believe I can come up with something."

"Good. I knew you'd rise to the occasion."

"Sit on my face."

"*What?*" I almost choke on my own spit.

"You don't want me to look at you from behind, and you're tired. So just hang on to the headboard, sit on my face and enjoy yourself."

What he's saying is scandalously hot. I've read about it, but never really thought about doing it. How does it work, exactly? What if I get too excited and accidentally suffocate him? Such an ignoble death.

Worse will be if I have to call 911. My emergency? Oh, it's just that I was riding my husband's face and now he's not breathing. I don't know if he's dead. He feels really warm. No, I don't know how to do CPR, which is why I called you...

Do men still maintain their erections when they're suffocated like that? I shake my head. *I'm from Nesovia, not Necrovia.* Just not happening. No way.

"Don't you want me to soothe the ache from last night?" Ares whispers, like Satan before the tree of good and evil. He runs his index finger over my folds and shows me the glistening fluid. "We wouldn't want you high and dry."

"I don't think that's going to be a problem."

He laughs. "Exactly." He strokes the dripping folds, and I bite my lip to contain the moan welling in my throat. "Come on, baby. Let me live my fantasy. I always wanted to have my wife sit on my face."

"You're lying." I aim for stern, but it comes out breathless.

"Never." He says the single word with such exaggerated solemnity that it feels more like a lie than the truth. "I thought you wanted to be a good wife." He dips his finger shallowly into my pussy, sending a small ripple of tingling sensation through me.

"I *am* a good wife."

"There you go." He looks at me. The good humor twinkling in his bright blue eyes is a relief. *He isn't upset,* and that makes it impossible to say no. "Just imagine how good it's going to feel. Doesn't your pussy ache a little from last night?"

"A little, maybe."

"Right. You're wounded, sort of. And you know animals lick their wounds to feel better."

I chortle, even as his hand is doing a great job of stoking my need. "That's the most ridiculous thing I've ever heard."

"I swear it on the Bible."

I gaze into his eyes. And to be honest, I'm a tad curious, too. But giving in feels like...a surrender of something far more than I'd like to give up, even though I can't put my finger on it. I sniff daintily. "Well... just this once."

"Yes. Just this once, unless you want to do it again."

The Accidental Marriage

"Like I told you before—if it sucks, there's no second time." The moment the words leave my lips, I flush.

"Oh, sucking is definitely going to happen," he says with a dark laugh.

I grip the headboard and position myself, a knee on either side of his stunning face. My cheeks flame at how lewd I must look—my legs spread and my clit and pussy visible to his unblinking, fiery gaze. All the moisture in my mouth dries, and I lick my lips. Then, carefully and slowly so I don't crush him, I lower myself.

"Good girl," he says with satisfaction. "Now, just a little more."

"But—"

"Come on, baby. You want to be a queen, right? My face is your throne."

He runs his hands over my ass, cupping it and leading me lower, encouraging me. His hot breaths fan against my inner thighs, and my muscles quiver.

"Ah yes," he groans—and strokes my wet flesh with his tongue.

I throw my head back as a shocking jolt of pleasure shoots through me. He continues to lick leisurely, like he's enjoying an ice cream cone. My thighs tremble as I resist the urge to lower my hips. *Can't—kill—my husband—*

His tongue flicks a couple of times over my clit. My back arches and my knees almost buckle. *Oh my God.* I didn't know they could do that when they're already supported on the mattress. He traces the curve of my ass with his hand, sending delicious shivers up and down, then pushes a finger into my pussy. But only slightly, to tease.

Devil man.

If it weren't for the scar, I'd turn around and tease him back. Pull his cock into my mouth and return the torment. He thrusts deeper into me, but retreats before I can really enjoy the sweet invasion. I wish I could draw in enough air to tell him to stop teasing, but it's impossible as I hang on to the board and try to not grind myself into his face like I want to—need to.

I vaguely sense him moving his arm down his body. His breathing shifts to something a bit tense. Is he touching himself?

The picture of him gripping his cock and thrusting into his hand while eating me out boils my blood until I'm hot all over. Even my *toes* tingle.

His free hand grips my pelvis, guiding me to ride his face. My inhibition whimpers surrender at his silent encouragement, and I rock against him. He doesn't hold back anymore, either. He devours me, his lips and tongue working over my hypersensitive flesh, his other arm moving harder and faster.

"Oh my God, oh my God," I pant as I crest higher and higher, my body taut with mounting pleasure. When the orgasm hits, I scream, my knuckles white on the headboard. Somewhere far away, hot fluid hits my lower back and hair, and I struggle to breathe.

My brain is barely functioning. But the part of me that wanted to go crazy over his face crows, *See—he's not dead,* while another triumphant voice that sounds suspiciously like Ares says, *You definitely can't walk back to "your room."*

Ares's hands are busy running the sheet over my back, wiping up the cum from his cock. I didn't realize it could shoot so far. He gently helps me lie down and recover.

"What do you say?" His question breaks my post-orgasm haze.

"Thank you?" I whimper, wishing I could rest for a while. Human bodies aren't designed to be tormented this much within a twenty-four-hour period.

"You're welcome. But no. Do you agree that you can't walk back to your room?"

I blink. Did he actually say that? I didn't imagine it? "Yes," I say, since I can't prove him wrong, and he seems very determined to get an honest answer from me. My legs feel like jelly.

Laughing with satisfaction, he places a kiss on my forehead. "I have to go to work now." Then he hops off the bed with a spring in his step.

Damn, he looks good. All that lean muscle rippling. His butt is perfect. The Renaissance masters would weep if they could see it. Still, it's unfair he's so full of energy. Is he an incubus sucking all my life force out through sex? Although... Well. Sex with him *is* amazing, so I can't really complain about his performance. I'm just not sure what to make of the fact that I'm so languid and lazy afterward.

Just as he's about to enter the bathroom, something pops into my head. "What am I supposed to do to keep myself busy?"

He looks at me over his shoulder with a shrug and a masculine smile that makes my belly flop. "Whatever you want. You have my black card. Be a good girl, rest and spend my money."

22

LAREINA

After Ares is gone, I lie in bed a bit longer. I'm not sleepy, but I'm also not in the mood to move, either. Should've known Ares would want to be proven right. *Lawyers.* I shake my head, smiling. Can't argue with him with words or actions.

Something buzzes on the nightstand on my side. I frown a little. What's that about? It continues to vibrate.

My phone!

I haven't had one for so long that I forgot. I grab it and look at the screen. An unknown number. Huh. Who could it be? Other than Ares, Lucie and Ethan, nobody has my phone number.

Oh no... Doris, Vernon and Rupert... I totally forgot about them, but they couldn't possibly stay away from me this long without making an attempt to figure out where I went and how to reach me. Although I'm not sure exactly how they've found my number, the possibility of losing out on sixty billion has to be motivating.

And I was feeling so good after that amazing orgasm.

"Hello?" My tone is terse. What are some clever things I can say to Doris? Ideally something so taunting that she'll pop a vein and die from swelling to the brain. I won't even gloat as she screams in pain, because I'm nice like that.

"Hello?" comes a soft voice. "Is this Lareina?"

"Yes," I say warily, trying to place the caller. She sounds familiar, but the only thing I can be certain is that it isn't Doris.

"It's Akiko. We met last night...?"

"Yes. Of course I remember." I sit up. How could I forget Ares's stepmother, who's shown me nothing but courtesy?

"Great." She sounds relieved. "I was trying to see if you're doing anything today."

"Um." I think about what I should do—other than "being a good girl and spending my husband's money"—then remember the stuff in the living room I need to make decisions on. Ares probably wants it out of the way as soon as possible. "I was going to try on some clothes Ares had delivered."

"By yourself?" She sounds scandalized.

"I guess...?" Ares is at work, and Lucie has a demanding career as a jewelry company CEO. Sadly, I'm the only person in my social circle without much to do.

"What fun is that?"

"It's more for practical reasons. I don't have many things to wear, so he probably thought it'd be easier to have his personal shopper send things over for me to pick."

"That boy." Akiko sighs. "He's such a *man*. Ridiculous to think that that's the proper way for a woman to shop, trying things on in a living room. And by *yourself*." She sighs again with disapproval.

"I'm sure he meant well." Loyalty is the cornerstone of a good temporary marriage.

"Of course, but it's so...sterile." She makes a soft tooth-sucking sound for a moment. "Why don't we do this? Unless there's something amazing in what his personal shopper sent, return it all and we can do some *proper* shopping."

Her offer is tempting. I've never really done any "proper shopping" —and part of me would love to experience it. Still...that living room full of clothes...

"You don't think he'd mind? There's enough here to open a department store."

She scoffs. "I doubt it, especially if you have that many things. He probably has no idea what was sent. We'll go to an actual *store*. I don't have the best sense of fashion, but I'm more than happy to ooh and aah."

I laugh. "I doubt that. I absolutely loved your kimono. And the beautiful plating of each course. You did it yourself, right?"

"Yes!" She perks up. "I knew you'd have a great sensibility for things like that. Most people don't appreciate it."

After a few more pleasantries, we agree to meet in a couple of hours, since I need to shower and make myself presentable. I swing my feet off the side of the bed and stand up—or try to. My thighs are *unbelievably* sore, like I spent hours in the gym yesterday.

Still, I don't have time to sit around. I drop my hands to the mattress to support myself, swing around and, groaning, lever myself up. Once I'm sure I won't collapse, I text Ares for another driver, then hobble to the bathroom for a quick shower. The hot water seems to help, although I think I'm going to be walking gingerly for the next couple of days.

Back in my room, I throw on a T-shirt and jeans, then go to the kitchen to grab a single-portion Greek yogurt and check my phone.

–My Knight: The driver's on the way. If you want, I can have him come over every day.

–Me: Thank you. Would you mind? Just until I learn to drive or something.

–My Knight: No prob.

–Me: Also, do you mind if your personal shopper comes by to pick up the things in the living room?

–My Knight: You already went through everything?

–Me: I picked out some items I want, but Akiko is taking me shopping today.

–My Knight: Okay. Whatever makes you happy.

Akiko was right about his not caring about sending them back. I swallow the last bit of the yogurt, then realize I've totally interrupted his day. Is it...not meddling and annoying? A wife who keeps busy wouldn't be texting him during the day to ask about setting up a driver, would she? On the other hand, he didn't complain, so...

Perhaps this is a trial period or something. But it's really confusing.

By the time I step out, the same limo from yesterday has pulled into the driveway. The driver opens the door. This time I make sure to get his name off the tag on his uniform: Javier.

I give him the address, and he maneuvers through the SoCal traffic until we reach a discreet square building without a sign or anything over a sleek black exterior. It brims with "if you don't know what this is, you don't belong here" energy. Even the double doors are made with smoked glass for privacy.

Feeling a little skeptical and unsure, I step inside. Pale golden marble shines on the floor, and thousands of fairy lights hang like chandeliers from a high ceiling, creating a warm glow that's inviting, luxurious and fantastical. Small indoor waterfalls gurgle over tiered white stones so smooth they look like well-polished jade. The music isn't a standard classical tune, but something soothing and likely original, with strings and a piano that remind me of Schubert's *Trout Quintet*. On the wall behind the crystal-top counter is an excellent imitation of Monet's water lilies.

"Lareina!" comes Akiko's bright voice. She gifts me with a sweet smile that I can't help but answer with a wide grin of my own. If she was traditional last night, today she's modern through and through. Her elegant jade dress with an ivory three-quarter sleeve bolero jacket slims her already slender figure. The nude heels add four inches of height, which she needs, since she's fairly short. But you'd never think she's old enough to be Ares's stepmom from the way her long black hair frames her flawless face just so, cascading down her back in thick waves. It's possible that Prescott married a very young second wife, but there's a temperedness about her that says she's much older than she looks.

Compared to her, I'm barely dressed. Now I wish I'd spent more time selecting my outfit—maybe a dress. And done my hair, too. It's a bit wild, since I didn't have the time or energy to blow-dry my own lengthy mane.

"You look so beautiful. I love those colors on you." If somebody else had said it, it might sound insincere. But Akiko speaks with such conviction and admiration that it feels real.

"So do you. How is it that you look so put together? Were you already ready to go when you called?"

"Oh, not at all. I just had a complete wardrobe to choose from, which you will too after we're done. Or at least enough of one that you can look and feel beautiful no matter the occasion."

We walk inside the corridor. I suddenly realize there's a short Asian woman in an azure jumpsuit following us. Her hair is cropped and spiked, but it looks shockingly good on her angular face.

Akiko notices me looking at the other woman. "That's Juliette. She's going to be helping us."

"Hi," she says, waving.

"Hi." I smile.

We sit on a big sofa, and the staff brings out a tray of fresh fruits, baked sweets and tea. Akiko takes a small fork and cuts a section of a pink macaron and tastes it. She does it systematically with everything on the tray, then uses a spoon to sample my tea. "It's all excellent, my dear."

A small lump clogs my throat. Although I told Ares and his family about my hang-ups, I didn't expect Akiko to pre-emptively test everything with such natural grace, as though it's an everyday thing for her to do. "Thank you."

"My pleasure. Factory-sealed food is fine, but it tends to be processed and stripped of nutrition. You must take care of your body and eat fresh fruit. Vegetables, too. If there's anything else you want to snack on, don't hesitate to let me know."

"I will."

"Catalogue, please." Akiko's voice is soft, but there's a command in it that makes it impossible to ignore. She turns to me. "Is there anything particular you'd like?"

"Um. Not really. As long as it isn't a white, flowing dress, I'm fine. I want some colors."

"Then colors you shall have." She smiles, and we flip through the huge stacks of catalogues. They're organized by style, season, occasion and material, and have everything from super fancy—the kind you might wear to a royal wedding—to shirts and shorts to nightgowns and underwear.

With Akiko's guidance, I pick out five cocktail dresses, four floor-length gowns and several shirts, shorts and skirts.

"You don't want to over-buy because dresses go out of style, and you might want to try something new and interesting later," she says. She also helps me choose shoes and accessories. "A woman *must* have a full ensemble. What you present yourself to the world is what you become."

While Juliette busies herself grabbing the items, Akiko turns to me. "I saw you came here in a limo. Is Ares being extravagant?"

"Partly. But I don't know how to drive."

Akiko cocks an eyebrow. "Ah. That makes sense, given what you said yesterday." She sighs softly. "I'm so sorry about what happened to you. I hope my reaction didn't make you uncomfortable. I didn't know what to make of it. I've heard of people doing terrible things for an inheritance, but slow poisoning..." She shakes her head.

"Yeah. I got used to it, though."

"You shouldn't have had to get used to it."

She pats my hand. The gesture is motherly—the kind my own mom might have given me if she were alive. It sends an achy pang through my heart, and I contain an absurd urge to ask Akiko to hug me.

"If you'd like, I can arrange for some driving lessons. No pressure, but I believe a woman shouldn't rely on money alone. She must be capable, and every bit of knowledge is another piece of the final work."

"I'd love that," I say, trying to contain the excitement at the idea of learning to drive and having a car of my own. "And...could I ask you for another favor?"

"Of course."

"Can you teach me how you did the flower arrangements at the house? They're really unique and beautiful."

She brightens immediately. "I'm so glad you liked them! In Japan, flower arranging is called *ikebana*. I'd love to show you how to do them. It's not that hard, and you have such good taste. I'm sure you'll learn quickly."

"How do you know I have good taste?"

"You loved my plating, remember?" she says, then joins me in laughter. "When you have time, you should visit our home again. We have a small art gallery inside with some interesting contemporary pieces. I think you'll enjoy it. I even bought a Susan Winters on auction last year."

I gasp. "You have one of my mom's paintings?"

Akiko blinks. "Susan Winters was your *mother*?"

I nod.

She covers her mouth with her hand. "Oh my goodness! What a small world. She's one of my favorites!" Then something else crosses her face. "Wait a minute. Are you from *the* Hayworth family? The one that owns Hayworth Logistics?"

"Yes."

She gasps. "Does Ares know?"

I laugh. "Probably not."

Her eyes widen. "So he doesn't know how much you're worth?"

I shrug. "I guess not...? He never asked. But he did bring up needing a prenup to protect his assets."

Akiko laughs until tears form in the corners of her eyes. "Oh my. That's so funny. I won't say anything, but I can't wait to see his reaction when he finds out."

I nod with a smile. This union between me and Ares may not last that long, but I don't have the heart to tell her.

"I imagine the marriage hasn't been what you dreamed of," she says, the mirth slowly fading from her expression.

I stare at her in shock.

"Don't look at me like that. I blame Ares for not giving you the kind of dream ceremony every girl deserves. Eloping in Vegas? With none of us there to witness and bless the union? Did you get married by an Elvis impersonator?"

I giggle. "No. Sinatra."

She leans forward, her eyes sparkling with curiosity. "Was he good?"

"Good at officiating. Not singing." I laugh and shake my head, remembering.

"See? That's exactly what I mean. Ares doesn't have a romantic bone in his body." Despite the rebuke, affection fleets in her gaze. "But in spite of that, he's a good boy. A good man."

"You care for him," I say softly.

"I love him. He isn't a child born of my womb, but he's a child of my heart. So are Bryce and Josh. I married so far from home, and couldn't have children of my own, but I regret nothing." She reaches into her purse and takes out a navy box with discreet silver embossing on the cover. "Here."

"What is it?" *Oh, no. Was I supposed to bring something?* I open the lid. Inside the box is a stunning set of pearl jewelry: earrings, necklace and bracelet. The white orbs are so flawless and lustrous, they seem to glow as though they harbor pieces of the moon inside. "I can't possibly accept them."

"Don't be silly. It's a set from my mother, and I always wanted to hand it down to my daughter-in-law. Generation to generation, woman to woman. I hope you can make Ares as happy as he makes you." Her smile is more brilliant and precious than the pearls she gifts me.

Guilt builds in my heart. Although Ares and I are technically wed, our marriage isn't real in the way Akiko clearly imagines. Not only that, I plan to divorce him within six months so he can have the ideal wife he told me about. The kind of woman who keeps busy, doesn't bother him too much and can share occasional dinners and bear him children who are smart enough to get into some fancy law school. Although I told him I was open to giving him kids in Vegas, it was out of fear he might dump me. I've never had regular periods—maybe because of the slow poisoning and all that. Actually...

Now that I think about it, the last time I had my period was almost a year ago. The realization is vaguely depressing and enraging. My body might recover, but it may never function correctly, denying me an opportunity to have children of my own.

Doris and her family owe me so much.

If Akiko notices my slightly blue change of mood, she doesn't show it. She has me try on the clothes—which I do, careful to avoid showing her my bare back—and asks me to slip on the shoes that seem to match my outfit the best, then coos like she's the one shopping. "You're so beautiful—everything looks amazing on you! Why don't we pair that with this cute belt?" She picks up a thin, faux-croc-skin belt that looks perfect with the lacy chartreuse dress I'm in. "I knew it!" She turns me toward the mirror. "Look how adorable you are!"

I flush with pleasure. It's almost like I'm her real daughter, one she can't dote on enough.

Wistfulness sends a ripple through me. What if my parents hadn't passed away so long ago? I could've had something like this with my mom. And with my parents' protection, I would've been able to lead a normal life—hang out with friends, eat whatever was in front of me without feeling like I might die from it, and date some hot guy then share every detail with my friends in breathless excitement. Things I've only seen on TV and YouTube videos could've been part of my life.

My grandfather often told me how much Mom loved me and wanted to care for me for the rest of her life. Akiko feels like somebody my mother sent to love me.

Unable to suppress the sudden surge of emotion, I hug her. "Thank you. You're the best."

She laughs, her face bright with joy. "So are you."

"I don't know what I would've done without you today. I... You're just wonderful." I smile, blinking hard to avoid spilling tears.

"So are you, sweetie." She tucks my wayward tendrils behind my ear with a smile.

But my warm feelings turn to a sort of horror when she has Juliette charge everything to her account.

"Oh, no. No, no, no. Ares gave me his card!" I say, shocked. If I'd known, I wouldn't have bought so much.

"If he wants to buy you something, he can come himself and swipe his plastic." She winks. "It's a mother-in-law's prerogative to spoil her daughter-in-law."

~

Akiko has all the items delivered to Ares's house, then heads to Huxley & Webber to meet Prescott for a lunch date. It's apparently something she does to keep things interesting.

"You should try it," she says. "Romance is like a flower. You have to nurture it or it will wither and die."

I wave as she gets into her Maserati. She's such a force to be reckoned with, but I know her advice doesn't apply to me. Ares and I are going to be done with each other soon. From little hints here and there, it seems like our marriage has something to do with his promotion. So okay, he chose me, but that doesn't mean he has to stay with me forever.

He made it crystal clear that I don't fit him. He only did his best with sex because it was part of our deal—and because he wanted to make a point last night.

I inhale and exhale deeply to expel the negative emotions. They serve no purpose.

Besides, I should look at the bright side. Soon I'm going to be free of my shitty relatives and be in charge of sixty billion dollars. There is so much I haven't been able to do—and probably won't be able to do because it's too late—like going to classes, making friends in school and going to dances and sporting events.

But there's a lot I still can. Travel the world. Do more art because I enjoy it. Maybe learn to cook from a master chef in Thailand because I always wanted to cook something exotic and interesting. On the way I might even meet the love of my life, a man who doesn't think I'm not a suitable wife and doesn't mind that I have eccentric habits and needs. He might even consider them charming, rather than look at them like flaws he had to tolerate in order to be with me.

I start toward the waiting limo.

"Hello, sweetheart."

I stop and look at the cool brunette climbing out of a flashy red Ferrari. A well-fitted white jumpsuit with black and gold accents drapes beautifully over her model-thin body. She's pale, but good makeup has left her cheeks slightly rosy. She struts over to me with the confidence of a woman who knows she's in charge. Dark sunglasses cover her eyes, but not her high cheekbones or the crimson lips stretched into a smile. My money's on the smile being practiced. She emanates too much coldness to be genuine.

"Hello, Zoe," I say. "What's up?"

She pulls off her sunglasses. Her blue eyes gaze at me with predatory intensity. "Is that how you greet your godmother?"

I raise an eyebrow and stare back at her. "How should I greet you?"

Her smile widens as she takes a step forward, invading my personal space. In response, I stay rooted to my spot, my spine stiff. Her eyes are just as cold as before. "Why don't we talk over lunch? You haven't eaten yet, have you?"

23

ARES

Bryce gives me a wary stare as he steps into the elevator late in the morning. "Why are you smiling?" His gaze drops to my coffee. "It can't be that."

I instantly pull the corners of my lips down. "I wasn't."

"Yes, you were. It's super unnerving, especially since I know it isn't because you fucked up Ethan Beckman."

My mouth tightens until I feel brackets forming around the corners. The mention stirs the annoyance I've pushed aside since yesterday, when I learned my wife hired that asshole. Just what the hell is wrong with *us*? We Huxleys live and breathe law, revel in gutting our clients' opponents and building liability-free empires for them. Hell, I would've done it for free.

Bryce peers at me. "Don't tell me he fucked you over."

I grind my teeth. "It's complicated."

"Nothing ever good follows when somebody says 'it's complicated.'"

"Lareina hired him."

"*Beckman*? Why?" Bryce says the word with half despair and half outrage, like a teenager who just learned that porn isn't real. "For what? A prenup?"

"To sort out her financial affairs and get the parasites off her trust."

Bryce's jaw drops. He'd be excellent at that. "She doesn't need Beckman for that! What am I, chopped liver?"

"No. Liver is nutritious."

"Not funny."

"Wasn't a joke."

"What does she see in him?"

"He came recommended."

"By whom?" Bryce seethes.

"Obviously somebody with terrible judgment."

The elevator stops on my floor and I step out, almost bumping into Kenna.

"Excuse me," she says with a small, embarrassed smile.

"My fault." I note layers of bandage wrapped tightly around her left wrist. Normally I'd ignore it—after all, engagement is encouragement. So many girls thought any sort of response from me was a sign I wanted them, and it led to some unpleasant endings. But I think of her scars, and the question tumbles out. "Are you all right?"

"What?"

I jerk my chin at her wrist. "The bandage."

"Oh, that? It's nothing. Just some wrist pain, probably carpel tunnel." She drops the arm and brings down the sleeve like a cover. "They have really nice cold-drip coffee," she says suddenly, pointing at the coffee in my hand. "Maybe one of these days you can buy me one." Immediately she turns red. "I meant I'd treat you to one."

The mistake should be charming, especially with the deep blush on her objectively pretty face. But my gut is quiet. "Why?"

"Um." She blinks a few times. "Don't you like free coffee?"

"I prefer to pay for my own." I turn around and head to my office.

Why are you doing this? She could be Queen.

I don't know, and don't want to dwell on it. I always thought if I ran into Queen again, I'd feel that unmistakable connection. But nothing like that wells in my chest, not even a little.

I spot Akiko near Dad's office. Must be one of their occasional lunch dates. She's looking chic and lively as usual, but then, she's always energetic. I've never seen her cry or look despondent. The woman is like human sunshine.

"Ares," she says, "you look good today. You have a court appearance or something?"

"Not that I know of."

"Oh, some free time. How nice." She smiles.

Is she subtly hinting for me to bill more hours? Although she's been in the States for a long time now, she sometimes reverts to her old Japanese habits and beats around the bush rather than getting straight to the point. She might've heard Dad say something about my promotional prospects. "Don't worry," I say. "I'm planning to work at my desk."

She purses her lips. "That... Well, work is very important, of course, but don't you think your wife might need some time with you?"

"Lareina?"

"She was a little down, trying on clothes all alone in your living room, until I intervened." Vague disapproval mars the perfectly smooth skin between her eyebrows. If she's too upset to notice she's wrinkling her skin, she's really distraught, which I hate to see. She might not be my biological mother, but I like her and respect her. She's done the best she could with the traumatized teenager she inherited when she married my dad.

"It's more convenient that way," I say.

"Not convenient. Lonely! What's the purpose of shopping if nobody's there to offer opinions?"

Akiko wants a specific type of response, but...what? I've never cared about what others thought. I buy whatever I feel like. "You don't need opinions, do you?" I ask gingerly.

"Of course I do! Nothing brings me joy like your father calling me beautiful."

Ah, I get it now. "I think my wife is beautiful."

"Have you told her?" Akiko asks.

"Yes, of course." *Have I?* I think I have... Haven't I?

"If you don't tell her, she'll never know. She can't read your mind." Akiko smiles. "Deep inside my heart, I know your father loves me. But sometimes I need to be told, reassured we're still on the same page."

I force a smile which hopefully looks natural. Dad, Grandmother and Aunt Jeremiah have probably guessed why I married Lareina, but not Akiko. She refuses to get involved in the inner workings of the firm, saying the American legal business is beyond her. "I'll keep that in mind."

She leans in conspiratorially. "Take her to that art auction," she says. "The one next month. It's going to feature a lot of amazing art. Buy her something pretty."

"Why not just jewelry?"

Akiko shakes her head. "Jewelry is cliché. Besides, I already gave her the pearls I got from Japan."

"The pearls I got from Japan" is how she always describes the heirlooms from her zaibatsu family. They give them to the women who marry into the family. The fact that Akiko is giving them to Lareina means not only am I fully a member of the family on her side, but so is Lareina.

Guilt needles at me. The marriage isn't even real.

Well. You could make it real by staying together.

But it's—

Suddenly my previous objections fade away. My wife makes me laugh. She even put a smile on my face without my realizing it. She's so vulnerable yet strong, like a tree standing tall and powerful in a hurricane, and I have this strange, instinctive need to protect her, so she doesn't break in the storm.

I frown. *Good God.* How have I become so sentimental? This is... unnatural. "I have to go now. Enjoy your lunch," I say brusquely to hide the need to run and hide from the disquiet welling in my chest.

Forcing myself to keep a measured step, I head to my office. My phone pings.

–Unknown: Just because you're trying to send me to jail doesn't mean it's over between us!

Oh boy. This must be Soledad, who finally figured out that I blocked her number over the weekend. Doesn't she realize that reporting her behavior to the police signifies our relationship has gone past the point of no return?

There are district attorneys who admire my grandmother. They wouldn't go easy on a "criminal," especially somebody who tried to harm Catalina Huxley's grandson.

–Unknown: I'm out. And in L.A. We need to talk. You should drop the baseless charges. You owe me that much.

I start to type, *I owe the DA on your case unshakable testimony to put you in jail for a while,* then stop. Engaging is encouraging. What she wants is my attention.

I delete my text and block the number. My phone buzzes again.

–Unknown: You're a stubborn child, aren't you?

Harvey or Mom. The possibility of the latter makes the nerve behind my eye twitch a little.

–Unknown: Do you think running is going to solve your problems?

Harvey.

–Unknown: Your wife isn't what she seems.

She can be whatever she wants. She kept me out of your clutches.

–Unknown: Do you know she's your mother's goddaughter? Didn't you ever wonder why she was so eager to help you? It's because she needs to, for Zoe.

–Me: I don't believe you.

If Lareina is really Mom's goddaughter, why didn't Mom do something to help? She could've swooped in like an angel, dazzled the poor girl who'd been abused for so long, then used her to fuck Harvey up. After all, Lareina is beautiful enough to attract attention, and Harvey's a sucker for a pretty face.

–Unknown: See for yourself.

A photo of Lareina and my mother at an Italian bistro half an hour or so from here. Lareina is in a T-shirt and jeans, her unbound hair falling behind her in waves. She holds a glass of white wine without drinking it. Meanwhile, Mom... She hasn't changed one bit. Still the same hair, although she dyed it auburn, to remind Vincent that she too is his flesh and blood. She must've realized by now that her father never loved her mother that much. He loves power and control, not his women or the children they bore for him.

I look for any signs of coercion or tension on Lareina's face, but there's nothing. My gut burns, even as I tell myself it's gotta be a fake. These days AI can produce all sorts of seemingly real images.

—Unknown: A photo fresh off the press, so to speak. They're still there, lingering over pasta and wine. Must have a lot to say to each other. Probably plotting a way to destroy you. You have a choice, Ares. You can either join me and destroy your mother or do nothing and become her puppet. Up to you.

24

LAREINA

The aromas of garlic, olive oil and basil hang heavily in the air. The Italian restaurant is bright with light colors that are mostly from sage and lemon cream palettes. Well-trained servers in crisp uniforms with permanently toothy smiles on their faces move among the tables—aspiring Hollywood actors and actresses, working to make ends meet before their big break. Every ten minutes or so someone launches into a short Italian aria—a bit clichéd, but it fits the ambiance.

Zoe twirls some spaghetti around her fork. The tomato-based seafood sauce on the long noodles looks like the ground-up bone marrow Doris once tried to feed me when I got stubborn about going to an art school.

To avoid the sight, I stare at the creamy chicken pesto pasta in a pretty white bowl in front of me, then glance at my chilled Riesling. Zoe ordered them, as though to prove she knows me better than I realize because I would normally love both. Or maybe she did it to show she doesn't give a damn what I want. Either way, she's succeeded in annoying the hell out of me. I can't afford to touch either one, but the smell of the food makes my mouth water. *Inconsiderate bitch.*

Of course, she wouldn't know that I can't eat anything that hasn't been tasted by another person first. So much for being my godmother, but she's never been around to notice much. If she ever sent me any gifts... Well, they could've been intercepted by Doris. So I won't hold that against Zoe.

Still, if she had no interest in being a godmother, she shouldn't have volunteered. From what I've heard, my grandfather brought it up with her father as a half-drunk joke when I was an infant, and she jumped at the opportunity. Probably because she thought she might be able to get at the Hayworth fortune through me—until she learned that my aunt is the one in charge of my trust. I can't imagine any other reason for how little interest Zoe's shown me in the last twenty-nine years.

Why am I surrounded by leeches? It's like somebody put a hex on me.

"What are you thinking?" Zoe says, pulling me out of my melancholy reveries.

"Leeches."

She frowns, then laughs. "Silly girl. Eat."

She thinks I'm joking. But if she knew me at all, she wouldn't. I move my pasta around without taking a bite. Zoe glances at me from time to time between bites, but doesn't comment. She might not have noticed I haven't taken a single bite. But then, that's how self-centered people are.

I really miss Ares. If he were here, I'd feel more secure—

Oh no. Stop it. When did I become so needy? I'm not the kind of person who waits around for a Prince Charming to come rescue her.

He's no prince. He's a knight.

Whatever, I scoff at my inner voice. Let's say he does magically show up—then what? I have to rescue myself, take care of myself and keep myself safe. Even as my head says the food *probably* isn't tainted, every time I look at Zoe's face, I get unpleasant chills and can't make myself put anything in my mouth. She's the kind of person who wouldn't think twice about poisoning me. And unlike Doris, she wouldn't bother calibrating the dosage. She'd dump in as much as she could, for the quickest and surest result.

"What are you doing in L.A.? Aren't you busy in Nesovia?" I pat myself on the back for keeping resentment out of my tone.

"I'm always busy, but how could I stay in Nesovia when Doris invited me to your wedding in Vegas? Guess she wanted some kind of mother figure for you, to make the ceremony look more complete."

Mother figure, my ass. "A real mother figure wouldn't have let me marry Rupert."

"And you didn't." Zoe's smile widens, cold amusement in her eyes. "Sadly enough, Doris forgot to mention that her son's so incompetent he lost the bride to another man."

"Why? Were you planning to help him?" This time, grievance bleeds into my voice.

She laughs. "What does Rupert's idiocy have to do with me? He could stab his own dick with a fork, and I couldn't care less."

I cock an eyebrow, inwardly agreeing with her last statement in spite of my misgivings about her.

"So. How's your marriage going?" she asks.

"It's none of your business, is it? We both know you didn't show up because you care about my personal life." I didn't mean to sound so petty.

"Sure it is." She props an elbow on the table and rests her chin in her hand. Her gaze glitters with icy satisfaction. "After all, you're my only daughter-in-law."

"I am?"

"Didn't Ares tell you?" Hurt flashes in her eyes, but then disappears so fast I can't be sure I didn't imagine it. But I'm not feeling generous enough to give her the benefit of the doubt.

"I met his mother already. Akiko."

"That *cunt*," Zoe spits. Fury burns in her gaze. If Akiko were here right now, Zoe might stab her with the spaghetti fork.

"If by *cunt* you mean *lovely person*, then yes, I agree."

Zoe shoots me a sharp look. "Are you on her side?"

"No. I'm on the side of truth."

She stares at me with absolutely soulless eyes. I don't look away. I can stare her down just as well as anybody.

"Do you honestly think you have what it takes to win Ares over?"

She might have followed her son and me to L.A., but knows nothing about our marriage. Otherwise she wouldn't make such a ridiculous statement. There's no *winning him over* because I'm not what he wants. And to be honest, the more I think about it, the less I'm convinced I can change into what he *does* want. I'm going to be thirty soon. When and how am I going to suddenly find a career that's going to keep me busy? I won't have to work to make ends meet. And nine to five, Monday through Friday, hoping he'll come home early enough that we can have dinner together? If I live my life like that, I'll probably begin to resent Ares.

I pick up the wine glass and swirl it gently. "I didn't marry him to win him over, Zoe. Generally speaking, people have already won their spouse over *before* marriage. You understand, right? You've been married before."

She narrows her gaze. I smile.

"You think you're so clever, don't you?"

I merely quirk an eyebrow.

All faux humor gone from her face, she leans closer and speaks in a low, soft voice, as if she's talking to an easily frightened and slightly dim-witted child. "If you're so clever, do you know how your parents contracted such fatal food poisoning?"

The question slams into me. It takes a moment before my brain can unfreeze from the shock. My heart thuds wildly, acid pooling in my gut. "What are you saying?"

Zoe pulls back with a condescending smile. "What do you think?"

"Did Doris poison my parents?" I demand in a low, shaky voice. I have to know.

"Do *you* think she poisoned your parents?" Zoe picks up her wine glass and drinks.

She studies me over the rim, a cat toying with a mouse. I inhale and exhale deeply a few times. She wants to shake my composure, break me by throwing out established facts without adding anything new. So what if she hints at some foul play? There's no guarantee she'll help me confront my aunt. She could easily claim that she didn't mean anything, and I overthought everything.

"How am I supposed to know?" My voice is shockingly steady. "I was just a kid at the time."

A mixture of respect and annoyance fleets over Zoe's face. "You don't have to be a child to be helpless, Lareina. Do you think you can keep yourself safe from Doris?"

"I've survived her and her ways so far, so yeah, I think I can hang on a little longer."

"You won't last for long without me on your side."

I stare at her. Confident much? A smirk tugs at her mouth. So much smugness. She thinks she's all that. "You mean longer than twenty-nine years?"

The smirk vanishes. "There hasn't been as much urgency as there is now."

"Uh-huh. And you can stop Doris and her family, just like that?" I snap my fingers. "Is that what you're saying?"

"Yes." She sounds almost too proud.

"So why didn't you, if I was suffering before?"

"I've been busy," she says smoothly.

"Riiiiight. Busy." It's an effort not to sneer. These sorts of scenes are starting to bore me. People only reach out when they want something, but look the other way when I need something from them.

"Haven't you wondered why Doris has been so quiet since you left Vegas with my son? Do you think she's just given up on your inheritance after all these years?"

I just look at Zoe. "You might be the one holding Doris back, but I'm not going to give you credit. Not now. It's too little, too late."

"You're such an ungrateful little bitch." A small rebuke. "Don't forget, Lareina—blood is thicker than water. And it's *my* blood that flows in Ares's veins. Your tenuous little link to him can be broken anytime, but the bond between my son and me is forever."

25

ARES

My thoughts are a jumbled mess, I rush to the garage, then drive like a madman on the road. The first thing that comes to mind is that the entire matter has been staged. After all, Harvey knows how much I hate my mother, along with her manipulations and anybody who might take part in facilitating them. But then logic questions how I can be certain Harvey's telling the truth about Mom and Lareina. He used Soledad to drug me. He'd have no problem using my wife to get me to agree to be his legal puppet.

Regardless, I need to see it with my own eyes to be sure. I trust nothing when it comes to my mother and uncle.

I get to the restaurant and walk right past the hostess, whose expression quickly goes from smile to shock, weave through the tables and booths until I find my wife—

And my mother.

The impact of seeing the woman I swore I'd never see again slams into me like a wrecking ball. Somehow I'm transported back to the cabin, tied up and helpless. She croons how much she loves me, then pours the "water" into my mouth, pinching my nose and forcing me to drink. She smiles like she's just won the Best Mom Award. I clench my clammy hands and glare at the woman, wishing I could strangle her so she will never appear before me again.

I hate it that Harvey's picture didn't do her justice. She's still beautiful, confident and immaculately packaged to hide the rot underneath. Her eyes—those fucking blue eyes that look just like mine—bore into Lareina, and I want to gouge them out so she can never gaze at anyone ever again.

"Don't forget, Lareina—blood is thicker than water. And it's *my* blood that flows in Ares's veins. Your tenuous little link to him can be broken anytime, but the bond between my son and I is forever." The words sound reptilian. Everything inside me tenses with loathing and denial. I don't give a shit about the blood bond she loves so much. She's not my mother—she's a monster.

But does Lareina see it that way? My exes often asked why my "mom" was Asian, then wondered about my birth mom and if I missed her. Some of them even suggested I should spend some time with her because I might regret it later in a misguided attempt to get me to open up and share what was on my mind. Harvey said Zoe is Lareina's godmother. My wife might have some affection for her and might believe she and I should forget the unpleasant past and get along.

I start to step forward to pull Lareina out of the restaurant. I have no desire to hear her response. And I realize I'm scared that she might agree with my mother. I don't want to see her differently because despite what I've been telling myself about her being strange or keeping me off balance, I like being with her.

But she's quicker.

"But Ares introduced Akiko to me as my mother-in-law. And neither he nor Prescott said a word about you. I guess blood isn't so thick in your family after all."

It takes a moment to process Lareina's buttery words. The tight knot in my gut eases as warm feelings surround my heart. Relief and peace—the likes of which I've never experienced—seem to envelop me in a bath of contentment. Although I've never said a word to Lareina about Zoe, it's like she knows what's on my mind and trusts that my judgment is correct.

It feels nothing less than life affirming. And I want to hold her and tell her how much I adore and cherish her.

But first...

"What the hell are you doing here with my wife?" I grind out as I step forward.

The cool mask cracks, revealing surprise and longing underneath. I don't buy any of it. My mother is a master manipulator who could give a lesson or two to Aunt Jeremiah.

"Ares. *My son.*" She smiles. "I was just saying hello."

I place a protective hand on my wife's shoulder. "Don't you understand I don't want to see you?"

"But I miss you! And I'm your *mother*! I'm entitled—"

"The only thing you're entitled to is a long jail sentence."

She juts out her chin, full of provocation and stubbornness. "You can't keep me away forever. Your brothers are thirty now."

"What are you going to do? Grab me again and drag me to the woods?"

"That was a long time ago! Nothing's happened since!"

"Only because the family managed to keep you away. I don't trust you. My last memory of you is your pinching my nose so you could force me to drink that drugged water. You left me to die."

"I didn't, I swear! I went back!"

I snort. She could tell me the ocean's salty, and I wouldn't believe her.

"Are you still looking for the girl who supposedly saved you?" she demands. "She never existed! Why can't you accept that? It was *me* who saved you! You just got confused from the drugs and the trauma."

Her sheer shamelessness is simply astonishing. She stares up at me with all the sincerity she can muster. "No," I say. "You're not her. You'll never be her."

"She was blonde. Like I was back then."

Lareina gives her a strange look.

"She almost died to protect you, didn't she? To spare your life?" Mom insists.

"Then why didn't you say something before now?" My tone is

ruthless, a lawyer cross-examining a witness he knows is committing perjury.

"Your father kept me away from you. He never gave me a chance."

"Mmm-hmm."

"Why won't you believe me? Do you think Prescott loves you?" I reach out to my wife and help her stand. Mom grabs my other arm. "Do you think Akiko actually *cares* about you?"

I drop my eyes to her white-knuckled grip. The fingers don't loosen. She glares up at me, her eyes red-rimmed with unshed tears. She should've gone into acting. She would've won enough Oscars to justify her sheer arrogance and chutzpah.

"Akiko has been more of a mother figure than you could ever be. Without her, I wouldn't have grown up to be the civilized human being that I am today. Do you think popping babies out of your womb is all that's required? You have to love and nurture your children, and you haven't done any of that."

"I *love* you. Bryce and Josh too. It's Prescott who won't let me be a mother to you. Why is it that you never condemn him for all that *he's* done wrong? You always hold me to such impossible standards."

"All you had to do to make me not hate you was not be a criminal. Have you ever considered the possibility that if you hadn't kidnapped me and left me to die, I might've liked you more? Maybe gotten in touch with you, spent holidays with you, whether you were married to Dad or not? Plenty of my friends have divorced parents, but none of them had to go through what I did. All you had to do was be a minimally decent person, and you couldn't manage that."

"What I did was all because I love you! To keep our family together! Why can't you understand that?"

I shake her off. "You don't love me or the twins. You only love yourself. We're just accessories that make you look good. You just can't fathom that we might have different desires and feelings and needs." I turn to Lareina. "Let's go, wife."

She nods and follows me out amid stares from the other diners. Mom continues to hurl words at me, hoping to convince me to change my mind. But none of them stick.

I instruct Lareina's driver to take the rest of the day off, and I put her in my car and pull away from the restaurant. Only the sound of the engine fills the Maybach for several blocks. I breathe deeply to hold my churning emotions in. Zoe Dunkel has been the worst kind of monster in my life for so long. Looking at her, I realized I've worked harder than anybody around me, *had* to work harder, just to ensure I'd never be taken advantage of by her again. No more kidnapping, no more manipulation. But facing those still-unhinged eyes somehow froze me in one spot for several moments.

Pathetically weak. Perhaps I'm not as strong as I thought.

"I'm sorry you had to see your mother like that. Are you upset I saw her?" Lareina asks suddenly, interrupting my internal one-way flight to self-loathing. "I didn't want to see her, but she sort of insisted. And she *is* my godmother." The briskness in her tone says the facts are unfortunate, but she has nothing to hide.

Her almost curt, straightforward explanation soothes my frazzled nerves. If she'd offered up a lot of awkward explanations, I would've become suspicious. "Do you know her well?" I ask.

"Hardly at all. And I have no plans to get to know her, regardless of what she claims. She's never done a thing to check up on me or protect me. But now, all of a sudden, she tells me she can 'help.' Except I'm married to you, and I don't need anybody else's help anymore. Funny timing, isn't it? If she'd offered even two weeks ago, I would've kissed her feet in gratitude. But now?" A careless shrug. "She missed her chance."

Relief pours through me. "You don't like her."

"I don't, but it's not about liking or disliking. It's about her making me feel used and manipulated. But"—the weight of her gaze strokes my face—"are you okay? I mean...she's your mother."

"I'm fine. Our relationship became irreparably damaged when she kidnapped me."

"I'm sorry." Lareina reaches out and pats my shoulder. "Did she really plan to...you know, kill you?" Her question is halting.

I have to think about it. "Probably not."

I flex my hand around the steering wheel and concentrate on breathing steadily. Everything about that time burns my gut, makes me want to scream and shout at the heavens for being unfair. No child asks to be born, but care could be taken to ensure the parents aren't complete sociopaths.

"Hard to say with her. In case you didn't notice, she's not quite right up here." I tap my temple. Then I remember how Lareina bravely bared herself in front of me and my family, and I want to return some of that. Besides, she's already heard a big chunk of the past thanks to Mom's blabbering. "When I was ten, Mom and Dad were going through an ugly divorce. A tragic ending, since they originally loved each other. But things quickly went bad because she didn't marry Dad only for love, but for connections, power and prestige." I keep my eyes on the road, not wanting to see my wife's reaction. It's a sordid past, and I've never shared it with any of my exes or friends. "When she realized she couldn't stop Dad from divorcing her, she decided to kidnap us kids—me, Bryce and Josh."

Lareina gasps, but doesn't speak, just squeezes my forearm. The muscles relax a little. Only then do I realize I've been clenching my hands.

"Thankfully, Bryce and Josh got away. But I didn't. She tied me up in a cabin in the woods. Tried to feed me drugged food and water, probably to get me to cooperate and say whatever she needed me to say to my dad. But I refused to eat. Finally, she lost patience and force-fed me some drugs and then left. While she was away, the woods started to burn, which then caused fire in the cabin. She never came back."

"How did you manage to escape?" Lareina's soft voice trembles with horror.

"A girl pulled me out. If it hadn't been for her, I would've died. Mom clearly doesn't want to believe that. But then, she always has been selfish and nasty."

"But *she* believes that she helped you out." Lareina lets out a soft breath. "Guess she's revised the past."

"Yes. Everything she did was for us—*for the family*—because she loves us. Loves me. What a joke." The bag of Wonder Bread was real. I ate it, tasted the slightly stale and chewy slice. Drank Queen's clean water. Had conversations with her that kept me sane during the days I had no idea when—or even *if*—I'd ever be free again.

"She won't give up easily. She wants to be part of your life again."

"My ass." Mom just wants to use me and my brothers to push Harvey out of the mob. She cares about us as much as it benefits her, and not an iota more. "I have her eyes, but that's about all there is to our relationship."

Lareina lets out a laugh. "You don't have her eyes."

"Of course I do. Everyone can see it."

"They're the same color, but they aren't anything alike."

"They're the same shape, too." I feel slightly annoyed that I can't let this go, and stupid that I'm pointing out something that's essentially a flaw. What kind of fool points out what's wrong with him when he wants the girl to like him?

Whoa. Do I want my wife to *like* me? I thought... When I first realized we were married, I only planned to stay tied to her until we both got what we wanted—financial freedom for her and the promotion for me. But I realize I haven't thought about my promotion much. Instead, most of my mental energy has been focused on her—wondering if she was okay, if she felt safe and if she was enjoying herself.

Lareina's eyebrows knit as she shakes her head. "I guess, but so what? It's not the same thing. Her eyes are cold and unfeeling. Like...one of those lizards that only has a basic brain. There's no conscience. When she looks at me, I just want to shudder and leave. But with you, it's the opposite. Your eyes are compassionate and honest. Smart, too. And determined. I thought it was amazing how you held yourself together in Vegas after your uncle drugged you. If your pupils hadn't been so wide, I might've thought you were sober. Not only that, when you look at me, I feel warm and protected. You have the kind of eyes that make me trust you. Eyes are more than just colors and shapes. It's about how they can make someone else feel. You have the most beautiful eyes, and believe me, they are *nothing* like your mother's."

My heart pounds. Emotions shake me, and my hands begin to tremble too much for me to continue driving. I pull over, hit the hazard lights and turn to her. "Say that again."

"Your eyes." She runs her fingers over the corners of my eyes with a tenderness that makes my heart ache. "They're nothing like your mother's. They're uniquely you, reflecting who you are."

A tight lump forms in my throat. Her words feel like a light in the dark—salvation after despair. I cradle her shining face, lean over and kiss her with all the tender emotion she arouses. She kisses me back, her thumbs brushing my eyelids, gentle as butterfly wings.

When she touches me like this, I don't care what Harvey said. I might not even care if she has an ulterior motive. If it's some sort of insane self-deception, so be it. I'd rather be lost in the sweet maelstrom. At least as long as it lasts.

26

LAREINA

Something has changed.

Ares is acting differently. He's still as attentive as ever, but there's a hint of tenderness when he gazes at me, like I'm his most prized treasure.

But why? *I* haven't changed. I'm still the same weird me—an eccentric heiress who can't eat food without having somebody taste it first, and who has a higher number of fingers than friends in her contacts.

I'm not okay with anybody seeing the scar on my back, either, including my husband, so I'm always careful when we're intimate. Sometimes a mix of wistfulness and disappointment crosses his face when I shift to hide it. Obviously, he wishes I wouldn't be so obsessed about hiding it, but that isn't going to happen. I always want to appear pretty before him, especially when we're only going to be together for several months.

Also, I don't have anything keeping me busy all day, like Ares told me he wants in a wife. Ethan and his team are doing most of the digging through my financial and legal affairs.

When I tell Ares about my idleness, he sets up a beautiful art studio in a sunny room with a fantastic view of the garden. It has three easels, all with differently sized canvases, an angled desk for sketching and a couple of comfy seats. A mahogany chest with four drawers holds all sorts of supplies, from paints to palettes to various brushes. It's even better than the tiny studio Doris made in the house in Nesovia.

He must've put a lot of effort and thought into creating this space for me so quickly. I hug him tightly. His arms go around me, providing a comfort and warmth I never want to leave. Why does he make himself so irresistible when we both know our accidental marriage is just temporary?

He gestures at a canvas that's taller than me and wide enough to cover a vast expanse of the wall. "Didn't realize one of them would be that big," he says sheepishly, his cheeks and ears turning pink.

He's absolutely adorable, and the vulnerability in his gaze melts my heart. Who would've thought a big, bad lawyer could be so sweet? "It's perfect. Just imagine what I can paint here."

"True. I'm looking forward to it."

"Don't. It's probably going to suck," I say against his chest, recalling what the experts Doris hired said about my talent while studying my artwork, ostensibly to figure out my "mental state" but most likely to find a way to label me mentally unfit so she could toss me into an asylum.

"So?" He runs his fingers through my hair. "You said it was something you did with your mother, and it sounds like you liked it. Do what makes you happy."

"What if I tell you I want to use your computer to watch things on YouTube?"

He looks puzzled. "What if you do?" Then he shows me how to log into an extra laptop he has in his office. "Yours. You can come anytime and use it."

"Doesn't it bother you that I might snoop around?" Doris would've never allowed me in her office without supervision. She was always paranoid I might discover something I shouldn't have, probably because there was a lot to discover.

He shrugs. "Client materials are kept locked when not in use. Not because I don't trust you, but because that's the protocol at the firm. As for the rest..." He shrugs. "Snoop away."

And he means it. I spend a few hours in the studio doodling in the brand-new sketchbooks—nothing's inspired me to actually pick up a brush and sit in front of a canvas. Then I browse the web to read about science or history. Sometimes art or music.

It's exhilarating to be able to learn *whatever* I want, *whenever* I want. Doris always restricted how long I could be on the internet and what kind of things I could read about.

Doris, you suck so bad. And my husband is amazing.

YouTube has videos on cooking Thai food! How cool! Maybe I don't have to travel to Thailand to learn how to make pad Thai after all. I study one by a Thai-Canadian named Pai and order the ingredients to be delivered. I'll try it tonight.

I text Ares about my plan.

—My Knight: Thai? If you're in the mood, I know a couple great restaurants.

—Me: I've always wanted to learn. I'm probably not that terrible. Otherwise, there's always takeout or delivery. Pepperoni pizza never fails.

—My Knight: I'm sure it'll be fine. But don't you need a wok?

—Me: I do? How do you know?

Does my husband cook Thai? Is there anything he can't do? I was going to use one of the many frying pans in the kitchen.

—My Knight: Because Akiko makes a mean stir-fry. I'll text and ask her to send you one of her woks. They're already seasoned.

—Me: You're the best.

I send the text, then look at it. It sounds so...affectionate. More personal than just a polite "thank you." Something about it bugs me—I should be more careful not to appear clingy or cringey.

That evening I time it just right so my first ever pad Thai is ready to be served as Ares walks in. I think it tastes all right, tangy and sweet with some salt to balance everything out. Still, my palms grow clammy with nerves. I've never had Thai food before—just heard about it. It's possible that what I created tastes okay, but isn't all that authentic. What if he doesn't like it?

My husband sniffs the air as he enters the kitchen with some vivid purple orchids and a brown bag that's moist with whatever's sweating inside. "Wow. Smells like Thailand."

"Really?" I look up at him, all hopeful and relieved.

"Uh-huh." He hands me the bouquet. I murmur my thanks, bury my face in the flowers and inhale the heady fragrance. "We just need some young coconuts." He grins and pulls out two huge green coconuts from the bag and sets them on the table. Then he plucks the biggest blossom from the bouquet and tucks it behind my ear. His fingertips brush the sensitive skin of my earlobe, making my whole body tingle with awareness. "There. A pretty flower for my pretty wife."

I flush. No matter how many times he calls me pretty, I can't seem to get used to it. The word always makes my heart flutter, like I'm a teenager experiencing her first crush. Everyone says your first crush fades soon enough, but the sensation only seems to grow stronger. What if it never fades?

Stop getting ahead of yourself. Time to serve the meal and see what Ares says.

I plate the pad Thai—nowhere near as fancy as Akiko's style, of course. But I think it's okay. I then sprinkle crushed peanuts around the noodles—yum—and arrange a trio of fat shrimp so they look fancy sitting on top.

We look at the green coconuts. "How are we supposed to eat those?" I ask, certain Ares will know.

"You have to cut off the top." He studies the round objects seriously. "I've never had to do it myself, though. The vendors always did it for me in Thailand."

"You've been there?"

"A few times. It's beautiful—soft sand and warm, gentle waves." He gives me a smile. "If you want, we can go."

"I do," I say eagerly, until I remember he turned down the vacation I proposed on our way back from Vegas to celebrate our future divorce. But maybe he's changed his mind. Or maybe he means we can stay friends and travel together at some point. I decide not to dig too deep in case it ruins the mood.

He takes the coconuts to the kitchen, then undoes his shirt cuffs and rolls up the sleeves. Thick, well-muscled forearms flex as he moves to take off a Patek Philippe watch. With casual elegance, he pulls out a huge butcher knife from the dark wooden block. The blade is spotless and so shiny, I don't think anyone's ever used it.

"We don't *have* to have the coconut," I say tentatively from the other side of the counter. I don't want him to get hurt. That knife isn't just big—it looks *very* sharp.

He shoots me a look full of confidence. "Don't worry. I know what I'm doing."

I merely smile, then watch as he brings it down once. Then again. And again. And again. The sound of the blade hitting the fruit is like a small tree getting chopped down. His brow furrowed in concentration, he shapes one side of the coconut, then sits it upright. A hard, horizontal strike, and the knife sticks into the hard shell.

I want to ask if the coconut is impossible to crack, but keep my mouth shut to avoid upsetting his ego. When I met Lucie for coffee last week, she said male pride is more fragile than a hothouse flower.

Her friend Yuna was there as well. "And not just any flower, but the kind that dies the second it doesn't get the sun and water it feels entitled to."

Incipient triumph gleams in Ares's eyes. He wiggles the blade, still stuck in the shell. The tendons in his forearms stand out, the muscles flexing. His tongue swipes quickly over his lips.

Damn. Why is it so hot in here? The stove's off, and the A/C's working.

I pull the hair off the back of my neck and start fanning myself. Ares notices, and a sexy, arrogant smile tugs at his gorgeous mouth.

The top of the coconut finally cracks open. He laughs softly, then hands me the whole thing. Our fingers brush, and my toes curl. What he's doing should be illegal.

"Careful. It's heavy." His voice strokes me like the softest velvet, delivering electric shivers.

Then he starts on the second one, working much faster than before. The strength, control and ease with which he handles himself is an aphrodisiac. Who would've thought watching your husband crack a coconut could be so erotic?

I squirm, shifting my weight left and right. It doesn't do a thing to relieve the aching pressure building between my legs. The only one who can help is Ares. If we didn't have pad Thai growing colder with every passing minute, I might be tempted to kiss him and let things run their natural course. Or if I didn't think he was hungry after a long day at work...

Stop acting like a nympho. We can always have sex after dinner.

I close my eyes briefly, trying to master my out-of-control libido, then carry my large, hard coconut to the table. Ares brings his, along with long straws for both of us. He smiles. "Bon appetit."

I toast by lifting my coconut and taking a sip. He digs into the pad Thai, and I wait for his verdict with a raw-nerve anticipation I've never felt before. What if it's awful? Although I thought pizza would be fine if I screwed up, I realize I want the first meal I've ever made to be delicious —and meet with his approval.

Is that normal...or clingy behavior? I debate for a moment. He's been so good to me that I don't want to do anything to disappoint or cause him distress of any kind. Relationships are so much harder than I expected, even if they're temporary. I wish I had more experience, because then I'd know exactly what to do and not overanalyze.

Actually... I only overanalyze with Ares, like his opinion is critically important to me. Does that mean I care about him? And...more than I should, given what he said he wanted from me?

The possibility weighs down on the light, fluttery sensations in my belly that started when my husband walked in. Something heavy and painful settles in their place instead. Mulling, I move the noodles around on my plate.

"Lareina." Ares's soft voice stops me. "Are you all right?"

27

ARES

My wife's fork stops, the prongs still buried in the perfectly cooked rice noodles. *What's wrong?* She seemed fine when I walked in with the flowers and coconuts. She flushed becomingly and watched me handle the hard-shelled fruit with a brilliant light in her gorgeous eyes. Does she have any idea how sexy she is when she watches me? Does she know how much I revel in her gaze, knowing that, in her eyes, I'm nothing like my mother?

My blood warmed, and I wanted to taste her lips more than the food. Hell, if she hadn't made dinner herself, I might've said fuck it and ravished her on the spot.

But I didn't want to appear as though I didn't appreciate her effort, especially since she's never cooked for us before. It's probably a sign she's beginning to think of this house as her home, too, after my effort to show her she can go anywhere and do whatever she wants. I don't ever want her to feel like she's confined to just the bedroom, living room and dining room.

As the silence stretches, I drop my gaze back to her plate. "Do you want me to taste it for you?" I ask gently. I should've thought about it, but since she prepped the meal, I assumed she wouldn't need anybody to check her food first.

She blinks, then laughs softly. "Ah...no. I trust myself not to put in anything dangerous. I was just thinking..." She hesitates for a moment. "This coconut you brought is delicious."

Her eyes meet mine, and she's smiling. But the light from before is gone, and my lawyer's instinct says she's only being partially truthful. Of course, whatever she's hiding is the more important part of the situation. Incisive, probing questions pour into my head, but...

Lareina isn't a hostile witness on the stand. She's my wife. If she's upset enough to hide something from me, I need to figure out a way to coax it out of her and see if I can fix it.

So I smile back. "They're better in Thailand."

She cocks her head, tapping the end of the straw. "How?"

"Just fresher there, probably. Or maybe it's the whole scene, the beach, the sun, the wind—lots of palm trees. There's something magical about the place. Akiko took me there when I was a kid, and we went a few more times. I also went when I was an adult."

"With Akiko?"

"No. Just by myself to relax. Plus a couple of times with my brothers."

"You didn't take your girlfriends?" Lareina sounds skeptical. *Maybe even jealous?*

When my exes started to get proprietorial, I ended the relationship. But with my wife, a sense of gratification swells. I like seeing proof that she cares—that she's possessive of me and doesn't mind showing a little claw to mark her territory.

"Why would I? I said to 'relax.'" My exes were never relaxing. I frown a little as a realization strikes me. They were like a chore, a checklist of something to be done to prove I was okay to The Fogeys. But if I'd been with Lareina...

I would've definitely taken her with me. Would've loved to see her frolic on the gorgeous beach, as white sunlight broke over her water-beaded skin.

"We should go," I say suddenly.

"When?"

I flip through my calendar and workload for the next few months.

The Accidental Marriage

"It'll take a few weeks to wrap up all the stuff on my plate. Since we're going to need at least ten days, maybe after mid- to late September?"

She nods slowly, which isn't the reaction I anticipated. What's that about?

She opens her mouth, then shakes her head slightly and gestures at the plate.

"How about the pad Thai? Better in Thailand, too?" Her tone is light, but the skin around her mouth tightens.

"It's great, and I can't say it's better in Thailand."

"How come?"

I reach out and shift the flower behind her ear—although it doesn't need to be adjusted—and stroke the soft curve of her earlobe. I just want an excuse to touch her. "Because I've never had any made by you. It's the first time you've cooked here in the house."

"I've never cooked *anywhere* before."

The implication sends sweet warmth through me. I'm glad I didn't give in to my baser urges earlier. "Then all the better. Nobody in Thailand cooked for the first time for me."

The bright sparkles reappear in her eyes, and I can't look away. Her shoulders finally relax as she takes a bite of her noodles, then smiles like the happiest woman in the world.

I freeze, unable to move as the air catches in my throat. I've never seen this expression on her before. She looks so content—her heart at home and at ease. The sweet sensation from earlier thickens, sending shivers along my skin. I wish that we could be like this forever.

The conversation for the rest of the dinner is pleasantly mundane. At one point I ask about what she did during the day, and she excitedly tells me about a Thai cooking channel she found on YouTube. "I always thought I had to go to Thailand to learn, but I can do it here too! The lady has so many recipes. Since you liked the pad Thai, I'll try some others as well."

Joy puts a rosy glow to her cheeks, and her eyes shine. Her enthusiasm is contagious. "Then I'll be your guinea pig. Somebody's gotta eat the food you make."

She nods with a laugh. "But you have to be honest about it. You can't just think, *Oh it's the first time she made this for me, so I have to flatter her.*"

"I swear, I'll be honest." I pause for a moment. "I'll always be honest with you."

She smiles. "I know. I think I knew the moment I ran into you in Vegas."

"Hmm. But back then you didn't know anything about me."

"I knew you were nice enough to help a strange woman who practically broke into your room. You even tried to give me money. And even though we got married accidentally and you have no recollection of it, you've decided to help me out anyway."

"I had my reasons," I mutter, somewhat reluctantly. But I don't want to take credit for something that isn't entirely true.

"That promotion? I'm sure you earned it. Jeremiah and Prescott don't seem like the types to give it to you otherwise." Suddenly Lareina frowns, eyeing our empty plates. "I didn't make anything for dessert."

"Why bother exerting yourself?" I get up, pulling her out of her seat.

"Do we have ice cream in the freezer?" she asks, somewhat hopefully.

"No."

Every cell in my body seems to sigh at the sensation of her bare skin against my palms. She's a lovely little witch—making me feel like I'm home and excited beyond measure at the same time.

I gently coil my fingers in her hair, giving her time to pull back if she wants. Instead she looks up at me, her eyes glittering with expectation. It's all the encouragement I need. I bend down to capture her mouth.

Sweet and salty with a hint of tartness. And woman, pure and beautiful. The taste of her hits me like the most addictive of drugs, and overheated blood flows into my cock, leaving me dazed.

I hold the kiss forever, desperate to get more of her. I can never seem to get enough to satisfy this hunger for my wife. She pushes into my mouth with her tongue, boldly erotic. My heart races faster, and I trace the sweet curve along her waist, slipping my hand underneath her shirt.

The feel of her taut, warm skin sends my senses spinning, as though my coconut held wine, not water. I trace the irresistible lines of her body

I adore so much. The pad of my thumb strokes along the little bumps along her arched spine, slowly gliding up, up, up—

Suddenly, she freezes and pulls back. "I don't think... Um..." She looks away.

Her back. She's worried I might touch the scar, discover the shape and roughness of it underneath the shirt.

The withdrawal hits me like a bucket of ice water. The blood in my body instantly chills. When she told me she didn't want me to see it before, I thought maybe she was just shy about it, unsure about my reaction. But we've been together long enough that she should have some trust in me, shouldn't she? I even promised I would always be honest with her.

I pull back as well. "Yeah, okay. I have some work to do anyway. Need to review a contract." I manage to say it calmly, although my throat is tight.

"Right! You want some more?"

"No, I'm good. Are you...?"

"I'm fine. Yup, fine. Why don't you go on up, and, uh, let me know if..."

She's pushing me away. Part of me wants to stay and argue, but I also understand that she won't tell me anything until she's ready. Even though she opened up about her past in front of me and my family before, she hasn't shared everything. Given her forceful personality, nothing will move her until she decides it's time.

The study feels lonely and oddly cold. Weird. I've never felt that way about the place before. It's one of my favorite rooms, designed for maximum comfort and productivity. Everything I need is within easy reach on the desk, and the bookcases have all the reference materials I might need. There's a comfy reading couch if I want to stretch out rather than sit at my desk.

But my focus, usually a strong point, is gone. The words on the paper don't make any sense. Twenty minutes in, I realize I've been on the same page since I entered the study. Sighing, I rub a hand over my forehead. *What am I doing here? I should go talk to my wife about—*

Lareina peeks through the open door. "Hey."

She's changed out of her shirt and shorts, replacing them with a blue dress that hugs her perfectly. *She probably doesn't want me touching her bare back again.* The realization is bitter. "Hey."

She blinks at my brusque tone, then bites her lip. "Mind if I sit here for a while?"

An overture. She doesn't want our marriage to be uncomfortable and weird. I draw in air. My uneasiness from earlier abates a bit. She's right about this point. Even if we have our differences, they shouldn't carry over.

When I don't answer immediately, she lifts a charcoal stick and a sketchbook in her arms. "I want to do some drawings, but need a little inspiration."

"Am I your inspiration?"

"Who else? Especially when I want to capture a man at work."

Despite myself, I smile a little. My wife has the most extraordinary ability to soothe any negative emotion. "All right."

"Thank you, Sir Muse." She grins and settles on the couch.

Now the room is filled with the sound of her soft breathing and the whisper of charcoal on paper. Suddenly it doesn't feel so cold and empty anymore.

Subtle electric currents run in the air, making my skin prickle. I try to focus on the contract, but I can't stop glancing at her from time to time. The blue is a good color for her, deepening her eyes until they stand out more vividly. She looks at her phone occasionally, but then quickly returns to her drawing. Her eyebrows pinch together, and she taps her chin with the end of the charcoal from time to time as she angles her head in thought.

Although she's changed clothes, she left the purple orchid in her hair. Perhaps she needs more time before she can really trust me. If the scar is a long-held trauma, we might need more than just a few weeks together.

Patience, I tell myself.

"If someone were to gift you a portrait, would you prefer that it be big or small?" she asks suddenly.

I straighten. Is she drawing me? "Small enough to carry in my wallet," I say without hesitation. I'd love to look at the little picture and

The Accidental Marriage

see what she sees when she looks at me. It'd be great if I needed cheering up. Or just because I was thinking of her.

Actually, a wallet wouldn't be a good idea, since the sketch could be damaged. I'll pull out the antique pocket watch Grandfather left me and put the sketch inside the lid. The watch is fancy enough to go with any of my suits. When I'm in something more casual...

Fuck it. I've seen people wear Rolexes with Walmart T-shirts.

"That's so small. It wouldn't take much time at all," Lareina says.

"Another advantage," I say, hiding my anticipation. She purses her lips seriously, doing a great job of acting nonchalant. She's so cute when she thinks she's being smooth. "I mean, you wouldn't want to keep the person waiting, right?"

"No. Okay, you're right. This is long overdue."

Long overdue? We haven't known each other for that long, and it's only been a week since I converted one of the rooms into a studio for her.

Her focus is wholly on the paper in front of her. I put down my pen, link my fingers and watch her over my hands. She's at her most beautiful when she's lost in something she enjoys. She glows with satisfaction and happiness from within, and that makes me want to put an impenetrable wall around her so nothing can shatter her joyful cocoon.

Of course, there's also an urge to kiss her and distract her from the task at hand, like a jealous husband competing for his wife's attention. I'm also starved for her. Every so often during the day at work, she pops into my head. And every single time, she's either laughing and wrapping her arms around me from behind, or pulling me toward her beautiful body clad in nothing but lacy lingerie and fishnet stockings, her lips shockingly plump and red. Today was particularly bad, especially after her texts. In my mind she was sprawled on my desk at Huxley & Webber, her darkly glittering eyes daring me as she spread her legs.

Although this isn't the office, it'd be hot as hell to put her on the desk and seduce her. Spread her wide and devour her. Then plunder her sweet pussy until she begs for mercy. But the desk would be wet with her juices and—

Her sudden exhale jerks me out of my thoughts. "Done!"

I jump from my seat. "Lemme see." But I'm only partly interested in the portrait. A larger part is ready to carry her to the desk and make my fantasy come true.

"What do you think? Pretty good, right?" she says, showing me the sketch.

Who is this? The question pops into my mind, but I silence it before I blurt it out and hurt Lareina's feelings. The man on the paper looks nothing like me. If I didn't know any better, it looks like—

"It wasn't easy to do without the model in front of me, but the picture helped."

What? "Your model was sitting right here the whole time." I gesture at the desk.

"No, I just wanted to capture your intensity."

What the fuck? I glare at the man in the miniature portrait. My brain is finally processing the features, from the smug look in his eyes and the annoying smirk on his lips—both of which I loathe and want to erase. "Ethan *Beckman*?"

She doesn't seem to notice my tone. "Pretty good, huh?"

"You drew that son of a bitch rather than me? For your first portrait?"

"Oh, it's not my first. I did one a few years ago for an online art class."

I glare at the picture. I hate it that he got to know her before I did. I despise that he got to be close enough to her that she drew his portrait all those years ago. The unfamiliar rage burning in my heart is startling in its intensity and animosity. I want to punch Beckman's face until it resembles something very different from the picture my wife just drew.

She continues, "He asked me if he could keep it, and I said yes, but apparently he never got it. When we met again, he asked me about it, but I don't have it anymore. So this is a make-up portrait." Her words are like gasoline. "He was really nice to me back then."

Their shared past is infuriating—especially since she and I don't have anything between us except an apparently ridiculous Vegas wedding that I don't remember. She claimed she hired him because he came recommended, but is that really all there is to it?

The fury burns until my vision turns red. "Did he see your back?"

She gives me a look. "What does that have to do with my sketch?"

Oh, wife, "no" would've been more than sufficient. Somehow her question seems like an admission that Beckman *has* seen it—or perhaps she's considered showing it to him.

I loop my fingers around her long hair as I lean over and take her mouth. Her soft gasp is crushed between our lips.

The sketchbook and phone fall to the thick rug under her feet. I put my arms around her and pick her up. She loops hers around my neck, her mouth still on mine as though she can't get enough.

Her hunger for me settles the jagged edges of my temper, even though I know it's just my body she wants. She loves the pleasure I can give her with my cock, welcoming me into her dripping depth every night.

I prop her on the edge of the desk, just the way I fantasized. Her swollen, rosy lips look like a juicy cherry on her pink face. The golden hair cascades over her shoulders, and the orchid petals—not part of my original fantasy, but I'll work with it—quiver over her ear, making her look like a wild goddess.

With easy snaps, I break the thin straps on the bodice, letting the dress slide down her torso, pooling at her waist. She pants, her gorgeous, bare tits rising and falling with each breath. The pointed nipples make my mouth water, my blood hot.

Her lips curve into a tempting smile of a siren. I claim her mouth, cupping her breasts in my palms. Her skin is cool against mine, but quickly heats as I knead the soft mounds. Teasing flicks of my thumbs across her nipples and her head falls back, exposing the sweet expanse of her throat.

I close my mouth over her pulse point, gratified at the rapid beating of her heart. I want to fuck her until she's too sated to do anything except cling to me. I want to keep her hidden from the world so nobody —especially not that asshole Beckman—can make any demands on her attention and care. The intense urges are so foreign and dark, they should be scary. Instead, they seem irresistible. What does that say about me? Am I as fucked up as my mother?

The thought pierces me like an icy shiv. I lift my head, my hands slightly shaking over her breasts. My eyes meet hers—and there's desire and something tender in her gaze. The sudden chill dissipates, replaced by a warm prickling that sends goosebumps over me.

She cradles my cheek and runs her thumb under my left eye. Only then do I realize that the skin there has been twitching.

"I don't know what you're thinking, but it's okay. We'll be okay."

Her soft words ripple over me like an absolution, cleansing and healing. I turn my head to kiss the center of her palm. "It's like I'm walking a tightrope. You keep me off balance, but somehow never let me fall."

"Just like you never let me fall." She smiles. "You caught me first, remember?"

"I do." I'll never forget the moment when she jumped onto my hotel balcony.

"Maybe that's when—"

"When what?"

She smiles again. "Nothing."

I bite back my frustration. She was about to say something important. I can feel it in my gut.

Her lashes flutter as she lowers her eyes for a moment, then lifts them with a small, sexy smile. "I don't think I told you, but I'm not wearing anything underneath. I had to take it off after dinner because it got so wet."

If she means to distract me from wondering about what she didn't say, she's done a good job. A weirdly bitter arousal flows through me. She's open to talking about her underwear, but not anything else that might bridge the gap between us, not to the point she's willing to show me all of herself, without any barriers.

But I'm also a man starved for my wife. I drop my pants and boxers and drive into her hot pussy. She's as wet as she claimed, and oh so tight. She gasps at the force of my thrusts. Her breasts bob. She moans when her nipples rub against my chest with each push and pull into her searing depths.

I fuck her with all the unspoken, dark desire in my heart, with a bittersweet need that makes it impossible for me to cling to any pride or dignity, desperate for any scrap of openness she's willing to throw me.

And as she climaxes over and over again with my name on her beautiful lips, I grit my teeth with an uncontrollable possessiveness that turns my vision hazy.

"Ares, Ares..." she pants as she convulses around me. "I— You drive me insane. I can't get enough."

The breathlessly spoken confession pushes me over the edge, my control slipping from my shaky grasp. I manage to pull out at the last second and then spurt all over her belly. But even as I shake and fight to drag in air into my heaving lungs, there's an emptiness that continues to gnaw at my heart.

28

LAREINA

I put down my brush and stare at the canvas in front of me. It's sizeable, suitable for a detailed piece.

The outline of a powerful man sprawled on a couch with a glass of whiskey at his fingertips takes the center. His dress shirt is unbuttoned, showing his powerful chest.

This is my first oil painting since I left Nesovia. I know Ares says he wants something small enough to carry around, but I can't capture him in such a tiny medium.

Besides, I can't give him a present that only took a couple of hours to complete. It wouldn't show enough care and sincerity on my part. He's done so much for me.

The canvas is manageable enough that I can finish it in the next four months. That way I won't linger for too long after my financial emancipation and his promotion. Doris told me unwanted guests who linger are like flies. And although I'm no fan of hers, I suspect she's right about that.

As for the biggest canvas, the one Ares was a bit embarrassed about... Well, I'm sure someone will make good use of it. Maybe his next wife.

Shoving aside the rather glum thought, I stand and take several

The Accidental Marriage

steps back to gaze at the canvas again. Many "experts" have said my work was only mediocre at best, but Mom told me art isn't just about technique. It has to have heart. "Computers have fantastic technique, but nobody buys those because they lack the human touch. Sometimes artists create something that looks like nothing but a huge paint splatter, but somehow the humanity shines through, and they're prized."

When I was little, I didn't fully grasp her meaning. Now that I'm older, I'm beginning to understand what she meant—and appreciate how wise she was.

I roll my shoulders just as my belly growls. Time for a lunch break—an individually packed bagel and whipped cream cheese. Ares tasted the latter before leaving for work. I sit and chew, then thumb through my phone to look at any emails or messages. No social media, since I don't trust Doris and her family to stay away. Zoe implied that she's "keeping me safe" from them, but I'm not dumb enough to rely on a sneaky bitch like her. Kidnapping Ares and leaving him to suffer like that—she's worse than I ever imagined possible.

My phone buzzes with a text.

–Unknown: We need to talk. Just because you're in his house doesn't mean it's over! You aren't even his real wife!

I purse my lips. Who is this? Some angry woman who got the wrong number? Should I tell her? Or is it best just to delete and block?

–Unknown: I'm right outside. We have to talk. Now!

–Unknown: Don't ignore me or I'll go to his office to talk about this.

–Unknown: I'm pregnant!

I raise both my eyebrows. *Wow. Talk about drama.* Now I sort of want her to keep going.

–Unknown: I'm not the mistress here! You are!

Oh, cheater drama! Guess I should stop her, since she should verbally beat up the guilty party, not me.

–Me: You have the wrong number. You should check so you can vent your ire on the right person.

Two seconds pass before another text pops up. But instead of an apology, it's a big middle finger emoji.

—Unknown: Don't play dumb. You think you won because you're in Ares's house?

I frown, then go up to the earlier texts. Is she implying Ares is involved in some kind of bigamy? *I'm not the mistress here! You are!* sounds like that's what she's saying, but Ares is a lawyer. Wouldn't he know that's illegal?

Even if he, for some unfathomable reason, doesn't care about the legality because he just wants to get promoted, *I* care. I can't have any doubt cast upon the reality of my marriage.

But in case she's dangerous, I stop by the kitchen to grab a sizable frying pan, then experimentally swing it a few times. *Perfect.*

I head out and see a skinny blonde in a dark burgundy mini-dress standing by the gates. Her arms are crossed, pushing enormous breasts up to create canyon-like cleavage. A pair of huge white wedge shoes elongate her toned and tanned legs. Actually, everything about her is toned and tanned. Her stomach is flat—so if she really is pregnant, it's still early.

She glares at me, her blue eyes flashing with anger and resentment. The shade is very similar to Ares's, but the emotions in them are ugly.

"Oh my God, you aren't even that good looking." Something about her face is weird as she speaks. She looks me up and down. "Are you his maid?"

"No." I flip her the bird with my left hand.

She turns red, and her face muscles twitch awkwardly.

I smile blandly. "Oops, wrong finger." I show her my ring finger. "Here."

"Did you grab it off eBay?" she sneers, then sniffs.

"No. Peery Diamonds. Perhaps you've heard of it. It's an exclusive brand."

"Oh, so you think you're all that just because you got yourself a hot sugar daddy?" She fumes. Or, at least, that's what I *think* she's doing. It's hard to tell with her face being so stiff. Then it finally hits me: she's recently had Botox. Doris was like this too when she sought to preserve what remained of her youth and beauty with my money.

"Are *you* upset you *lost* a sugar daddy?" I ask. I can *almost*

The Accidental Marriage

sympathize with her plight now that her meal ticket is gone. She's able-bodied, so why doesn't she get a job?

"Pfft. I'm rich! I don't need his money."

"Well, congratulations. Now you don't have to worry about not having Ares around."

She puts a well-manicured hand over her belly. "I'm *pregnant!*"

"Tell that to the father. There's nothing I can do for you or the baby. I'm not an OB-GYN." Then I tilt my head. "By the way, what's your name? I wanna see if my husband ever mentioned you."

Vindictiveness gleams in her eyes. "*Soledad.*"

I feign consideration, then shake my head ruefully. "Never heard of you."

She turns red. "You bitch!"

"Look, Soledad, if you were really somebody Ares was in love with and you were carrying his baby, you wouldn't be here. You'd be in his arms, pampered and protected. So, why don't you go stir up trouble elsewhere? Better yet—go home, *stay* home, and let the rest of the world enjoy some peace and quiet."

"Do you think you're clever because you can say shit about me on the other side of these gates? Look, loser. You aren't that special. You're naturally blonde, right? Yeah, thought so. And your eyes—they aren't fake either."

I frown. "What are you trying to get at?"

"Ares has only ever dated blondes with either blue or green eyes."

"So? He has a type. So do I. I like my man strong, wide-shouldered and beautiful, with a sharp mind and beautiful blue eyes."

"Idiot. He's been searching for his 'true love' all these years. Countless PIs have been hired to look for her. At least once a month they report to him, and—"

"And how exactly would *you* know that?" I interrupt.

She scoffs, crossing her arms in a way that says, *Isn't it obvious?* "Don't you sometimes check his phone to see what he's up to?"

"No. But I can see why he isn't with you anymore if *you* did." Maybe she's the reason Ares is so hung up on respecting boundaries.

"Only naïve fools don't keep tabs on—"

"But what does that have to do with his relationship history?" I ask, trying to steer her back to the topic.

"He's been dating women who look like *her*. You and I—we're just substitutes. Get it?" Soledad sneers. "There's no eternal happy ending for you, just like there wasn't for me. Not even the baby is going to change that." She pauses, giving me a chance to process.

Her words claw at me—my pride...or my heart... Or it might be the tiny kernel of hope I've secretly harbored that one day Ares would care for me—and wouldn't mind that I'm nothing like the ideal woman he's described. I keep forgetting our union isn't about love.

That asshole. He's too nice! And it's unfair. He even called himself my knight, even though at that time he wasn't quite sober. Shouldn't he have treated me with respectful indifference? Kept himself busy while coming home early enough for dinner once in a while? Not worried about what I can or can't eat. Not cut a young coconut for me or say that he'd love to take me to Thailand. Not buy me canvases or a set of beautiful paints or brushes and set up a studio in a sunny room that looks out over the garden full of blooming lilies.

He keeps making me feel special. But...

Come on, Lareina. You're smarter than this. Don't let this ex with a grudge get to you. You don't know Ares's side of the story. This woman could've made everything up.

Soledad stares at me, chin raised. She clearly has an ego. She'd never put herself down by calling herself a substitute. No matter how painful the pang in my heart is, I can't let her win by acting like I believe her.

I put on another bland smile. "Substitute? Says who? What makes you think I'm not the original?" I tilt my head. "That ever cross your mind? I'm not only blonde, but have both one blue and one green eye. Up till now, he had to *settle* for either blue or green eyes because most people don't have one of each like me."

The color drains from Soledad's face.

"The only substitute here is you. I'm his *wife*. The *real thing*. Now, if you don't have anything interesting to say, leave before I call the police."

At the mention of the police, she grows even paler. Then she turns and runs.

That afternoon, Ares doesn't text. And he's still not home when I finally go to bed at midnight.

29

LAREINA

THE NEXT DAY, I step into a bustling dim sum restaurant. I always thought, based on videos I've seen, that a place like this would be busy and have very Asian-themed décor—dragons and phoenixes or something. Instead, the hall is inlaid with frosted green jade pieces designed to look like a life-sized bamboo forest.

A host comes over, and I give her the name of my lunch date. She leads me to the back, and I wave when I catch sight of Ethan.

Since our previous meeting, we haven't had much contact. I did mail the small sketch to him, but face-to-face time wasn't really necessary, since he knew what I wanted. After all, I'm not paying him to check up on me, just help me claim what's rightfully mine. And after that, punish Doris and her family. There probably isn't enough evidence to make them pay criminally in a court of law, but there are other ways.

Ethan's in an exceptionally well-tailored navy suit that fits his shoulders and lean torso well. The only splash of color is the burgundy tie, but his confidence helps him carry off the otherwise bland ensemble. Now that I think about it, Ares only wears black, blacker and maybe navy. Must be the lawyer uniform, although Jeremiah seems to like bold colors in order to make a statement.

"Hey," Ethan says with a smile. "Thanks for agreeing to meet on such short notice."

"No problem. Thanks for letting me pick the cuisine." When he asked to meet for lunch to discuss my trust, I suggested dim sum. With Zoe, I didn't care if I couldn't eat a bite, which oftentimes makes the other party uncomfortable. But Ethan's another matter.

"No problem. I haven't had Chinese in a while. This'll be good."

We order. He goes mainly for the dumplings, but I choose fried rice, noodles and veggies that have to be shared from the same plates. Then we agree to get a large pot of jasmine tea to split—thank God. The service is brisk, and soon our food comes out.

Ethan serves me crab fried rice, while I pour tea for both of us. I wait until he takes a bite of his portion before I chew on mine. *Ah... Heavenly.* The perfectly blended flavor of Dungeness crab meat and freshly chopped veggies is chef's-kiss good.

"So. What's this about?" I ask. Ethan is a busy man. He didn't ask me out just to eat. "I thought the entire process would take about three months?"

"It's probably going to take longer. Nesovia recently passed a law to force probation when a woman reclaims her inheritance through marriage."

I purse my lips. "Those damn politicians. They never do anything useful. When I get a hold of my money, I'm bankrolling whoever runs against them."

"Amen." Ethan grows serious. "But in the meantime, it gives your aunt an opportunity to file a petition and tie the process up in court for a while."

"How much time are we talking here?" I pray it only adds a couple of months, but it's the legal system, which churns slowly.

"Maybe a year?"

Ugh. No! "Even after I turn thirty?"

"Yes, because the process started *before* you turned thirty."

"Fuckers," I mutter, thoroughly annoyed with the lawmakers of the damn country I had the misfortune to be born in.

"But Doris says she'll sign an affidavit to give up the right to contest if you'll sign a transfer agreement."

Rage flares. "She's not getting a penny out of me!"

"If she wanted money, I'd advise you against it. But that isn't what she wants."

"Oh?" I can feel my eyes narrowing. "Doris loves getting my money as much as spending it. Why would she give it up? What's the catch?"

"She wants you to agree to transfer ownership rights to any and all items you've decided you don't want to keep anymore."

That's even more confusing. "Like what? My clothes? Shoes?"

"Examples in the agreement include notes, scraps of paper, doodles, your old stationery items, although that's not an exhaustive list."

"I'm not giving them my old stationery for the rest of my life. I might have some private stuff written there."

"It's whatever you *don't* want. She wants to get this done as soon as possible."

What's Doris's deal? This doesn't make any sense. "Do you see any gotchas in the agreement?"

"Actually, I don't. They're literally asking to take your trash, in a sense." He takes a shrimp shumai from the steamer.

I look at the Cantonese soy sauce fried noodles and swallow a sigh. Ethan hasn't touched them yet. I get more fried rice instead. I need more carbs if I want to think clearly. "What do you think she's trying to pull?"

"Unless you're throwing away a treasure map, I don't know. By the way, if you have one, you should give it to me, not them."

I laugh. "No. I don't have anything of that nature. Hmm."

"In any case, you can take your time and decide on what to do."

"Well, you're my lawyer. What do you think?"

"I'm of two minds about it. If all they really want is your old, unwanted stuff, maybe it wouldn't be such a bad idea to let them have it. In return for expediting the process to get your trust sooner, of course. But I also recognize they could be setting a trap, or...maybe they're hoping to get something of value from your castoffs." He shrugs.

"They know it'll be nearly impossible to touch my money. I'm not just married—my husband is a Huxley. That might've made them change their tactics." Or did Zoe have something to do with it? I hate it that a small part of me wonders if she should get some credit, all because of her cryptic remarks. But Zoe's family is dangerous, and Doris, Vernon and Rupert don't want to cross the Dunkels.

"Very possibly."

I sigh. I loathe making decisions when I don't have all the facts. "The smart thing to do might be to sign the agreement. But part of me doesn't want to give them anything, even my trash, you know? They've taken so much already." I look down wistfully at the so-far-untouched noodles. Will I ever be able to do something as mundane as eating out without worry, like everyone else?

Resentment, frustration and anger start to boil, and I expel a breath to hide the emotion. "To be honest, I'd prefer that they be out on the streets with nothing but the clothes on their backs."

"Then that's what you should do." Ethan's smile is neat and perfect —the kind designed to inspire confidence and relief.

"Thanks for understanding. I know the way I want to do it makes things more complicated."

"It's all billable." He winks.

I finally pick up the noodle plate and serve Ethan some. "This looks so good. You should try it."

"Well, this is cozy. When did you become so familiar with my wife, Beckman?"

I glance up. Ares is standing at the side of our table with an expression so dark and gloomy, it wouldn't shock me if it started to thunder and rain inside the restaurant. Bryce and Josh are behind him and waving tentatively at me, then they throw Ethan an ugly look. All three are in black suits—the lawyer uniform!—and are obviously here to enjoy their lunch.

"It's business," I say.

"While serving food to each other?" Ares's stormy blue eyes are still on Ethan as he speaks.

"He was helping me eat."

Ethan raises his eyebrow slightly at my explanation. I cringe inwardly. I should've phrased it better. Now it sounds like Ethan's been feeding me like a baby.

Since I don't feel comfortable discussing this with Ethan and my brothers-in-law present, I stand up, loop my arm through Ares's and drag him away. His expression is still taut, but he seems to thaw a bit.

"If you were craving dim sum, you could've asked me," he says finally when we reach the relatively deserted hall to the bathrooms.

"But you're busy, and I didn't want to disturb you."

"You're my wife. You're supposed to disturb me." A mix of shocked realization and agitation crosses his face. Why is he so upset about my being considerate?

"That isn't what we agreed to," I remind him. He has so many important clients and cases. The little conditions to our temporary marriage of convenience might be so minor they just slipped his mind.

The muscles in his jaw bunch together. Maybe he hates being told he's mistaken about something. He *is* a lawyer, after all.

Then I remember something I've been meaning to tell him. "By the way, Soledad came by yesterday. She said she was pregnant with your baby. You might want to check up on her." I mentally pat myself on the back for sounding so placid.

But instead of thanking me for letting him know, Ares looks at me like he wants to scream. "Why didn't you tell me sooner?"

"I was planning to, but you came home late. Not that I'm blaming you for working late, because things happen. And this morning you left for work early, and I didn't want to bother you, since whatever case you're working on must be critical. But if Soledad is that important, I'll text you as soon as possible next time."

"*Next time*? Is that all you have to say?" He sounds terrible, like somebody's dragging the words from the depths of hell.

"Um..." I shift back and forth.

She said I was a substitute. Am I? Who do you see when you see me? When you said you wanted to be my knight, did you mean your true love or me? What happens if you find her before we get what we want out of this marriage? Do you care for me at all, even a little bit?

Except all the questions sound so clingy and ridiculous, the kind you might ask your real husband, in a real marriage. "Yeah. I guess...?" I say, trying to sound as neutral as possible. I've already given up on changing enough to be the ideal wife he spoke of, but I should do what I can.

He looks at me with all the agony in the world, his complexion paler, his eyes losing the gorgeous spark that never fails to mesmerize me. I don't understand why, but somehow it feels like I'm at fault. "I'm really fine, Ares. You don't have to worry about me."

I shouldn't have added that. His beautiful face crumbles, like he's a man whose last hope has been dashed.

30

ARES

INSTEAD OF GOING HOME, I stay away for the next few days. I text Lareina to let her know, praying she shows a hint of unhappiness...a tinge of disapproval. Even Akiko, as supportive as she is of Dad's career, sighs a little when he has to pull all-nighters.

–Lareina: Thanks for letting me know! Hope you have a productive evening!

I stare at the text, then read it again, slowly. Then glare at the two sunny exclamation marks.

I breathe in and out slowly to settle myself and read it again, with more focus and attention than I gave to my constitutional law final.

No matter what interpretation I force on the words, she doesn't sound upset. I'd even say she sounds happy.

Fuck.

I said I wanted *respectful* indifference, not disrespectful apathy. If Lareina were the kind of wife I told her I wanted back in Vegas, she would've asked why I was working so late, offered to stop by the office so we could grab dinner together.

She almost sounds like a woman who's happy to have her husband working late so she can hang out with another man. Like Ethan Beckman. The only reason I'm not barging into our home without notice is that the fucker's busy dealing with a nasty countersuit involving two Hollywood celebs with more fame and money than brains or common sense. They're exactly the kind of clients you would wish on your worst enemy.

But I'd take them on if Lareina would be even half as jealous as I was when she mentioned Soledad.

Fucking Soledad. I'm going to make sure she serves jail time for what she did in Vegas. I don't care what strings her dad tries to pull. I not only know how to cut them, but pull my own to make her miserable. If she flails enough during the process to take Harvey down with her—well, that's doubtful, but one can always hope—so much the better.

I glance at the desktop clock. Is Lareina working in her studio again? I bought multiple canvases, one of them ridiculously large. Although I was a bit shocked at how enormous it was, I was also secretly glad. It'll take her a while to paint all three, beyond the next few months. Maybe a year or longer. At least, Google seems to think so.

I come out of the office to stretch my legs and grab some coffee. As I make a turn to reach the break room, I almost bump into—

"Ack!" The coffee in Kenna's hand begins to tip forward, but she suddenly twists her wrist. The dark brew spills on her pale beige blouse. I start to reach for her, but she staggers back a step or two and looks down at the huge stain, her eyebrows pinched and mouth open.

I feel bad for her, since she obviously tipped the hot drink on herself to prevent it from spilling on me. I keep a spare suit and shirt in the office just in case, but I doubt she does the same.

"Are you okay?" I ask. "Let me get you some paper towels."

"No. No!" She pulls back as though I'm a leper. "I'm fine. Really."

What's that about? Earlier she was telling me about some great drip coffee place, and now she's acting like being near me will give her cancer. Her gaze flicks to something behind me, then her complexion turns chalky.

I turn and see... *Josh?*

"I gotta go." Before I can say anything, Kenna spins in a half-circle and trots off.

"Did you do something to her?" I ask my brother.

Josh smiles sweetly. "Why, good afternoon to you too, Ares. Yes, thank you, I'm having a great day."

My suspicion radar is pinging hard. "Cut the sarcasm and answer the question."

"I haven't *done* anything. Just saw her outside the lobby with some thuggish guy. A debt collector."

I frown at the visual he's painted. "A loan shark?"

Josh shrugs, but it feels like an affirmation. Wordlessly, we walk toward the break room.

"She's lucky it wasn't Aunt Jeremiah who caught her," he remarks.

She would've fired Kenna on the spot. My aunt believes perception matters more than reality and doesn't tolerate anything that could damage the firm's reputation.

"But that doesn't explain why she was fleeing like that." I give him a look. "Unless she owes you money."

"She doesn't, and even if she did, I'm a nice guy. But maybe she's scared *you* might tell The Fogeys. After all, you're inflexible and humorless."

I snort. The two adjectives are what almost everyone at the firm uses to describe me when they don't think I can hear.

"I had a word with her about that, too," Josh adds.

"That isn't like you." My brother doesn't give a shit about most people's problems...unless they're paying clients. Or family or close friends. His unusual behavior piques my curiosity, but I stomp on the feeling. If he wants to explain himself, he will. If he doesn't, nothing can make him. If I push too hard, he'll spin some convincing bullshit story. "Besides, I wouldn't have ratted her out to management."

He makes a noncommittal noise. "I wanted to step in before you did something you shouldn't." He pours us two mugs of black coffee and pushes one to me. I take it with murmured thanks. "I saw the scar on her back."

"So?" I feign nonchalance, but what is he getting at?

Josh takes a sip of his coffee. "I know the girl you're looking for is scarred. On her back, to be specific."

"Where did you hear that?"

"It's been over twenty years. You've been careful, but nothing stays hidden for that long, especially when you searched for her so desperately."

Suddenly, I realize Greg hasn't sent a report about Queen, and I haven't been thinking about her over the last few weeks. Sudden guilt pierces my heart like broken glass. *Am I forgetting her? Abandoning her like The Fogeys would like me to?*

At the same time, the voice that sounds awfully like Grandmother says, *It's time to let go. Sometimes things are simply not meant to be. Pursue a happiness that's close to you rather than one far away. Queen wouldn't want you to spend so much energy and effort searching for her if the cost is living a good life. She didn't rescue you for that.*

Queen was too young to think that far ahead—but she might be disappointed now if she knew the amount of time and money I've spent on looking for her over the last twenty-two years. I learned a long time ago that there are certain things I can't do anything about. However, it's bittersweet to consider the possibility that she and I may never cross paths again.

"If you never find her again..." Josh sighs. "I don't know exactly why you're looking for her. You can't possibly think you're going to fall in love with her and marry her, or something far-fetched like that. But if you're hoping to pay her back, just pay it forward instead. If she's the kind of woman worth searching for over twenty years, she would love that."

I nod slowly. "Yes. She would." The realization comes with pain and disappointment. It isn't easy to let go of something I've been obsessing over for so long.

He clasps my shoulder. "Anyway, I gotta go wrap up some motions. You coming to poker tonight?"

"Of course. Wouldn't miss it."

Contrary to what I told my wife this afternoon, I don't have to work past seven thirty today. Actually, tonight is the monthly poker night with my brothers, with Bryce hosting it at his place. Although we see one another regularly, it's mostly at work, and all of us are usually too busy to spend more than a minute or two saying hello.

Besides, it's a tradition we've kept since the kidnapping because the therapist said we needed a way to cope with our emotions—me dealing with the trauma of the near-death experience, and the twins struggling with the guilt that they left me behind when they fled with my help. I told them after my return that I was glad they weren't stuck in the cabin with me. I was older and bigger, and it was my job to keep my baby brothers safe. But they still couldn't let go.

The therapist suggested a game night, saying spending time together without talking about the kidnapping or its aftermath might be useful. Just once a week, and we weren't allowed to dwell on the past event anymore. Behave how we would've without the kidnapping—without guilt or pain or loathing or self-recrimination.

We tried a few different board games, but eventually settled on poker. We were all about equally good at it, the game could go on as long as we wanted to play, and we liked to test our luck.

But deciding on a game wasn't the hard part. It was learning to let go, which took years. Then we gradually started to talk about things that most boys would—cars, sports, anime, manga and girls. Well, the last was never on my list, but it was on my brothers'. We even continued our poker nights at Harvard once the twins started college, then later in law school.

I head to Bryce's place after taking care of a couple of emails from anxious clients. He lives not too far away in a mansion that's more of a fortress than a home. Stone walls and turrets and windows that are probably bulletproof. His garden is full of succulents. He says he likes his landscape low maintenance and pretty.

On the round table in the dining room, the various cheeses, sliced roast beef, pork and crackers that Bryce had catered sit on a lazy Susan. There's also a humidor full of Padrón Cigars 1926 Serie Maduro, two bottles of Pétrus 2020 and a Hanyu 2000, which goes to show just how much Bryce loves us; the distillery shut down in 2004, and there isn't any more lying around to buy even if you have the cash. But he's never letting us touch his Hanyu Ichiro Malt card series. His love only extends so far.

"You look like shit," Bryce observes lightly as he checks his hand.

"He always looks like shit." Josh puffs on his cigar while glaring at the cards he's been dealt. I'd assume that he got a shitty hand if it were anybody else, but not Josh. He'll bluff and lie like a heartless dog to win.

"Don't like what I have." I look at mine again. A pair of fours. If one of the community cards is a four, I'll have three of a kind. Not bad.

If only I had a bit of the luck that I have with poker with my wife—

The acid I've become familiar with after marrying Lareina burns in my gut. I seethed with jealousy at seeing her being so chummy with Ethan Beckman, and she couldn't have been calmer when she talked about Soledad. Not a ripple of interest when she casually mentioned my ex's "pregnancy," which is a damn lie. Barnyard animals will stage *The Nutcracker* before Soledad gets pregnant with my baby.

"By the way, what were you so smug about this afternoon?" Josh says to Bryce.

"Me? Smug?"

"You looked like a cat after a successful hunt," Josh says.

"There was some kind of commotion," I say, trying not to dwell on my situation with Lareina. The whole office buzzed about it, whispers rising from every desk.

"Well." A corner of Bryce's mouth lifts. "An uninvited guest interrupted my day, and my assistant did her best to keep her out, but..." He shrugs, then deals the community cards.

The four of clubs. Great. I toss another chip onto the pile. Each chip is worth a hundred to make the math easy. Bryce and Josh toss in a couple to call.

"Who managed to get past Amélie?" I can't think of anybody who would barrel into his office like that, especially with his assistant in the way. Amélie might look like a delicate flower, but she can be a battle-ax when she needs to be.

"Fiona Oberman."

I raise my eyebrows. "*Fiona?* Doesn't she know you hate her?"

"Yeah, but when I was young and dumb, I made a promise to do her one favor. She finally came to collect."

"Wow. But still... She couldn't find anybody else to turn to for help?" Josh says.

"What did she want? Not representation, right?" I ask. "She would never trust you that much."

Everyone knows the level of distrust and animosity between the two. Not sure why, because Bryce was interested in her when they first met. So what if she was involved with some loser frat boy and distanced herself from Bryce for a while? My brother isn't the type to dislike a woman for dating whom she wants.

"She wants to borrow money."

I almost choke on my whiskey.

"Did you tell her that if she can't pay you back, you'll want a pound of her flesh?" Josh asks.

"Of course, especially when she begged so prettily." I sense a sliver of annoyance and frustration underneath Bryce's derisive tone.

Another card dealt. The king of hearts.

Not a flicker of an eyelash from my brothers. I raise just for the hell of it. They call.

"Did she take your offer?" Josh asks.

Something passes behind Bryce's eyes. "Too much fucking pride. Funny, considering her family's on the verge of bankruptcy."

Lying asshole. The sardonic smile on his mouth betrays him. He didn't offer her shit, just enjoyed taunting her. Nobody's said she got on her knees, but I wouldn't be surprised if he pushed it that far.

I stuff my mouth with cheese. As the sharp flavor spreads on my tongue, I wonder if Lareina is having dinner. Somebody needs to make sure she can eat. Now that I think about it, it's irritating that the fucker—Beckman—didn't notice she wanted to eat the noodles. He should've tasted them before she had to serve some on his plate.

Bastard. This is why I'll always hate him.

You've hated him since long before you met your wife, an inner voice points out.

Fine, I'll hate him *more*.

"She'll come around, though." Bryce sighs nonchalantly. "What other choice does she have?"

"A sugar daddy?" Josh says. "SoCal is full of 'em. She doesn't even have to limit herself to single men. Mistressing is a lucrative business."

Bryce snorts. "Don't be ridiculous. She's too old for that."

"She's barely thirty." I look at my brother like he's intellectually challenged.

Josh adds, "And she keeps in shape. She looks like she's twenty-two. A lot of guys would tap it."

"That's disgusting," Bryce sneers. Another card dealt—the queen of diamonds. *No help.*

"Not my fault she's a babe," Josh says.

I throw in more chips.

"You seem confident," Josh says.

"I'm always confident."

"You taking your wife to the art auction exhibition?" Bryce says, probably not wanting to have Josh continue talking about Fiona and her prospects as a trophy wife—or mistress.

"What exhibition?"

"The one for the art auction two weeks from now. Susan Winters's paintings are going to be up for sale, and you might want to grab one or two for your wife," Josh says.

"Why?" I ask. "Is she Lareina's favorite?"

Bryce and Josh look at each other. "Ares, Susan Winters was Lareina's *mom*. Haven't you done a background check on her?"

"Well, yeah, but..." Greg sent it a couple of weeks ago, but I didn't read it. Curiosity compelled me to peek, but I refused. The report would tell me every fact there is to know about her—age, birthday, family relationships and educational background. But that feels forced. Couples should get to know each other by spending time together. When I saw the report attached to Greg's email, I realized I wanted to learn about my wife organically. "Wait a minute. How come *I* didn't know about the exhibition? Don't the organizers want me there?"

"Akiko mentioned it, but you probably forgot as usual, since you hate going to events like that. The organizer probably didn't bother to invite you either," Bryce says.

"Assholes. Don't they know who my wife is?"

"Most likely. They might've invited *her*."

Bryce meant to soothe me, but it does the opposite. Why didn't she say something about the auction? Does she not plan to go? Or worse yet, go with someone else? *Like Ethan Beckman?*

I jerkily puff my cigar. Just because she doesn't act jealous over Soledad doesn't mean I'm going to behave the same way.

Besides, didn't we promise to be faithful? What she's doing seems like Cheating Lite.

"She'd probably love to see her mother's art, unless she hated her mother," Josh says. "Not only that, if she's into art, she'll enjoy meeting one of the latest up-and-coming stars, who'll be at the event. She's selling her work there too. Parker Jacoby. Her paintings are already getting a lot of buzz right now."

Art exhibitions aren't my scene, but my wife seems to like art in general. She spends hours every day drawing.

"Fine. I'll take her." Maybe it'll provide an opportunity for us to become closer.

31

LAREINA

I GLANCE at my phone screen. Since telling me that he needed to work late, Ares hasn't texted me or anything. Did I sound too cold in my response? I want to be a considerate wife, so I sent him a reply full of cheer, even though I was a little disappointed that he was busy—again.

I look at the colors starting to fill the canvas. Unlike my previous work, the shades are mostly dark wood tones with green and blue. The last is an exact match for Ares's eyes. He doesn't like his eyes, but I adore them. I've spent so much time making them perfect in the portrait.

The phone buzzes.

–Lucie: Wanna join me and Yuna for an evening get-together? Our husbands are out of town, and the kids are with their grandparents. Just us adults. I know it's last minute, so if you're busy, that's fine.

–Me: Actually, I don't have anything to do—and my husband's working late. So let's do it!

–Lucie: Awesome! Here's my address.

I get out of the smock and change into a clean shirt and jeans, then ask Javier to drive me to her house. It's a stunning mansion, sprawled out like a sleepy giant. The garden is massive, and there's a greenhouse full of lush flowers. Lucie greets me at the front entrance, the double doors large enough to serve as a gate to a medieval castle. The foyer boasts a high cathedral ceiling with a surprisingly delicate chandelier.

"Thanks for inviting me. I love your greenhouse," I say as Lucie leads me past two kitchens. She's dressed casually in a round-neck T-shirt and stretchy cropped pants.

"Seb decided to build one because I was studying 'flower language' for the Korean market. He said it'd be inspirational."

"Which was faster? The greenhouse or your mastering the language?" I ask.

"The greenhouse. The man can make things happen when he's determined." Lucie's eyes grow dreamy. It's clear she's crazy in love with her husband.

Good for her. But my happiness for her doesn't quite soothe the ache from realizing that the kind of mutual affection she has with her husband won't be mine.

Don't think too much about it. You're just infatuated. After you're divorced, you're going to find the other half of your soul.

"He had to be like the Terminator, or he would've lost you back then," Yuna says, then waves. "So glad you could join us!" Her auburn hair falls over her delicate shoulders, and she's in a red sundress that looks amazing against her creamy skin.

"Do you like Korean food?" Lucie asks. "I should've checked before I invited you, but I got distracted. If you aren't into it, we can grab sandwiches or salads or whatever. Or we can do Mexican."

"No, I can do Korean," I say, not wanting to be a bother. I've never tried it, but why not? As long as somebody's willing to taste the food first.

"Thank God. Mom totally overpacked." Yuna rolls her eyes a little, but her big smile glows with affection. "My mom's visiting to see the grandkids, and of course she had to bring her chefs with her. They cooked all sorts of stuff. When I told her I was visiting Lucie, she packed a bunch of things, saying we never eat enough when we get together."

"Not true. I feed my friends well," Lucie says, leaning toward me.

"According to my mom, unless I'm a butterball who has to be rolled home, I'm 'starving.'" Yuna turns to me. "But if I gain weight, she'll ask why I'm letting myself go."

I giggle. I can just imagine the scene. "Difficult standards to meet."

"But I still love her. What can I say?" Yuna shrugs with a big grin. "Besides, she thinks all my friends are like her own kids. So if you ever meet my mom and she starts to mother you, just nod and go along with it."

I smile at the lovely picture Yuna's presenting. She sounds a little abashed, but I think it's sweet of her mother to care for her friends, too. It isn't something I experienced—or even thought possible—while living in Nesovia under Doris's guardianship. Even when she was doing her best to fake being nice, it wasn't convincing.

We head to the dining room. I relax a little when I see a family-style spread on the table. Some glass noodles, stir-fried beef, some sort of rice and veggies wrapped in seaweed, pickled vegetables and soups, all with tongs and ladles for serving.

"Are there more people coming?" I ask.

"No, just us three. Mom thinks we can eat all of it by ourselves." Yuna shakes her head as she pours chilled chardonnay for everyone.

"Wow. But okay. It smells amazing."

"Tastes better," Lucie says.

I wait for Yuna and Lucie to grab theirs first, then serve myself to ensure I don't take anything nobody wants. Thankfully, they get a little bit of everything.

I wait for them to take bites then eat. I've never had Korean food, but it's quite good—lots of flavor, with a good balance of sweet and salty. The noodles are to die for, so chewy and tasty. "Your mom's chefs are angels."

"They probably sold their souls," Yuna says with a contented sigh and a sip of wine. "I almost feel bad for my dad because he has to eat the backup chefs' cooking. They aren't bad, but just not as good as the ones Mom brought here. But what can he do? He loves her, so he let her do what she wants. He says whoever loves more loses in a relationship."

Her father's observation hits me like a brick in the face. I never considered it from that angle, but is *that* why I'm feeling...restless? I'm falling for Ares and he doesn't want me at all?

"That's so cynical," Lucie complains. "If you keep saying things like that, it's going to kill my jewelry design mojo."

"You don't design them, you run the company that sells them," Yuna says. "Besides, it's true, isn't it? He lets her take the best chefs. If he didn't love her, he wouldn't."

"So if you stay, you know, *indifferent*..." I say, then try to push more noodles into my mouth to hide my trepidation. Half the forkful drops on my plate, but hopefully Yuna and Lucie will chalk it up to my unfamiliarity with glass noodles, not nerves.

"Then nothing." Yuna shrugs. "I mean... I guess they'll eventually seek the companionship and love they aren't getting from their spouses from someone else. There are plenty of marriages like that in Korea. Of course, you have to be extra cautious and discreet, because getting caught is embarrassing. There's a big difference between loving somebody who isn't your spouse and getting exposed for it."

"Good God. If you're going to do that, why stay married?" Lucie says with disgust.

"Family alliances? Money? Power? Convenience? Needing a socially acceptable spouse to present?" Yuna shrugs again. "Could be anything."

I say nothing, but my heart seems to turn to lead because it sounds just like my marriage with Ares. He was so clear on what he's getting out of the marriage—his promotion. And he knows I'm getting control over my money. Does it bother him that our marriage is so transactional? Is that why he's been a little distant recently?

I grab more noodles, then notice a François sculpture set in a protective case bolted into the nook. "Is that an original?" I ask, hoping to turn the conversation away from love and marriage.

Lucie immediately brightens. "Yes. My favorite. And my prize. It used to be in the living room, but I had to move it here. Harder to reach. The case is shatterproof and bulletproof."

"Did somebody try to steal it?" I ask in shock. "This area's safe, isn't it?"

"Very, and nobody has tried to rob me. It's just that I have a young child, and she has no respect for art."

"Ah."

"Kids never do," Yuna laments. "They're like puppies, but slower to mature and train. I'm skipping the auction this year because Liam almost destroyed a painting I bought for Declan for Christmas."

"Oh no." Lucie shakes her head. "That's why I already commissioned a special case to store the one I'm planning to buy next week." She turns to me. "Are you going?"

"I'm...not sure. I didn't even know about this auction. What do they have?" The idea is intriguing. I've seen movies with exciting auctions, but I've never been to one.

"Some really interesting pieces. And you can go to the exhibition before actually buying anything. I thought you might like to because they're going to have a few of your mother's paintings up for sale. Apparently, a couple of them have never been seen by the public before."

Mom's work is being sold? "Really? My mother's art? Since when?"

Lucie looks at Yuna. "I don't know. Over the past ten years or so? But your mom's paintings *are* actively sold at auctions."

I grind my teeth. I had no idea, and nobody was going to inform me of anything in Nesovia.

The sales are likely Doris's doing. Based on our increasingly hostile relationship, she must've figured she needed a backup plan in case she couldn't get me to marry Rupert. The next best thing would be to sell all the antiques and paintings that aren't part of my trust behind my back. That would give her money she could hide from me.

Guess nobody told her that those items belong to me, and it's an act of theft to dispose of them without my permission.

Is this why Doris tried to get me to sign the agreement, giving her ownership rights to my "trash"? She'll try to dispute who owns what, tying everything up for years. After all, it'll be all hearsay, and she can get Vernon and Rupert to testify I threw those things away. And my public eccentricity would work against me in court.

Greedy, greedy bitch.

"I want those paintings, but I want to see them first." I want to make sure they're really works that my mother left for me before I report Doris for theft and sue her. There's a *miniscule* possibility Mom gave some to Doris.

"It might get pretty pricey if you plan to buy them all," Lucie says. "I've heard rumors that there will be about five pieces, and your mother became very popular recently. I think the latest work was auctioned for almost two million, and it was a fairly small painting."

So if all five were sold for the same price, that'd be ten million. Not a terrible amount of money for Doris and her family. Not as nice as sixty billion, but not bad—although terrible for me, since they're pieces of my mother's legacy.

The stress of dealing with my relatives' greed is suddenly crushing, weighing me down until my shoulders bow. I want to bury my face in my lap and close my eyes and pretend the world doesn't exist.

"What's wrong?" Yuna asks.

"You want your mother's paintings," Lucie says.

I nod, a hand still covering my face.

Lucie lets out a sympathetic noise. "And let me guess—the trust is still tied up?"

I nod again.

"Well, it's an easy problem to fix. Just get your husband to buy them for you." Yuna pats my back gently. "After all, his money is your money."

"No..." His money is definitely not my money. Ethan's almost done with our prenup. He said it was taking a while because my assets are extensive and he wants to be thorough. But I've read an earlier draft. According to the agreement, anything bought belongs to whichever spouse that financed the purchase, unless it's designated as a gift from the very beginning and documented as such.

Which I suppose means I won't be taking anything from the studio, either. But that's okay, since the portrait's a gift for Ares. *My mom's paintings, though...*

"Oh, come on. If you think he's going to object to the amount, just rub him like a genie." Yuna waggles her eyebrows. "Unlike the usual cheapo genies who only let you rub them three times, your man will give you what you want *every* time you rub. Hehehe."

"Exactly. Works like a charm." Lucie giggles. "And you can add some kisses for better results." She purses her lips and makes a kissing sound.

I give them a wan smile. Easy for them to say, since their husbands are apparently crazy about them. Mine is...well...

Mine is complicated.

The Accidental Marriage

That night, I stay up until Ares comes home at one. He raises his eyebrows when he sees me.

"Hi," I say. "I was waiting for you to come home."

He smells of alcohol and something smoky. Not cigarettes. Cigars? Was he at a business dinner and had to return to the office? I press my lips to contain the questions. They aren't as critical as what I want to say.

"Did you need something?" he asks. "You should've texted."

"You said you were working late. I didn't want to bother you, since it sounded important."

He hesitates for a moment, then lets out a soft sigh and nods. "My fault. I should've made it clear that it's no bother. Nothing is more important than you."

Sweetness starts to shiver through me, until shock flares in his eyes. Suddenly I realize he didn't mean to put it that way. He probably regrets it now.

Sudden resentment surges. I hate it that he's confusing me, telling me he wants respectful indifference, but then acting all caring...and regretting it. I think of all the things he's done for me without my having to ask. Is he sorry he did them?

But right now, I don't want to talk about it. That's not why I stayed up, and I have a feeling that if I broach the topic we'll end up arguing.

"There's an art auction next week. I want to go," I say. "Not sure about the protocol for something like that in a marriage like ours, but I'd prefer to go with you. But if you don't want to, that's fine."

He stares at me as though I just slapped him. Then he runs a hand over his face. "Of course we'll go together."

"It's okay if you're busy—"

The muscles in his jaw bunch. "I'll go with you."

32

ARES

Lareina is acting strangely for some reason. I agreed to take her to the auction. So why behave so stiffly, like that wasn't what she wanted after all?

I didn't say anything I didn't mean that night. I find her even more important than my work. As soon as the words slipped from my lips, I froze in shock. I hadn't realized it until I said it, but somehow she's become more important than I can imagine.

"What do you do when your wife is upset?" I say over an after-work drink with Huxley Lasker, my cousin. Despite having graduated Harvard Law with honors, he refused to join the firm because he'd rather be in advertising. Grandmother and Aunt Jeremiah still can't believe it, but nothing they said or did changed his mind.

Most people don't realize we're related when we hang out together. Huxley looks more like his degenerate Hollywood mogul father than his mother. He got his dark hair and square jaw from the old man. The brain and good taste, on the other hand, are all Jeremiah. His father was so unbelievably lazy and stupid, he named his child after our family's last name. Who does that?

On the other hand, he didn't kidnap his own child and leave him to die in a forest fire. So on balance...

"Why? You in the doghouse already?" Hux says.

"No, there's no doghouse." I still sleep in the same bed as Lareina. "I just feel like we got off on the wrong foot."

"Okay. How did it happen?"

I glare at him. I hate it when people ask me a question I can't answer. He purses his lips, then clears his throat.

"Maybe you should start over," he says.

"Start over? How?"

"Buy her some piece of jewelry that symbolizes a new beginning."

I snort. "You sound like your half-brother." Sebastian Lasker is the CEO of Sebastian Jewelry. *Again*—that father of theirs naming kids after their mothers' family business or names.

"Seb isn't usually wrong about things like this. There's a reason he runs one of the most successful jewelry companies in the world."

"She won't accept a ring."

"For a good reason. Too cliché. Buy her something she wants."

"Like...?"

"I don't know. She's *your* wife." He shrugs and spreads his hands. "A yacht?"

So she can sail away by herself? I don't think so.

He continues, "Don't you already have one that you barely ever use? Just draft a transfer agreement. You won't even need to hire a lawyer."

"She already *has* a lawyer."

"Who? Bryce?"

I wish. "No. Ethan Beckman."

Hux nods with approval. "Yeah, well. He's not bad if you're going to hire somebody outside of the family."

I shoot him a death glare. "Whose side are you on?"

He spreads his hands again. "*Side*? What side? Look, just figure out what she wants and give it to her. Easy. You're overthinking this, and that won't help you figure out why she's upset with you in the first place. Harvard Law was great at teaching logic, but there's no logic to love."

Is what I'm feeling, love? My heart beats funny—too fast and too irregular. Not to mention my chest feels uncomfortable and tight. My mind won't focus, either, constantly distracted by thoughts of my wife.

I don't like it. But I can't imagine getting rid of the disruptive emotions, either. Somehow, they feel more vital than the air in my lungs.

A hint of regret fleets over Huxley. "If your mother hadn't messed you up so bad, you might be doing better. More experience."

I don't think experience is the problem. It's more a fear of being out of control—being so off balance when I'm with Lareina. Her smile makes me warm and her sweet words are a balm to my battered soul. When she told me my eyes were nothing like my mother's, I thought my heart would burst. When she twines herself around me at night in sleep, I want to pull her closer and hold her tighter, rather than push her away with a shudder like I used to with my exes.

I love it that being with her feels natural and wonderful. But sometimes I feel like it's a sandcastle about to crumble. Especially when she keeps me at arm's length without a discernible reason. Or when she acts like another woman claiming ownership over me doesn't bother her at all. She'd show more possessiveness over her old underwear than me.

Still, I take Huxley's advice to heart. Despite a rocky beginning with his wife, right now they're very happy together. Almost disturbingly so.

So I drop by Sebastian Jewelry and select a set of stunning sapphires, since Lareina seems to be partial to them. I get stones that match my eye color—she likes them, and I want her to be reminded of me often. I want to occupy her mind the way she occupies mine.

Should I just pamper her with money? Would that work?

She reacted favorably when I talked about going to Thailand. I should take her there and show her the stunning beaches, feed her delicious food and pamper her with hour-long massages. It's beautiful all year around, so all I have to do is find some free time.

I flip through my calendar. Twenty days in mid-October. Should be perfect. I send a quick note to HR.

Still, it seems too far away. People need something more immediate to feel appreciated.

The art auction! Bryce and Josh mentioned it during our poker game. That's the ticket. It's in a week or so, and Lareina will appreciate it. Akiko told me before that those things usually have an exhibition for committed buyers, so they can examine the works up close before the actual bidding starts. I should take my wife and see if there's anything that interests her.

I text Akiko—she's really into art collecting and will know everything there is to know about the exhibition. I want to plan it well so all Lareina has to do is show up and buy what she likes.

On Friday, Ethan Beckman finally delivers the very belated prenup to my office. "Took you a while," I say.

He gives me a bland smile. "Her assets are extensive."

"Or maybe you're just a slothful lawyer. You didn't have to waste your time hand-delivering it like some lackey, by the way."

Instead of firing back, he says, "I had to meet with Jeremiah's client to discuss a settlement. Otherwise, I wouldn't have bothered to come. Anyway, sign it. Or else I'll tell my client you just want her money."

Asshole. And stupid to boot. "Did you forget I'm worth at least two billion dollars? If anybody wants money, it's my wife."

Beckman lets out a condescending laugh. "Wow, two whole billion! That's cute. But never mind, you'll find out soon enough." He makes a show of checking his watch. "I have to get going. Got an appointment with your wife soon. A coffee date." He winks.

"For what?" I bristle. This asshole is spending way too much time with her. Dim sum and now a coffee date?

"To discuss financing some big purchase."

"How big?" She has my black AmEx.

He shrugs. "Not sure yet. A hundred million? Maybe more?"

"What the fuck?"

He just raises an eyebrow and walks away. I clench my fists and glare at his retreating back. If I didn't care about law at all—or my career at Huxley & Webber—I'd punch him just on principle.

A hundred million plus. And my wife is running to Ethan for it. Of course the fucker doesn't have that kind of money, so he'll have to finance it for her.

It chaps my ass she hasn't said a word to me. She knows I have the money. Why won't she ask *me*? My money's just as good as whichever banker Beckman introduces her to. Actually better. *I'm her husband!*

–Me: Can we meet?

As soon as I send the text, I realize my wife might not see it in time. I call her. I'll be damned if she takes a penny of money that Ethan Beckman arranges for her.

"Hello?" She sounds innocent, as though she isn't about to have a coffee date with the enemy.

"Can we talk?"

"I saw your text and I was about to respond. Is this about the prenup? I heard Ethan just delivered it to you."

My knuckles whiten at the warm way the fucker's name rolls from her lips. "I haven't read it yet."

"You should. How about in an hour or so? I can stop by your office, unless you're coming home early today?"

"Now. I want to talk now."

"*Now* is not a good time." I can hear an infuriating frown in her voice. She makes me sound unreasonable. "I'm meeting someone in a few minutes."

"Ethan Beckman?"

"How did you know?"

"Because he came here to rub it in. Don't do anything stupid. I'll be there in a minute."

I hang up, then open a tracking app on my phone to see where she is. The phone I bought her isn't some innocent model. I put an app on it to track her movements because at the time I thought she could be linked to Harvey or Mom. But I've never checked up on her with the app.

Until now.

I hate that I'm acting like a jealous husband, but what I hate more is how crazy she drives me. Me, leaving the office at two, when I'm supposed to meet an important client in an hour. Instead of prepping for it, I'm chasing after her like a puppy about to be abandoned.

Lareina is sitting in a booth at the newly opened specialty café that some of the assistants were talking about in the break room a few days ago. The place is all dark wood and windows. Little figurines featuring famous landmarks in Italy—the Colosseum, the Tower of Pisa, Duomo di Milano, St. Peter's Basilica and more—line a shallow shelf behind the counter, above bags and bags of freshly roasted coffee beans.

She's heartbreakingly beautiful in a pretty pink dress that brings out the natural flush in her face. She tucks a wayward strand of hair behind her ear, and the gesture is natural and perfect. The glint of the wedding ring on her finger soothes my monstrous possessiveness, but only a little. After all, she's still here to meet with Beckman.

He brings a tray of two slices of cake and two coffees to her. He smiles like a used car salesman or ambulance chaser, and my wife smiles back at him as though blind to his smarminess. He sips his coffee, and she merely warms her hands with hers. See? He has no fucking clue she can't eat or drink what he just gave her. He doesn't even notice anything wrong. She isn't swapping plates, either, obviously not comfortable enough to do that with him.

If I were there with her, I would've tasted both her cake and her coffee. Then I'd offer to pay for whatever she needs because she's my wife and she shouldn't have to beg.

Fury sweeps through me like a powerful storm. *She should've never hired Beckman.* She shouldn't have let him get near her, and she shouldn't be relying on him so much.

I step inside the café. The bell over the door chimes. The lanky guy at the counter starts toward me, but I ignore him and turn toward the booth where my wife is.

"I can use my trust as collateral to borrow the money," she says, not noticing me at all since her eyes are so intent on Beckman, like he holds the solution to her problem. Raw, bitter possessiveness bursts through my veins. She's mine—*my wife*. She shouldn't look at some other man like he can fix whatever's broken in her world. That's *my* job, *my* privilege and *my* prerogative.

"We can probably—"

"You don't have the money for it," I say coldly. "Give it up before you embarrass yourself, Beckman."

"Ares," Lareina says. "What are you doing here? How did you know I was here?"

"Easy. He told me." I jerk my chin at Beckman. "Your lawyer has a big mouth."

"I didn't tell you where," he says defensively.

"Didn't have to. I just followed you." Hux said I don't have much experience, but I'm smart enough to know this isn't the time to tell my wife about the tracking bug on her phone.

"Regardless, this doesn't concern you."

"My wife's matters concern me a great deal." I turn to Lareina. "When do you need the money?"

"Probably in a week?" She shrugs. "I'm not totally sure."

I turn back to Beckman. "Can you get her the money she needs within a week?"

He looks away briefly before glaring up at me. "No. It'll take a while to underwrite and—"

"I don't need you to tell me the steps involved. I know them as well as you," I say. "Stop wasting her time when you know you can't provide what she wants, when she wants it. People like you are the reason lawyers have such a bad rep."

Lareina's eyes shift between me and Beckman. I hold out my hand. "Let's go. He can't do anything for you, but he'll bill you six hundred bucks an hour for taking the time to tell you so."

She bites her lip, then glances at Beckman. Is she seriously considering refusing my hand?

I stare down at her, willing her to take my hand. I can't guarantee what I'll do if she doesn't.

Finally, she sighs. "I guess it's more complicated than I thought. Thanks for your time, Ethan." The friendly way she says his name grates on my already over-frazzled nerves.

But when she places her hand in mine, I can forgive her for almost anything.

33

LAREINA

Given Ares's reaction to seeing me with Ethan at the café, I assumed he'd stay upset for a while. But instead, he offers to take me to the exhibition Lucie and Yuna told me about. I agree readily, trying to gauge his mood, but I might as well be trying to read Aramaic.

Since it's our first fancy social outing as a couple, I spend hours selecting a dress and fussing with my hair and makeup. Lucie told me husbands can't stay unhappy for long when their wives look hot.

–Lucie: Sort of like how it's hard for me to stay mad at Seb when he's looking particularly delicious after a good workout. He knows it, too, which is why he gets a good pump and flexes his muscles when he finally realizes that I'm annoyed with him "for some reason."

By the time my prep is finished, my eyes are smoky and come-hither. The lip tint I picked out is blood red with an undertone of burgundy. My cheekbones never looked so sharp, and I pat myself on the back for a job well done. Makeup is a lot like painting, it's just that one's face is the canvas.

My hair's pulled back into a chic updo, and a few tendrils frame my face just so. The cape dress Akiko and I picked out drapes over my body like a silken waterfall, showcasing my long limbs. I slip on strappy heels and silently walk down to the living room. Ares stands in the center, looking out the window, in a black suit and shark-gray tie.

I pause to take him in. The high forehead to the straight slope of his nose. The gorgeous, talented mouth with a tongue too clever for my own sanity. The intense blue eyes that always ensnare me like a trap and won't let go. I noticed them first when I met him, and I still think they're his best feature. I know he always thought that they were like his vile mother's, but I hope he no longer believes that after what I told him.

Suddenly, he turns his head in my direction, like a wolf scenting his mate. Our eyes meet, and the brilliant blue grows darker with heat. I flush with pleasure at his reaction to the way I look. It was worth the time and effort.

He slowly comes toward me. I start to lick my lips out of habit, then immediately catch myself. Can't wipe away the tint on my mouth.

He wraps an arm around my waist, pulling me into his delicious body heat. "Mrs. Huxley."

"Hello, Mr. Huxley. You look fantastic."

"And you look good enough to eat." His eyes drop to my mouth, and my whole body tingles in response. "Do we *have* to go to the exhibition?"

I put a hand over his chest. "Yes. As much as I'd love to spend time with you, I also want to show off my handsome husband."

Something soft and indulgent crosses his face. "Unfortunate." But his tone is tender.

"We all must bear our crosses."

He nudges my nose with his. "Mmm. It's going to be agonizing."

"We don't have to stay long. I just need to check a few things." Once I take a look at my mom's paintings, I can start to make an inventory of the items Doris and her family stole. Then I'll decide on the best way to pursue the matter. Since it's separate from my trust, I'll ask Ares for advice. He seems unhappy that I continue to turn to Ethan for legal help, probably perceiving it as some sort of snub. I only asked Ethan because he's my lawyer, and it was easier. Plus, I didn't want to bother Ares when he was so busy at work.

"Let's finish getting you dressed for the evening," he says.

"Um... Am I missing something?"

He picks up a box with the Sebastian Jewelry logo on it from a coffee table near us, flips the lid and shows me the contents.

Inside is a set of stunning sapphire chandelier earrings, necklace and bracelet. Their shade is the most beautiful blue. The stones are huge without looking gaudy, and the diamonds embedded in between add to the brilliance of the set.

Touched by the extravagance and thoughtfulness of the gift, I look at his unreadable face. Suddenly, I'm tired of the awkwardness that's been brewing between us, and I want it to disappear. Why did I cling to doubts and angst over what I couldn't change? I always knew this was a temporary marriage and that I'd never fit the ideal woman he has in mind. Who cares that I might be the substitute for the woman he really wants? He's kind to me now. We could have a great time until he gets his promotion and I get my money. I should let it go so we can both enjoy the time we have together.

Suddenly the questions and uncertainties swirling in my head disappear, and I feel sweet warmth all over, like the time in Vegas when he caught me on the balcony, then later helped me escape my aunt. "Put them on me."

He gently rubs my earlobe, the touch sending sensual frissons down my torso to pool between my legs. He replaces one earring, then does the same with the other. I squirm to ease the ache starting in my flesh. Why am I feeling the heat when we had wild sex last night, where I orgasmed four times before I quit counting? Am I an undiagnosed nymphomaniac? Is nymphomania even a medical condition?

His warm fingers brush the back of my neck. I bite my lip to hide my reaction, but from the low, satisfied growl in his throat, he noticed the goosebumps on my arms. The sapphires are cold, creating a shockingly erotic contrast to the heat of his skin.

"I can do the bracelet," I murmur shakily, lowering my lashes to hide my eyes. My emotions are too vulnerable and exposed.

He places his index finger under my chin and tilts my face up until he can peer into my eyes. "You can, but why should you?" He loops the bracelet on my wrist, somehow managing to stroke my beating pulse point at the same time. "Perfect."

"So are you."

~

THE EXHIBITION IS HELD in the grand ballroom of the Aylster Hotel. There are more people than I expected. Some collectors, some dealers, representatives for big art galleries and connoisseurs who prefer to remain anonymous, and a few reporters covering the art scene. The crowd is similar to some of the private showings Mom took me to when I was little.

Ares and I hold hands as we casually browse what's available. Most are postmodern pieces with vivid colors, some with interesting brush technique. I move closer and squint at a delicate dappling of red, which somehow looks rough, like churning waves, if you stand a few feet back.

Ares leans in. "Like it?"

"I find it fascinating. But I'm not sure if I want to buy it."

"We can get it."

"Not right now." I do some math. Ethan messaged me after our disastrous coffee appointment that if I want to buy something, I can probably arrange for financing after the fact, although he said it isn't always ideal. The banks in Nesovia won't underwrite a deal in the millions for art because they're scared of not getting their money back. The U.S. banks won't want to bother with collateral made up of overseas assets because they're harder to assess.

The easiest way to get the money is through your husband, he advised me. He has two billion. Everyone knows it, and it'll be fast and easy, whether he pays for what you want outright or finances it.

At the time, I was hesitant. But now...

Maybe I'll ask, promising him to pay it back when my trust isn't tied up anymore. I remember him mentioning interest when he punched Rupert the second time. Yeah, I'll definitely offer him interest as well.

We make a turn. I stop abruptly at the sight of familiar impressionistic paintings. Although they appear to be abstract blends of color, if you look closely you can see a chubby, golden-haired toddler playing in a field of wild flowers, from different angles and in various lights. Her rosebud mouth is pursed in single-minded concentration in some, smiling in others.

My eyes sting, and I blink rapidly to ease the pressure. Although I knew there was a good chance Doris stole my mother's paintings, I didn't realize the impact of seeing her crime in person. I only considered how I'd use my money to get them back and punish Doris and her family. But seeing the works with my own eyes feels like a gross violation of my soul and the love I've kept in my heart for my mother.

"Shh, love, what's wrong?" Ares says.

"I just..." I sniffle. He carefully brushes his thumbs over my cheeks, and I realize I'm crying. "I haven't seen them for so long." *And they shouldn't be here! Fucking Doris. I'm going to make her pay.*

"Why the tears?"

"I just miss my mother." I smile to let him know I'm okay, even though my heart aches and grievances rake their talons across my chest. "These are Mom's works."

"All of them?" He sounds impressed, then takes another sweeping look at the paintings. Mom did impressionistic art, but unlike Monet or Renoir, many of her pieces are abstract. Not only that, there are hidden pictures underneath the surface. It takes a while to figure out how many pictures each canvas holds, and no one can ever be sure that they've discovered them all. Art critics called her the puzzle master. I call her a genius.

"Yes. Although most of them shouldn't be here," I murmur through the thick lump in my throat.

"What do you mean?" Ares frowns, then glances down at my hand and takes it in his, warming my chilled skin. Only then do I realize I'm shaking.

"They're pieces that were put into the private, climate-controlled storage. Mom never sold or gave them away, and so their ownership came to me. Except *they're here.*"

He tenses. "Doris stole them?"

"Probably. Mom gave her some for birthdays and I think once on Christmas, but the ones on the walls here weren't gifted to anybody. Ballsy, isn't it? Doris is trying to sell my mother's paintings in L.A., *knowing I'm here in the city.* It's like she's daring me to call her on it."

"The auction won't stop unless you can prove ownership."

"I know." And that's the only reason I'm not making a scene right now. Doris is likely ready to show she has the legal rights to sell these paintings. And given how weird Nesovia's laws are—with complex guardianship for unmarried women—it might even look like she's in the right. If an American court recognized her as the legal owner, it'd be very difficult for me to get the paintings back. I need to be ready before I fight.

You never fire the first shot unless you know you can win decisively.

With a soft pang in my heart, I step forward and look at a pencil sketch of a little girl making a sandcastle on the beach. I don't need to read the description attached underneath to recognize *My Love on the Beach.*

"You?" Ares gestures.

"Yup. Building a castle so I could have a kingdom of my own to rule. I was always an ambitious child." The memory brings a smile. It's one of the happiest moments of my life.

He squeezes my hand. "Not ambitious. Regal."

I laugh softly.

He grows serious. "Is it also stolen?"

"Not sure. Mom gave it to Dad on Father's Day, and I think he later gave it to Grandfather. I don't know what happened afterward, so it's possible it was legitimately sold or transferred." I pull out my phone and scan the QR code next to the sketch. An overview pops up, explaining that it's owned by Orville Black's estate. "Okay, not stolen for sure. Orville was Mom's cousin. He was one of the nicest men ever. Always carried me on his shoulders so I could feel tall." I smile fondly. "I heard he passed away three years ago, but never got to attend the funeral. His widow probably wants to cash out." Although I was little when we spent time together, I understood instinctively that Orville never had a lot of money. He was rich in friends and family. His wife might need to sell the sketch to make ends meet in her old age, and I don't begrudge her for it.

Out of all the works, this is the only one I can be certain isn't stolen. Not only that, I want it desperately. It's the simplest sketch, but all the more precious for that. It captures a spontaneous moment in my childhood when I was happy and loved unconditionally. I turn to Ares. "I want this one. No matter what it costs, I have to have it."

His eyes flare with something like surprise and heat. "Say that again."

"I want it." I keep my eyes on his. "No matter the cost." I place my hand over his chest, where his heart thumps hard against my palm. "Get it for me? Please?"

His pulse quickens, beating wildly. "I love it when you turn to me for what you want." He puts his hand at the small of my back and pulls me close, creating our own private cocoon in the midst of all the people in the exhibition hall. "You're hot when you're direct and demanding."

"Hot enough for you to give me whatever I ask for?"

"Absolutely," he says.

I look up at his darkening eyes, need for him heating my body. When he gazes at me like I'm the center of his universe, I feel like I matter. And I want him to feel the same sense of importance.

Rub him like a genie. Yuna's laughing suggestion flashes through my mind.

I surreptitiously run my hand over him. *Oh, hello.* His cock is already hard. I smile up at him like a siren. "And I love it when you show me what *you* want."

He lowers his head until his mouth is at my ear. "Jesus, do that again," he says huskily, his breath hot against the sensitive skin.

I run my hand over him, and his breathing breaks. Thrill sizzles. The knowledge that the simplest touch can make this large, powerful man shudder with need sparks excitement. And a sense of my own power.

"Yuna said something about rubbing one's husband like a genie to get what you want," I tease, then stroke him again.

"She's wrong," he says. "You're supposed to lick the genie."

I laugh softly. "We'll get arrested before I get to licking," I whisper in his ear. "Not even your brilliant legal arguments will keep us out of jail."

He chuckles, his eyes hot. "Don't worry. I'd never let you spend a single minute in jail."

34

ARES

THE DOOR LATCHES BEHIND US. The small closet near the ballroom is empty except for a couple of brooms and mops. A flick of a switch and a single bulb glows above us.

My wife kisses me, her hand on me. Now her touch is bolder, her fingers tracing my shaft through my slacks and boxers. Despite the layers of clothes, her strokes seem to brand me. The heat flows through my veins. My skin feels too tight, nerves sensitive.

She caresses the tip of my cock, then goes on her toes, wrapping her other hand around the back of my skull and pulling me down for a kiss. Her mouth is hot, her tongue eager. Electric streaks run down my spine all the way to my balls and the tip of my dick.

I rock against her hand, feeling like a horny teenager, and run my fingers through her hair as she fumbles with my belt. Lust shoots through my veins, my entire body tingling. More blood flows south in anticipation of her hands on my bare dick.

The hiss of a zipper. A whisper of silk. Rough, shallow breathing.

Her lashes cover her eyes as she bites her lower lip in concentration. *My siren.* As soon as my cock's free of confinement, she grips the shaft in her hand and gives it a gentle pump. I drop my forehead against her shoulder and groan softly. She's never done this before, and I get the feeling that if I say anything she'll vanish like a startled rabbit. I thrust into the tight sheath of her fingers, silently letting her know how much I love what she's doing to me.

She continues to move her hand, then lowers her lips until she's running her tongue over the erratic pulse point on my neck. I shudder. Who would've thought having your neck licked could be so erotic? Then she slides lower, her movement sinuous and graceful—

Her breath fans my cockhead.

My dick jerks, and I clench my jaw at how good it feels. She looks beautiful on her knees, her eyes lifting briefly to gauge my reaction. She sticks her tongue out—*oh God, yes*—and licks the tip experimentally, tasting the clear fluid. Then she runs her tongue over her lips and gives me a small, wicked smile that hits me hard, leaving me dazed.

She pulls my cock inside her mouth slowly, then hollows her cheeks. The sapphires around her throat sparkle like a priceless collar, marking my possession of her. I caress her brow tenderly.

"Good girl." Suppressing an urge to shove myself into her mouth, I move my pelvis gently. "Look at you, taking my cock. Beautiful."

She moans softly in her throat, the vibration passing through my dick. I groan in pleasure and grip her hair hard. The muscles of her jaw and neck are too tense. "Relax, baby. Breathe through your nose and set a rhythm."

She opens her mouth slightly and pulls me in deeper, moving her head along the shaft. Her pace is tentative and awkward, likely her first time—but that knowledge is heady and sexy as hell. The fact that she wants to go down on me heats my blood until I can barely see. My balls tighten, and I know I'm already ready to come.

But not yet.

"Put your hand under your dress and touch yourself, baby," I coax her.

Her mouth wrapped around my cock, she flushes as though pleasuring herself is too embarrassing. The sight is touching in its vulnerability.

I caress her temple. "Come on, baby. I'm dying to know how you're enjoying this."

Her cheeks scarlet, she lowers her hand until it vanishes under the dress.

"Are you wet? If you are, open your eyes and look at me."

She hesitates for a moment, then looks up at me, her eyes glazed with lust. Her getting wet from sucking me off is one of the hottest things I've ever experienced. The pleasure sharpens, an orgasm ready to slice through me. I can barely hold back.

"Pump yourself with your fingers. Remember how my fingers felt inside you? Do that. Make yourself feel even better."

She moans against my dick as she pumps herself. I cradle her gorgeous face. Hot bliss spreads over her, making her furrow her brow as she searches for the right spot and the perfect rhythm. Reining in the urge to go balls deep, I thrust shallowly into her mouth.

"That's right. Pump yourself and touch your breasts. Knead them, tug and pinch the nipples."

She hesitates a little.

"I can maintain the pace. Stroking your breasts will feel amazing." I feel like a devil tempting the innocent.

She drops the hand and slips it underneath the bodice. Her groans get stuck in her throat. During all this, she remembers to keep her jaw relaxed.

"Good girl. My beautiful, perfect girl."

I drive deeper into her mouth, watching closely to make sure she doesn't choke. Her movements grow more frenzied underneath the skirt. She's absolutely stunning when she's chasing her peak, her entire body trembling, and her eyebrows pinched in focus. If we didn't have to go back out to the exhibition, I'd love to come on her face, mark her as mine and mine alone.

Her breathing is shallow and labored. She's so close. Her orgasming while getting fucked in the face with my dick sends a hot ripple through me. She might be on her knees, but she's my goddess, my queen. I will lay the world at her feet.

A long groan tears from her throat as her body shakes in climax. I grip her hair hard as an orgasm crashes through me. I release into her hot mouth, sensing her tighten and relax as she swallows.

She's simply too magnificent. I pull her up gently and straighten her clothes and hair. She's completely languid now, her arms almost limp as she wraps them around me.

"Are you okay?" I ask, stroking her back soothingly.

She nods with a small smile that lances my heart, as sweet as Cupid's arrow.

I kiss her hard.

"That was amazing," she murmurs. "I can see why you like using your mouth on me." She places a soft kiss on my cheek. "We should do it again, but first, let's go back to the exhibit and see if there are any more of my mom's paintings."

35

LAREINA

Who would've thought a blowjob could be so potent?

My whole body buzzes. There was something extremely powerful and charged about controlling Ares's pleasure with my mouth. The raw taste of him was shockingly exciting. And the low groans he emitted, the praises he heaped on me and the erotic cajoling...

Was it really cajoling, though, if he was giving me license to do what I wanted to do anyway? Hmm...

I admire my husband for acting like nothing's happened, although it's been only a few moments since he was shuddering in my mouth. My knees, on the other hand, shake. If he didn't have his arm to support me, I'd probably look drunk.

Eventually, my legs grow steadier. But I still pretend I can't walk on my own. I like having Ares's heat enveloping me. And he smells good. Why shouldn't I enjoy my husband's presence?

There aren't any more of Mom's paintings. We only have one more section to check, but I'm ninety-nine percent certain her works won't be there. The auction house grouped the pieces by artist and then by theme. Still, can't hurt to check, just in case.

Right as Ares and I are about to enter the nook, we bump into Lucie and her husband. He's tall—tall enough that she can wear heels and not tower over him. A handsome man with dark hair and square jaw, he's laughing at something Lucie just said.

"Hey, Lareina!" Lucie says with a big grin. "Awesome to run into you."

"Yes! Hello!" We hug and exchange air kisses.

"This is my husband, Sebastian Lasker. Seb, this is my friend, Lareina Huxley."

"Ah. The lady who managed to get Ares to commit." He smiles. "It's late, but congrats on the wedding. And hey, nice earring and necklace set." He winks, and we all laugh.

"Yeah. My husband got them from a *great* jeweler." I wink back. "So, did you find anything you like here? I think you said you were going to buy something?"

"Yeah, that piece." She gestures at the section Ares and I haven't been to yet. "It's called *Passion Series Number Three*, and is just *so* intense. I love it. There are six pieces in the series, and Barron Sterling already bought the first two. I'm determined to get the rest."

"Good luck." I mean it sincerely, although I'm not sure it can be done. Barron Sterling is an old billionaire with too much free time and more money than God could spend. The rumor is he's so influential he has the Pope on speed dial, and he's not even Catholic.

Since Lucie spoke so highly of it, Ares and I decide to check out the painting. Lucie and Seb follow us in case I have questions about the piece.

Ares lowers his head so he can speak quietly into my ear. "You aren't planning to bid on it, are you?"

"Nope. Even if I like it, I won't. She called dibs first. Besides, I already have my sights set on *My Love on the Beach*."

The section only has four paintings, but I stop abruptly as soon as we enter, my breath caught in my throat. My temples begin to throb.

The first one is titled *Orange Dream*. A giant orange fireball is set against a green and blue background with black streaks running through it like bolts of obsidian lightning.

The second one is *Maze*: a boy and a girl are running through black and orange walls and traps.

The third is *The Wonder*—an empty Wonder Bread bag left on a rock in the mountains. The grass around it is charred, like from a campfire. Next to me, Ares inhales sharply, flexing his hand against my side. Does he like that one? It's the only one in the set with an ordinary, everyday scene. But somehow it fits with the previous two.

The final one, *Passion Series Number Three*, is layered with dozens of different shades of red, but if you look closely, you can see shapes beneath each coat.

"Wow. Just…wow." My brain is doing its best to process what I just saw and failing rather badly. Emotions are surging, but I can't even decide what they are. I feel like an empty canvas that's having buckets of paint dumped on it.

Ares is giving me a look, sensing that something is off. "What's wrong?"

I look at the description for each work. Everything's by… "*Parker Jacoby?* Are they *kidding*?" That talentless, brainless, shameless tart?

"You know her?" Ares says.

"Oh, I know her. Do you?"

He shakes his head.

Lucie steps forward. "She's an up-and-coming artist," she says helpfully. "Getting famous now. Catherine Fairchild—Barron Sterling's art curator—recognized her talent and bought the first couple of her works, which made her a rising star. Catherine has a rep for discovering diamonds in the rough. She was the first to sponsor and promote François before he became *François*."

"I see…" The more I learn, the angrier I become. Now I understand the reason Doris was so eager to have me sign the agreement. These paintings are my "trash." The ones I created to release my emotions and "reinterpret" my nightmares per the therapists she hired. Parker is a front—she's young and pretty enough. The public will love her.

But I'm sure most of the proceeds from the sale of the paintings I created never went directly to Parker. At best, it was a fifty-fifty split. Given how greedy Doris and Rupert are, Parker probably got much less, but she wouldn't object too much, since impersonating an artist is still better than getting an honest job.

Besides, who could resist the lure of fame and adulation without putting in any effort?

The Accidental Marriage

"How much were her works sold for?" I ask.

Lucie looks at her husband. "The last one fetched two million, I think? Is that right? It made a stir in the art world. Yuna was upset because she wanted it, but didn't want to bid quite that high. She collects because she likes art, but she also wants them for investment value."

"Two million dollars, just for a single painting," I murmur. "Not bad." I've created so many pieces. Sketches. Thrown them haphazardly in a storage closet because I didn't care that much about them. After all, the art experts who saw my work said I wasn't talented. But who paid for their assessments? Doris—*with my money.*

If she could get me to transfer them all to her, legally, she could be wealthy, even without my trust fund.

She's obviously decided that will be easier than trying to force me to hand over the sixty billion or force me to marry Rupert now that I already have a husband. After all, she can't hope to win a legal fight for my money against the likes of Huxley & Webber or Highsmith, Dickson and Associates.

Doris, Doris, Doris. You stole my mom's work and now mine. No way you stopped there. How much have you stolen from me?

"Are you all right?" Ares asks. Lucie and Seb are also looking at me with concern.

"Like my paintings?" comes a soft taunt.

Lucie and Seb start. Ares's head swivels and he stiffens, wrapping his arm even more protectively around me. I turn and face Parker, who's standing there with a shit-eating smile. Her arm is looped around Rupert, who's doing his best not to glare at me—he's greedier than his stepmom, and probably bitter he won't be getting the sixty billion he somehow feels he deserves.

Parker looks pretty good. She's had some professional help. Her dark brown hair is artfully curled, and she's in a sparkling black dress that shows off her surgically enhanced cleavage and long legs. Filler has done wonders for her normally thin lips, and the makeup kicks her appearance up another notch or two. Her hazel eyes look down at me as she tilts her chin arrogantly. She's practically daring me to say something. *You can't prove anything.*

"*Passion* is nice, although poorly titled," I say. *Let's see how deep she can dig her own grave.* I'd bet my ovaries that she has no clue of the secret behind the paintings she dubbed the Passion Series.

She twirls her hair around a finger. Rupert scoffs. "Too bad for you that she's the artist."

"Watch your tone, Fage. You're speaking to my wife." Ares's voice is cold enough to insta-freeze blood.

Parker clears her throat. "Have you met Catherine Fairchild?"

A brunette who was looking the other way turns to us. She's so gorgeous that she almost doesn't look real. Her face is perfectly symmetrical, and every feature on her is delicate. But what could be a porcelain-like fragility is counterbalanced by the cool steel in her eyes that says she's nobody's doll. The black cocktail dress is flattering—a potato sack would be flattering on this woman—but also businesslike. Apparently Ms. Fairchild isn't the type to mess around.

With Catherine facing us, Parker is barely noticeable. It's an unusual situation; Parker generally likes to stay away from women who make her seem like a deformed squid by comparison. Ah, the things people do for money and fame. Bet she has lots of admirers.

"How do you do? I'm Lareina Hayworth Huxley." I smile and extend a hand.

"Catherine Fairchild." Her handshake is firm, her greeting warm. The smile that she gives me has enough wattage to light up half of Orange County.

"What's your take on *Passion Series Number Three*?" I ask with genuine curiosity. After years of gaslighting and lies, I want an unbiased, professional opinion.

"I love the intensity of pain the colors represent. Although Parker named the six-piece set *Passion*, so much pain and rage just pour off the canvases, it's like you're under a waterfall of unadulterated emotion from the artist. It gives me the shivers to look at any of the pieces."

"I see." I fling a cool smile at Parker. "What would you do if you knew somebody stole them from the real artist?"

Catherine looks at me with bemusement. "That simply isn't possible. The body of work she's accumulated over the years shows growth and progression as she matured as an artist. I even saw some of the oldest sketches from when she was a child."

"How would one prove she didn't do them?" Lucie says diplomatically. Her eyes dart at me with concern.

Ares also senses the tension and shifts to stand half a step in front of me like a shield.

"As I said, impossible. Besides, I expect Parker to produce even greater works in the future," Catherine says.

Parker pales a little, but she doesn't back down, not with Rupert's arm around her. She nods. "Of course. You can look forward to it."

Shameless bitch. "Catherine, I hate to tell you this when we've just met, but you've been deceived. Parker didn't create any of these paintings. I did." My voice comes out so calm, it surprises even me.

Parker laughs incredulously, while Rupert glares at me like he'd love nothing more than to rip me into pieces right now. Ares, Lucie and Seb stare at me in shock, then Ares tightens his arm around me in a show of quiet support. Catherine scrutinizes me, her gaze serious. "If this is some sort of joke—"

"No joke," I say. "It's true."

"Can you prove it?"

"I'm not drawing something just to prove myself. I shouldn't have to do that!" Parker says swiftly.

I almost roll my eyes at her outburst. "That's ridiculous. Who has time for that? I can prove it with the Passion Series you're so proud of."

Uncertainty and doubt cast shadows over her face before she quickly shakes them off. "How?"

"Catherine clearly knows her field, because it's correct that every piece in the Passion Series is full of pain and rage. They're *my* pain and rage at the treatment I've suffered."

Ares squeezes my hand, his expression stony. He obviously recalls what I shared during dinner at his parents' house.

Parker laughs. "Oh my God, that doesn't prove anything."

"Parker's right," Catherine says quietly.

"Doesn't prove anything *yet*. But every painting in the series has a little secret, something only the creator would know." I glance at Parker, then step closer to the canvas. "Do you know what it is?"

She scoffs. "Stop making stuff up. You were always jealous of me, and it's ridiculous you're taking it so far as to claim these paintings are yours!" Her voice goes almost shrill toward the end.

Catherine frowns. She probably doesn't want to believe she's been supporting an imposter. A couple of onlookers have gathered, shooting skeptical glances at me.

I didn't expect people to believe me blindly, but it's a little disappointing that they aren't even open to listening to the truth.

"My wife is not a liar."

Ares's firm declaration surprises me. I look at him in shock.

"I'll personally vouch for her," he adds, and warmth swirls in my heart.

The disappointment from just moments ago dissipates. With him on my side, the situation doesn't seem so daunting. Besides, who cares if the others don't believe me now? I can always prove I'm the true artist later.

"I believe her, too," Lucie says. "She has no reason to lie."

Sebastian looks at his wife, then coolly settles his eyes on Parker. I wouldn't want to be on the receiving end of that look.

My heart grows impossibly light as I realize I actually have a team behind me. My confidence soars. *So this is how it feels to belong.*

Catherine looks at Ares, Lucie and Seb for a while, clearly conflicted, then turns to me. "Okay. If you believe there's a way to authenticate the true creator, why don't you email it to me? I'll check it out."

"No need for email." I pull out a small pen from my clutch and jot down the painting's secret on my palm, then show it to her. She furrows her brow. "Is this true?"

I nod. "Do you think I'd lie about something that could be disproven so easily?"

"I don't know you. But...no. It would be a particularly stupid move." She turns to Parker. "Do you have anything to say?"

Parker's smile is stiff, but she doesn't lose her composure. "There's no secret, Catherine. How your heart resonates is what matters. My paintings are all about how you feel when you look at them. If you're happy, then that's what the work is about. If it makes you sad, then that's the theme. I don't have any formal art training. I just rely on instinct and emotion. Viewers should let go of any preconceived notions and enjoy the work the way it's presented, rather than trying to imbue it with a meaning that isn't there. Blue curtains in a story don't mean the character is depressed or the author was subtly commenting on her mood. The curtains are just blue, and how you feel is what's important."

"Okay." Catherine nods.

"I believe my girlfriend. I've seen her working on these with my own eyes," Rupert adds.

Catherine shoots him a brief glance, then texts something on her phone for a minute. We spend the next half-hour discussing art before an out-of-breath hotel staff member shows up with a flashlight. "Here you are, Ms. Fairchild."

"Thank you." She takes it and raises her voice. "Everyone, please stay calm. We're going to turn off the lights for a few minutes."

The hotel shuts off the lights in our section of the ballroom. I move closer to Ares in the sudden darkness.

Catherine clicks on the flashlight. Black light is cast over the canvas, sections of it glowing a bright bluish color, stains shaped like splatters and forming a V.

Ares inhales, and Parker lets out a sharp cry. Rupert curses. The light in Catherine's hand trembles. Her phone buzzes, and she glances at it, then gasps.

"Do you believe me now?" I ask.

"Oh my God. Turn the lights back on."

I blink a few times as bright light floods the exhibition hall again. Catherine's complexion is chalky, except for the bright red of her cheeks.

Parker points at me, her finger trembling. "You threw some kind of fluid on it behind people's backs, didn't you? Why else would you tell Catherine to test it with black light? You've always hated me, but defacing my work like this is too much! I'll sue!"

"This isn't the only one that glowed in the dark." Catherine's voice is terribly cold. "I had my assistant at Barron's gallery check. *Passion Series Number One* and *Number Two* also glowed. Trust me, since the works have joined Barron Sterling's collection, nobody's had an opportunity to touch them or alter them in any way."

The color drains from Parker's face. "Fuck," Rupert mutters.

Ares looks at me curiously. He's probably wondering the exact nature of the secret.

"You have lied to me, stolen from the real artist and defrauded Barron Sterling," Catherine says. "Artworks worth millions."

"Catherine, no! Don't you trust me?"

"Trust? How when you've lied and refused to admit to it? If you were the true artist, the black-light reveal would have been the first thing you told me."

"Art theft is a federal crime," Ares says helpfully. "Along with transporting stolen artwork and defrauding the public. And unfortunately for you, the statute of limitations hasn't run out. Enjoy your time in the federal penitentiary."

I nod with satisfaction. That doesn't seem like a terrible outcome for the duo, especially since I'm not sure if I'll be able to get them for being part of the conspiracy to poison me.

"It wasn't me! I didn't want to do it!" Parker shrieks, then points at Rupert. "It's him and his stepmom and dad! They said nobody would notice, and we'd all get rich! It's just trash." She gestures wildly at my paintings. "I just picked them up and sold them. Like garage sale! It's no different."

A bitter mixture of victory, sadness and contempt drips through me. It's such karmic justice, albeit ugly. Parker is going to drag everyone down with her. Keeping her mouth shut has never been a strong point.

"You stupid bitch!" A loud smack of flesh hitting flesh cracks the room.

Parker cradles her cheek and stares at Rupert in disbelief. Everyone else does too, except me. I know he's always had a problem controlling his temper—it's part of his entitled personality. Everyone should do what he says or else suffer the consequences. He gets away with it in Nesovia, using my money as a shield. But here in America? He picked the wrong stage for his outburst.

Less than two minutes later, hotel security shows up along with a couple of uniformed police officers. Parker points at Rupert. "He hit me! Arrest him for assault!"

Ares leans forward. "Battery," he says, sotto voce.

Catherine speaks in a low voice with one of the officers. He nods, and they grab Parker and Rupert and cuff them.

"Why are you arresting me?" Rupert says. "I didn't do anything! She's the one who stole from my cousin. I had no idea the paintings weren't—"

"I thought you saw her paint them." I tilt my chin at the painting hanging in front of us.

He turns red and shoots me a murderous gaze. I stick my tongue out. The gesture is immature, but I've always wanted to do it to him. Just to see if maybe a vein will pop. One throbs visibly on his forehead, but unfortunately, I don't think it's going to burst.

"By the way, officers," I call out with a sweet smile. "Don't forget to nab Doris and Vernon Fage. They're deeply involved in the whole scheme."

"You have no proof!" Rupert shouts.

"Sure I do. They tried to get me to sign a transfer agreement involving my artwork." I turn to the police. "If you need more information, you can always contact my lawyer, Ethan Beckman, at Highsmith, Dickson and Associates. He has a copy of the agreement and a *lot* of information to share with you."

36

ARES

THE EXHIBITION ENDS NOT ONLY with arrests, but with the organizers announcing that the auction will be delayed in order to re-evaluate and reassess every piece. The fraud perpetrated by Parker Jacoby and Rupert Fage and his parents leaves many people shaken. Catherine in particular looks to be in a kind of shock, then asks to speak to Lareina later.

I regard my wife with surprise, respect and admiration. When she spoke of painting, she made it sound like she dabbled. She downplayed it every time she talked about what she'd done, like her talents weren't particularly remarkable. Does she have any idea what a big deal it is to be recognized by someone like Catherine Fairchild? Or have your work end up in Barron Sterling's collection? Even I've heard of the man's impressive private galleries.

The most amazing part is how calm and collected she was during the entire time Parker and Rupert tried to provoke her and call her a liar. My wife must have nerves of steel.

You just realized that now? a small voice in my head mocks. You didn't realize that when she free-climbed the façade of your hotel seventeen stories up in a wedding dress?

By the time we arrive home and change into more comfortable clothes to wind down for the evening, I get a text from one of the contacts within the police department I pinged earlier to get an update about the case.

—Francisco: Nabbed Doris and Vernon Fage. Not only did they commit international and federal crimes, they also broke a bunch of state and local laws. The DA is happy because she needs a big, juicy case guaranteed to convict.

What a perfect timing. The woman wants a win to tout during her re-election campaign. "They arrested Doris and Vernon. They're going to jail."

"Perfect. Thanks for letting me know." Lareina smiles as she settles on the bed.

I lie next to her. "So. Now that it's been resolved to your satisfaction, can you let me know the secret?"

She frowns. "Secret?"

"The one you shared with Catherine."

"Oh. That?" An awkward clearing of her throat. "Okay, this might sound a bit morbid and weird, but keep in mind I painted the so-called Passion Series when I was sixteen or seventeen or something. Teenage angst, basically." She looks down at her fingers.

"Okay." I nod, since she looks unbelievably nervous, but it's touching that she cares so much about my reaction. Her vulnerability makes me want to take up a shield and protect her, so nobody can ever hurt her.

"If you put all six paintings in order and use the black light, you can see the hidden message. S-A-V-E-M-E. *Save me.* I used my own blood to write it because it seemed, I don't know...more dramatic that way."

I stare at her. She nibbles on her lower lip with embarrassment, but I'm horrified she had to experience that. How desperate she must've been. How confused and hurt and upset. No wonder she said the paintings are about pain and rage. The fact that she's overcome her past makes her the most amazing woman ever.

She scratches the tip of her nose. "It took a while to complete the letter for each canvas because it really hurts to stab your fingertip enough to bleed like that. But eventually, I realized I had the wrong idea. Nobody was going to come to save me. I had to save myself."

Her soft, self-deprecating words cut like glass shards. I hug her tightly, hoping she can feel how hard my heart beats for her. I wish I could go back in time and shield her from her God-awful aunt and the rest. "How did you endure it for so long without going crazy?"

"Because I knew it wouldn't last forever. I made plans, thought of ways to make my escape. And it was my luck and blessing that I found you along the way. Don't get me wrong, I'm not going to forgive any of them for what they've done, but I'm not going to live the rest of my life angry and resentful either. I'm still young and pretty! And soon I'm going to be rich, especially with Doris out of the way. With no one to contest my petition to take over my trust, why *shouldn't* I live happily ever after?"

I laugh at her exuberance.

"My mom and dad would want me to be happy. So would my grandfather—and everyone else who ever loved me." She grows quieter. "I want to live happily ever after for them."

"You will."

She smiles and brushes her fingertips over my cheek. "Thank you." Then she blinks like she's just remembered something. "By the way, did you get to review and sign our super-late prenup from Ethan?"

"He brought it to me, but I haven't had a chance to review it."

"You want to take a look? You can ask me if you have any questions."

"I don't feel like getting up."

"Oh, come on. You're such a baby," she teases.

"Mmm... Can a baby do this?" I lift her nightshirt and kiss the side of her waist.

She jolts and shrieks with laughter. "Stop! I'm ticklish there!"

"Never!" I kiss the spot again.

She tries frantically to push me away, her small arms straining cutely against the top of my head. "Come on! I have it on my—agh!—tablet, so you can read it *without leaving the bed*!"

"Oh, all right." I reluctantly push away from her so she can grab the tablet. I shouldn't have given her the black AmEx to buy stuff. Who brings work to their bed?

She taps a few times and hands it to me. Glumly, I start to read, all the while mentally cursing. That fucking Beckman. He could've given it to her next week.

The agreement is fairly standard. Nothing egregious. Beckman probably whined that she should be more ruthless about taking my property. After all, he thinks I'm just a spoiled trust-fund baby.

Then I get to the section about her assets.

What the—?

The trust she's fighting for is worth *sixty-two billion*? It isn't a typo or math error. I add up everything in my head just to be sure. Then there's a matter of the real estate, antiques and works of art that come with her family's estate. The estimated value of those dumps another billion or so onto the total.

I stop reading and just stare. I've seen big numbers before, helping clients move hundreds of billions of dollars in transactions and deals. But to think...

When Lareina said her aunt wanted her money... No wonder they were willing to poison her to get it. I should've asked about the extent of her inheritance sooner and arranged for bodyguards. I didn't think of it because Doris, Rupert and Vernon had been quiet since our marriage. But if they hadn't been plotting to steal Lareina's paintings instead, things could've gotten ugly.

Suddenly the memories of times I thought Lareina might be after my money fleet through my head. *Ugh. Talk about embarrassing.* I want to kick the blanket, but thankfully I've never said it out loud. It'll just be my secret shame.

I shake my head. "I've never thought I'd say this, but I feel kind of... poor."

"What? Why?"

"Uh, sixty-two billion...?"

"Yeah, the trust grew a bit. Surprise!" She shrugs with an awkward smile. "Does it matter that I have more money than you?" She peers at me earnestly.

I smother the laughter bubbling in my throat. "Does it matter that I have less money than you?"

"No!"

"There's your answer. You'll always just be Lareina to me."

"Aww." She sighs softly, resting her cheek over my heart and looking into my eyes. "And you'll always be Ares to me. My knight."

37

ARES

I NUDGE MY WIFE, who's resting on her side, then nuzzle her neck. She raises her shoulder, then pulls the sheet all the way to the base of her skull.

"Come on, babe."

"Don't you *come on, babe* me," she says, her words sluggish with sleep. "I'm tired."

"We gotta celebrate your victory."

"Which we did last night. Twice. And again just an hour ago."

"Well, yeah. But I think it deserves at least one more encore."

"No." She buries her face in the pillow. "Besides, I want to do something other than just thrash around in bed all day, as fun as that sounds."

"Like what?"

"I want to go to an amusement park."

"You... What?"

"An amusement park. You know, a place with a haunted house and roller coasters and stuff."

"I know what it is. Why?" Amusement parks are my idea of a nightmare. Strapped to a machine that doesn't give a shit about gravity that you can't control and hope for the best. No thanks. My aversion grew stronger after the firm took on a massive liability suit against one because five people died from willful negligence.

"Because I've always wanted to go and ride a roller coaster when I was finally completely free from Doris. Please?"

When she flutters her eyes like that, I can't say no. "Okay."

"Awesome. You're the best." All of a sudden full of energy, she throws the sheets back and hops out of bed. Perhaps she feels like a brand-new person after her shitty aunt and her family went to jail. Along with that fraudster Parker Jacoby. I make a mental note to see if I can acquire *The Girl on the Beach* somehow. Which then leads me to remember...

"Hold on a sec. Aren't we forgetting something?"

She stops at the door to the bathroom. "What?"

"You have to rub me like a genie to get your wish."

She laughs. "Afterward! I promise!"

The infectious sound makes me laugh too. We get ready, and I drive us to Magic Mountain, since she specifically mentioned roller coasters.

The noise, crowd and the long wait times make me realize why in the movies rich guys rent out the park for the whole day. I'm already not a fan, and having so many people around with the cacophony everywhere gives me a headache. The only reason I don't turn around and leave is the joy on my wife's face.

She stares up at the crazy roller coasters and tugs at my sleeve. "Come on! Let's ride that one!"

"Um." I press my lips as shrieks pierce the air with the massive dip of the machine. "You sure?"

"Of course! We didn't come here just to *watch*. Let's go!"

I look at the machine dubiously. Intellectually I understand it's probably safe enough. The liability case was an exception, not the norm. But I hate the lack of control. The inability to jump and save myself and my wife if something goes wrong because we're so high in the air.

Come on. You can do this for her.

The safety mechanism pins us to our seats. I hold Lareina's hand. It's surprisingly dry and warm, while mine is embarrassingly clammy. She smiles at me. "You can squeeze your eyes shut and scream. I won't tell anybody," she whispers.

"No. I'd never," I scoff.

She just nods with a big grin.

The roller coaster begins to move. Slowly at first, to lure the passengers into complacency. Then with more speed, along with maddening twists and turns that make me think my brain's about to fly from my skull. I hate the way it climbs high, then drops like the track just ended—even though in my head, I know it didn't. My heart pumps like I've run three marathons.

I peek at Lareina. She has her eyes squeezed shut, but she's grinning. Then, during the final dip, she covers her face. I pull her close. She must be scared. Even though my stomach is dropping just like the ride, I try to lend her my strength.

Something damp soaks my shirt. I pull away and see tears streaking her face. I hold her tight, feeling like a failed husband for exposing her to something scary like this. Even though she said she wanted to do it, I should've said no for her sake.

When the ride stops, I manage to climb out fast despite the shakiness of my limbs, then help Lareina out. She collapses into my arms, then buries her face in my chest.

"Hey, it's fine," I murmur, stroking her hair soothingly. "I got you."

I don't know how long we stand there. But from the way her shoulders shake, she's obviously overcome with strong emotion, although she isn't shedding any more tears.

Wordlessly I pick her up and carry her away from the ride. She loops her arms around my neck, then lets out a sigh. "Thank you."

"For what?"

"For coming here with me. The last time I went to an amusement park was when I was little, with my parents. I remember being upset because I missed out on so many rides—I was either too young or too small. I think I spent most of my time pouting."

I picture her as a little kid with her mouth pursed and sticking out. "You must've been adorable."

She laughs. "I doubt my parents thought that. But I promised myself that we'd have another family outing at an amusement park when I was big enough to ride everything. It's just that I didn't get to until now."

She smiles at me, her eyes glowing softly. "I wasn't free of Doris, but more importantly, I was alone, without a family of my own."

Her softly spoken confession clenches my heart. *Family.* The word sounds unbearably sweet. I look at the woman who's survived so much. "I'll always be your family. Always," I vow.

The smile she gives me is brilliant, but tinged with sadness. Perhaps she's thinking about her parents. It breaks my heart that she didn't grow up with their love.

I give a determined stare at one of the bigger and crazier roller coasters, then squeeze my wife. "The day's still young. We'll ride every damn coaster in the park."

38

LAREINA

THE SCANDALS SURROUNDING Parker Jacoby go viral. I guess you can't keep anything hidden if it involves defrauding major art collectors.

Parker, Rupert, Doris and Vernon look like hell in their mugshots. Parker apparently cried before her photo was taken, and Rupert glares at the camera like an enraged ax murderer. Doris's mouth is tight—she's probably angry she got caught—and Vernon, well, he is sheer venom. But despite always acting innocent, he's the worst of the bunch. He hides in the background, not doing anything overt, but always hinting and egging others on to do things in order to benefit himself.

I have the misfortune of having my name and picture splashed across the tabloids, too. Did these reporters *have* to pick my least flattering side? From the worst angle possible? My face resembles ghostly, pudgy dough, with huge, smoky eyes that make me appear manic. If I didn't know it was my own picture, I'd think the woman looks like a serial killer.

Reporters camp outside the gates. More try to contact Ares and Huxley & Webber to get in touch with me. "Aunt Jeremiah is so annoyed she's grumbling about getting restraining orders," Ares says with a smirk over dinner.

"Can she? If she could, I'd like to have her get me one for the those 'journalists' who keep following me everywhere."

"I doubt it. But she might surprise us. She's very good at bending the law to her will. If there's a loophole, she'll find it."

"Why won't they leave me alone?" I whine. I'm not used to this kind of scrutiny.

"You're the hottest story right now," Ares says. "You're young, beautiful and a mysterious heiress from another country. Also the only child of the renowned Susan Winters, and you had your artwork stolen by relatives over the years, only to finally be discovered by the world for the truly amazing artist that you are. Why wouldn't they love you? I'm a little surprised more of the vultures haven't shown up, to be honest. They're obsessed."

I stir my chicken Caeser salad, flushing at the way he looks at me with adoration. Doesn't he know the only one whose love I want is him? I cradle my chin in my hand and gaze at his gorgeous face—the stunning blue of his glowing eyes and the sensual line of his smile. Is *he* enamored of me, too? Does *he* feel obsessed? It's impossible to tell if he's including himself or not.

Which is the problem. He hasn't told me how *he* feels. Our marriage is still set to expire soon. Wouldn't he have said something if he wanted us to be together?

The thought ripples through my heart, and I forcibly push it away. I'm not going to dwell on it and turn what remains of our time unpleasant. "The media's interest is the most annoying thing *ever*, but I also feel like it could be an opportunity."

His expression says, *That's my girl*. "What are you thinking?"

"I can give an exclusive interview and talk not only about the art theft but about how Nesovia's archaic laws made it possible for my relatives to take advantage of me. The country always promises to make changes, but it never does. However, they are *very* conscious of their image as a refined first-world country, so some international public shame might do the trick. And even if it doesn't..." I shrug. "Saying my piece about those crotchety old lawmakers will be worth it."

"If you need help getting ready, I'm here for you," Ares says. "And everyone at Huxley & Webber is at your disposal."

"Thank you." I smile. "I'll definitely take advantage."

I prep my statements and clarify my goals. Ares's cousin Hux, who's in advertising and a genius with creating the perfect public persona and PR campaigns, advises me to use a podcaster he's picked out because she has the best reputation, reach and audience for what I want. The woman used to be an investigative reporter, then a DA in a county in Connecticut.

The day of the podcast, she asks a lot of great follow-up questions to draw out aspects that I hadn't considered. What I love most about her is that she didn't come to the interview trying to spin a narrative or use me as some kind of symbol for her cause. She's sympathetic, but fair, treats me like a person, not a victim to be coddled or an artist whose talent people should blindly admire.

By the time I'm done with the ninety-minute talk, I'm worn out. I haven't talked much about my past before, not publicly, anyway. I never thought people would believe it—it's inconceivable to all that my relatives would try to poison me, gaslight me and force a marriage on me... Isn't it? Part of me always feared that people would not only not believe me, but actually turn their backs on me. The idea was terrifying, and always left me feeling too vulnerable to say much.

But the result is immediate and worth every bit of my discomfort.

There is immediate public outrage and quick clarifications by some of the lawmakers in Nesovia, especially those who have pretended to care about women's rights and equality. And the scrutiny makes it harder for Doris and the others to escape the hammer of justice. I hope they get crushed like a nail made of balsa wood.

Ares comes home early and holds me the day the interview goes live. "I listened to the whole thing. I hate it that you had to suffer alone. I hate it that I wasn't able to be there for you."

"You didn't know. We hadn't even met back then." I lay my head on his shoulder, content to be with him, his comforting body heat seeping into my bones. "Besides, all that led me to you. And I'm not going to live my life thinking about what could've been."

"Lareina." He presses kisses over my eyes. Each touch is so tender, like he cares deeply about me. "I don't know how you can sound so calm."

"Maybe because I'm at peace with you?" I smile. "I'm fine. Really." I wrap my arms around his waist, hoping the close contact will give him the same ease and peace I'm feeling.

But that night he has a dream, and he calls for Queen. It's always the same. "Queen. Where are you? Don't leave me."

I turn over and face him in the dark. Which one is his real feeling? The sweetness he shows while he's awake that makes me think he might love me...or the urgent calling of that name in his sleep?

When he's awake is what counts, the part of me that wants to be loved by him insists. But when he calls for Queen, it's hard to listen to that voice.

~

MY BROTHERS-IN-LAW's texts arrive the next day.

—Bryce: You know you should've told us about all that shit.

—Josh: The family always comes first. Pietas et unitas. You're one of us now.

—Me: Thank you, but I honestly didn't realize they were stealing my paintings. I thought the poisoning was the worst thing they'd done.

—Bryce: I know a guy who knows a guy.

—Josh: Stop it. You don't know anybody.

—Bryce: He's just jealous of my connections. But honestly, nobody messes with one of us and get away with it. Ares is your husband, don't forget. You have the entire Huxley clan behind you.

More buzzes. This time from the elders of the family—The Fogeys, as Ares calls them.

—Prescott: I'm always on your side, my dear. We should have dinner later this month when we aren't swamped.

—Akiko: I saw the interview. I'm so sorry. I couldn't stop crying. Remember—you're my daughter too. Next time someone hurts you, you come to me.

—Catalina: Simply unconscionable. The entire might of Huxley & Webber is behind you. My connections are at your disposal. I'm going to do everything in my power, call in favors, to ensure they get the maximum sentences.

—Jeremiah: Why don't we have the death penalty in our beautiful state anymore? It's heartbreaking.

A bittersweet warmth unfurls in my heart. Their acceptance is absolute. As far as they're concerned, I'm their family in every sense of the word. Of course, they don't realize I'm not the one Ares really wants by his side. I force a small smile, because I'd rather smile than cry when so many people are behind me. I'm going to miss this when I leave.

Unlike my uber-busy in-laws, Lucie and Yuna manage to get past the reporters and sneak through the gates. They just hug me for a moment without a word.

"You're one of the strongest people I know," Yuna says finally. Her voice is choked up, but she doesn't shed tears.

I squeeze her again.

"I'm so sorry you had to go through that alone. But don't forget you have us now," Lucie vows.

"Appalling. Absolutely appalling." Yuna shakes her head.

"Don't worry, they're going to pay," I say.

"Oh my gosh, I'm so sorry." Lucie smacks her forehead. "Why are we making *you* console *us*?"

"You're not. You're showing me you care, and I'm showing you I appreciate it." I put a hand on her shoulder and pull her close. "Do you know I never had friends I could talk to? And now here I am, with not just one but *two* amazing friends who rush to see if I'm okay?"

We lunch and chat, mostly about my life back home, my plans for the future. I avoid talking about my marriage, but ask about their families and who they recommend to manage my money and so on. After all, I'm going to need advisors of my own soon.

Ethan calls to let me know that the process of claiming my trust will take much less time than anticipated. Doris can't mess it up by filing motion after motion while she's in jail in America when she needs every bit of money and mental energy to defend herself and her family. She's probably going to throw Parker under the bus, but the latter won't go quietly. She's easily crazy and angry enough to go scorched earth on everyone.

"Even the probate in Nesovia will be shortened. There's so much interest and speculation that even if the court justifiably delays the

The Accidental Marriage

process, it'll look really bad. Those people are way too image-conscious. Why don't they always do the right thing?" I can hear the head shake in Ethan's voice.

"So it doesn't matter if I'm married or not? Or reach thirty or not?"

"Doesn't look like it. Technically you don't have to maintain your marital status until you get control of your trust, especially if there's no one challenging it, like your aunt. And Ares can't touch anything, since he signed the prenuptial agreement. I expect it to take maybe two, maybe three more months? Then you'll be fully in charge."

"Thanks. That's good to know." My voice is slightly hollow. Once Ares gets his promotion, we really have no reason to stay married. "Hey, when do most law firms announce promotions and stuff?"

If Ethan's surprised by the question, he hides it well. "Our firm announces publicly in the next two weeks, before the month is over. Huxley & Webber do, too. Don't know about other firms."

"You sure about Huxley & Webber?"

"Oh yeah. Rivals," he says. "We all know about each other so we can rub it in each others' faces."

"Oh. That's...soon." I thought—I was *hoping*—it wasn't for another month or two...or a couple of years. I clear my throat. "Just in case... Um. Can you prepare for a divorce?"

This time an edge of surprise comes through. "I'm sorry?"

"It's *just in case*. Ares and I...might not have a reason to stay married anymore." He might not become a partner, even though he seemed fairly certain all he needed was a respectful wife. I bite my lip, hating myself for wishing even for a second he wouldn't get promoted. Just what kind of shitty person am I? I got what I wanted when I married Ares. I should want him to get everything *he* wants.

"Uh... Yeah. Of course. But maybe you should wait until you're sure about it first. It's not a cheap process. If you still want to proceed, I can start, though. Anyway, take a few days to think about it."

We hang up, but my phone rings again soon. Wondering if Ethan forgot something, I answer it without checking the screen.

"Not bad, my dear," comes Zoe's voice, tinged with a hint of reluctant respect. "You're much more resourceful than I expected."

I stiffen. "A girl learns fast when she never had much to work with." *Thanks to people who turned a blind eye, like you.*

"They aren't going to pay for poisoning you, though. And how about their supplier? It's someone fairly close to you. And me, of course."

Is she implying Harvey was Doris's poison dealer? And does she think I'll believe her? A woman who drugs her son and leaves him in a forest alone is just as capable as Harvey of handing out poison for the right price. Thank God Ares has a wonderful stepmother in Akiko, and his father is sane. "I honestly don't care, Zoe."

"Don't you want to know about your parents' deaths?"

The air in my lungs freezes. I take a moment to gather myself. I can't afford to show any cracks to Zoe. "The food poisoning?" Despite my resolve, my voice is shaky.

"Yes. Don't you want to know if it was just bad luck…or something more sinister?" she says, drawing out each syllable.

My first gut reaction is *yes*. Unequivocally yes. I'd love to know if anybody played a hand in taking my family away from me. Then I'd love to make them pay.

And yet…

I clench the phone until my knuckles whiten. Zoe expects me to jump at this chance, especially when I'm riding high after dispatching Doris and her family.

Zoe's doing this because it benefits her. She wants to dangle this in front of me and manipulate me. She wouldn't have bothered otherwise, just like she looked the other way while Doris and her family abused me.

Loathing and resentment surge inside. I draw in air slowly to calm the churning emotions. As much as I'd love to know the truth, I'm never going to give Zoe any power over me. Mom and Dad aren't coming back. The only one with the motive to hurt them is Doris, and she's already sitting in jail, awaiting trial. Even if she doesn't get sentenced for poisoning my parents—assuming she actually did that—she'll still rot in prison. "It doesn't change the past," I say coldly.

"Well, aren't you the Machiavellian one? I like that about you. Sentimentality is *so* cheap."

"Too bad, because I don't like anything about you. By the way, what

I said applies to you too. You can call and bug me all you want, but you'll never have Ares's respect and love again. He despises you."

A sharp inhale, followed by a low hiss, full of venomous fury. If we were facing each other in person, she'd probably slap me. "Don't get too cocky," she sneers. "Do you honestly believe I have no reach outside of Nesovia? Do you think just because you're in America, you're untouchable?"

"Why not?"

"Don't be so complacent, my child. In my experience, the most unexpected blows come just when you think you're at your happiest."

39

ARES

"Hey, there he is! The brand-new junior partner!" Barry says with a big grin as we pass each other in the office.

A huge grin splits my face, and I high-five him on my way toward the break room to grab another coffee. "Thanks, man."

The firm has officially announced who's getting promoted and made the list public. It's a longstanding tradition at Huxley & Webber. If you can't stand open competition where everyone knows where you rank, this firm isn't the right place for you.

Some say the firm should be renamed Sink or Swim, either jokingly or dejectedly. Either way, seeing my name on the list of associates who made junior partner is deeply satisfying. I've worked hard at my career to get to where I am. Although my responsibilities have shifted from initial associate-grind to actually acquiring new clients and managing existing client relationships, I have no doubt I'll be successful. I *am* Ares fucking Huxley.

"Congratulations, Ares," says Aunt Jeremiah, who pours black coffee into her blood-red Huxley & Webber mug, then raises it. "You made it."

"Thank you."

"I wasn't sure about your wife at first, but I've decided I like her. She exerts a stabilizing influence on you, which is excellent. Every man needs someone like her."

I grin at the approval in her voice. It isn't always easy to get a passing grade from Aunt Jeremiah. The woman embodies excellence in almost every aspect of her life, and perfection in the courtroom—and demands the same from those around her. "She's amazing."

"She'll be even more amazing once she ditches Highstrung, Dickhead and Associates." She narrows her eyes. "Tell her I said so."

I laugh. "I will."

I already signed the prenup agreement, and since then I haven't had any contact with Ethan "Pain-in-the-Ass" Beckman. Hopefully Lareina has let him go. She doesn't need him, not when she has me.

The interoffice messenger beeps.

–Bryce: Congrats, bro. You coming to happy hour to celebrate?

–Me: Thanks. I'd love to, but I'm heading home early to celebrate with my wife.

–Bryce: Nice. A private celebration!

–Me: But next time for sure.

I look at the message thread with a mix of amusement and confusion. If the promotion had happened before marrying Lareina, I would've definitely gone to happy hour. After all, it's a great opportunity to network and see what's going on. Doing good work and billing a lot are important, but so is knowing what's happening around me and in legal circles.

But the person I want to share this joy with—on the same day I received the good news—isn't at the firm. It's Lareina. My wife.

I finish work half an hour early and head home. On the way, I pick up some gourmet smoked venison ham and cheese. They'll go well with the Pétrus 2018 I've been saving for this occasion.

The moment I open the door, a heady aroma of basil and tomato sauce hits me. The latest song by a popular band, Axelrod, blasts from the Bluetooth speakers in the kitchen.

I stop in the entrance and just watch my wife. Her hair's tied into a messy knot, her shirt has splatters of paint on the left shoulder—she probably forgot to change after spending hours in her studio—and drawstring pants cling to her ass in just the right way. Her face bare, with bright eyes and full lips, she looks just as beautiful as she did when she got all dolled up for the exhibition.

I want to tell her to forget the dinner and ravish her on the spot. At the same time, I feel bad about wasting her effort. Besides, today might be a significant day for her, too. Like maybe she's finally getting her hands on her money.

She taps the edge of the boiling pot of water, staring at the phone screen. "When is he going to get here? It's been forever since Bryce said he left the office."

"Who are you waiting for?" I ask with a laugh.

She starts, then leaps at me with a big smile. I embrace her, enjoying the soft, feminine feel of her in my arms.

"What a welcome," I say with a laugh. "What's the occasion?"

She widens her eyes. "You're asking *me*?"

I nod.

A beat of hesitation. "Were you planning to hide your promotion from me?"

"What?"

"I'm doing homemade pasta from scratch to celebrate. My cooking is still only so-so, but I wanted to do something nice for you. I didn't add any salt, though. So you'll want to sprinkle some on it to get the full flavor."

"Did Bryce tell you about the promotion?" It's obvious she's been in touch with my brother.

"Yes. But he wasn't the only one. I think everyone wanted me to give you a surprise celebration." She smiles brilliantly. "I'm so happy for you. I know you've been working really hard for this."

"I have, and thank you. I couldn't have done it without you."

For a second, her eyes seem to dim, which surprises me. But before I can ask what's bothering her, she's back to beaming so brightly that I wonder if I actually saw anything.

"I'm glad," she says, placing a kiss on my cheek.

Guess it was just a trick of the light. "Is there anything I can do to help?" I ask, shrugging out of my jacket and rolling up my shirt sleeves.

Her gaze drops to my forearms. "I feel like you're hinting at something."

I cock an eyebrow. "Got a forearm fetish?"

"Of course. When a man rolls up his sleeves... Mmm." She does a chef's kiss. "Those coconuts were great before, but what made them better was the way you cut them open. I could see the muscles..." She fans herself while fluttering her eyes.

"Look all you want." I flex my forearm muscles.

"Damn." She bites her lip. "I'm trying to cook here. But no matter how sexy you'd look stirring the sauce, I can't have you cooking your own celebration meal."

"You can have me do whatever you want." I put my hands on either side of her against the counter and cage her. She smells so good—all lemony, with a hint of the herbs she's been using to cook. I bury my face in her neck and nibble a little. She lets out a soft, infinitely erotic gasp.

I'm hard and ready. I press against her, letting her feel how much I want her.

"How hungry are you?" I ask against her ear.

"Not...that much. You?" she says shakily.

"I can wait."

"Well." Her gaze darts to the bubbling sauce and boiling water on the stove. "I guess I can always reheat it." She cuts the gas.

"I love the way you think."

I kiss her. I've been thinking about this all day. Hell, I think about kissing her all the time. Don't need a reason. I breathe and I want to kiss her, hold her and pamper her. It's the strangest thing.

Maybe it's fate. It's not like me to be so sentimental, but I don't know what else it could be when she literally fell into my arms in her wedding gown. She fuses her mouth to mine, her tongue aggressive. Her enthusiasm is the most potent aphrodisiac. I pull her close and slip my hand underneath her shirt, palm her taut skin, reveling in the supple warmth. When I move higher and cup her bare breast, I groan. If I'd known she was braless when I walked in, I might've just tossed her over my shoulder before we could even exchange greetings.

I set her on the edge of the counter and push the shirt up. Her breasts never fail to catch my attention, so plump and soft, tipped with gorgeous, rosy points. Part of me wants to go slow and drag it out, but another part of me wants it fast and furious. She plunges her fingers into my hair, pulls me to her chest. I close my mouth around the nipple. Her cries of pleasure are better than the finest whiskey, hot and potent. I knead the other breast, enjoying the pleasant weight in my palm. Her breathing grows shallow, and a moan tears from her slender throat where her pulse flutters wildly. Lust turns monstrous at her openly unabashed desire.

"Please," she says, her eyes narrowed and glittering with need. "I want you right now. I'm so wet." She takes my hand and leads it beneath her pants.

Her impatience fuels mine. Overheated blood pumps through me. The fire in my veins burn away my control. I kiss her with unrestrained greed, stroke her, caress her and rub her, making her thrash and beg and rock against me.

Her pants and underwear fall to the floor. She undoes just enough of my slacks to grip my naked dick and bring it to her pussy.

"Wait, no condom."

"So pull out and mark me." She throws out the answer carelessly before gliding her slick flesh over mine.

I clench my teeth, but it can't contain the groan when she positions the opening of her pussy against the tip of my cockhead. My vision blurs red, and every tendon in my neck and shoulders stand. A tiny sliver of sanity says pulling out isn't the most reliable method. That's how Hux's half-brother got his wife pregnant. I should—

"Don't you want me?"

Okay, fuck it. Her breathless question shatters all my prudence, especially when she looks at me like something's breaking inside her. I drive into her hot depths with one powerful stroke, throw my head back and moan at how amazing her pussy feels against my cock. She's so hot, so wet. Without a barrier between us, I'm aware of every little spasm of her inner muscles around my shaft.

Sweet Mother of God.

I dig my fingers into her pelvis and grind my teeth. She grips my shoulders, her nails marking my skin. The pain is shockingly erotic. I pound into her. Her head falls back, her mouth parted, her eyes rolling up as she loses herself in pleasure. Her breasts bob up and down; I take a nipple into my mouth and suck hard.

"Ares!" she screams. She convulses around my cock as an orgasm seizes her, and she's even wetter, her juices soaking me to the balls.

I continue thrusting, not giving her a chance to come down from the high. Her already pleasure-softened body responds beautifully, hitting another peak with ease. When her inner muscles grip me, my balls tighten and the base of my spine tingles, signaling an impending climax. I'm not going to be able to stop it—

I pull out. "Fuck," I groan as my cum spurts all over her belly. The sight of the white, sticky fluid hitting her and sliding down drives me feral. My cock stays half hard.

I could take my wife all night long. All day long. Hell, all forever long.

Cradling her beautiful, flushed face, I kiss her with all the taut emotion inside me. She runs her fingers over my face, tracing every line tenderly. Sweetness tinged with something wistful fleets over her. A hot surge of adoration fists around my heart. Her eyes are so brilliant, like stars are shining within their depths.

I start to speak, "Lareina, I love—"

She puts a finger over my mouth. "Let's get divorced."

40

ARES

My heart stops. My tongue freezes. My brain quits.

Lareina looks up at me, her eyes still brilliant and tender, the smile heartbreakingly beautiful.

"What?" I say, laughing shakily. *I couldn't have heard that right.*

"Let's get divorced."

I blink. The post-orgasmic flush lingers on her cheeks. My cum is still warm on her belly, and my dick's still wet from being inside her. I look around, wondering if I'm in some bizarre nightmare, separate from the evening I walked into. The sauce remains in the pan, and the water waits to be reheated. A small bag of pasta sits next to Lareina's ass on the counter, ready to be boiled.

"Why?" My voice sounds far away, muddled, as though I'm hearing it submerged in water. The euphoric heat has left, replaced by a sense of extreme foreboding.

Her face freezes, and she looks at me like she doesn't know what to say. "I just think... Well, we both got what we wanted. I have my money—and safety—and you have your promotion."

"But—"

"I think it's better this way. I'm not what you have in mind for a suitable wife or ideal marriage."

Fuck. She's throwing my words from Vegas back at me. When I was being an arrogant dick.

"And this"—she gestures vaguely with her hand—"isn't what I want for our future either. We would be much happier away from each other."

"You don't know that." But even as I insist, I don't know exactly what she means by "this" or how to change her mind. Part of me says I need to pin her down, but I'm also afraid. What if she says the past few months have been a trial, and it disappointed her?

"Yes, I do." Her gaze is steady. "I know *exactly* what I want from my life, Ares."

"And you think... You want..." My breath shakes. I run my hand over my mouth roughly, feeling utterly at a loss. The D-word rolled from her lips so casually, but I can't even say it, not in relation to us. When we were in Vegas, we spoke of our marriage as something with a time limit, but as time went on, I painted her into my future: her in her smock, paint splatters all over, our beautiful children and us growing old together. She'll have gray hair, and wrinkles will cover her skin, but she'll still be the most beautiful woman in my eyes, and I'll love every line.

"You're just a little shocked right now," she says, patting my cheek. "But it won't be long before you realize I'm right."

∼

I tuck my dick back into my pants and leave. I can't stay in the house with her talking about divorce so calmly—not when the very idea tears at me like a vulture's talons.

I drive aimlessly until I reach the beach. Moving on autopilot, I climb out of my car and sit on the damp sand. The waves pound into the ground, and the horizon is invisible in the blackness. I stick my fingers into my hair and clench hard.

What the hell just happened? How did things go so wrong? Weren't we *happy*? Is she still upset about what I said about marriage?

I've never been caught this off guard before. Not since Mom kidnapped me.

If Lareina asked me if I meant what I said, my answer would be yes. At the time, I meant every word. I couldn't even bear it when my girlfriends wrapped their arms around me and clung. I always thought I wanted a dignified, respectful marriage, like what my father has with Akiko. No crazy drama.

But if Lareina asked me how I feel *now*, I'd say I can't imagine life without her. Her strength, her bright personality, her decisiveness and daring—they all attract me in ways I've never felt before.

Why did she spend all that time and effort trying to make a nice dinner and celebrate my promotion just to ask for a divorce?

My thoughts spin in circles. God, I feel so *stupid*! How can I not figure this out? Lareina's serious about divorcing me.

As I inhale more of the salty air, the gears in my head finally start to turn. My wife isn't a fickle woman. She's not cruel, or prone to cutting people out for no reason. Because there are so few people close to her, she cherishes every friend she has. She must know that if she divorces me, she could lose my family, too.

Other than the idiotic things I've said, what's the problem? Something else that told her this was the right moment to bring up divorce—

The answer hits me in the face with sudden force. My promotion!

We both got what we wanted. I have my money—and safety—and you have your promotion.

I jump to my feet. She already had her money, but she waited until now because she wanted to make sure I got my junior partnership. And all this time I thought she stayed because...

I exhale harshly. Logic says I should take the promotion. I deserve it. I worked hard for it, practically slaved for it at times.

But...

I picture myself as a junior partner. I'll be in a bigger office. Maybe with more hours from admin support. More money. More clients. More cases. But I'll go home to an empty house, an empty bed and an empty life. No more getting up in the morning and making sure my wife has something she can eat. No more tasting her food and watching her smile like I'm responsible for the sunrise. The moment she told me how beautiful my eyes were, how they were nothing like my mother's, plays in my head like a movie I can never forget.

My heart feels like it's beating wrong. I clutch my chest in pain. I can't picture my future without Lareina in it now. But I *can* picture myself living perfectly well without the junior partnership. Logic says I should argue my case and have both the partnership *and* Lareina, but her expression was too resolute when she asked for the divorce. She won't change her mind. Not unless she learns I didn't get what I was supposed to out of our marriage deal.

I pull out my phone and start texting.

–Me: I decline the promotion.

It takes less than a minute before I get a call. It's Dad. The moment I answer, he booms, "What the hell was that?"

"I told you. I don't want the promotion."

"Did Harvey drug you again? Or is it your mother this time?"

"Neither. I'm perfectly *compos mentis* and don't want it."

"But why? You worked so hard for it. You threatened to go to another firm if you didn't get it. You even got *married*!" The final statement is a loud shout. He's probably about to have a stroke. Thankfully, high blood pressure doesn't run in the family.

"Yes, and that's why," I say. "My wife thinks I got what I wanted out of our marriage, and now she intends to divorce me."

"I told you to be nice to her." I can hear Akiko practically moan the words next to Dad. *Great. He put me on speaker.*

"So let me get this straight. In order to keep your wife, you're going to give up the promotion? Do you know how that makes us look? Jesus, the next time you want to get promoted—forget it! In fact, there won't *be* a next time. You're done at the firm!"

"I don't care."

"You won't even be able to go to another firm. What are you going to tell them if they ask you why you didn't become a junior partner even though it was offered to you?"

"The truth."

"You idiot! It's going to make you sound like some pussy-whipped loser who can't tie his own shoes without his wife's permission!"

"People can think what they want. Compared to losing my wife, it doesn't seem that bad."

Dad's breathing grows loud and fast. "You will absolutely *not* decline this promotion! Not until you've given it *at least* seventy-two hours of sober consideration."

"But—"

"Non-negotiable, end of story, Ares!"

When Dad is like this, it's impossible to reason with him. Not only that, he'll turn Aunt Jeremiah and Grandmother against me if I push. "Fine. Seventy-two hours. But I'll still think keeping my wife is more important than any promotion." Then I hang up and send a quick text to Lareina before she does anything rash.

41

LAREINA

I BURY my face in my hands. How could I have blurted it out like that? *I ruined everything.*

The kitchen is empty. The passion Ares and I shared has long gone cold, and I shiver. Sudden exhaustion makes even the simplest movement seem like lifting a mountain. I just...

Finally, I sigh and force myself into action. I slide slowly off the counter, wipe the white goo off my belly with a paper towel and drop it into the trash.

My heart is heavier than lead. From the way Ares left, he's probably not coming back tonight. I could've waited for a better time to spring it on him. It's just that when he held me like I was the most important treasure in his life, "I love you" surged in my throat. But I just couldn't say it, not when I knew this was the end of the marriage and he can't quit thinking about the woman he calls Queen.

The kitchen is too fresh with our recent lovemaking. I trudge toward the garden to breathe in some fresh air and clear my mind, shedding pieces of my shattered heart along the way. Does it make me a totally shitty human being that I almost wish Ares didn't get the promotion so I'd have a reason to stick around?

It's ridiculous that I seem to be unable to just tell him what's on my mind. I didn't hesitate this badly when I was debating climbing over to Ares's balcony in Vegas. There, failure meant death. The end. But at least I wouldn't have had any pain or lingering regrets haunting me. But with Ares? I don't want him to pity me or avoid me out of awkwardness or—worse yet—fear that I might try to cling to him like his ex. If I loved him a little less, I might've found the courage to confess my feelings.

I reach the garden and remember that stunning purple irises are blooming in the back. Maybe they'll cheer me up a little.

The scent of the flowers tickles my nose, and I breathe in the earthy smell. The deep violet, even darker at night, somehow reminds me of a lullaby. When Ares returns, I'll take a moment and explain to him why I chose divorce over staying together. He's upset now, but he'll understand that continuing this marriage wouldn't be fair to either of us when he learns that Queen still haunts his dreams.

The irises to my right rustle. I turn, but see nothing in the shadows. The night lights seem a bit dimmer than usual. Did a bulb or two go bad? I make a mental note to look into it later.

My phone buzzes. I glance at the screen, my heart jumping to my throat. *Ares.*

–My Knight: There's no promotion. The partners made a mistake.

What?

–Me: I'm so sorry. Are you okay?

Three dots appear on the screen. He must be devastated. Now I feel like a complete bitch for asking him for a divorce. I should've kept my mouth shut. I have to take back what I said.

Yeah, but now you can stay married to him!

I shake my head at the shameless thought, consumed with guilt and self-recrimination. How can I be so selfish when Ares must be feeling absolutely crushed?

Besides, he might not want to stay together now anyway, since being with me didn't get him the promotion he wanted. He said "nice and respectable wife," and I might not have fit that definition well enough to satisfy the firm.

The wait for the dots to turn into actual words seems interminable. I want to know what's on his mind, but at the same time I prefer to bury my head in the sand and stay ignorant. What if the error has something to do with my suitability?

Finally, a new text pops up. I glance down at it, my attention wholly on the message.

But before I can finish reading, something pungent and nauseating covers my face. I can't even hold my breath before the fumes permeate my nostrils and mouth.

Everything goes black.

∼

"Fucking cunt! Wake up!" A slap.

Pain explodes across my cheek and my head snaps to the side. The coppery tang floods my mouth.

Something sticky and rough is biting into my wrists and ankles. A dull pain in my shoulders says I've been sitting in the same position for too long.

Where am I? What happened?

There's a fog in my head and my vision is hazy. I squirm, and the chair wobbles a little on uneven legs. A nail—or something—is sticking out in the back and scratching my shoulder blade. With my luck, it's rusty and will give me tetanus. There's a smell of moldy wood and loam. A campfire crackles on the unfinished floor, and a lone, naked, broken bulb hangs from a slanted ceiling with a hole big enough to see a blurry moon.

I blink, trying desperately to clear my vision. Sticks fan around me on the floor like sunflower petals. *What the...?*

"You bitch! You ruined everything!"

Rupert? "Aren't you in jail?" I manage to rasp. My eyes finally adjust.

"You wish! Cunt! Fucking cunt!" he screams in my face. He's in a ragged T-shirt and cargo shorts—clothes he would've never been seen in before. His hair is messier than a bird's nest. In the bright yellow fire, his eyes glow red like an enraged demon. He suddenly straightens, takes a deep breath. "But guess what? You aren't the only one with somebody on your side. I got somebody big and important helping me, too."

Do you honestly believe I have no reach outside of Nesovia? Do you think just because you're in America, you're untouchable?

"Zoe?" I ask.

Rupert sneers. "This is what you deserve. You could've just been nice. Married me like you were supposed to. I didn't even want to touch you. Parker is my true love." He speaks like he was going to do me a favor or something.

Am I supposed to thank him for that?

"Once we realized you'd gotten married, did we make things difficult for you? No! We just wanted to take the things you didn't want anymore—your trash! They weren't even worth that much, not compared to the money your father and grandfather left you. With a bit of fame, Parker and I could've been happy." His eyes contain a gleam that reminds me of ice.

"You were going to get rid of Doris and Vernon."

"Duh! Why the fuck would we keep them around? All this mess because they couldn't even kill you and your parents right!"

I gasp. Although Zoe hinted at it, the bald revelation sends a shock wave through me. Decades of injustice and grievance twist my gut into a tight knot. I feel hot tears dripping down my cheeks. "Did they poison my parents?" I whisper shakily, wishing I could break the knots and strangle him with my bare hands.

"Well, *duh* again! You were supposed to die, too, but they fucked it up. Ugh. If all three of you had just *kicked off*, Doris could've taken the money. Why are you so fucking persistent? You're like a cockroach that just won't stay squished! Why did you have to ruin it for me and Parker?"

"*I* ruined it? For *you and Parker*? You stole from me! You killed my parents for money!" I shoot back, rage shaking through me.

"Hey, wasn't me. Doris and Vernon did that. Believe me, if *I'd* done it, you wouldn't be involved in this conversation!" he says arrogantly.

"You think you're so clever? You couldn't even slow-poison me right."

He shakes his head, pacing. "Partners! Fucking partners. Have to do every goddamn thing myself if I want it done right."

The Accidental Marriage

"How about marrying me, like you were planning? Couldn't do that, either," I sneer.

"So what? You're here now. At my mercy!"

I can't argue with this nonsense. In his mind he's the greatest, smartest, most wonderful and deserving, no matter what.

"You should've died in that fire twenty-two years ago. You were always out, running around and coming back to the cottage disheveled, like some hillbilly mountain girl. Dirty. Then you came home in a charred dress, scarred in the back. Probably a punishment for seducing who knows what."

"Wasn't I eight?" I don't recall what he's talking about, but I want to make sure I did my math right. A headache from whatever drug he used to knock me out is hammering at my skull.

"So? Lolita was the same age!"

Lolita? "Like in the book? She was twelve—"

"Shut up, bitch! Doris should've have stopped me when I told her I should just beat the resistance out of you and have you the way I wanted. You were always just a tool and should've been taught your place." He heaves air. "But no. You wanted to have things *your* way. Well, since you wouldn't serve your purpose, now I have no choice."

He's gone completely insane. "What are you going to do?"

"Something I should've done a long time ago." He grabs a red canteen and pours the clear contents all around me in a circle. Only then do I realize the sticks on the floor are kindling. "Parker says she doesn't want to die, but not me. I'd rather be dead than live in some cage with nothing. But I'm not going alone. I'm taking you with me." He tosses the empty container away and lights a match.

My palms slicken with cold sweat. I struggle, trying to free myself. But there's no give. The chair wobbles violently, and I stop. Toppling over won't do me any good.

The wavering yellow flame from the match lights Rupert's eerie smile. Then he lets it go.

42

ARES

–L*areina*: *Are you okay?*

No. I haven't been okay since you mentioned divorce.

My default response—*I'm fine*—comes to mind, but I hold back. Lying won't help anybody. She isn't a fool, and she knows I'm upset. *Are you okay?* is her way of asking if I'd like to talk about it, and *I'm fine* would be the clearest way to shut her down.

–Me: Not really. But we can't get divorced. I didn't get what I want. We have to talk, Lareina. Don't do anything rash and don't move out or get a lawyer. Definitely not Ethan Beckman.

That asshole would rub his hands together with glee if he filed for divorce on her behalf. My misery is his joy.

–Me: Wait for me. I'm coming right now.

I climb into my car and floor it. The phone stays silent—hopefully she's digesting what I told her. After all, I just delivered a major blow to her plans.

If Lareina were some other woman, I'd be confident that "I love you" might be enough to convince her. But she's anything but ordinary. She has her own internal logic and way of looking at things. If I can't change her views, she won't cave. No matter what. I need to delay the divorce and use the time wisely to show her I'm worth keeping.

The Accidental Marriage

As for the promotion, fuck it. The firm can give it to me next year or the year after. Or if Dad is too pissed to make me a partner, I'll just stay an associate for life. Better yet, I could quit and be a man of leisure, spend all my time with my wife. We haven't even had a honeymoon.

What an idiot I've been. I should've taken time off and spoiled her. She's spent her life trapped in a house in Nesovia by her evil aunt. I could show her the wonders on every continent, see the world again through her eyes and discover new beauty.

My car squeals as I turn and brake. I kill the engine, hop out and run inside. The house is silent, although lights are on in the kitchen and living room.

"Lareina?" I call out. "Honey?"

More silence.

"Lareina?" I call out again, louder.

Still nothing.

Apprehension slithers down my spine. It isn't like her to avoid me like this. Where did she go?

I pull out my phone to check her location.

What in the world? Is this thing broken? Why is she stuck halfway between here and the citrus grove owned by the Pryces? It's just an area with a bunch of woods and crap. And she doesn't even have a driver's license yet.

Did she take one of the cars out anyway, to clear her head? But it seems irresponsible—not something she would do, no matter how upset.

Heart pounding, I rush to the garage. The sensors turn on the light.

"Lareina!" I shout desperately, hoping she'll hear me no matter where she is. The name echoes, but there's no response.

My eyes sweep over tens of gleaming vehicles. None is missing.

Something's wrong. The fine hair on my back stands. Terror burns my gut. I check the app again. Lareina's location hasn't changed.

What Grandmother said once flashes through my mind. "I love undeveloped areas with trees and wildlife. But sometimes I feel like they're the city planners' way of accommodating serial killers who might be living in the community."

It's not a serial killer. I haven't seen or heard anything like that on the news. But the tension in my belly tightens like an overstretched violin string.

I get inside the Cayenne and speed off. On the way, my phone rings. I answer immediately, praying it's Lareina calling because she didn't hear me from the bathroom or something.

"We got a problem," Francisco from the LAPD says. "Rupert Fage escaped."

I run an impatient hand over my face. Why is he calling me? What does he want me to do about it? "How? Did you get him back?"

"We'll get to the bottom of that soon enough." Translation: *We don't know, and we don't want to admit it.* "And no, he's out and about. Very dangerous. He's been missing for at least five hours."

The blood in my veins turns to ice. *Rupert's out, and Lareina disappears?* I flex my fingers around the steering wheel as rage, fear and frustration claw at me. "Five hours? And you're telling me this *now*?"

"Calm down. We're sending a couple of cruisers over to your place, just in case."

"Forget it. My wife's missing! Her phone says her last location's off the road to the Pryce Citrus Grove. Hold on. Let me give you the coordinates." Taking advantage of a red light, I go to the tracking app and rattle off the numbers. "I'm going to need you there. Now!"

Lareina...

The light hasn't changed to green yet, but I hit the gas hard, leaving a wake of honking cars behind me.

Hang on. I'm coming.

43

LAREINA

THE INSTANT the match hits the gasoline-soaked kindling, a circle of fire goes up around me. Black smoke billows upward, choking me. I cough, shaking my head. The acrid fumes rub against my throat and lungs like sandpaper. The air in my chest grows thinner.

I'm going to suffocate before the fire burns me alive.

I need to get down as low as possible. I swing my weight left and right. The legs on my chair wobble. The nail on the back pokes at my shoulder blade, scratching it with every sway. I grit my teeth. I'm going to survive this, *and then murder Rupert*. It'll be justifiable homicide. Self-defense.

The chair tips over. I crash onto my left shoulder. The impact knocks the breath out of me and I lie there, dazed. The smoke isn't as thick on the ground, but the air is still too hot, too dry and too thin. Not only that, the fire is spreading. Unless I can free myself, I'm not making it out of here alive. The nail digs deeper into my flesh too. Warm liquid trickles down my back, where my scar is. A vague and completely irrelevant thought pops into my head: *Now it's going to look even more hideous.* I push it aside and focus on what's important.

If only my arms weren't tied...!

Sweat beads on my hairline from the heat. My lungs are starved for air, but there isn't much, just smoke. My vision blurs as my mind goes somewhere between reality and a dream. I gaze at a spot beyond the fire—at something hazy and illusory. I stare at it like a ghost observing a scene.

A child is tied to a chair—who is it? No clue to indicate his identity. At least his arms are free. The front of his shirt is wet and smells like sweat, yeast and artificial vanilla that's so cheap it feels off.

Unlike me, he doesn't resist or try to escape. But then, he's just a kid. His chest moves shallowly, but if he stays like this, he's not going to make it. A small blonde girl appears and shakes him. "Wake up! We gotta go!" the girl says.

The fire burns brighter. The light from it obscures the moon. She manages to free him, but he isn't walking well. Is he injured?

My head throbs. I squeeze my eyes shut, breathing shallowly to avoid inhaling the acrid air too deeply. My body doesn't feel right—like I'm weightless and slowly spinning in the air like an astronaut in space.

Somehow the girl is gone and I'm rescuing the boy now, so short the smoke isn't in my face. But I don't relax. Anything could happen. A giant wolf jumps from the wall, above the door. It tries to attack the boy, but I push him out of the way. The beast takes a bite of my back.

Pain blooms. Air clogs in my throat. Tears spring to my eyes, but I pretend to be brave.

The boy and I are out of the shed, but it's no good. The entire place is surrounded by fire. I blink. I try to lick my parched lips, but my tongue's too dry to make a difference. The boy has vanished. *Where did he go?*

I thought there might be a lake where I could lie down and rest, but no. Tears trickle from my eyes and bitter regrets weigh upon my heart until I want to just drop to the ground. If I'd known my life would end like this, I would've waited until I had the celebratory dinner with Ares. Or at least I would've told him, "I love you," face to face, so that my last words to him weren't "Let's get divorced."

Somewhere in the dancing flames, Ares lunges forward, coming through the fire like a wolf. His blue eyes are fierce as he crouches over me. He touches me, trying to support my body and right me, then stops. He raises a blood-soaked hand. His handsome face crumbles, twisted into something sad, furious and terrifying. He cries out something, but my hearing is too muffled to understand.

I don't want him to worry. It probably looks much worse than it really is. I try to reassure him by smiling. But my smile must be awful, because his expression only grows more appalled.

Strength oozes away, bit by bit. My body relaxes, and I blink up at him. I'm glad the last thing I see is Ares before my vision turns dark.

44

ARES

Oh fuck no.

Denial screams in my head, then terror thunders in my heart. The coordinates on the phone's tracking app lead me to a burning shed. It's so old its door is hanging drunkenly by only one hinge. Flames blaze inside, and I rush in, realizing it could be a trap but not caring. I have to make sure my wife is safe. If she's stuck inside, I have to get her out. No time to check for traps or wait for the fire department.

Dense smoke makes it nearly impossible to breathe. Despite the painful sting in my eyes, I keep them open and spot Lareina on the floor, tied to a chair, like I was when I was ten and Mom kidnapped me. The scene is so eerily similar, I feel like I'm back in time, twenty-two years ago.

Soot and dirt cover my wife's face as she squints up at me. The wan smile she manages smashes my heart into shards—I know she's trying to soothe me even though she's the one in pain.

I try to free her, but stop when her warm blood drenches my hands. I pull her torso away from the sharp end of a nail that's sticking out from the back. Her shirt is tattered with holes, and I pull it away from the wound so it doesn't get stuck to her skin.

Then I see the scar on her shoulder blade—a burn that left a beastly canine mark on her otherwise flawless skin. Caught in the maw is a stylized H for the Huxley family, the one Mom put into the silver wolf head she commissioned to prove her devotion and loyalty to the family—anything to stay with Dad.

My jaw slackens as I stare at the bloodied scar. I always thought that, when I finally found Queen, I'd be elated. Instead, I'm just reeling. How could Lareina be my Queen? I've been looking for her for so long. It doesn't feel real.

My hands shake. "Queen?"

She doesn't seem to hear. Her pain-glazed eyes blink at me, but nothing seems to register.

"Queen!"

Her lips twitch. Either to say something or to smile, I can't tell which. But she's fading fast. A terror I've never known before mauls my heart.

Quickly, I rip the duct tape binding her to the chair away. She curls up on the ground like a wounded kitten. I reach for her—

"You fucker!"

At the seething voice, I turn around. Rupert Fage, in person, swinging a big branch at me. Rage sparks, blazes like hellfire. I need to pour out my grief and fury, and he's the perfect target.

Placing my wife on the ground, I duck, catch the stick and kick him in the gut. He folds with a grunt, and I smash the back of my foot against his spine. Something cracks, and he drops to his knees. "Fuck!" he screams.

I punt him, aiming for the nose. It crunches, and he covers his face, blood gushing between fingers. The inside of the shed is hot enough to roast a swine. Flames lick the support beam across the roof.

Time to get outta here.

I pick up Lareina and carry her out. She lies limply in my arms, and I place her on the passenger seat of my Cayenne and put a finger under her nose, needing to confirm. *Please, God, don't let anything happen to her. I just found her.*

Featherlight breathing tickles my skin, and I slump to my knees. *Thank God.*

The roof caves in. Huge chunks of the walls collapse. No sign of Rupert.

Still, I hold my wife protectively and guard her until the wailing sirens pierce the night.

45

LAREINA

THE NEXT TIME I open my eyes, I'm in a white room with blue curtains over the windows. The air has a hint of disinfectant, and the lights above me are harshly fluorescent. An IV bag is hooked into a vein inside my elbow.

I'm also surrounded by Ares and every one of his family: Catalina, Jeremiah, Akiko, Prescott, Bryce, Josh, Huxley and a woman I haven't met before. They all wear expressions of relief and concern.

Ares squeezes my hand. "Hey."

"Hi." It comes out as a croak.

"How are you feeling? Anything uncomfortable?"

I consider. My throat is raw, and my eyes are gritty. My back hurts like hell, like somebody rubbed it raw and poured salt all over it. "I'm alive, which is what matters."

"How did that asshole get you?" Bryce asks.

"He put a cloth with something over my face, and I passed out. He blamed me for everything and wanted me to pay." I turn to Ares. "But I don't think he was planning to contact you for ransom or anything. How did you find me?"

His mouth parts, but nothing comes out. His family all stare at him, then look at each other.

"Perhaps we should give these two some privacy. I'm sure they have quite a lot to discuss," Catalina announces.

"Thank you, Grandmother," Ares says sincerely.

"If you need anything, all you have to do is push the call button." Jeremiah gives me a meaningful look.

I smile at the blatant way she sides with me, to let me know I'm not alone.

They file out, and Bryce, who's the slowest, probably hoping to catch something, closes the door behind them.

"Well...?" I raise an eyebrow.

Ares shifts, then looks away briefly. "Iputatrackeronyourphone."

"Uh...what?"

His eyes dart to me before dropping to the lilies and roses in their vases. "I put a"—he clears his throat—"tracker on your phone."

I stare at him. "That's a blatant violation of privacy. Furthermore, it isn't exactly respectful."

"Nope. Or indifferent." His chin juts out.

I search his face, but there's nothing but inscrutable determination. He looks like he's about to face off with the biggest antagonistic force in his life, except I'm the only one here. "Okay, I just don't understand. You confuse me, Ares. You tell me you want one thing, but then do the opposite."

He looks sucker-punched for a moment, then blinks a couple of times. He exhales, rakes his hair and sighs. "I didn't mean to. Look, I wasn't lying when I said I wanted a marriage of respectful indifference. Back then, I really believed that's what I wanted. But being with you made me realize I was wrong. You changed me, Lareina."

The earnest sincerity in his voice takes my breath away. It's the sweetest thing anybody's ever said to me, but I can't forget him calling for another woman in sleep. "What about Queen?"

Shock cracks his composure, and sudden pain pushes into my heart like shards of glass.

I continue, "You call for her at night."

His shoulders deflate. He knows he's caught. Bitterness fills my mouth until I can't help scrunching my face. Why did he have to embellish so much, trying to make me believe he cares?

The pain is like acid over my skin. I close my eyes briefly to hide the heartache.

"I suppose Soledad told you."

I nod.

"Yes, there's a woman I call Queen. I call her that because she never told me her actual name, and she said she preferred being a queen over a princess. Queens are in charge. Princesses aren't."

I frown up at him. That's very similar to what I told Ares while running from the bad guys in Vegas.

"She was my salvation, my only anchor to sanity when my mother kidnapped me. She came by with Wonder Bread and shared her food with me so I wouldn't have to eat the drug-laden food Mom left so she could manipulate me. You know the burn scar on my arm?"

I nod.

"I got it when she pulled me out of the fire. It started after Mom fed me some nasty stuff and left me alone in the shed. I was drugged and really out of it. If Queen hadn't been there, I would've died."

I cover my mouth and stare at him. He told me about the kidnapping before, but not the details of his rescue. I just assumed the police had found him or something. But it also makes me realize there's no way I can overcome the attachment he has for Queen. She's his savior—or, as he put it, his *salvation*.

He looks deeply into my eyes as he continues the story. "After the rescue, I looked for her. It wasn't easy. I not only didn't know her real name, she'd completely disappeared. The only thing I could tell the people my family and I hired was that she has one blue eye and one green eye, and a burn scar on her back, which she got while saving me. There was an ornamental wolf's head in the cabin where I was being held, and it fell as Queen and I were making our escape. When she saw the head falling toward me, she pushed me out of the way and let it hit her instead."

My mind works, and the pieces start to fall into place. My heart begins to hammer. Is he telling me *I'm* the Queen he's been looking for? It seems so unbelievable.

"I saw the scar on your back. It's just like the one she got—the teeth from the wolf bust and the H in the center. For the Huxleys."

"H? It isn't an I?"

He snorts. "Who told you that? Haven't you seen the scar yourself?"

I shake my head. "Not really. Only Doris and a couple of sitters I had saw it clearly. They all told me it was hideous and I should hide it from everyone to avoid disgusting them."

Fury and revulsion burn in his gaze as he curls his lip in derision. "Well now *I've* seen it, and they lied to you. It isn't hideous. It's a physical manifestation of your bravery and character. Even as a small child you couldn't ignore a person who was suffering. You were willing to risk your life to save someone else. That's not shameful, it's admirable." He rests his forehead on mine. "Queen."

I let out a soft sigh. The nickname runs over me like a sweet elixir.

"Lareina, I don't want to get divorced. I want to be in your life, always. Even before I knew you were Queen, I wanted to be with you."

The revelation both surprises me and warms my heart. Perhaps he subconsciously knew when he saw me in Vegas that I was his Queen. After all, while he was high on Harvey's drugs, he called me Queen and promised to be my knight.

My heart near bursting with joy and love, I smile. "Ares, I was already going to stay with you until you get promoted, so you don't have to worry about it."

He places a finger over my lips. "I don't want you to stay with me for my career. Not because of some deal we made. I want you to be with me because you *want* to." A rueful smile crosses his stunning face. "I lied about the firm making a mistake about my promotion. They didn't. I told them I didn't want it—"

"*You what?*"

"—because I wanted a reason to tie you down. But then while you were lying here in the hospital bed, I realize that that would make me no better than your aunt. You should never be lied to or manipulated for someone else's gain—not even mine. I want you to *choose* to be with me. I want you to *choose us*." Holding my hand, Ares drops to one knee. "Lareina, my Queen, will you let me stay by your side, love you, cherish you and protect you as long as I live?"

Holding the fathomless blue eyes that shine with infinite love for me, I cradle his beloved face and kiss him. "Yes."

46

LAREINA

A CLOUDLESS BLUE sky stretches over a verdant field full of flowers and the scent of fermenting grapes and grass. This is Ares's and my second ceremony. It's only fair to have our friends and family witness our renewed commitment to each other.

Ares is so handsome in a black-and-white tux. The formal wear fits his broad shoulders and thickly muscled body perfectly. *My knight in satin armor.*

I'm wearing a white backless dress. I've never worn anything like it before, but it seems fitting. After all, the scar doesn't make me ugly. Ares is right. It's a physical sign of my bravery back then. And honestly, I think it marked me as *his*, just as the scar he got from the same fire marks him as *mine*.

Ares's family beams with approval. Prescott slips Jeremiah five hundred dollars. He apparently wagered that "Queen" wasn't real, and Jeremiah said she was. Jeremiah's smile is extra wide. The woman loves to win. But Prescott doesn't seem too upset as he sits with a hand swiping over eyes that are glistening with tears.

My friends Lucie and Yuna join us, along with Catherine Fairchild, who's decided to champion my career. Even Barron Sterling shows up with his girlfriend Stella Lloyd, which causes quite a stir. Apparently, the elderly billionaire art connoisseur is capricious, private and autocratic. But he gives a great hug.

When the singer sings Sinatra's "Love Is Here to Stay," Ares and I have our first dance. Our lives are only going to get better.

47

BRYCE

Ares dips Lareina to the Sinatra tune. A huge grin splits his face, and the old guilt inside me eases a tad.

I haven't seen my brother this happy since the kidnapping incident. If he'd tried to drown himself in women or booze, I would've understood, but he's led an ascetic, almost monk-like life, focusing on his career and not much else.

My phone pings. I look down. A photo from an unknown number. It's Fiona, in a bride's gown. There's another ping—and a photo of a guy who I presume is the groom. Suddenly I stop cold and stare at the screen. *What the fuck?*

The smarmy face of Jude Morven stares back at me. I wanted to break it in high school and college, and I still want to break it.

–Unknown: Perfect groom for the perfect bride.

Is this her answer? Her pride is so great that she'd rather marry this piece of shit than try me one more time?

But then, she's always been crazy about Morven. I'll never forget her crying her eyes out, one hand clenched over her heart, when he was hit by a semi and almost lost his life. *What does she see in him?* He's always been a complete asshole to her, treated her like garbage. And she always just lowered her eyes and took it, no matter what he asked of her. But with me, I couldn't even look at her wrong before she snarked.

I shut my phone off and drum my fingers on the table. *I should just let her be with that creep.* It's what she deserves—the life of a doormat.

And yet every drop of acid in my gut churns. I simply can't understand—

Ignore it. She wants that asshole.

I forcibly turn my attention back to my brother. But—

Fuck. I get up and start to walk away. I have a wedding to go fuck up.

~

THANK you for reading *The Accidental Marriage*. For exclusive bonus epilogues and more, please join Nadia's newsletter at http://www.nadialee.net.

TITLES BY NADIA LEE

Standalone Titles

Beauty and the Assassin

Oops, I Married a Rock Star

The Billionaire and the Runaway Bride

Flirting with the Rock Star Next Door

Mister Fake Fiancé

Marrying My Billionaire Hookup

Faking It with the Frenemy

Marrying My Billionaire Boss

Stealing the Bride

The Lasker Brothers

Baby for the Bosshole

My Grumpy Billionaire

The Ex I'd Love to Hate

Contractually Yours

Finally Forever

Still Mine

The Unwanted Bride

The Sins Trilogy

Sins

Secrets

Mercy

The Billionaire's Claim Duet

Obsession

Redemption

Sweet Darlings Inc.

That Man Next Door

That Sexy Stranger

That Wild Player

Billionaires' Brides of Convenience

A Hollywood Deal

A Hollywood Bride

An Improper Deal

An Improper Bride

An Improper Ever After

An Unlikely Deal

An Unlikely Bride

A Final Deal

The Pryce Family

The Billionaire's Counterfeit Girlfriend

The Billionaire's Inconvenient Obsession

The Billionaire's Secret Wife

The Billionaire's Forgotten Fiancée

The Billionaire's Forbidden Desire

The Billionaire's Holiday Bride

∼

Seduced by the Billionaire
Taken by Her Unforgiving Billionaire Boss
Pursued by Her Billionaire Hook-Up
Pregnant with Her Billionaire Ex's Baby
Romanced by Her Illicit Millionaire Crush
Wanted by Her Scandalous Billionaire
Loving Her Best Friend's Billionaire Brother

ABOUT NADIA LEE

New York Times and *USA Today* bestselling author Nadia Lee writes sexy contemporary romance. Born with a love for excellent food, travel and adventure, she has lived in four different countries, kissed stingrays, been bitten by a shark, fed an elephant and petted tigers.

Currently, she shares a condo overlooking a small river and sakura trees in Japan with her husband and son. When she's not writing, she can be found reading books by her favorite authors or planning another trip.

To learn more about Nadia and her projects, please visit http://www.nadialee.net. To receive updates about upcoming works, sneak peeks and bonus epilogues featuring some of your favorite couples from Nadia, please visit http://www.nadialee.net/vip to join her VIP List.

Made in the USA
Middletown, DE
08 July 2025